"You never seen a shadow dancer?" Harley asked, shivering. "Now *there's* one to give you the creeps."

"I heard the name used," I told him. "What's it mean?"

"That's what we call 'em on the street. They're all real young, real pretty—but they got hooked on something *scary*. Not like dope—they're like, well, *slaves*, damn it. Fast Eddie Small pimps a string of 'em, they wash his car, clean his house, and with the dates—Eddie has fun making them do *disgusting* things. An' they don't care. I mean, you look in someone's eyes—even a loony, a wino, a junkie—and you see a *person* there. You look in their eyes and there's nothin'. Not even hope. Shadows of pretty girls dancin' to Fast Eddie's tune.

"You stay away from them, Brandy. I don't want to ever look in your eyes and see only a shadow dancer there."

Stay away? I couldn't tell Harley it was my job to *find* these shadow dancers—even if I ended up as one.

THE SHADOW DANCERS

Tor Books by Jack L. Chalker

JACK L. CHALKER
THE SHADOW DANCERS

G.O.D. INC. NO. 2

A TOM DOHERTY ASSOCIATES BOOK

For Will F. Jenkins,
who as "Murray Leinster"
took the parallel world concept
and made it infinite so the rest of us
could play in his yard.

THE SHADOW DANCERS

First printing: July 1987

A TOR Book

Published by Tom Doherty Associates, Inc.
49 West 24 Street
New York, N.Y. 10010

ISBN: 0-812-53308-9
CAN. ED.: 0-812-53309-7

Printed in the United States of America

0 9 8 7 6 5 4 3 2 1

1.

A Summons From G.O.D.

Cleopatra Jones stared down at the twinkling lights of the city from her luxurious penthouse apartment; her city, the city she protected and watched over. Her slim, glamorous face and form reflected back from the window, a ghostly angel of perfection against the night scene . . .

Oh, hell, who was I tryin' to kid, anyway? Yeah, it was dark and I was lookin' out the window, but all cities look glamorous and mysterious at night, even Philadelphia, and only thing the woman starin' back at me in the glass had in common with tall, lean Cleo was that we were both black females who'd come up in the world.

It hadn't taken me long to put the weight back on that I'd lost back in that Garden place, though I wasn't as bad as I had been. Truth is, the most fattenin' stuff in the world is also about the cheapest, and when you're dirt poor you wind up with lots of peanut butter and real fatty stuff 'cause it goes further and fills better. Oh, the tummy was still okay, but the hips were growin' and so were my tits, which seemed oversized even when I was down at my model weight (thanks, Ma!). At five six, with a naturally round face and lots of bushy hair (I know it's not in fashion but it's the only way I could ever control it without spendin' two hours a day on it) I looked, well, *plump,* anyway.

I guess we was the only self-made poor folk in the Camden ghetto back then. Daddy was a retired Army colonel; he coulda done better by just bein' retired—there weren't too many retired black colonels then. But, no, he'd been a cop in the Army and he was a little too old to be a cop after and a little too black in that day and time to be a commissioner or police advisor, and he had this dream.

1

Back then there wasn't a single black-owned and operated private detective agency in the area—those that had the background didn't have the bread to get started. He pumped it all into settin' that agency up. Not much—a dingy office overlookin' a side street in one of the lousier sections of the ghetto even back then, some secondhand furniture and files, and a phone and a sign on the directory and the glass door to the office. *Spade & Marlowe, PI.* With Ma as his secretary he got enough clients to pay the bills, with a little help from his pension. Trouble was, the clients weren't exactly the well-to-do types and we pretty much got peanuts even when he did his job right—if we got anything at all.

My comin' along pretty well finished off any surplus, although I always knew that I was the one thing Daddy loved as much as that agency. We got by, but then Ma died young—she always had a real blood pressure problem and never did much take them pills—and he had the agency and me and the agency was the money for us to live. I dunno, I guess maybe I wanted all his attention and got very little, since he was in and out at all hours and I had to be pretty much on my own. I got to be somethin' of a wild child, runnin' with a bad pack, never carin' 'bout school or the future or nothin', just blowin' reefer and drinkin' booze and gettin' into lots of trouble. Just about the only thing I really paid attention to was makin' sure Daddy didn't know—we used to steal blank report cards and fill 'em out real convincing-like, and I could always come up with the right answers for his questions. I guess now I was rebelling against him in a way, and maybe against the whole world as I saw it, but I didn't see no future and no purpose to nothin'. Lost my virginity real young, too; when I finally got knocked up good, I stole some stuff from a store and hocked it for enough to get an abortion. It weren't no easy thing to do, but there was no way to keep a *baby* from Daddy's knowin', and that settled that.

That kind of neighborhood you was always around users and dealers, pimps and whores, and they weren't no creatures of evil and sin to me. I knew 'em by their first names, and they knew me. To a kid like me, they were romantic kinds of figures, and if nothin' else they was the only black folks who seemed to me to be makin' it. I'd slept around so much by the time I was sixteen that all my fantasies were about bein' a hooker. Dress up real sexy-like, and have the dudes *pay* you to get laid. Easy money, easy work. Only who my Daddy was kept me from either joinin' up with a string or bein' taken in by a pimp. Ain't no way no pimp in that part of town wanted the Colonel as an enemy.

Finally, of course, Daddy found out about it. Had to, sooner or later. We had one big hell of a scene, and for the first and only time in his life he actually beat me good, and I was ready to pack up, run away, and go to some other city like New York and sell myself on the streets, but I got so mad I came out first to tell him, knowin' it would hurt him, and I couldn't find him at first. Then I figured he was in the bedroom, and he was, only I didn't go in or show myself and my bad mad just kinda faded out.

He was cryin'. Colonel Harold Parker, U.S.A. (Ret.), one of the toughest dudes in the world, was cryin'. John Wayne woulda cried before Daddy. It must have been the first and only time in his life he did it. This was the man who had dug a bullet out of his own side with a knife, then driven himself twenty miles to the hospital.

Pretty soon, I was cryin', too, and I ran into him and we held each other and cried it out. After that, we made a deal. I didn't want to go back to school, and he didn't want me in with that crowd no more anyway, so he agreed, though he didn't like it, to let me come in and take over Ma's old job as the secretary, receptionist, you name it. In exchange, when things got straightened out in the office and we got a little ahead on the bills, I'd take some night classes, get my G.E.D. high school equivalency, and maybe more if we could figure a way to afford it. 'Cause I was his business manager, he'd know where I was and what I was doin', and our free time would be *our* free time.

Well, I never did take to school, and I never got through eighth grade, but I managed. I always read—Ma and Daddy had seen to that from early times, and I kept doin' it even when the gang made fun of it—so I had a leg up on some of them kids who have high school diplomas and straight A averages who couldn't spell *cat* or write much beyond their name. I got a big vocabulary, but I never could keep all that grammar shit right. Well, you know, you speak black English on the streets and white English around Daddy and it's kinda like thinkin' in one language and talkin' another. I got one of them ghetto-southern accents I ain't never gonna lick, and I gave up years ago tryin' to correct my grammar. It's a lost cause. I'm a low-class hick with a big vocabulary, so sue me.

I got the bug, though, helpin' Daddy on cases and gettin' things mostly in shape. The files might not have had the best grammar but they was complete and up to date. I never was no good at math, but after we got the free calculator for subscribing to *PI Magazine* I always knew we was deep in a hole. Still, I learned the business, for what it was worth. It's a damned dull, boring job with no respect and few rewards, no matter what the books and TV and movies tell you. No big action, either. Daddy had a gun, a big magnum, but he almost never carried it and I don't think he ever fired it as a PI. I did a lot of practicing with that sucker and I got pretty good, but that thing has a *kick* they don't show you on them TV shows and it ain't much good at any range. I also took karate and judo lessons at the Y and got pretty good at that, though I never had much call to use 'em.

I also just about cut out any social life. It weren't none of Daddy's doin', it was just me. Truth was, I just didn't have much self-image, as they call it. Never did. When Ma died and Daddy was away so much, I couldn't be on my own, so I got into the gang and did what the gang did. I figure now that's what all that fantasizing 'bout bein' a hooker was all about. Any girl who has that trade as her sole ambition ain't got much sense of herself. When men pay, then you got worth, right there, in dollars and cents. I was fat and slow and no matter how good a shape I whip into I ain't never gonna be no Tina Turner.

Daddy and the agency, then, became my whole life, my whole identity. I don't blame nobody, but it's just the way I am. I can't change that any more than I can change how I look or how I talk. Nobody would believe it if I told 'em, anyway—except maybe Sam, who knows it but just can't figure it.

But one night Daddy didn't check in—the cops did, and I had to go down and identify the body. He hadn't even taken his gun with him on that job, but he got far too many holes to go anywhere afterwards. It was kinda weird standin' there, in the morgue, lookin' at his water-soaked and bloody, bullet-ridden body. One part of me said it was him, but with all the life out of him he just didn't look *real*, somehow. I couldn't even cry, but all through that night and the next few days I just got madder and madder. The cops had no real leads and he'd been pretty closemouthed about it all even to me, 'cept that it was something big, bigger than he'd ever had before.

I cracked the case, after two months, when the cops couldn't, and I got some reputation as hot shit for it but it wasn't all that damned hard. Sure, I didn't know anything about that case, but whoever it was didn't know that and I just began to put out the word that I had leads and knew more than I did and set myself up as a target. The cops thought it was real gutsy of me, but truth was I'd just had all I had left in the world snatched from me and I didn't really care if they killed me so long as I got at least one of the bastards involved. Detective shit is more guts and dull routine than anything else; there ain't no real Sherlock Holmeses. The only thing is, most of the crooks around ain't all that smart, either—they just got smart lawyers. I set myself up, got invited to a meet just like Daddy, and I went, just like Daddy, only I took the magnum. 'Course, the gun didn't do no good, but the fact that I also called the cops helped nab the triggermen in the act of tryin' to kill me and led eventually to the indictment and conviction of a popular young black politician on the way up who just happened to be in the mob's pocket.

All that didn't help, though. Fact is, I got no new cases worth much and lost some old clients even though I got a reputation as a PI at least as good as Daddy out of it. Big Tony and the mob never did get touched by it all, even though they ordered it; the white folks had gone scot-free and the black folks had taken the fall, as usual, and for some reason I got blamed for that. Crazy thing was that the only folks who would toss a case or two my way were the smalltime crooks in the ghetto. Seems they were impressed and wanted me on their side.

Still, not enough came in to make even the basic bills,

and I sold the house and lived on that for a while, takin' a one-room dump near work. I was just goin' through the motions, though, and I knew it. I just didn't know anything else to do. Oh, I had a bunch of relatives, mostly cousins, in the area, but about the best I could hope for was some kind of job as a domestic or cab driver or something. I didn't have no skills to speak of, no real contacts, no diploma—and you needed that just to collect garbage—and only me as a job reference. Couldn't get no unemployment—I was self-employed—and welfare didn't mean shit unless you had a couple of illegitimate kids. The only guys I knew who might be marriage bait were either ones I couldn't stand, ones who wanted some kind of house nigger, or ones that were already as high as they were gonna go and were like street cleaners or handled the drive-in window at McDonald's.

Here I'd done somethin' the cops couldn't or wouldn't do, and dumb luck or not I done it good, and instead of gettin' the gold stars and thanks and all the rest I got shut out. I got to admit that my fantasies turned back again, and every time I passed one of the hookers I got more and more tempted—and without Daddy around I had offers from a couple of local pimps.

The cops, though, had at least a little soft spot for me, since I'd given them some good collars. I mean, a couple of white cops got to bust a bunch of meddlesome black dudes in Camden, and that was gold stars on them. That's why, at just about this time, they sent Sam around to me.

Sam was older than me by a good ten years, pudgy, balding, but kinda cute. He was also the first white man I ever took a liking to, and a big shock. It was the first time I found out Jewish white guys could be about as poor and out of it as me. He was a cop from Bristol, up north a bit in Jersey, and he was down tryin' to track down a ring that snatched little kids and turned them into kiddie porn objects. Fact was, I took to him right off, not just 'cause I needed somebody right then but even though he was white and Jewish he reminded me one hell of a lot of Daddy. He had that same sense of moral outrage Daddy always did, more than I ever could bring up, and when he was after bad guys he wanted their asses bad. He also had a real passion for the old detective stories and for all them old detective movies on the Late Late Show starring Bogart or Robert Montgomery or Lloyd Nolan, the kind my Daddy always loved and grew up on. And, like me, he wasn't too thrilled to be a detective, he just didn't know how to do nothin' else. He also had a college education and real brains. He goes on them brains, too; I go on feelin's and sometimes guts but I ain't never gonna be no brain and I know it.

In the end, we busted those suckers, got back one kid, and exposed a crooked cop who shielded them, but it didn't stop there. Fact was, I knew what I saw in Sam, but I never will know just what he saw in me, but he's the only white man I ever been around who never showed one ounce of racism or racial hangups. Sam quit the Bristol force—he never was too comfortable on the vice squad anyway—and came down with what little he had to try and make the agency work. We kinda hoped if maybe a white ex-cop was around some of the black folks would give us more business, and it did bring in some, but not nearly enough. We got married at city hall—the bride wore jeans—and even that had a price. My relatives didn't approve at all, and his relatives were even madder than mine. I was still poor and broke, but it didn't really matter no more.

Fact was, I grabbed for Sam 'cause I needed somebody bad, but I really fell in love with him. Real bad. I ain't never been in love with nothin' or nobody before or since like this. From the moment we moved in together, he was the only thing important in my whole life. He kept the agency goin' by sheer willpower mostly for my sake, as it turned out, and he never would believe me when I told him I'd be happy if he got a salaried job doin' most anything and I played house and mommie, but it's true.

I know, I know—on the outside it looks like black woman makes it in the cold world, but I never saw my case written up in *Jet* or *Ebony* or even the *National Enquirer*. If you got the brains and the education and the skills and the drive then go for it, baby, but I ain't ever gonna have them things and I just ain't one for crusades. If Women's Lib wants to nail me for it, that's all right, but I didn't see no cases from them when I was a woman-owned business. Sam told me he didn't mind if I kept my name, but *I* minded; outside of the bed, it was the only way I could really show him just how much he meant to me. Besides, I like the look

I get from people when they find out somebody who looks and talks like me is Brandy Horowitz. A Jewish American Princess I'm not.

The trouble is, my life's still all cliffhangers. I was about to pack it in when Sam showed in the nick of time and saved me. When we both were gonna pack it in as detectives and him take a security guard's job down in Delaware and me be a housewife, in walked a case that changed everything. Started out as a little mob-related thing and wound up with us discoverin' the biggest secret since the A-bomb, maybe bigger.*

Don't ask me how it works, or how it's possible, but it's so. It ain't possible, but it is and that's that. Sorta like if God came down and worked miracles in front of everybody —it would convince even most atheists. Well, this thing's like that. I ain't sure I believe in flyin' saucers, neither, but if one landed in front of me and little green men got out and asked for directions, I think I would.

There ain't just one universe, there's millions of 'em, maybe more, and they all exist smack dab on top of each other. No, that's not right—they're all in the same place, only nobody and nothin' in one can see or hear or sense the existence of the others. They all started from the same creation, but they spread out at different speeds and don't ask me no more. I ain't the smart one, and even Sam can't really explain it. They say there seems to be no end to them—they stretch onwards to eternity on both sides of us. Because there's so many, almost anything that mighta happened in our universe but didn't happened somewheres else. Like, everybody says how lucky I am—I always seem to get better when it can't get no worse, like I told you. But there's maybe a couple of hundred other worlds so close to ours that I exist, and this is the only one in which I married Sam. The other me's wound up whores and maybe addicts or stuck in lousy marriages or dead or somethin', but I'm the lucky one.

Now, not too many people know about this, but one world found out that this was so and figured out a way to go

---

*For a complete account of this case, and all the gory details, read *The Labyrinth of Dreams,* Tor Books, 1986.

between the worlds. How the hell they ever did that, or even figured out that the other worlds existed, I can't imagine, but they did. This network to go between is kinda weird, like a long tunnel, but it runs mostly like a railroad, with switchmen and stations and stuff like that. Of course, even the ones who run the thing, called the Labyrinth, which Sam tells me is a word that means a maze and comes from one of them ancient mythology stories, only have stations on a few hundred, or maybe thousand, worlds. They're pretty closemouthed about that. They keep explorin', keep lookin' in at ones, until they find ones that have somethin' they might need. Might be an invention, or just a bright idea, or some raw material they need—anything. When they find somethin' like that they set up a station and put in a permanent crew and then they also recruit locals to help run things.

They don't really care about the worlds they move into, 'cept as how they can make a profit from it, and one of the things they move into and eventually take over is organized crime, which seems to exist one way or another everyplace. Like here the Mafia and a bunch of other big crime groups are really wholly owned and operated by these dudes from another world—and most of the crooks don't even know it. They also got a legit arm, the General Ordering and Development Corporation, or G.O.D., Inc. as we all call it when we don't just say 'the Company.' You may never have heard of it, but chances are you're one of their customers. You know all those things they advertise on late-night UHF TV stations and all them cable stations—knife sets, pen sets, crazy gadgets that never really work, discontinued and outdated merchandise, cheap imports, that kind of shit. You know what I mean. They have an 800 number to call to order or an address at the station, but down right at the bottom, in real small print, they have to put their name and headquarters address of who they really are and where they're really at. Well, that's where you find General Ordering and Development, Inc.

Most all the folks who work for that company don't know who or what it really is, neither. Just the ones at the very top, and some of the company security people, and them that run and secure the stations.

They can't have a station just anywhere. First of all, most places each world is totally isolated from the others, but there's always a bunch of weak points. A lot of disappearances, people bustin' into flame, visions, ghosts, you name it come from them weak points. Most of them ain't too useful, though; I mean, you build a station in downtown Philadelphia somebody's gonna find out sooner or later. They go for the isolated, middle-of-nowhere places, which are few and far between these days, and they also got to be ones they can buy up lock, stock, and barrel. The big station here's out in a hick town in redneck Oregon called McInerney—the only place they could buy up and control that was away from everything and everybody. They got a second little station up near State College in Pennsylvania, which is also middle-of-nowhere wilderness, but since they stuck both Penn State University and the biggest state pen up in there it ain't the favorite spot. It's mostly automated and used only when necessary.

They got the company headquarters smack in the middle of downtown Des Moines, Iowa. It's on a weak point, but they can't risk usin' it. All they can do there is send messages back and forth through it.

They don't have but a fraction of the worlds with stations. They only been here since the early fifties, and not in force till later'n that. I guess it was only then we came up with somethin' worth stealin'.

The Company and the Mafia and whatever pay real good and more than pay all expenses, and also cover up whatever it is that faraway home world wants here that we got and they want to steal. Don't ask me what it is—that's a closely guarded secret.

Still and all, we came out winners from that one in spite of a bunch of close scrapes and even more cliffhangers. We also did the company a big favor by exposing some rotten apples, and unlike the last time we got somethin' out of it. A fair amount, really, considerin' where we came from. We got a small suite of offices for the agency in a midtown Philadelphia high rise the company owns rent-free, our old bills paid off, several thousand bucks in seed money, and we also got some pretty good payin' clients referred to us by the Company or their people.

Not that the cases were any different or any more thrillin' than the old ones were, but there were *lots* of clients and they all paid and paid real good. At rates that started at two hundred and fifty bucks a day plus expenses, we did all right. Got us a fancy two-bedroom apartment in one of the new developments right in town, too, which is where I was that night, lookin' out the window and wishin' Sam were around. He wasn't, though; he was in Pittsburgh until the next afternoon, checking out an accountant livin' way beyond his means.

It was crazy, but right then, with a lot of what I'd always dreamed of all around, I was thinkin' 'bout quittin' the business. It was really Sam's anyway, now—I just helped out and gave support and advice now and then. Fact was, I was what the bankers call more a liability than an asset. We was movin' in higher circles and higher society with these clients. They was all educated, well off, rich—and I ain't talkin' 'bout race here, since some of 'em was blacker'n me. I wasn't the good-lookin', glamorous type, didn't know what fork to use or what wine went with what—in my old circles, Thunderbird was a step up—and it was like them and me come from different parallel worlds. You didn't have to walk the Labyrinth to find that kind of thing. All I had to do was open my mouth and I was low class, uneducated, ignorant. Most folks thought I was the receptionist anyway, or maybe the cleaning lady.

Oh, Sam made a big thing about how he needed me, couldn't get along without me, and all that, and I think maybe he believed it himself, but it wasn't true. Just goin' in to work was gettin' more and more depressin' every day, even when I had a lot of work to do. We needed more people, sure, but we needed nice, clean-cut young folks who were college grads and talked just right and all that. Most of my friends, the few I had, were from the old neighborhood in Camden or among some of my cousins all over the place. Now that we had money I was discoverin' just how many relatives I had, too. I could sure buy company, but none I felt good with.

In the end, I guess, it was just that I was beginnin' to feel useless and without much to do. We was just too removed from what I'd been used to and brought up with. All this new wealth built a wall between me and the kind of poor folks who were all I knew all my life. I could drop over there, but it was never the same. I had what they wanted and probably would never have and they knew it. Crazy thing was, too, I didn't really feel safe over there anymore.

See, that was the reason for all the trouble I got in, and maybe the reason a lot of black kids get screwed for life. I mean, there you are, a kid in a neighborhood where there's so many poor folk a lot ain't got nothin' to lose and a lot more just give up. Crime's real big and deep rooted there, simply 'cause it's the only real source of jobs and steady income. Most folks there don't wanta kill you, they just don't think two steps ahead. If you're wearin' a jacket and one wants it, he'll just go up and off you and take it. The only way a kid's got any real chance if they don't wanta be like that themselves is to join a gang. I guess it's always been that way. I seen *West Side Story* twelve times. The boys in the gang, they give you protection 'cause it's the code, and the girls, well, they give the boys whatever they want. Most times, you're as safe as you can be, but you grow up feelin' dependent on folks and with no real confidence in yourself, even though you wind up actin' tough and talkin' tough so nobody knows how scared you are, and the boys grow up thinkin' of girls as dependent, weak, *things* and not people.

The leaders of them gangs ain't got much smarts; they're all muscle and nerve, so they don't like anybody to be smarter than they are. You gotta talk gutter talk, like what they like, do what they say. That way you wind up with your first kid at fifteen or so and a life on welfare.

That's why when Daddy took me outta the gangs he also took most of my protection, my security. By the time he took me out, I was set, you know. A part of me will always be that little girl, and I'll always talk and act like I had to all them years.

Over there now, though, I was nothin' but a target. Nailin' Daddy's killers got me some respect but it didn't do nothin' for my nerve deep down. When I was with Daddy, or Sam, or the cops, it was somethin' else, but all alone I'm just a scared little ghetto girl.

I never was much for church goin', neither, so I didn't really have that to fall back on. Most of 'em I knew were either preachers on the make for some kind of political office or cause or decidin' on how the blacks got to hold a revolution or make some new country somewheres, while the rest just sat there and sang and prayed and said we might be down now but wait till we die and then we'd be in the Promised Land. Well, I never seen where that country was gonna be, and they wouldn't let Sam in, anyways, and I just ain't so sure about no Promised Land, or at least if they'd let me in when I got to the gates. Lookin' at the folks who were sure it was there and sure they'd get there, I ain't so sure a place filled with them types is where I want to be trapped for eternity, neither. Daddy never did have much belief in God, even on the battlefields, but he belonged to a church 'cause it brought in some business. Maybe that's why men got more power in business than women—they make better hypocrites.

So, I was cut off from my old neighborhood and people, and my relatives weren't no damned good to me when I needed 'em and I didn't see why I should be so damned good to them, now, and I didn't feel comfortable anywhere in the business society of most all our clients—Sam didn't like 'em none, but he could pretend he did for the money and jobs—and 'cause I was rough and foul-mouthed and talked like a poor ignorant nigger I wasn't invited to no parties or social occasions.

Not that I wanted to go back where I was. Uh uh. I ate real good, the sheets were satin, and I had a jacket in the closet there that was genuine mink, and folks who woulda laughed in my face a while back now kept tryin' to get me to take their credit cards. We was doin' real good—maybe eighty grand a year or more, before taxes, and we had a shitload of deductions. It was crazy. Years and years I worked like a dog and got nothin' but poorer and poorer— I'd'a made a profit goin' on welfare—but now I had all this stuff and not only didn't I have to work for it, it was better I didn't. If Daddy had this agency the way it was now, then maybe I'd'a grown up fancy and speakin' all clear and nice like some TV newsperson and have gone to all the right schools and I'd be right up there now. I mean, I seen some of them high-steppin' black folks around, and they seem to be real in and real popular. They're even more uncomfortable when I'm around, though; guess I remind 'em too much of their roots or what they beat. Maybe kinda like that sergeant in *Soldier's Story* who thought black society couldn't afford blacks like me no more.

Thing was, them oreos wanted to forget where they came from; I couldn't help but bring it with me.

That left Sam as the only important person in my life. He was my lover and my best friend, but he was really my *only* friend. He was everything rolled into one, but when he wasn't around I had nothin'. I needed something of my own, some place where I'd feel comfortable and something to do I felt important at.

I'm also not gettin' no younger. Oh, sure, with our connections with the Company we can get a lot of fancy stuff that keeps us lookin' and feelin' better than we should and maybe give us real nice lookin' old ages, but I never yet seen a drug that didn't have a price and I sure wouldn't start on them things if I was gonna have kids. I'm thirty-two now, my clock's tickin' on that no matter what magic they can pull, but I don't want to bring up no kids in a downtown apartment. They'll have enough problems bein' half black and half white, and I want them schooled and brought up so they at least'll be comfortable in this society where only money really matters.

We're makin' out good but we're spendin' good, too. Hard to stop when you ain't never had it before and never thought you would, and that's both Sam and me. If I got to be my own universe I want a nice, big house with lots of land, like out in the new-money sections of the Main Line.

Well, I always get down in the dumps when Sam's not around. I had to do something, though, and I knew it. I'd quit smokin' 'cause we couldn't afford it and now I was up to two packs a day and, as I say, the weight was comin' back fast, but I just couldn't bring myself to put myself on some diet. Who the hell was I tryin' to impress, anyway?

I just settled back on the bed and was goin' through the TV cable guide when the phone rang. It was late, so I figured it had to be Sam, but it wasn't. It was Bill Markham.

Now, we hadn't seen or heard from Bill Markham in quite a while, so it was a pretty big surprise. He was head of security for the Company here on our Earth, a native of here, too, and while he helped us get where we were he also was one of them folks whose nuts we'd pulled out of the fire when we stumbled into this. Without even a Christmas card after all this time, I figured that if Bill called it wasn't to see how we was.

"Brandy, is Sam back yet?"

"Uh uh. Not till tomorrow afternoon, last I knew. Why?"

"We've had something come up that might be up your line. Company business."

"I can tell him to call you when he gets in."

"Uh uh. No, this concerns both of you. You, really, more than Sam."

I was curious, at least. "Anything you can tell me now?"

"Not over the phone. It's not a security problem here—yet—but it's better told in the office where you can see the materials I have. Sam might as well be there, because he can have a role, too, if he wants, and I can't see this going off or you agreeing to anything if he's not in."

"You might be right," I admitted. "We'll see. Sam's due to get in to the airport 'bout three-forty in the afternoon, and I know he's plannin' to come straight in to the office."

"Fine. Why don't the two of you come straight over to my offices in the Tri-State Building? We'll talk there."

"Uh, yeah, sure, Bill. No hints?"

"Not now. Tomorrow. See you then."

"Yeah, okay," I responded, and he hung up.

Now I really got to wonderin', and worryin' a little, too. Me more than Sam. That was the real puzzler. I mean, we been damned lucky all in all, and we were even luckier when we fell into our lone case with the Company so far. We shoulda died or been marooned forever in one of those parallel worlds more than once.

Trouble was, all that we had here and now we owed to the Company. Everything. They gave it to us, but always with a string. Every once in a while the Company might, or might never, ask us a favor, but we sure as hell were expected to jump if it did.

That phone call wasn't no request for a friendly get-together. It was an order.

2.

A Puzzle for a Lone Hand

Sam seemed as happy to see me as I was to see him, but he looked real tired and not up to keeping on the go the rest of the night. He wasn't at all happy to hear about our appointment with Markham, not just 'cause he didn't feel like doin' anything much but also 'cause he felt it had to be bad news.

We quickly got his stuff in the car and I drove him into town. He's not too thrilled about the way I drive, so if he let me he was real tired.

"He didn't say what it was about?"

I shook my head. "Nope. Only that it was me he wanted. You're just there 'cause he knows I won't do it if you say no."

He sighed. "Yeah, that bothers me, too. I don't like this, babe, not one bit. If this is anything like the mess we had last time it might be real bad. We can't always luck out of these things."

"I been thinkin' the same thing. Look, Sam, do we have to take it? I mean, I'd kinda like to see some of them other worlds sometime, I admit, when we know what they are and what the hell is goin' on, but gettin' back into that shit they get themselves into—that's somethin' else."

"Well, we have to go to the meeting, anyway," he replied. "Look, we gotta face facts. We're doing real good right now. Real good. And the whole business is growing. Thing is, though, it's doing good and growing only because the big boys have us on the approved list. One word from good old Godawful, Incorporated and we're back in Camden fighting roaches if we're lucky. You remember *The Godfather?*"

"Sure. Saw it three times."

"Well, that's what it's all about. We did them a favor,

16

mostly by accident, and they offered a favor back." He went into his Brando impression. Sam was great for impressions. *"Someday, and that time may never come, you might be asked to do a small service for me in return.* Well, this time G.O.D. is Godfather, Inc. We been called."

"I think that considerin' what all we done for them, we're even."

"So do I, but all that does is mean we'll get to live our natural lives out. Once you take, you get taken. There's no such thing as a *little* graft. Still, I don't feel any obligation to get my head blown off for them, and even less obligation to let them get *your* head blown off. They set us up, but Spade and Marlowe isn't a subsidiary of G.O.D., Inc., although, Lord knows, everything else seems to be. We been down before, we can be down again. I love this now, yeah, but I love you and life more."

I woulda kissed him for that if I could keep from crashin' the car, 'cause he meant it. Still, I'd been doin' some figurin' of my own.

"Look, Sam—suppose it *is* a big risk? You know I been feelin' kinda trapped, and even though we're livin' good, we ain't got no reserve and if we have to make the agency bigger we'll have ta put most of our money there for a while. Ain't neither of us gettin' no younger, so this might be a chance for a score. We'll hear the man out, but I promise that if we both don't go for it then I won't go it alone. Fair?"

"Fair," he agreed.

Bill Markham was one of them tall, good-lookin', sandy-haired guys who usually is the sales director of some company on the way up or maybe some jock sellin' running shoes on TV. I knew he was older'n me, maybe closer to Sam's age, but he looked real *young* and he talked real smooth. Knowin' Sam was tired and we both was curious, though, he got straight to the point. There was just us in his office, door locked, everything off. Real private.

He reached into his pocket, pulled out a little box, and put his thumb on a small square just about big enough for it. The box opened, and he took out a small opaque cube about the size of a thumbnail. It looked like cheap polished plastic, and 'cept for a brown circle on the bottom there was nothin' to mark it.

"This is what's known as a parium capsule. I don't know

where the name comes from, but they all look pretty much like this except for the color and sometimes the size. Basically, it's a needle—a substance is sealed inside in some kind of suspension when it's made, then you put it where you want to inject it on bare skin, with this little circle down flat against the skin, and press real hard. Anything inside is injected directly into the bloodstream. It even has a little bit of logic, so if it needs to find an artery it'll do it. No needle marks, no pain, no infection, not even much sensation except a little suction feeling when it fires. Then you toss it away. The Company's field medics and others with a need for it have them around. They're small, stackable, easy to store, and you can have a whole pharmacy in a shoe box. This one's used, so feel free to take a look at it, but don't touch the little spot."

We both looked, but neither of us felt like handlin' it. You didn't know what had been inside, and none of them gadgets get a hundred percent out; leastwise, none I ever knew.

"The machine for loading them is small and very portable and has its own internal power. It's a highly restricted device, but as with all highly restricted devices it's not impossible to get one or many if you really want them and you have Company or home world contacts."

Home world. That was the world that was supposed to be some kinda paradise off what it ripped off of all the other worlds. They didn't invent nothin', but what he was showin' us wasn't of this world for sure.

"It's real handy. You can take something—a drug, for instance—and transport it almost any way you like in bulk, then just load it into the little machine, load a bunch of these in as well, and press start. At the other end, the little capsules come out filled with whatever dosage you put in as the load, all precise, stacked and arranged like sugar cubes. These things themselves are tricky to perfect, but once you have the mold in silicon anybody can turn them out."

"I never liked shots much, but so what?" Sam asked. "It's not too far off what might be around here in a few years."

"Maybe. Maybe not. Think about what this might do in, say, the heroin racket, or freebase, or anything like that. Measured doses, different strengths, all safe, and everybody gets their own fresh needle every day so there's no chance of infection or contamination."

"I'd make a guess they already have," I put in. "Otherwise, why tell us about it?"

He shrugged. "They haven't come in here, anyway. There was a move to get them into the narcotics trade here simply as a safety measure, something we could do, but that talk's all but died out now. But elsewhere, we're facing something new, something even the opposition is a little nervous about."

The opposition. That meant any folks in the Company or workin' for it or on the home world who didn't like things the way they was and wanted changes, by fair means or not. Control of the whole multi-universe business was really in the hands of just a very few people, nameless and faceless to us, who were called the Board of Directors, and from what they told us this Board was basically one big family. It was kinda like a kingdom, with the same few families holdin' all the top jobs and top power, and that always left other folks unhappy. Anytime you had this much power in so few hands you was bound to have a lot of lower-downs after your hide. That was one reason why gettin' in to the home world was so hard and so restricted, and why them Directors never left.

"A drug?" I prompted him.

"Yeah. A drug and more than just a drug. You two have been around. You know what the usual drugs will do. There's a fair number of addicts who couldn't get off if they wanted to, and if they need a fix bad enough they'll kill their own grandmother."

We both nodded. We knew that all too well.

"There's a new drug. At least we call it a drug, although it doesn't act like any drug anybody has ever seen. It acts a little like it's alive, although if you saw it under a microscope you couldn't believe it could be. It looks almost like water, maybe just a touch brownish, and if it is injected anywhere into a Type Zero human it heads straight for the brain, checks it out, takes over, then moves in and starts doing its thing. It actually manufactures duplicates of enzymes in your brain and then replaces your natural enzymes with its duplicates. The duplicates are of the same sort, but not exactly. They're purer, actually more efficient. When they first take over control, whatever those enzymes control gets a pure jolt of what it likes and so do you. There are pleasure centers in the brain. When stimulated, the body sticks in these enzymes and you feel pleasure. In this case, the pleasure would be prolonged and absolute."

"That's a fairly simplified description of the way drugs like heroin work, Bill," Sam noted. I got to admit I got a little lost with all them enzymes but I figured the result.

"That's true, but that's because the plant enzymes, highly refined, are injected directly. In this case, the process is indirect. We have a controller, almost a control center, that uses the body's own materials to make what it needs, but *it* controls things. With heroin, rejection sets in, the plant substances or chemicals are expelled, and it's kind of like an engine suddenly losing its oil. Unlike the engine, your body will eventually replace and start making those chemicals again, leaving only the memory of the stimuli, but between the time the enzymes or chemicals are expelled and the time the body needs to replenish and regear it's like running an engine with very little oil. It gets very, very sick."

That was the best way to explain withdrawal to a lay person I ever heard.

"It *does* pass, though, without killing or doing real harm to the body," Sam pointed out. "You only *wish* you'd die."

"True. But a lot of what we do is based on pleasure-pain stimuli. The memory of the rush, just how great you felt, remains, and a fair number are inclined to get hooked again even if they're forced off. Now this stuff is different. It's more like a parasite. It spreads over your body, but doesn't duplicate itself to the extent of harming any part of it. It gets what it needs from the body, and it's pretty stable once it's complete, but it knows you. Don't ask me how that's possible, but it does. If it gets into the brain it sort of takes over. The body abruptly considers it natural and normal. Your body defenses won't fight it. It survives by controlling that chemical balance, the blockers and the enzymes, in your brain. If it needs sugars and starches for some reason, it'll stimulate its host to eat particular things. Ditto for things rich in various minerals and whatever. It can suppress urges, emotions, desires, or heighten them to near compulsion."

I got to admit I was gettin' a real sick feelin' inside. "You mean it takes over, makes the body a slave? It *thinks?*"

"No. I doubt if anything like this ever could think as we understand thought. And it just manages the body and stays where it is and gets what it needs and it's happy, leaving the host to still be him or herself, subject to its requirements. There actually are some microscopic life forms like this here on Earth, but all in the lower animals and all known here so far in marine organisms. We think this is a natural organism. We think that on some world, somewhere, it was allowed to evolve so that it reached a very high state and operated on the highest life forms, and on land as well. You can't just catch it, like a disease. A specially organized cluster—still microscopic but definite—must invade the new host. Its remote cousins here reproduce by sex between two hosts—and it can compel its host to have sex, and does. The trouble is, from its point of view, it doesn't work that way in Type Zeros, so we think this is from a world quite different from ours."

I didn't remember much from our lessons on the Company, but I remembered what he meant by Type Zero. That was the type that the home world was—which also happened to be the type *we* were, too. Just plain folks. The further away you got from us, though, on both sides, the more real strong differences came on. Humans developed in different places than here, or with maybe different ancestors. Some of 'em was ugly as sin and looked like folks from a bad horror movie, but they was still basically human anyway. They just went to show how different we could have turned out with just one little thing goin' another way. Those they called Type One, and no matter how weird they looked, they was all close enough to us that we could probably have sex and produce somethin' neither of us would really like to claim. Sorta like you can breed a lion and a tiger, or a cow and a buffalo; like that.

Type Twos came from different ancestors and weren't close enough to breed with us. At best they'd produce sterile offspring—like mules—and mostly nothin' at all. Type Threes and beyond were so far off us that they might as well be from Jupiter or somewheres for all we had in common. We couldn't even catch their colds.

Trouble was, there was millions of worlds side by side that was only different in smaller things, then millions of Type Ones on both sides of them, and so on. A lot more than the Company could count, let alone know everything about.

"So we can catch it but we can't give it," I said. "That's somethin'."

"Yeah. It means real addiction. We think it's a Type One organism, but we haven't been able to locate where it came from and considering the number and range it might take years, even decades, if all resources were put on doing just that. It's a needle-in-a-haystack proposition. On our own, we'll find this one only by the kind of luck you have hitting the lottery. Now it does a nice, neat job inside of us, but we're not what it evolved in and it runs into problems. Something in our air, or our body chemistry, or whatever gets to it after a while. It begins to slow down, then break down. The only thing that can restore it is a fresh module of itself. What it does inside the body is very complicated; suddenly it can't handle the task. It starts cutting back. It starts to die and it tells you about it by hitting the pain centers. It also becomes a massive infection in the brain, fighting off all comers and struggling to survive one more minute. The withdrawal becomes the ultimate agony—and the host dies before the parasite does."

Sam was kinda disturbingly clinical, but, then, he'd been a vice squad man. "How long before this breakdown?"

"About thirty hours, give or take with the individual. Never less than twenty-four and never more than forty as near as we can tell. Our samples have been very limited, our information mostly second-hand or eavesdrop or observations by people not trained in this sort of thing. Withdrawal takes another six to eight hours of increasing agony before you pass out and the heart stops. Brain tissue disruption or destruction begins shortly after the pain button is pressed, though, and accelerates from there. We think that's what kills, eventually. The autonomic nervous system—heart, breathing, whatever—is disrupted. Let it go too long and a fresh infusion will get the body going again but it won't repair whatever brain damage you get. The effects are wide ranging and inconsistent from individual to individual. There could be memory loss, or some sensory loss—vision, hearing, taste, smell—or some motor function problems or intelligence, talents, abilities—you name it. But pain's the last to go."

I listened, not understandin' all the biology shit but understandin' the effects on the people good enough. "Bill —how do you know this?" I asked him. "The only way you could know this is if it was done on people."

"It was," he said softly. "But not by us. This isn't something we'd *ever* fool with. It's too scary."

"Can you kill it?" Sam asked. "Without killing the addict, I mean?"

"Sure. You can kill anything. If we had enough cases, we could easily isolate whatever starts breaking it down. Without tipping off the opposition and letting them know we're on to them, we just don't know for sure if we could cure it or not and if so what the price would be. We got hold of some raw samples, strictly by accident, and ran them through every test and every expert and computer the home world has. We have been unable to make it grow in the lab, and it ignores test animals, even chimps. The only way it'll reproduce is inside a human, and since the reproductive clusters humans produce lack something it needs and can't get, they aren't any good, either."

With that kind of setup, Bill Markham then let us have the whole load.

I got to admit I don't understand the Labyrinth, and I ain't sure nobody really does. I sure can't figure out how them early scientists guessed it was there, let alone built this network, this inter-world railroad. I been in it a few times, but I still can't figure what's happenin' in there. It's like a real long tunnel, stretchin' out in all directions, only you're inside a cube with windows. Windows up top, windows beneath, and on all sides 'cept the ones that keep you in the Labyrinth. That means you always got a choice of four worlds to exit to. Every once in a while, there's a switch junction, with a control room and Labyrinth in all directions. That switcher punches his buttons and you go which way he decides, into a whole set of new cubes in all directions until you get to other switch points.

Sam and me we went to a bunch of 'em, and we always

walked, but there's enough room in there to drive a truck through—if you could figure out how to make a truck go up or down instead of just forward, back, left, and right. Of course, it probably ain't left or up in there; none of the usual rules mean much inside there, 'cause you're outside every-place else. They must have some kinda trucks or flyin' saucers or whatever they use, though, 'cause they move trainloads of shit through that thing.

Three guilds, which I guess are sorta like unions or somethin', run the thing. One controls the switch points, one runs the stations, and a third moves the cargo through from one point to another. Ain't no way the biggest, baddest computer in creation could look at all that stuff all the time, though, so security mostly monitors the switches 'cause just about everybody and everything has to pass at least one of 'em.

The first way they check is that everybody who has any real business in there's got some kind of code thing in your bones. Fact is, there might be a whole hell of a lot of Brandys, even with the same fingerprints and eyes and all that, but they ain't the same person no matter how alike they are. I got a code planted somewhere inside my bones—don't ask me how or where. They stuck me in a thing like an iron lung, punched a bunch of buttons, I didn't feel nothin', and that was it. But now any switchman can look at his or her board as soon as I'm inside that cube and read out not only who I am but *which* I am. The code's big, random, and total nonsense. It's all in computers, of course, but they tell me that even if you got into the computer you couldn't find the numbers.

If you don't have no number, and you look suspicious, they shoot you off to some siding, someplace on a world where people just never came about, and you sit there till they're ready for you, if they ever are. We had that happen. If you don't have no coding but you sound like you know what you're doin', you can sometimes bluff 'em with a convincin' destination, but they can send messages at about the same speed as they can send you, and they call security on both ends. At least, you could, 'cause we did it, but I'm told they tightened that up now. No code, and you get dumped no matter what.

They tightened up a lot of other shit when we breezed through their system. Now before you go in you got to file a destination and any stops with the stationmaster who sends it to the security computer, and you're checked as you go along. Guess they were kinda sloppy and cocksure of themselves till we screwed 'em.

Still, somebody first found the world with this drug disease thingie, whatever it was, then figured out how to bottle or can it or whatever and brought it down the line to the Type Zero—our type—area. There ain't a lot of switches up in Type One and Two territory, and lots of unexplored worlds in between them, so it was possible that somebody could be goin' from one legit point to another and stop off just long enough to pick up the goods.

That meant there had to be somebody who knew just what they was doin' in the world where this shit came from, then somebody who could get messages back and forth without security knowin' to set up the deal and the pickups, then somebody in the transport guild to actually pick up and carry the stuff, disguised as part of legitimate cargo, and drop *it* off at its destination, where other big plotters would make use of it. Pretty complicated stuff.

The Company didn't know who discovered it, or how, and how they managed to both figure out what they had and keep it quiet, even settin' up this scheme. They didn't know how long it had taken to set up. They *did* know that it was well organized and involved some real bigwigs someplace and lots of corruption, but that was it. They just bumped into it, when they had an accident or something in one of the cargo haulers or whatever that they use and found it strictly by luck. They didn't let on they knew, and it seemed like the transport guild worker was innocent. They'd already switched it and he was now on a legit run. They put a tracer on it to see who'd pick it up, and somebody did.

"Rupert Conrad Vogel," Bill said, showin' us a photo of a guy who looked like a fugitive from a cheap World War II movie. "He's a stationmaster, which means administration and a Company man, or so we thought. He got the shipment, took a lot of it, then sent some back disguised as something else, again looking very routine. The pickup courier was legitimate, but he encountered another courier along his route and somehow that second courier got the package and dropped it clandestinely at a world where we didn't have a station but did know. We picked this courier up, stuck him in a hypnoscan, then erased any memories he had of being picked up and discovered and let him continue. He didn't know much. He just got some nice little extras all in things he and his family could enjoy but we wouldn't particularly notice, and for that he got a message slip passed into his pocket now and then that a shipment—he didn't even know what it was, nor cared—would be with so-and-so as unlisted or misaddressed cargo. He'd meet the other courier, either get the parcel or note that it was wrong and offer to take it back to headquarters for resorting, then drop it when his route took him near this other world. That was it."

"You dead sure this ain't just the tip of the iceberg?" I asked him.

"Pretty sure. Their supply is limited. There's no clear routine as to when the shipments come, but that's probably just to disguise their origins. Vogel's their dispatcher. He gets it, he holds on to it, and then he sends it out in measured amounts. As far as we can tell, he's handling the real experimentation himself, and very effectively and ruthlessly. He's well placed to be able to do so, as you'll see in a minute."

"And the other place?" Sam asked.

"A world not too far from this one and very similar in a lot of ways. They're getting only about three thousand doses every twenty to thirty days, so there's only enough to sustain maybe a hundred people. They appear to be going to a local organized crime underboss who's never had any known connection with us and shouldn't even know about the Labyrinth. He, in turn, has one man supervising it and they seem to be using it in a very low-level way, to maintain a group of young women as prostitutes. This thing's ready-made for that on a petty level—I mean, this thing *compels* you to have sex a lot. We don't know what connection they have to Vogel, or why they were picked, or why they're being allowed to use something like this for such a petty and ordinary thing. Company people don't go there, except our wayward courier, of course, and we've had a monitor on that gate ever since and nobody but that courier ever approached. We sent in a small team of agents, and they couldn't find anything odd, either. There's a connection there, but we can't find it."

"But they know about the Labyrinth," Sam noted.

"Yeah, they do—but not many," Bill replied. "The big boss has had a lodge up near the central Pennsylvania weak point for years, and this place happens to be one of those on the way from here to there that's weak enough that when we open that Labyrinth route it can be accessed without a station—like the dead end you two were shoved into that time."

"Yeah, only here nobody jumps in but something gets tossed out. All we could find was that they were being paid off to do just what they're doing and ask no questions. There's lots of ways you can do it when you have a crime boss on the hook, including checking close other worlds, getting inside information he can use, and feeding it to him. You can feed him just enough, wrapped around the parcel, to keep him quiet and on the hook."

"You mean," I said, "that somebody just pops up once and bribes this crime boss into this? We'll pay you if you find fifty or more girls and hook 'em on this?"

"That's about it. We don't know why. Makes no sense on its face, and except for the fact that most but not all of the girls they hooked are relatively young, there's no connecting thread between them. None. There's no reason to think they know much. Just hired help, like the courier—but a lot harder to snatch and interrogate. You see what kind of a bind we're in?"

We could see, too. "You can't snatch any addicts for information 'cause they'd be dead in two days," I noted. "You can't take out the courier without killin' all them girls and lettin' whoever's doin' this know you're on to 'em. Ain't nobody in this chain that knows anything worth knowin' 'cept this guy Vogel."

"Yeah. Vogel. He knows a lot, even if he doesn't know it all. He had to be directly contacted if only to corrupt him. He had to be sold on becoming a traitor, which is much harder considering the risks. He's got one hell of a racket where he is that fits his peculiarities to a T, and he's got a reliable reputation. He'd have to be offered something really big to switch. He also knows exactly what he's got because he's in charge of the experimentation, and as a stationmaster he's well positioned to move people and goods when he wants."

"Why not just take him out, then?" Sam asked. "Get him out of there on a pretext, fry his brain, and then take what results he has as well?"

Bill Markham sighed. "I wish it were that easy, Sam, but it's not. This is a class A operation all the way. They're very good, whoever they are. Vogel will spook and run at the first suspicion, and probably has people there working for him even *he* doesn't know about whose only job is to take him out if he gets nabbed or exposed. The labs, the whole place he's got, are wired for one hell of a big explosion should anything go wrong, and we don't even know who might trigger it or how. We could kill him, of course, anytime, but that only buys us time until they can set up another site like his that we don't know about. We've tried tricking him out, but he's always come up with a plausible excuse not to leave. If we press too hard, he'll blow that joint and split to a safe line."

Bill sat back in his chair and sighed. "You see," he continued, "he's our only real lead and he's eggshells. He's no good to us dead. And we *have* to know what the hell is going on. We don't know what this stuff is, where it comes from, who's bringing it in and how, and, worst of all, we don't know what they plan to do with it. We have a lot of pieces, very few real live suspects, and none of them fit. Why go to all this risk? What's it all about? All we know is that clearly they can't synthesize it, either, so they're pretty limited, and that means they have a very specific plot in mind—but what? Something big, real big, or they wouldn't take all these risks. Very big people are involved just to do what they've done. Who are they? How did they manage it? What are they planning? You see?"

I did see. Bill had one hell of a problem on his hands. "But, Bill—you got agents, all that technology, all that power. Surely you can do a snatch-and-grab with this guy," I said.

"You'd think so, wouldn't you? The trouble is, this guy's

stationmaster and he's smart. He wouldn't have turned traitor without taking that into consideration. He knew what he was up against, and who. Cranston was a stationmaster, too, you remember, and he'd even set up a resort on a weak point with a Labyrinth substation in his basement, and he came damned close to getting away."

We remembered. We had to chase the bastard through the Labyrinth and he still almost killed us.

Markham slipped some switches and the room went dark and a panel came down in back of his desk. Another button, and some slides appeared on the back, the first of a really *enormous* mansion that looked like a cross between a fancy home in the country and Fort Apache.

"Looks like a federal penitentiary with a nice house in the middle," Sam noted. "Are those machine gun towers on that outer wall?"

"They are, and you have three rows of fence before you even *get* to the wall. The distance between the first two fences is wide enough for men with nasty dogs to go through, which they do, and there are sensors on the fences for any kind of disturbance. Even a rabbit brings the dogs running. The third fence line is electrified with enough juice to fry anybody. Then there's the wall, which has both machine gun coverage and is thick enough for riflemen to stand between the towers. A hundred and eighty-six guys held a far less secure wall against five thousand infantry for twelve days at the Alamo."

"But they eventually lost," Sam pointed out.

"Yeah, they lost—but you could hold this place for a while, anyway. Long enough to realize you were going to be overrun, burn the papers, get out of there and blow the whole complex. The entire estate is honeycombed with tunnels packed with explosives that would leave a crater half a mile wide."

"There's gates front and back," I noted.

"Not much better. Built like Sam's prison. Reinforced metal and concrete and heavily defended so that any assault on the gates would have to be over open ground. We could use a small missile to blow them, but we'd never get enough people inside without tremendous losses and, of course, enough time to blow the place."

"Air drop?" Sam suggested.

"Again, possible, but he's got radar and air defenses that could pick up a pigeon at half a mile. A small force could get in, we think, but it would be hamstrung. It'd have to move to get him, and to do that it would have to pass a spider's web of television monitors wired to a central security control in the basement of the place. We can get them in, but we can't get to him and take him out without discovery no matter how hard we figure it."

"Bill—if he don't know you know he's gone bad, why this fort?" I wondered. "I mean, this ain't what the average station has."

"You're right, of course. That's the station there, to the back and left of the main house. Maybe fifty yards. The other outbuildings are quarters for the guards and supply houses and—other things. The reason it is the way it is is basically because Vogel lives in a world where that kind of thing is necessary for the health of somebody in his position. In fact, we helped set up some of the defenses initially to protect the station, and we figure he's made a lot of changes since then to protect against us as well."

In the world of Rupert Vogel, it seemed, we lost World War II. I ain't too clear on the history, neither, but it goes somethin' like this: the Germans didn't get bogged down in Russia because they attacked in the spring and won before winter set in, finally gettin' the Japs to attack Siberia and put the squeeze on. Then they turned back to England and with so many men and airplanes they finally wiped out the air defenses and invaded. We, on the other hand, spent almost all our time goin' against Japan. We mighta done somethin', too, but the Germans got their missiles goin' and managed to use the time to perfect the A-bomb ahead of us. We got it about the same time they did, but they had the way to deliver it, off ships and from friendly places in South America or somethin'. They nuked Norfolk and San Diego and places like that and that was the end of it.

Not that it weren't real messy and bloody when they came in, but we never had to face this kind of army before, one that didn't care who it killed or what it had to do. Everybody got IDs and papers, and couldn't sneeze without bein' checked. Then folks got classified, kinda South Africa style. The Jews all got shipped to camps in Georgia and Nevada and it was pretty clear what happened to them there. The folks with good German or Italian or even English names and backgrounds, they got the best treatment if they was cooperative, and lots were. We was beat good. These folks got to be the managers and bosses if they wasn't already. Then the rest of the Europeans, they got a second-class thing and they did the work in the factories, mines, you name it. All the Orientals got shipped to Japan or China or someplace.

That left the ten percent who was black, and there was a lot more of us than there were Jews or Orientals. They put us in the camps like the rest, and millions died, but they also used us. It was like they turned the clock back a hundred years. We became the lab animals for their experiments and medical stuff, others were trained as personal servants—slaves, really—to the big boys, and some of 'em, the big Nazi lords, even kept us like pets and bred us. The whole thing made me sick to my stomach, and Sam wasn't lookin' none too good, neither. He sure wouldn't survive in this new world, and his parents woulda been gassed. Thing was, a Bill Markham woulda come out pretty good unless he was one of them patriotic principled types. With his name, looks, and background he would probably be headin' up a storm trooper division at least.

"The Nazi-style culture is based on conflict, competition, and combat," he was sayin'. "They've had a lot of tension with the Japanese over the years but no real wars with them mostly because they just don't have enough people to manage all the lands they have now. Eventually they'll go to war for the rest of the world, but there is just no way the Germans and all those whom they've conscripted can both hold their control and expand. Taking over a continent and population this size was almost more than they could chew. When that kind of thing happens to people like these, they start going at each other's throats. Tiny putsches, minor coups, knocking off the local *statenfuehrer* and his boys and replacing them with a new lot just as bad or worse. The Reich allows it, since it bleeds off steam and there's a feeling that anybody who's sloppy enough to get knocked off or overthrown deserved it—the strong replacing the weak. How much power and strength you have is the sole measure of importance there after racial background, and they can get pretty hazy on that if they need people."

"So he's trapped inside his own fortress, afraid of his own people," Sam noted. "Some paradise."

"It's not as bad as all that. Probably no worse than guarding the President here against nuts. But when he's at home and in control, he wants to make sure that nothing happens to him and his, and, of course, we couldn't allow a station to fall into the hands of somebody we didn't control. That's why we went along with the mining and explosives part. As usual, our people set ourselves up as the standard. If we can't crack it, then it's safe, and we did a good job here. Trouble is, we never allowed for having to crack it ourselves. We can blow him and the Labyrinth station to hell, of course, but that won't get us anywhere. *We need Vogel alive.* He knows the results of the experiments. He knows the plot, at least the outlines of it. He might know just about all of it."

"You're sure he's not the ringleader?" I asked him.

"No, he can't be. He's never had any experience outside Type Zero lines, and he hasn't been involved with anybody who has. He's also a field man; he works stations, not the Labyrinth. He wouldn't have the knowledge or ability to set this off, although he's an important man in making it work."

"You think this is actually the competition, or is it maybe either an attempt by some Type One culture to take over down here?" Sam asked him. "Or, could it be some internal plot among the bigwigs of the company for control?" The 'competition' is what Company types liked to call anybody not workin' in their best interests.

Markham shrugged. "Who knows? Whoever this is is certainly in league with the competition. Vogel may know. That's why we need him so badly."

I shifted in my chair. "Look, Bill, I see this puzzle of yours and it's kinda interestin', but what's it hav'ta do with us?"

"I was getting to that. I've described to you how it's impossible to make an unobserved entry to Vogel's lair. Even inside the manor house, there's TV cameras, hidden monitors, you name it, and security all over the place.

There's only one place where the snatch could be put on Vogel, and that's a medium-sized room that's dead center of the second floor of the house. It's called the Safe Room, and its double-insulated, soundproofed, and unmonitored. It's entered, if you can believe this, through Vogel's private bathroom, and the door itself can be locked and secured from the inside. You could live through a bomb blast in there, and you could also not hear a full-scale invasion. It's his retreat—the one place in there where he feels totally safe. It's reinforced top and bottom as well, and is as secure as a bank vault. He spends a lot of time in there. We built it that way because the records and codes for the Company and Labyrinth that are the sole privy of the stationmaster must be kept somewhere safe and it was the easiest and safest point at which we could modify the place and install such a thing without ripping the old building down."

"Yeah, but so what?" Sam said a little cynically. "Even if you had some way of getting somebody in there with him, somebody who could take Vogel—and I'm not sure you can—then what? You can't get him out. I'm sure the place has no windows. So, anybody would have to take the leader out the only door, and all he'd need to do was give some signal, some indication, and you were dead."

"Give us some credit. We weren't going to build a place like that where the stationmaster, in a crisis, couldn't get out before it all blew. There's another door—an exit only, in the floor. Not even Vogel can use it to get in—it's booby-trapped and designed to jam and trap somebody inside who tried it. One way only. An emergency exit. It leads down through the walls to the basement area, then into a tunnel that runs out back of the house and all the way to the station, coming up here, near the control room stairway. The final defense is very simple, really—a bunch of rods that support a particular part of the tunnel ceiling. Even try opening or blowing your way through from the station end and the rods collapse—and so does half the tunnel. From inside, though, you only have to throw a few levers to move the rods to a safety position, allowing the door to open. When it closes again, the rods slip back into place. One way only, as I said."

This was suddenly gettin' interestin', although I still wasn't too sure I liked where it was goin'.

"What we propose is this," Markham went on. "Two separate actions both timed to the second. One is a diversionary attack on the wall from outside. That'll draw security's attention and most of the security personnel. At the same time, our team will use a command force from the Labyrinth to enter the station even if it's not operating. With the gate open, we can tap whatever power and forces we need. We'll be in our element. We could hold that place for an incredible length of time, even against direct bomb hits and worse."

"How long?" Sam pressed. "If you need a diversion it means they'll know they've been had even if they can't get to you. How long can you hold it before you'll have to withdraw or risk being blown up?"

"I doubt if they'll blow up the whole complex with an external attack jeopardizing their escape routes, but we figure thirty, maybe forty minutes tops."

"Uh huh. And what about Vogel? He's not going to know there even *is* an attack if he's as isolated as you say, but if he does learn it, he's also going to know that it's the Company because they have the station and he's not going to exit that way. He'll hotfoot it out of there a different way and make for a hidden substation just like Cranston did."

"No, it won't be as easy for Vogel as it was for Cranston, who built one of his houses over a weak point and assembled a substation there. This isn't Oregon, it's Pennsylvania —central Pennsylvania. The nearest weak point he could make for that would be accessible to him would be hundreds of miles away at either a point near Asheville, North Carolina, or even further away up in Newfoundland. Des Moines is too small, and too well covered inside. You're right, though. He'd try and get out overland to one of those points somehow if he knew the station was taken, but he won't know. We egged on and supported an overambitious major—I think his name was Ryland—to move against Vogel, and we studied the drill. If they're attacked and Vogel isn't in the Safe Room, he goes there immediately. If he's in there, he stays there, and gets sent a blinking light alarm. Then he can plug in a phone that connects through a direct wire to security in the basement and get the details and decide on a course of action from almost complete safety."

"Neat," I said. "This Ryland—I guess he didn't make it."

"His people got a pretty fair way, but they eventually were killed or captured. Vogel had the captured ones hung up alive on hooks suspended from the outer wall and left there until they died. He left the bodies to rot as an object lesson. Ryland tried to get away in a helicopter and they shot it down with a surface-to-air missile."

"Nice guy you got there," I said sourly. "No wonder he went bad."

"Uh uh. It *is* a wonder he went bad, and part of the puzzle. It takes an ugly, brutish, but smart man to survive and hold on to power in that kind of society. He was carefully picked because *our* Vogel was so much like *their* Vogel, all the way through, only *our* Vogel was stuck as a low-level administrator. Thing is, he's exactly right for that kind of role in that kind of world and he has everything he ever dreamed of. If he finally was tired of the price in lack of privacy and whatever that the position demanded, he could always have asked to be replaced as stationmaster and retired to a world that still fit him. Now, he's forbidden to ever be a member of the Reich Council or Führer—in spite of his German name and lineage he was born in Pittsburgh, and you have to be a native-born European German to get those kind of posts, or even get into the position where you might get them. He might well become Leader of the Western Reich someday, though, if he plays it right and survives, so he has a lot to lose by crossing us. What could he gain?"

"The only way you can pay that kinda dude is with power. Real big power," I pointed out. "What's he care 'bout bein' no new Hitler when he knows how many worlds there are?"

Markham nodded. "And that means that this whole business is real big, about as big as can be. They're careful, really patient, limiting their experiments, getting it right even if it takes years."

I thought a moment. "If they could hook whole worlds on this shit, you'd have the ultimate power trip."

"You would, but I doubt if that's their intention. We have—what? Four, maybe closing in on five billion people just here alone, right? That's four billion doses a day, every day, forever. The distribution and supply alone would drive you bananas. Somehow, though, it's an attack against the Company, probably near its heart to go through all this. Think of men like Vogel, all of them, in total control of the technology, the knowledge, and the Labyrinth itself. I don't know what or how, but I feel it in my bones. Something very dangerous is going on here and Vogel's the only key. We think we finally figured one way to nab him."

I looked over at Sam and he looked back at me, and I guess we both thought at the same time, *here it comes at last.*

"Vogel is a man of heavy sexual needs, but he's also a total paranoid because he has to be to survive. He has a project, a hobby, that's highly offensive to anybody but something he does anyway. It's called *schwartzenbrood,* or something like that. He acquires, trains, and even breeds black women. He picks them according to rigid criteria, acquires them only from other area *gruppenfuehrers,* and they alone are his personal household staff. They prepare his meals, and test them first, and they make his bed, dress him, even bathe him. He treats them more like pets than people. When he gets new women, he always spends some time with them in the Safe Room."

I got that ugly twinge in the pit of my stomach. "You want to slip me in as one of *them*? And take him in the Safe Room and get him to the Labyrinth through the tunnel?" He didn't say nothin', so I added, "You *got* to be *jokin'.*"

"He's arranged to purchase three women from a man he's done business with many times before down in southern Virginia. He trusts this man as much as he trusts anyone, because he's got concrete evidence that the man is both a thief and a traitor, which he is. This man's under constant watch by the secret police; he only lives from day to day at Vogel's whim. We, however, can pull a substitution there thanks to our own agents and resources. Vogel's men then pick them up and take them, and you, to the manor. One of the girls is nearly a dead ringer for you—not identical and probably not related, but so close that it's mostly a matter of switching fingerprint cards. You get in, and he takes you to the Safe Room. We'll be monitoring you all the way thanks to a tracer we can put inside your body that even Vogel's best won't discover."

"He'd never buy it," I told him. "Hell, Bill, I'm kinda fat and without my glasses I couldn't see *you* behind your desk, there. I know I don't talk real good, but I sure as hell can't keep up no *Gone With the Wind* act for maybe days or weeks. If he's as careful as you say he's gonna check anyways. And even if I got that far, how am I gonna take him? He looks like a pretty big guy in that picture there."

"You forget our technology. When we snatched that courier and interrogated him, we had to make him forget that he was ever found out, let alone questioned, and do it so that even somebody else with our technology couldn't discover it. Otherwise, we couldn't have taken even that risk with him. You will be absolutely authentic so that even drugs and hypnoscans will not show you as anything other than what we want you to appear. Only when you are actually in his rooms will everything suddenly come back to you, clearly, completely, and thoroughly. At that point, you'll be able to switch the *persona* on and off as needed or required—but, of course, you wouldn't stand hard interrogation from that point. We've done it before. We also might be able to temporarily increase your vision by certain techniques, at least for a week or two. Not twenty-twenty, but much better than now. We don't dare apply any sort of contact or surgical correction, of course. Somebody there might notice. What do you think?"

"I think it stinks," Sam growled. "How big is Vogel, anyway?"

"About six feet, maybe two hundred thirty pounds."

"You think he takes 'em in there to play house? How does she get a weapon? Brandy's pretty strong and she's okay in the chop-chop stuff, but you can't depend on that in this case."

"We don't intend to. We have capsules that will defy a dentist's examination and X-rays. We'll put one or two in, immunize her against the agents, and all she has to do is kiss him and within two minutes or less he'll be the most cooperative, docile sort of fellow you ever want to meet. The cruder, less certain methods would be strictly backup."

"And I'd have like twenty minutes to lay this guy low, then at most another half hour to get him through the tunnel to you, right? That ain't much of a margin when anything might go wrong," I noted. "What if he decides to stick one of them little cubes on me? Or has somethin' done to my *brain* before he takes me up there? We got a lot of chances for things to go wrong for good here, and only real short margins for it all if it goes right. Maybe if them Nazis were invadin' here right now, and Sam and me are both candidates for the gas chambers, then this would be worth the risk, but it *ain't*. I'm sorry 'bout this world, but it ain't *my* world and it's gonna be just as shitty with or without me or Vogel. It's my life or at the luckiest the rest of my life as a slave. My ancestors was slaves once, but they sure as hell didn't volunteer."

Sam nodded. "She's right, Bill. The puzzle's a good one, and I'd like to help solve it, but you're asking her to risk everything in a very slim chance of this in the name of saving some company bigwigs from an eventual threat that, if it affects us at all, probably won't until we're old and gray. The last time they were working *our* city in *our* world. I'm sorry for these people, but I just can't believe this kind of James Bond plan has a ghost of a chance."

Markham hardly blinked. "I'm authorized to offer one million dollars cash, taxes paid, no strings, to take the case. All money up front, win or lose."

I got startled and just stared. A million bucks tax free . . .

"What good's the money to me, Bill?" Sam asked him. "Damn it, Brandy's worth more than that. If she's not here to spend it with me it's sure as hell not worth it."

I really loved Sam for that, but Bill really got me in my greedy part. A million bucks, cash, tax paid. 'Course, a million ain't what it used to be, but it's pretty good. I was beginnin' to wonder just how possible this thing was."

"I can't pretend this is risk free," Markham kindly admitted, "but I can cover some of the bases. If she's in there more than five days we'll come in, take her out, and blow the joint and the hell with Vogel. Guaranteed. We can also set what's known as an anxiety threshold on the tracer. We can get her pulse and blood pressure from it. If she's threatened with anything like surgery or this drug, it'll trigger her out of the *persona* and her pulse rate and blood pressure will shoot sky high and then we go in and get her right then and there and bye-bye Vogel. If we're down to ten minutes and holding the station and she doesn't show, we'll blow through that place and force whoever's in that Safe Room to come out one way or the other. I don't say you can't get hurt or killed, Brandy, but we'll do everything to keep it from happening, that I swear—and under no circumstances will we strand you there."

I looked over at Sam. "If it was you and not me, would you seriously give it some thought? Honest, now, Sam!"

He sighed. "If it was me going in, I have to honestly say I'd give it some thought, yes," he admitted, knowin' he couldn't fake that kind of stuff with me. "But a million bucks is not worth losing you, babe."

I looked at Bill. "You wanta leave us alone for a couple of minutes?"

Markham took the hint and left. I think he figured on it right off. I don't even think he was listenin' in someplace.

"I won't let you risk it. Not alone!" Sam said as soon as Bill was out of the room.

"We're good, Sam. We proved that."

"Yeah, we're good. As a *team.* He was painting the best damned picture of this cockeyed plot he could and he still made it sound like a sure march to the guillotine. And even if it worked, the odds are you're gonna get beaten or raped or all of the above. The only thing worse than losing you would be having you come back looking the same but not there inside. This is the kind of guy who trims your fingernails starting at the knuckles when he needs a few laughs, and he's surrounded by hordes of like-minded individuals. We're doing good now."

"Yeah, now," I echoed. "But not if we say no and you know it. We're makin' more now than we ever dreamed we'd have, and we're in hock up to our neck and you're workin' twelve-hour days and I'm a kept woman with nothin' to do on her own and less and less to do with the business. And don't give me no bullshit about my bein' a vital part of the business. It ain't true and you know it. I was happier and felt more like a real, useful person when we was in the damned slums starvin' to death, 'cause it was a real partnership and we was *together,* damn it. You got what you want now, but this is my chance to break *out* without losin' what we already got."

"You really think this thing has a chance? That *you* do?"

"I don't know," I admitted. "I only know that we been lucky for two born losers. Every time one of us sunk, somethin' happened in the nick of time to save us and make things better. You remember what we found out. There's hundreds of us out there, someplace, but none of us are havin' this talk now but you and me. I'm the only Brandy that married you. I'm the only one that didn't wind up some whore or junkie or dead. Just you and me gettin' together at the right time, and hittin' it off, or Little Jimmy showin' up and offerin' us that case, or gettin' stuck in a siding world that just happened to be between one world and another so the Labyrinth opened up and we saw and heard it and got out. What's the word? Implausible. Unbelievable. All of it. Everybody's got all sorts of shit in their lives that changed them for better or worse and they're all implausible, impossible, unbelievable. That's what this whole parallel worlds thing is *about*. I'm the one so far who done everything *right*. The *only* one."

He stared at me. "But those things just happened, one at a time. This is different. This is a clear choice of very high risk and for you alone. The other times, it was both of us."

"Well, you sure as hell can't get in the way *I* can, and probably not any other way, neither. I wouldn't risk my *toenail* for the damned Company and to hell with any threats, real or not, but this is a big score, Sam. Look, say we get outta here and I get hit by a car out front. What you got?"

"Ten grand from Home Beneficial Life Insurance. Okay, but the odds against that are a lot better than the odds here, and you wouldn't *jump* in front of the car."

"Maybe not. Know what I done while you was off in Pittsburgh? Went down and scored some high grade pot and sat around that apartment starin' at the walls and keepin' high as a kite and eatin' a ton of chocolate candy and I was *still* depressed. Now gimme that million and we hire on 'nuff people to take the caseload and we get us a big, fancy house way up the Main Line with lots of room 'n trees 'n luxury, and we get some kids and we enjoy life a little. Maybe I even set up my own business."

He looked at me hard. "Things really that bad for you? I knew you had some problems, but I never had any idea it was this bad. I guess I just wasn't looking at the flip side. Damn it, I'll quit the business. We'll move somewhere with whatever we've got and start a security business or something far away from here and G.O.D., Inc. I mean that."

"I know you do. Hey—you think I *like* this shit? I mean, gettin' killed, that's always a risk when you're after a real bad dude, but what you said, 'bout bein' beat or raped or have my brain scrambled—that's *scary*. But if I can do it, if I can really do it, really pull it off, then I ain't never gonna doubt myself again." I stopped a moment. "Besides, anytime before they put me under I have real doubts, really think that there's no way this can be pulled off, I'll pull out. And I want you there to make sure they listen. Hear?"

He sighed. "Okay. It's not that I don't trust and have full confidence in you, babe—it's just that I don't trust or have *any* confidence in *them*. And I'll be there—all the way through, just to make sure they hold up all the ends of their bargain, and Bill's gonna be there as well. He's gonna pay if it goes wrong because of *his* end."

Sam went out and found Markham and brought him back in.

"We made a decision, and it's firm," I told him. "Five million, same terms."

I was afraid Bill was gonna choke. "You *have* to be kidding!" he managed.

"It's chicken feed to the company if this is really that important, and if it ain't, then I ain't gonna do it."

I never saw a white guy turn red before, but he finally got hold of himself. "All right. By shifting some here and some there I can come up with it. Five million. But not as before. Two and a half now and free and clear, come what may. The other half only when a live Vogel is turned over to my security agents."

"Done," I told him. "And both Sam and you are along on the scene from the word go. That's the other part."

He looked puzzled. "I figured Sam would want in on the action, but why me?"

Sam looked up at him and gave a really evil grin. "So if your people act with the incompetence and unreliability that they've shown in the past and because of it anything happens to Brandy, I won't have to go far to wring your fucking neck."

3.

Heaven Is for Thieves

I remembered to stop the mail and papers and get the bills paid up before we had to leave. We had three days if we needed them, since all of this plan was based on the time them girls was to go from that bastard in Virginia—that other Virginia—up to Pennsylvania. Sam managed to tie up two cases, one of which was gonna send up that little accountant for a long stretch, and pass the others off to other agencies he trusted. Considerin' this was two and a half million bucks no matter what, he didn't mind much if he pissed off a couple of clients.

The morning of the third day we met Bill and went down to the airport and caught a flight west. First class, too, first time I ever rode that, and it was real nice. The seats are real wide, the drinks are free, and the service is great, but the food's just the same—they only make it look a little fancier.

At San Francisco, we changed to a private Learjet for the ride up to Oregon, which was even fancier and more luxurious, but we wasn't on it long enough to really enjoy it. Then, at Bend, the final switch to a standard four-seat helicopter for the ride up to McInerney, the little town in the middle of nowheres high up in the mountains that was the main station at least for *our* North America.

Considerin' how crazy this all was, and how, odds were, I was takin' my last ride, I really just relaxed and enjoyed things and didn't think too much 'bout the end of all this. Not that I was puttin' it outta my mind, it just wasn't nothin' to think about. I done all that when I made the decision to take the case.

I mean, in a way, it weren't no different than dressin' up like some whore and goin' undercover in the bad dude's hangouts, and I done that more than once. Either way, they catch on or somethin' don't go right and you're just as dead whether it's some Nazi nut on some crazy other world or some small-time hood in Philadelphia or Camden. It was true that I had more to lose this time, but I also had more to gain. Sniffin' out some missin' girl to see if she was on some pimp's string or findin' some runaway daddy who was hidin' out in the worst places, the kind the cops don't go in, for twenty to fifty bucks was crazier than doin' this for millions. No risk, no gain. I just made sure high risk was high gain, that's all.

Sam was a lot more worried, mostly 'cause in this case he had no control. He was strictly backup, but he was still important to me and both he and I knew it. If it did go bad, and I could get that word out, it was his job to pull me outa there no matter what.

McInerney was still the little town on the little road along a pass where the railroad came through with the one lousy diner and the one small motel and the Company's station just outside, lookin' like a cross between a railroad yard, which it was, and lots of warehouses, which it also was. 'Cept, of course, one of them warehouses was the station and not for trains.

And that's what the place looked like, even inside. One big, empty warehouse with a concrete floor and lots of dirt and stains and lots of see-through walkways and stairs of steel criss-crossin' overhead. Bill had decided not to waste no time once we got in; he wanted to get us where we—or me, anyways—could start work. That took a lot of high-tech prep, and the best and most secret place to do it was at the Company headquarters—the home world. Few folks who worked for the Company or even rode the Labyrinth all the time ever went there; it was strictly controlled and mostly off limits. I got to admit I was always curious about what the place looked like and what its people were like, but I never expected to find out. Bill had been there twice before, so he at least knew his way around a bit, but this time he wasn't bein' ordered there by the bosses but by us. He didn't really seem to mind, which helped the nerves a little, I guess. 'Course, he didn't have to get his mind fucked and go undercover in that slime pit.

Bill was a nice guy, but you always got the idea that if he could get somethin' done a little quicker by killin' you it just wouldn't enter his head to do nothin' else but shoot you right then and there.

It's always kinda impressive to watch the Labyrinth come on, partly 'cause you still can't figure out what it's doin' or how and it's kinda pretty. You stand over in the safe zone of this big warehouse floor and some folks up in a control room high and to one side throw the switches and it starts with a rumblin' under your feet that sorta shakes the whole building, like a vibrator. Then this line is drawn, straight up and down, just a little above the floor, in a kind of blue-white light. It just starts from nowhere, then draws itself to maybe fifteen or twenty feet high. When they're happy with it, they throw more switches and more lines start kinda branchin' off from the other line. Like half the line just falls away and then you have an L, then another from it to make a squared-off U and finally a top, so you got this big square of light.

Then the whole square slips off and you got two sides, then it splits again, and again, till you got a cube of light just sittin' there. Then it really starts goin' fast, foldin' and twistin' in and out of itself until you got a whole mess of cubes connected together. All of it looks like just lights; there ain't nothin' to be seen, but it's kinda neat to look at.

Then you walk right into the mess, even as it twists and turns, goin' to the middle of the thing, until everybody's in the same cube.

From inside, it looks different. You're in this cube of light, all right, but it seems kinda hard and solid somehow. You can see a cube or two ahead or behind, but you can't hear nothin' at all. It's like all the sounds just go away.

When we first fell into this thing by accident a coupla years ago, we only went forward or back, but you can go other ways, too. If you look at the top of the cube, then keep lookin' at it as you walk, the cube kinda, well, *rotates,* if you can imagine it, and you walk through the top; same with the bottom or sides. Wherever you look when you start walkin', that's where you go.

Startin' almost with the next cube, though, not all them

cube faces are blank. You get, well, *flashes* of places, or things. Sunsets, green hills, you name it. They ain't exactly real when you look at 'em, more like reflections in a mirror, but you know they *are* real and that if you go to that cube you'll come out there. Some—a lot—are dark. Sometimes where you're lookin' is the inside of a hill, or maybe up in the air with nothin' below, dependin' on what happened to the spot you're standin' on. That's really the hard part—you don't move all that much for all the walkin' you do through the thing. You can come out just where you went in, but a hundred or a thousand worlds away.

And you can come out some other place, but not without goin' through a switchin' cube. You can always tell a switchin' cube. All the faces but one are dark, and that one has somebody in a room, just a room, sittin' in a chair, lookin' at a whole mess of switches, dials, and screens. If they talk, you can hear 'em, and if you talk, you can be heard, 'cept you sound more'n a little dead and flat.

Lots of them switchers ain't human, neither. At least, they ain't *our* kind of human. First one we got to was a guy with hair all over his face and a real animallike look; sorta the Wolfman in some fancy uniform. Bill says most of the switchers are from the Type One worlds 'cause many of 'em got better hearin' and can see more stuff than we can and for some reason that's important. They don't speak English, neither, or any other language we know, but thanks to some little gizmo when we talk it's translated to their language and when they talk it's translated to ours.

Keeps things simpler. When I think of the number of languages they talk just on our world, then you got to figure how many there must be goin' through here.

"*Amitash fridlap!*" said the hairy guy. It don't translate till it knows both languages to use, of course.

"Headquarters, please," Bill responded, just like he understood that crap. "Special Agent Markham, world thirteen twenty-nine two stroke seven, with authorized encoded personnel from the same coordinates."

"English, huh?" the switcher grunted. "Okay, I've got you identified on my screen. You're authorized to the next switch module. Go through."

He turned some funny dial and one of the black faces opened up and we walked back into the quiet cubes with the many mirrors again.

The flashin' pictures on the walls, though, were different now. We sure wouldn't come out in no Oregon no more if we walked through one. The skies looked different, somehow, and the land was flatter, the green stuff a darker green. The trees looked big but all twisted 'round, and their leaves, when they had them, were real dark.

Now, some of them paths was just to different exits, but some of the places now already didn't look much like what I knew back home, even if they was Africa or Siberia. It was kinda wild to look at them and know that on most of 'em there was billions of folks all goin' about whatever normal folks did there, livin' and lovin' and dyin' and havin' babies and all the rest, all thinkin' they was the center of creation.

We went through three more switchin' stations, each one with a man or woman or something like that at the controls, but only one was what we'd call normal, and that's only from what I could see. She was kinda plain but with bright orange spiked hair that matched her eyes, so you can see what I mean.

This time, though, she was more of a boss lady than just a worker. "You are authorized onto the headquarters siding. When you get there, follow all instructions. No exits other than headquarters entry will be permitted from this point."

"I understand," Bill told her, and we went on. The Labyrinth took on a real odd look from this point, though; suddenly the walls of the cubes didn't just look like mirrors reflectin' strange places, they *was* mirrors, and they reflected back just us, then us again from the other sides, and so on, so there was thousands of smaller and smaller "us's" just goin' back until we got so small we disappeared, and that was on all the walls 'cept only the one ahead, which was black. Suddenly, though, we stepped out and into a really big cube that was *all* mirrors—even the way we came in was a mirror.

"This place gives me the creeps," Sam muttered, and sounded normal.

"It's designed to unnerve people," Bill replied. "It gets

more unnerving as you go along. This isn't the Labyrinth anymore—it's a special security entry room. We're here."

"Identification and purpose, please," came a real boomin' man's voice from all 'round us, kinda like the Voice of God. I jumped.

"Bill Markham, Brandy Horowitz, Sam Horowitz, on Security Committee business. We are expected."

"Remove and drop all clothing and anything else brought with you to the floor and stand at least arm's length from one another," the Voice commanded.

"I wondered why we didn't even bring a suitcase," Sam muttered.

"He means *everything*?" I asked, seein' Bill already droppin' his pants in public.

"Everything," Markham replied. "Except for special communications channels and the area for cargo quarantine and inspection, nothing is allowed in or out. Don't worry—we'll get new clothes when this is done."

"But what 'bout my glasses?" I protested. "I'm damned near blind without 'em."

"Those, too, I'm afraid. They'll fix you up when we get through."

Well, I never was all that shy, so in a little while there the three of us were, stark naked, and spread out in a room that reflected us in all directions into forever. I couldn't see too good—even Sam was a little blurry and he was closest —but I could see what happened next.

Suddenly the place was filled with a whole series of colored lights. They didn't feel like nothin', but one or two tickled some, and they seemed to come like see-through globs of color from all the mirrors. The first one was kinda lavender, then pink, then purple, and there was reds and blues, too. Then they switched off, and the mirrors did, too. Now it was a creamy white all 'round us, and I looked and our clothes and stuff was gone. I didn't know how they did that and I wasn't sure I wanted to know.

A part of one wall went back with a little whine, and we followed Bill through into a second room. This one was kinda warm and had real plush furry brown carpeting on it and a gizmo that looked like a cross between a doctor's scale and an eye doctor's gadget. Bill stepped up on it, stood straight, and looked through the two lenses of the thing. I really couldn't see the thing much till I was led up to it by Sam. I looked through it, then got a sudden little flash in my eyes, and that was it.

"Well, that done it," I muttered. "Now they've gone and made me completely blind."

"It'll wear off," Bill promised. "It's not as much as a flashbulb. This thing is a final check of our identity. They know who we are, and they can take a basic code reading even at the switch points, but this is detailed to the last billionth of a millimeter. This thing makes absolutely sure that you're not only Brandy but the Brandy they expect to see and no other. Nobody has ever fooled it. The encoder implanted in you long ago is almost like a tiny, microscopic computer, and it even monitors and records changes in your body as they happen. Never mind the rest," he said, seein' my blank look. "Just believe that the best and brightest of security, computers, and electronics have tried to fool this system and never have."

When Sam got his okay, he took my hand and another one of them doors appeared. This one actually had some people there, two men and a woman. They was kinda blurry to me, but they looked both human and not real human, dressed in some kind of satiny clothing. They had one for me, a kind of sari that went on real neat and fastened without no buttons or snaps or anything. Funny thing was, though, it kept me up, big tits and all, even though it seemed kinda soft and, well, *breakable.* It was cream colored and felt a lot like silk. They also had sandals that were so light you hardly knew they was there, but held with only one small strap that also seemed to know its place all by itself.

They also handed me a pair of real thin, light plastic glasses that also looked kinda shiny, and I put 'em on and at first couldn't see no change 'cept everything was tinted a little bit rosy. The longer I wore 'em, though, the clearer I could see, till in a little bit I was seein' better than I ever did with my regular glasses.

I could see the people of headquarters real clear. The best way I can describe their complexion is *golden,* deep but real goldlike, not just yellow or light brown. They had thick lips and them Japanese kind of eyes, and looked kinda Oriental, but not really. Their eyes all seemed to be jet black and kinda shiny, and their hair was all thick, dark brown. None of 'em seemed to have any face or body hair 'cept, of course, on their heads, and I guessed that none of the men ever needed to shave, nor the women, neither.

They wasn't small like the Chinese and Japanese usually are, but about average height. The girl was maybe a little taller than me, the men both about six two or three. What really hit me when lookin' at 'em was that none of 'em seemed to have a single mark or zit or nothin', now or in the past. All three seemed to be teenagers, but their skin was soft and smooth and *unworn* as a baby's. The girl wore a sari pretty much like mine, but of satiny crimson with golden designs in it. The two men wore a different kind of getup, kinda like a cross between what you wear for your judo lessons and what the politicians wear in all them Roman Empire movies. You know, the kind where the guys wear skirts and still look real normal.

Both the men and the girl were *gorgeous,* too. They had the kind of looks everybody always dreams of but nobody ever has.

I looked over at Sam and Bill and had to laugh. They was both bein' dressed in cream-colored versions of what the golden boys had on and somehow it just didn't look the same with their white skin and hairy legs.

Sam gave me a look but Bill just chuckled and said, "Don't worry, Sam. Since everybody wears these things here, you'll get used to it."

One of the golden boys said somethin', and the girl nodded and also said somethin', both in a kinda soft, pleasant, singsong kinda voice. The words didn't sound like nothin' human, and I knew I for one could never make them notes.

"I think we're being told to move on," Markham told us. "Their language is unique and nearly impossible to learn or even understand. I think their vocal equipment includes a few things ours doesn't, but don't worry. They do that for their security, too. The folks we'll be with will have been prepped and know English by now, at least as long as they need to. I can assure you, too, we've been observed by security, both people and machines, since we came in the entry room and *they* understand English quite well, or any other language."

"Quite right, sir," said a man's voice from another of them doors that just opened. We looked over and saw him come in, wearin' the same kind of Roman-karate outfit as the rest, but he looked a little different. For one thing, he looked older, though not *real* old and real good for his age, and his clothes seemed fancy and tailored even if they was the same style. He also had two gold-plated thick watches, one on each arm, or at least they *looked* like watches. He went up and shook Bill's hand.

"Folks," Markham said, "May I present Executor Aldrath Prang. My boss. These are the Horowitzes."

He shook Sam's hand then took and kissed mine. It was kinda sensual and neat. He got right to the point, though, in a neutral American-type accent that coulda been from anywheres. I guessed he learned it all by machine.

"We must go quickly," he told us. "We need to allow others in and I really would like to get you out to Vice President Mayar's estate as quickly and quietly as possible for security reasons. The fewer who know you're here, the better. We don't want any slips."

I could agree with *that* tune. "What about them here?" I asked, suddenly gettin' a little nervous. I didn't bargain for no public sessions here at headquarters.

"Everybody you'll meet outside the estate works for me," Aldrath Prang assured me. "They get their minds probed and cleaned so often they don't think of it as anything more of a big deal than taking a shower. Now—come."

We made it over to an elevatorlike contraption, but you didn't have no feelin' you was goin' up or down. One last security precaution, I guessed, and this Executor read my mind.

"All the weak points are well covered and blocked," he told us. "All but this one, which happens to be very deep inside a mountain of granite and basalt. Even if somebody managed to infiltrate and blow their way through and capture the station, it would do no good. They can't get into the world any way but one, and we control that from the surface. It's nothing personal, but it's somewhat ironic that we must isolate ourselves pretty much from any universe but our own even as we master the others. All our records are here, all the knowledge is here, all the computer controls and administration are here. Our culture is also very tight and devoted to our mission, and we dare not have it polluted lest some culture without our sense of responsibility come in and take control."

"You mean you never leave this world?" Sam asked, amazed.

"I don't, no. Particularly not me, although I was out when I was younger and didn't know too much. Some of our people go out, of course, particularly when they're young and idealistic or ambitious. We have research projects all over the place, and special needs and interests, and it's essential that those who will have the responsibility of running the Labyrinth and the Corporation get a sense and feel for just what we're dealing with—not just its size and complexity, but its differences. You see, there's been no disease here of any kind for generations. That's why you received a sterilization treatment among others when you arrived. It kills any microorganism that might be harmful to us and at the same time virtually halts mutation, freezing in place those which our bodies must have to help in digestion, for example. There also hasn't been a war here in thousands of years now, nor any kind of unpredicted natural disaster, nor famine nor in fact even real crime as you think of it, except for crimes of passion."

We saw. A whole world of peace and plenty with none of the dirty shit. If you just grew up here, and lived here your whole life, how would you ever be able to understand them other worlds, let alone make decisions that might cost lives? If you ain't never felt no pain or sufferin' or misery firsthand, if your idea of bein' hungry is that you're stuck in a city after all the restaurants are closed, if you never had nobody look at you funny 'cause your skin was black or you talked funny, then how you gonna understand the problems and see the big picture. Not that these folks would care in the end if they killed a bunch if it was for somethin' they wanted, but at least they had to look into the faces of some of the folks they'd be doin' in.

They'd been at this a long, long time.

We got to the surface and saw that the whole place had been cleared for us. We walked across a kinda lobby area that looked like some luxury airport waiting lounge, out a side door, and right into a funny-lookin' big car with no wheels that just kinda floated there at the door. A side of it was dropped down so there was steps leadin' up and in. The whole thing looked like some roast beef plate with a half a cigar on top. There was windows all the way along, although it'd looked solid from the outside. We could see out, but nobody could see in.

Inside it was kinda like a millionaire's camper van. Nice furlike carpets even on the walls, real plush recliner chairs around a table that looked like polished marble, and compartments all over the place. I expected the thing to wobble when we got on, but it was steady as a rock. I couldn't figure what was holdin' it all up.

There wasn't no driver, neither; not even a driver's seat. This fellow Aldrath—we found out quick that they said their first names last and last names first, like the Orientals do—he just went up front, took some kind of card out of a little pocket in his toga, and stuck it in a slot. The door closed, and off we went, no seatbelts or nothin'. You had to look outside to see that we was even movin'—and *was* we movin'! Up, up, and away real fast.

I could see the place below us clearly now, just a little round dome of a building in the middle of a bunch of trees in the middle of a bunch of low mountains kinda like the Poconos, but with no roads, no power lines, no nothin'.

It was a sunny day with just them cotton candy clouds, but we stayed just below them, so you had a right good view of the country below for miles and miles. Here and there you could see round towers and groups of domes and cubes and other funny shapes, but none of the places were real big and there was no roads at all.

Aldrath punched something in one of them compartments and brought out some drinks. I kinda figured they was somethin' like that. He saw that Sam and me were mostly lookin' out and down at the country, which didn't look the least bit familiar but really didn't look all that strange, neither. Sorta like central Pennsylvania or upstate

New York, only before all them folks stuck all them roads and wires through it. 'Course, if your cars and buses and trucks all fly like this thing we was in, you don't need all that.

"If you are looking for major cities, we have them," Aldrath said, "but not in this area. Our cities are mostly in the subtropical and tropical climates. When you can control or eliminate all the pests and divert big storms and manipulate the rainfall, those places are like gardens. This is mostly an area of wilderness and balance, with a few towns for special purposes or simply because people like to live here, and a number of broad estates mingled with forests and game reserves."

"I'd've thought sheer numbers would have populated a lot of this," Sam replied. "Or is the population stable?"

"It's stable, but reasonably large. We keep it worldwide at about a billion, which is more than adequate to preserve what should be preserved. It's not that we're restrictive, but we have many outlets for a population, both in settling and preserving certain other Earths that are truly wonderful places to live but which never developed a higher race and also the planets and to a limited extent the stars."

Even I was startled at that one. "You mean you don't just go next door, you're also up *there?*"

He smiled. "Getting to the near planets is no great trick, nor is colonizing a place like Mars. The stars are trickier, and we're still in our infancy regarding them, but who is better qualified to go than we if there are in fact alien civilizations out there? It provides us with a limitless and exciting future, you see. The parallel worlds go from infinity to infinity, and each universe is in itself so vast and varied it will end before anyone can explore more than a fraction of it. That's the secret to keeping a civilization as successful and prosperous as ours from rotting and decaying, you see. There is always someplace new to go, something new to learn, something wonderful waiting to be discovered. We have never become jaded or yielded to rot."

Yeah, it sure sounded like one of them—what'cha call it?—utopias, all right, and maybe it was about as close as we get, but I couldn't help think that we'd gotten sucked into all this 'cause some folks with real power, probably right here on this planet, ran at least one and maybe many rebel groups that tried to sucker and screw up and take over parts of the Corporation's territories and worlds, and we was here at all 'cause there was at least one known traitor and he had some boss higher up. They was askin' me to risk my mind and my neck against them folks, so I figured I had a right to bring that up, and did.

Aldrath shrugged. "Humanity is by nature imperfect, and so perfection is not attainable without also costing humankind the things that are most important to it. Creativity, a measure of freedom, curiosity, drive, willpower. We can remove these things, but then we make not perfect humans but perfect automatons. In spite of the fact that the lowest of the low here have things your richest and most powerful people would envy, we have classes. It is a part of our culture and our heritage. Our very language, our accents, are differentiated by class so that merely by a person's speech we know their station. Our very names are actually descriptives chosen for their poetry, their symmetry, and their meaning. My name is actually—" He gave one of them pretty songs. "The names we give you are rough transliterations of these sounds according to English rules. The corporate chiefs are the highest class and marry only among their own families. The professional, or managerial class does the same. The working, or common class is likewise separated not merely by name and accent but by family and society. As always, this causes strains."

"And I don't suppose there's anyone really anxious to let people move up," Sam commented.

"Not many. I, for example, am from the professional class and would not be anything else. The big limits are all on the corporate class—the people you will be meeting. They have all the real policy-making power, but they can not abrogate that power or that responsibility. That's determined almost from birth. They have very little choice in their lives and much of it is quite boring. I, on the other hand, am what I am because that's what I wanted to be. I could have chosen any profession I liked, and if I made the grade I'd have gotten it. If I didn't, or found I hated it, I could have chosen another. I work as hard as I like to work—and I very much like working—and get tremendous benefits. I don't have a private estate here or elsewhere, but I can avail myself of the desirable parts of any of them."

"Yeah, that's all well and good for you," I said, "but what about the common folks?"

"Those who greeted you today are so-called common folks. There's no heavy labor; it's mostly a service and maintenance economy here, and most of what we have that's really odious is automated. We automated everything once, but finally cut back so we automated only what people shouldn't ever be required to do. They, too, have a choice of many jobs, no real stress or pressure they don't wish to take upon themselves, and much in the way of benefits and opportunities. For example, how old would you say that trio who met you were?"

"No more than eighteen for the oldest," Sam answered.

The security chief laughed. "The girl is thirty-seven, and the two boys are thirty-one and forty. When you do jobs you enjoy and have conquered all the diseases and defects inherent in our ancestry, it's amazing how long a span you can have. I, for example, am sixty-seven just last month. From your standpoint I'm probably about half that, which is the way I feel and act. The average lifespan here is about two hundred and nine years, and you begin to get gray hairs and a few wrinkles at about ninety, but you really don't start looking old until you're about a hundred and sixty, and I know several two-hundred-year-olds who still swim a few kilometers a day and do mountain climbing for a hobby. That's true no matter what class you're in."

"Yeah, but what if some commoners think they can run things better than you, or maybe want to be scientists instead of lab assistants or something like that? What then?" I asked, gettin' an idea of how even this kind of society could get rebels.

"That's what I meant by outlets and expansion," Aldrath replied. "If there are commoners who believe they have superior talents and abilities and can demonstrate them, there are ways for them to be educated every bit as good as, say, my own son. We just can't have them here, since that would upset the system and the balance. They are welcome to go to a colony where they might find a place, or even found their own. Only the corporate level is closed absolutely, since there can be only one set of people controlling the Labyrinth and they are born, raised, and trained to do that and safeguard both us and the other worlds from one who might use that power for evil. We are not dictators to other worlds and cultures, Madam Horowitz. We are thieves. We steal things we need, and, most of all, ideas, art forms, even stories from unique and different cultures. In exchange, we keep the would-be dictators and oppressors of universes out, and we try as hard as we can to preserve worlds that have not destroyed themselves from doing so. Other than that, we do not tip balances."

"But you're much of organized crime on many worlds, including ours," Sam noted. "That's sure as hell interfering."

"I didn't say we didn't interfere. I said we do not *tip balances*. Those things were there before we came and would be there with or without us. We don't even increase their efficiency, and we leave it in local hands. Think of the alternative. We could easily take over any government, even all of them, and thereby safeguard everything, but we do not. We do not actually even take over the criminal societies, we just use them to help us covertly get what we wish. The vast bulk of the criminals do not know or even suspect us."

"Yeah, but you still got traitors and rebels," I pointed out. "I mean, we only got into this thing 'cause some folks from here got ambitious."

"That's true," he admitted, sippin' his drink. "As hard as we try, there are just some people who'll never understand the system. You see, we're *thieves* as well as explorers and preservers. We get a lot out of this. Our medicine, our power systems, this vehicle—all stolen ideas. To preserve this wilderness, we import raw materials we need and which we buy at a fair price and never in quantities that would impoverish a world. There are some who, nonetheless, see us as inherently superior to everyone else. Our religion teaches that all the gods of all the universes are real, and that together they form a powerful overmind, a Supreme Lord. We were selected by the Supreme Lord to master the Labyrinth and oversee the universes. Some take that a bit too far, and see us as the natural and Supreme Lord's choice as *rulers* of all the universes. They simply never grasp the essence of the system: *thieves never steal everything from the last rich man on Earth.* If we came in and took over, destroyed cultures and replaced them with an autocratic government, they would soon all be like us, only under us and never able to attain freedom again. Without that freedom, there is no creativity. If you make them subjects, they will reflect your own will imperfectly and, as a result, will never produce anything new or unusual or creative. In short, nothing worth stealing."

It was a real crazy way of lookin' at things, but it made a kinda lopsided sense. I turned and tried the wine, which was real sweet and went down *good.* I always had a thing for sweet stuff; it's why I ain't never been able to keep weight off.

"So what's next?" I asked the man. "Why bring us here?"

"We have some time, and we thought we'd make the best use of it," Aldrath told me. "There's no place more secure than here, although nothing is absolutely secure. We are going to Mayar Eldrith's estate, which is both private and isolated. He is a senior vice president of the Corporation and chairman of the Security Committee. His staff were all handpicked and are constantly checked by me and are as secure as we can get. We have all the medical-techinical apparatus needed to prep you for this job, and we'll do that as well as practice the system as best we can. When we're ready, we'll also be ready over in Vogel's pesthole of a world."

The flyin' bus turned and started down, and below we could see a real big house, a bunch of smaller houses that were still bigger'n most of what we had back home, with gardens and woods and stuff. It was the kind of country place you might expect the Queen of England to have, and the kind I always dreamed about. There weren't no funny cubes and circles here; this place had real charm and the outside, at least, looked like real wood, though it was real modern-lookin' and had all kinds of crazy angles.

We was met by a small group of young people all of which looked just as beautiful and just as perfect as the ones in the station. I was already feelin' real self-conscious about my looks, kinda like bein' the only black in an all-white town someplace out west. They wasn't white folks, but they was all the same and they was sure different than any of us.

The main house was *big*—I think it coulda been the biggest hotel in Philadelphia with room left over, though it was only four or five floors. It just went on and on forever. They didn't take us there, though, but to a smaller place down a hill and in some woods.

The inside was *gorgeous,* anyways—all wood paneling, thick carpeted floors that felt and looked great, real modern-type furniture, soft lighting that seemed to come from everywhere and went on when you came in and went down when you left—all that. The upstairs rooms all looked out on a balcony onto an *enormous* livin' room, kinda like in them luxury hotels.

"We use this place when we want privacy, even from the main house, where there are a lot of comings and goings," Aldrath told us. "You'll find clothing and the basics in the closets and bath upstairs. Your meals will be prepared by my security staff and served below in the dining alcove. If you wish to go outside, please limit yourself to the walks out the back of the house and do not go to any other buildings or speak to anyone not on the staff without my permission. We have very little time and much to do. I know you must be tired now, so Bill and I will leave you for now, but we start bright and early tomorrow morning and the sessions will be long ones."

I had thought Bill would stay here, but it looked not. The whole place was ours. "Now, this is somethin' *else!*" I breathed. "The kinda place I always *dreamed* of havin'!"

Sam was glum as usual. "Yeah, they treat the condemned with all the luxuries. I still got a bad feeling about all this. It's too complicated."

"Five million bucks, Sam! We can have our *own* place like this."

"Yeah—if we don't pay too high a price for it."

His name was Jamispur Samoka. He was another of them beautiful people, fifty-one and lookin' maybe in his twenties, and wearin' a pale pastel blue outfit that seemed to be the same here as lab whites were back home. He wasn't no doctor—they didn't have doctors here like we did—but he was the same kind of thing. His workroom looked like some mad scientist's shit from old horror movies, but they was all designed to do different things to and for people. I was scareder of him than of the mission.

"Much of this equipment was developed because our own people need some modifications before venturing into other worlds," he told me. "Also, it's often not possible to get an exact replacement for someone else when we need to infiltrate a place. This equipment can make a close match seem an exact match. It can't work miracles but it can do wonders. Fortunately, we have had the opportunity to get all the physical and genetic data from the woman you are to replace, and that makes it a lot easier."

That didn't sit well with me. "How much of a change will there be? I know I ain't no beauty queen, but I kinda like me the way I am." *Five million bucks,* I kept tellin' myself. *Just think of that.*

"It's important to emphasize that there is nothing we can do here that can't be undone here," he replied. "The trick is doing it in the first place. Whatever we do we have an exact record of doing and so we know the way to reverse it. In your case, we do not need to do anything really major or radical, anyway. The biggest problem here, which we don't face all the time, is that you might be subjected to tests available to someone who knows of and has some access to our technology. In effect, it must be so perfect that even we can't detect what we've done. This fellow Vogel is a paranoid and sadist at best. You must hold up to get close to him, and even though he doesn't know we've made him as a traitor, he's bound to have been even more cautious and paranoid because of his fear of discovery. Let me show you something." He reached down, pushed a button, and pointed.

The place where he pointed flickered, then took on an outline of a woman that quickly faded in and became solid and real three-dimensional. It was a black woman, stark naked, and still as death.

"That is who you have to be," Jamispur told me.

I looked hard at the woman, seein' now that it was just some kinda 3-D photograph. "Don't look much like me," I said. "That hair's long and straight. I never could get mine straight long enough to do much with it. Complexion's wrong, too, and she got a damn sight better figure than me or what you're gonna get out of me in two weeks."

"You underestimate yourself. No one really sees themselves as others see them. I know you're not all that modest about yourself or you wouldn't have taken this job. Will you disrobe and go stand next to the image, on that small dot in the floor, there?"

I did it—hell, he was gonna see more of me than this—and went over. The woman's picture didn't look so real right up close, kinda faded and with lines like bad tuning on the TV. There was a click, and he said, "Now come back over here and we'll look at what we've got."

I came back over and turned, and saw *two* women standin' there. The other one was me, but the doc was right—it really didn't look right, somehow. I started thinkin', *is that the way I* really *look to Sam and the others?* And I started makin' little critical notes to myself. Fact was, I *was* kinda cute, though, and I didn't have much different a figure than she did after all. A little more hip and thigh, that's all. The face, hair, and skin tone, though, just weren't right. I looked taller, but that might have been the bush hair.

And then he started puttin' me in his machines. They didn't hurt none, but sometimes they used drugs and sprays that might have hid just about anything. They was *fast*, though. I got the feelin' that if I broke my leg in the mornin' I'd walk out whole in the afternoon.

At the end of three days, Sam, who'd been spendin' his time with planners for the mission, was a little uncomfortable. I was changin' more than either of us bargained for. For the first time in my life, my hair was straight and silky-black like it'd been born that way, and it was growin' at one hell of a rate. By the end of five days my hair was thick and down below my shoulders and was just as big a pain to comb and wash as I always figured. It *really* changed my appearance, I'll tell you. My skin was a little lighter and almost a uniform chocolate brown. A couple of old scars and lots of stretch marks were gone; so was my vaccination scar, and my skin was a little oilier, almost shiny. I was also gettin' thinner, back in shape. The doc said the machines used my own body to do and lock in a lot of the changes, and that it took from the too fat parts. Not that I was skinny—but she wasn't, neither. Still, every time I looked in the mirror it was some strange girl starin' back.

It got worse, though, when the dental stuff started. I had more than a few fillin's, and they was wrong and had to go. They put me under with somethin', and when I woke up I was almost a stranger. The stuff in my teeth, and one or two new teeth, now felt a little dead in my mouth, like caps might, but there was no way by lookin' or even X ray to tell that them teeth weren't the way nature intended. My nose looked different, and so did my smile. My round face seemed a little more oval. I also always had a deep voice, but they tuned it a bit—it sounded funny when I talked, a little higher and a lot huskier. The new face also done somethin' to the way I could talk, too. I had real trouble with *s* and *r* sounds; it was a hell of a lisp. Still, in only five days, when he took another picture of me and put it next to that one of the other girl and I stepped away and looked, we was close. Damned close. It was more the way she held herself, and that idiot's smile on her, than anything you could measure.

"You thure you can change thith all back?" I asked him worriedly. "I nevah thought 'bout thith kinda thuff when I took the job."

"In the same five days," he assured me. "Except for the lost body weight, of course. That you will have to replace yourself, if you want to."

"I thure don' wanna talk like thith the west of my life."

Sam couldn't help but make fun of the lisp till he saw how self-conscious I was about it; then he stopped. "Remember, you agreed to do this," he said. "You don't like the price you paid so far—and neither do I—but this is the easy part."

"I know, I know," I grumbled. "I already got to the point where I just wanna get goin' and get thith over with."

I think what disturbed him most was the last thing they did. It was on the inside of my left palm, and it was nothin' more than a long number tattooed there in purple ink. Sam had an uncle and a coupla cousins with numbers like that, souvenirs of Hitler's camps.

And, in the end, that was the bottom line of what was buggin' him. This world I was gonna get dropped in was a Nazi world, a world where the Jews had been wiped out and *we* was the new Jews. It was like I was volunteerin' to be a Jew at Auschwitz. That didn't set none too well with me, but none of *them* had Sam just outside holdin' a gun on G.O.D., Inc.

Not that I wasn't startin' to get nervous. I was. The closer the dates came, the more doubts I had, the more second thoughts, and the scareder I got. I began to really wonder if Sam was right all along. I wasn't no Cleopatra Jones, no Jane Bond. Undercover was always the hardest and riskiest thing any investigator could do, and this was undercover in a whole *world* that considered me no better than a pet monkey and would treat me the same or worse.

Then we started through the simulation exercises. They had a room in the big house rigged up kinda like they thought Vogel's Safe Room was—but they wasn't sure—complete with secret passage, and they took me in there naked and in light but limiting arm and leg chains to where a big guy about Vogel's size and weight played the mark. The first three days of this, twenty times a day with analysis, I never even come *close* to takin' him, and I got *real* discouraged. Still, every time I blew it they took me aside, showed me a recordin' of the whole thing, and explained what I done wrong, what tricks I fell for, what opportunities I missed. I learned quick—this was my ass on the line, and I wanted to live to spend that bread. By the fourth day of trainin', I took not only the fellow playin' Vogel but two other guys even bigger and meaner about half the time. By the time there was only two days left, I was takin' all comers in that room three out of four times.

It wasn't good enough, but it had to do.

We also had all sorts of briefin's, goin' on and on and makin' us all memorize everything till we talked it in our sleep. Timing, other things, and most important the emergency procedures in case it went down wrong. I knew just what was gonna happen when and if, and there were only a few things they didn't tell me, 'cause if *I* didn't know then I couldn't be made to tell Vogel.

That night, we got dressed up in fancy-colored silks for

the last real night we'd have until it was over. The way I talked, the last thing I wanted was guests and a dinner party, but this weren't no last meal. The ones comin' to dinner were the folks with the five million bucks—the Security Committee.

"You got to do all the talkin'," I told Sam. "I couldn't open my *mouth* 'round nobody now."

"Yeah, well, I'll try, but you're what they've come to see and neither Aldrath nor I like it much."

"Huh?"

"Babe, these guys dreamed up this thing and passed the job of actually doing it down to Aldrath, who passed it on to Bill and then to us, but until now it's just an abstract thing to them. Beyond Bill, Aldrath, Jamispur, and a tight circle of security personnel who have their brains laundered every morning to make sure they're secure, nobody knows who is doing this, or when, or anything else. Now all of a sudden the whole damned committee shows up and demands to meet with us. They're all corporate class people— untouchable even by Aldrath unless he catches them with a smoking gun in their hands standing over a freshly dead body. They're all ambitious up-and-coming corporate types, sort of like Congressmen. They're a potentially leaky bunch and you can do a lot in forty-eight hours."

"But thurely the Thecurity Committee is checked out!" Trouble was, I was startin' to get used to talkin' like a black Elmer Fudd.

"People leak things for their own advantage. If one of 'em gets concerned with a bigwig he's trying to impress and gets pressed on what's being done about this security threat, he might blurt it all out just to make an impression, or leak it if there's rumors going around that he hasn't been very effective. Now, we're going to block out that whole time line from the Labyrinth, so nobody and no messages go in or out until you're safe, and anybody who leaves here not on our team will be monitored like a hawk, but these are big shots used to intelligence work. It's an extra added pain in the ass."

I couldn't help but notice that the Security Committee was all male. In fact, I found out when I pressed, just about all the senior officers were men. It wasn't that this place was out-and-out sexist, but women somehow never made it to the top spots. Some of it was that these guys tonight were mostly in their seventies and maybe had a hundred years or more before there was much of an openin', and the Chairman of the Board, they said, was a hundred and five and nowhere near retirin', but I think there was more. This sorta trickles down, too. If women aren't in top spots, they don't tend to be treated as good further down. Kinda like Russia, where all women are equal and work at jobs, but never get high up in the government 'cept as the head of culture or arts or somethin' like that, and are still expected to come home nights and clean house and cook dinner.

Here, nobody really *had* to work, and a lot of women didn't, stayin' home with the kids and stuff. Lots of the artists were women, I found out, and dancers and entertainers, and lots in the common classes had all sorts of regular jobs, but almost never on top unless they was the absolute best. Nobody seemed to care 'bout this, though. They all had one of them religions that believed in reincarnation, and you was a man one life, a woman the next, and so on. Me, I was thinkin' I might like to be a housewife and full-time mother to some kids, 'specially if I had lots of money, but I sure as hell would hate to be *required* to do that.

They trooped in, one at a time, and got greeted like one of them diplomatic receptions. More of them beautiful golden people, all of 'em, only lookin' a little older and maybe a little shiftier, like politicians or salesmen. Mayar Eldrith, our host, was tall and strong and real slick lookin'; he brought his wife, Eyai, who looked somethin' like some Hawaiian goddess. She had that special smile and way of talkin' that all politicians' wives seem to have, and Mayar talked like he was some big shot Senator runnin' for office. Real smooth voice and delivery.

He was followed by Hanrin Sabuuk, who looked and sounded enough like Mayar to be his brother, then Dringa Lakuka, who looked older and wiser and was a real quiet type but with real bright eyes. You got the feelin' he was some god slummin' and havin' a ball doin' it. Then there was Basuti Alimati, the youngest and newest member— only fifty-seven and lookin' a good thirty—who seemed real stuffy and businesslike. They told us he was the only one of them who never married and never seemed to fool around, neither. They wasn't very hung up on sex here—you could have as many wives, or even husbands, as you could talk into it, swing with either or both sexes, and have unlimited lovers on the side. This guy, though, was never even known to swing with himself.

The last one and just slightly older than "young" Basuti, was Mukasa Lamdukur. He looked much like the others and was maybe the most human of the bunch, and he was the only one who brought along others, much to Sam's and Aldrath's distress. They looked so young I figured it was his kids, but they weren't. Mukasa's job was keepin' the records straight and generally runnin' the committee on a day-to-day basis, and Dakani Grista, a real young hunk of a boy, and Ioyeo, who was a little small as the women went here and looked maybe sixteen or so, were the administrative assistants, or so we were told. Only Dakani was of the manager class, though; Ioyeo (their women never seemed to have but one name, all vowels—I guess it was the way things was translated) was actually a commoner class person whose big talent was that she was oversexed and not real bright. She had one *hell* of a figure, though, and that sari looked painted on, and I guess that's one of the things they wanted around the office. Even on a world of beautiful women, she was a real stunner, and she even had one of them dumb blond voices—you know, high-pitched as all get-out and whispery to boot—and all the right moves. I had to poke Sam more than once that night to get his mind back where it should be.

They all treated her kinda like some servant, though, but she fetched and smiled and giggled and didn't seem to mind. I couldn't help thinkin' that if there was a leak or a traitor at the top, that's the one I'd look first at. Nobody was like that in real life.

The talk was mostly small talk, and I did almost none of it.

"So, tell me, what's your world like?" Mayar Eldrith asked Bill Markham.

"A stroke seven world, sir," Bill replied pleasantly.

"Oh, yes—atomic weapons, superpowers, big and little

wars," Mukasa put in. "An interesting world. Not at all boring."

Bill choked down what he might really wanna say. "Yes, sir, it is definitely interesting. You've been to a stroke seven?"

Mukasa chuckled. "Long ago, when I was very young. They were fighting a big conventional war then, and there were lots of diseases and abysmal ignorance about them. I remember that. I suppose it must have been your world, since that's the only stroke seven we've developed for many years so far. Who won that war, anyway?"

"Depends on which one it was. If it was a world war, then it was probably the U.S., England, and Russia against Germany, Italy, and Japan. The U.S. side won. Now they and the Germans, Italians, and Japanese are on the same side and the Russians on the other."

"Fascinating," Hanrin put in. "I should like to see a full-blown war one day—from a safe distance, of course."

"They're very destructive and not very pretty or glamorous," Sam couldn't help but put in. "In fact, they're the ugliest side of human nature."

"Perhaps, but they are incredibly valuable. Progress and inventiveness accelerate a hundredfold during a war. Most great inventions and ideas come out of them, you know. I fear it is the nature of the human beast and just as necessary to him as love."

"I notice there haven't been any wars here," Sam noted, a little ticked off at this.

Mayar Eldrith sensed Sam's irritation. "Come, come! Yes, you're right, we don't have wars here, but we're a pretty static culture because of it. Our progress comes from what we learn from others. Still, we are not ignorant of the horrors and cost of wars. The Labyrinth came out of a war, in fact—the last war fought on this Earth between our people. In point of fact, it was terribly ugly. It destroyed in the end all human life on this planet. Only a small band of brave pioneers managed to escape through the Labyrinth, a very primitive thing then, and wait it out. When they were at last able to return, they found a wasteland. All that you see—the animals, trees, flowers, everything—they imported from other worlds. They redesigned the entire planet into a garden, and they swore that never again would violence sear us. Out of that came the Corporation and the system we now have."

That sorta explained a lot, like why most everybody looked like everybody else. Ten to one that class thing was really who was related to who when they came back. That was more'n a thousand years ago, but if they lived a couple hundred years plus each it was to them like maybe the World Wars were to us.

"Ancient history," muttered Basuti, the cold fish and also youngest at fifty-seven. "We're too damned fat and lazy for our own good, I say. No discipline, no motivation. We've become a bunch of whores, that's what."

"Now, Alim, don't start that again," Dringa Lakuka put in. He turned to us. "Basuti, there, was a priest and holy man until his older brother was killed in an accident, forcing him to assume obligations in the real world. I think he'd only be happy if we turned the entire world into a monastery."

"Many of us here would be far better off if we were closer to the gods than the flesh," Basuti muttered, giving the eye to Mukasa and his girlfriend.

"We strive for balance on committees as vital as this one," said Mayar Eldrith, clearing his throat nervously. "I humbly suggest that we confine ourselves to pleasantries for now. Our disagreements are none of these people's affair, nor their concern. What concerns us is whether or not we are vulnerable to evil. Someone very powerful has gone to a great deal of trouble to import this alien organism and test it. We must know why. It surely isn't to take over a mere Earth or two. Anyone with enough power to do that is hatching something aimed clearly at us."

Sam and I exchanged a look, and I knew we was both thinkin' along the same lines. All of a sudden, with two days to go, I felt like one big, fat, brown worm on the end of a hook. Somebody real powerful set this up. Somebody like one or more of the folks in this room. Somebody—Aldrath or maybe Mayar—already figured that one out. To keep that shit comin' down without tippin' off security as to where, it had to be somebody with a lot of knowledge and power in security. One of these guys. So they was trottin' out their sacrificial lamb and lettin' whoever have a good look, then they would all be watched like nobody ever been watched before, hopin' somebody would try and tip off Vogel.

I mean, guys who thought other folks' wars were neat and ran criminal syndicates on a bunch of worlds sure as hell didn't give a shit about me. I started feelin' a little sick and forgot all about eatin' or my talkin' or anything else.

"You have to excuth me wadieth and gentamen," I said softly. "Unweth theah's thomething vewy impowtant foa uth to tawk about, I have much to do and thith ith my wath night with my huthband foah a wong time." *Damn!* It was gettin' so bad I couldn't say no *l*'s, neither. Mix that with my usual accent and I must sound like an idiot!

"Oooh! That's a *cute* way of talking," Ioyeo whispered loud enough for me to hear. "What did she say?"

That did it. I kinda rushed away and nearly ran upstairs to the room. I felt so damned miserable I was cryin' before I hit the bed, and still cryin' when Sam came into the room.

He closed the door, came over, and just started gently rubbing my back. He always knew what I needed, and I could feel his own hurt and shame. Damn it! I'd *asked* for this! I really wished now that I'd listened to him and not spent all my time feelin' sorry for myself. I never wanted dear old Philadelphia and that mink-lined apartment more than now, and I'd've even given it all up and moved back to roach heaven in Camden right then.

"I'm sowwy," I sniffled. "I juth—it ain't what I thought it would be."

He sighed and kept on rubbin'. "I know, babe, I know. But it *is* just like putting on the hooker outfit and staking out the hourly motels. It's just a higher league. They can make the disguise so perfect it's scary. When you figure they can make themselves pass for us, and learn English in their spare time with a gadget, they just don't think of what it can do to us poor primitive mortals."

"I'm thcared, Tham," I told him. *"Weal* thcared. I want to caw it off."

He sighed again. "You saw them down there. You saw how they regarded us, how they talked about the other worlds. We're their toys, their playthings. They want this Vogel because he's a threat to *them,* not us. Their only opening is in two days. Not enough time to recruit and train somebody new."

"They can't *make* me do it!"

"You want to walk down and quit? Come on, babe, get hold of yourself. There's nothing I'd like more than for you to cancel out. They'd send us back, but they'd be damned angry at being inconvenienced. They'd have to come up with a different, even trickier, plan and maybe risk the necks of some of their own. They'd send you back just like you are now, and then they'd cut us off completely. You'd be stuck looking as you are now, speech impediments and all, and we'd be out on the streets with nothing."

I turned around and looked at him with this strange face. "And what if I did that anyway and they did that? Would we thtill be togetha?"

He kissed me. "You're still a pretty woman, babe, just different looking than I'm used to. But you're still you, inside, and that's who I married anyway. As for the money —how many Brandys can I buy for two million plus bucks? None. I started out with nothing, and I'll probably end up with nothing no matter what. If money mattered to me I'd be top salesman at my uncle's car showroom in Harrisburg, or maybe starting my own dealership by now. Or I'd be a comfortable cop with a heavy pad."

I hugged him and kissed him and never have I been more in love than right then and there. I just wanted to give myself to him, to fuck his brains out, and I planned to, but first I said, softly, "Tham—do you think it can be done? Do you think *I* can do it? Sthrait anthwa, now. No jive."

"It's possible," he answered, and I knew he was tellin' the truth. "And if anybody can pull it off, you can."

"Then, I'w'l do it, juth to thee them have to fork ova that money."

And *then* we made love for a long, long time.

I didn't get much sleep, and neither did Sam, even after we got done, but I was somehow real wide awake that mornin'. We *did* get to talkin', though.

"You think one of them'th the big twaita?"

He nodded. "And so does Aldrath. I think you're safe, though. Whoever's behind this is a big risk taker but he's no fool. He'll know he's been set up and sit it out. They've been on the hot seat, whoever they are, since the word came that Vogel was exposed, and they haven't dared try to reach him with any messages. They're stuck. They *have* to let this go down and work around it."

"But if Vogel knowth who, then they *hav'ta* act."

"You'd think so. But I just can't see any opening now that wouldn't just relieve us of the job of making the snatch. Aldrath is good at his job and I htink he's a basically honest man, or as honest as you can get in that line of work. He wants this higher-up so bad he can tàste it. It's almost like something personal with him."

"Which one do you think it ith?"

"Hard to say. Ioyeo and Dakani are the obvious choices, but Aldrath can haul them in and pick their brains without their even knowing it. He says Dakani's ambitious but hardly treasonous, and that Ioyeo really doesn't have anything in there except animal passions. She's not as dumb as she plays, but she's no heavyweight. No, it's one of the five. I keep thinking I should already know which one, even from our brief meeting, but I don't know why."

"Funny. Me, too. But I juth can't get a hand on it."

"Well, one job at a time," he sighed. "I'll work on that angle while you follow yours. If we can hand them Vogel *and* his master, now *that's* an IOU!"

I wasn't goin' nowhere right off; it was Sam who was leavin', for the team was already pretty much in place. They had to be all set up and ready to go before I even got there, which was fine with me, 'cept it was gonna be a real lonely, scary couple of days.

That day they introduced me to the hypnoscan, and I was real glad Sam wasn't around. Not that it was much of anything bein' in it—you sat down in this real comfortable reclinin' chair and they put sensors and stuff all over you and then packed your head in somethin' soft, so you could breathe but you couldn't see, hear, or know much of anything. It was all done by computers, of course; they load what they want in, then you just sorta drift off, and in what seems like a couple minutes it's over—even though it takes hours.

It was a little weird, too, 'cause even when you woke up

you didn't have no idea that anything was changed. The doc, he brought me over and made me walk this way and that, and I thought his voice sounded real fancy and cultured. Then he brought me over and handed me a sheet with words on it and asked me to read it.

"Hey, Doc, ev'body know we can't read," I responded. I felt nothing odd at the idea I couldn't read; I did feel some relief that my speech had improved some. In fact, I had changed radically.

The thing was, they'd wiped out any way I had of gettin' to a lot of my knowledge and skills. My ignorance was appalling, and I just took it for granted. I was also childlike and eager to please or do whatever I was asked to do without question, but I walked and moved like a two-bit whore. Any deep thoughts were just gone; so was any real sense of self-identity. I didn't know where I was or who I was or anything, but the worst thing was that it *didn't matter* to me. I had no questions. Later on, lookin' at myself in a mirror, I saw only me reflected back with this idiotic smile. They left me in a room for a while with the doors wide open and it never even entered my head to leave or go anyplace I wasn't told to go.

The Nazis had forty-plus years to experiment on us in that hell world, and that was plenty of time to take and raise children in cultural isolation and experiment with mind-dulling drugs that left permanent marks and methods of trainin' and all the rest. These wasn't slaves who was born in chains and wanted freedom; these were the ends of experiments on humans that nobody on our world would *ever* allow, born and bred as less than human and in their master's image.

And that was just stage one. Stage two put me out till I woke up in hell as somebody else, somebody completely different, somebody with a past and memories only of bein' property on that evil world. Somebody so ignorant they didn't even know it was hell they was in.

Preparation and trainin' was over. The mission was underway.

4.

You Can't Think of Everything

I ain't too clear on what came next. Oh, sure, I remember it, but not like it was real. More like a dream, you know? That's 'cause I was *her,* and she didn't think about much. It's only when I think back on it with what I know as myself that I can put it into any kinda picture that makes sense.

I woke up in a kinda dingy, smelly dormitory. It didn't have much in the way of lights and none in the way of privacy, but it had like twenty naked girls sleepin' on cots. Down at the end there was a long basin and a row of open toilets. It looked and felt perfectly normal. This was my tribe and these were my sisters. The hard part for even me to get into now is that I had no sense of personal identity, of self, at all. I had a name all right—Beth it was—but there was no sense of bein' a particular person named Beth.

We got up, took our shits in turn, walked under these open showers and wiped each other off with lard soap, dried each other off with towels, and combed each other's hair with carved wood combs. The showers were cold and while there was a lot of noise there wasn't much said. We could talk, all right, in a kind of strict pidgin southern that made a lot of uses out of few words, but there wasn't no need.

Then we went out, naked, on a cool gray day, and we did exercises and ran around this dirt track like schoolgirls at play. Some white folks watched us from off a ways but we didn't pay 'em no mind. Then we all went into this other building where there was tables and benches on which were dishes and let the sisters who'd gotten up early serve us. I can't tell you what the food was; you drank this thick, real sweet drink and you ate these different kinds of cakes. Lookin' back I figure it was some kinda cheap health food, full of vitamins and minerals and all that.

Then we all pitched in to clean up, makin' that place not just clean but *spotless*. Then it was back to the exercises and the track again, only this time it was more playful and less organized. All this with no boss, no supervisor, not even any orders.

This day would be different, though. In late morning, a black truck pulled up at the big farmhouse off in the distance and after a while two black-clad storm troopers armed with pistols came over to us and we stopped and waited, curious but not afraid. White folks were afraid of these kind of men; to us they were just more white folks. With them was Jenner, one of the supervisors at the farm. He pointed, then drawled out, "All right, you girls! Listen up, now! I'm gonna call out three names. If you hear your name, then you go in and you shower and then you come back out to us. The rest of you just keep on with whatever you was doing."

I was just as shocked and scared when they called Beth as if I were really Beth—which I thought I was. Still, I went with Daisy and Lavinia and took the shower and then reported back. We didn't say nothin' to each other—we was all too scared and confused for that. The black-clad men looked us over like we was horses or somethin', then Jenner said, "You all been sold to a man up north. You go with these men and follow their orders."

That was it; no good-byes, no nothin'—just go on, get in the back of the truck, and off. Well—not quite. When we got to the truck the men put chains on us. They didn't feel heavy, so I guess they were some kind of strong new metal—they felt like aluminum but were hard as steel. They cuffed us hands in front, with about a foot's worth of chain between, and they cuffed our legs with maybe two feet of chain between. I don't know why they chained us—where was we gonna go?—but they did, then loaded us into the truck, which was a kinda pickup truck with one of them caps on the back. It wasn't no camper, though; it was heated but you just sorta sat on the floor and that was it. There was a coupla boxes in there, too, but we didn't dare open 'em. Crazy thing was, I got a little thrill, even got a little turned on, by wearin' the chains.

Once we started off, though, we all got to cryin' a little. It was like bein' torn from the only family and world we knew.

After a while, though, Lavinia kinda took charge. She was more aggressive than we was. She even went to the little window and looked out, and after a while we did, too.

The impressions of the trip are just that—impressions. The highways looked real fancy, like our interstates, and had a lot of little cars on 'em. We went through a city, I don't know which, and it looked real ugly, all sterile gray with block after block of tall, dirty buildin's and lots of even uglier industry belchin' smoke into the gray day. Most of the people we saw moved like they was always tired, dressed in plain clothes. Clearly the white folks here didn't have much fun, neither. The good life, if it existed at all, was for the big shots.

And that, maybe, was the craziest thing of all. The more we saw of that white world, the less we wanted of it. We had no responsibilities, little work, no cares. Nobody would want to escape into *that* world. Even bein' wrenched and sold we were still secure and safe. No decisions, no responsibilities. It's scary to me to think that people can be brought up and conditioned to think that way, even now. Still and all, it was that world that did it, partly. It was a gray world filled with people with gray souls; a world without hope. They was all property, all slaves, white and black. The only difference was, nobody expected nothin' from us.

They stopped the truck off and on, to stretch their legs and ours. They had one of them porta-potties for us and the boxes had cold, hard versions of the cakes and sweet stuff they'd fed us back at the farm and a jug of water. That was all for us. Every once in a while they'd stop the truck someplace and get out, sometimes for quite a while, just leavin' us inside, while they ate or whatever. They were pretty ordinary-lookin' white men 'cept for their fancy uniforms and shiny boots, but we'd flaunt it a little for 'em.

"Tempted to take 'em all on, Pete?" the one asked. "They might be too much for you."

"Nigresses? You got to be kiddin'. I ain't that hard up. Why? You tempted?"

"Yeah, sorta."

"Well, forget it. Vogel'll run 'em through every test in the world. You know the rules. He gets 'em first. Don't trust no real women not to cut his balls off."

"Aw, what's he care? These ain't virgins. Look at 'em."

"Well, you do what you want, but the last guy who did that wound up dangling from a meat hook on the walls."

They didn't, although truth was we wouldn't have minded. Oh, they did a little fanny pattin' and tit grabbin' now and again, but overall they probably treated us better than they did their own kind. They even hauled out some old blankets when the chill got greater so we could wrap 'em around ourselves.

Fact was, the three of us did a lot of it in the back, there. It seemed normal and natural to make out, it felt good, and helped pass the time.

Eventually we got there, not over highways but back country mountain roads. We didn't really see the place till we was inside it, but when we got there and the door opened it was clear we was at our new home. Big place, but with lots of buildin's, grounds, and people. We got took into the basement of the big house where they let us shower, fed us, then put us in this tiny room with no windows, a bare light bulb, and a big old mattress on the floor that was big enough for the three of us. We was exhausted from the trip and just slept. They left the chains on.

The next day they processed us. There was a couple of people in lab whites and one older guy in black uniform who wore glasses. He came up to me. "Name?"

"Beth, suh."

He looked on his chart, then started in. First he tried to get me mad by makin' nasty comments, then he both scared and hurt me a little. I said "Ow! You huhtin' me, suh!" but that was about the extent of my rebellion. Finally they gave us a bunch of shots with this injector gun, took X rays and scanned us with something, then took us in to a hypnoscan, although as Beth I had no idea what it was. It was definitely something Vogel was not supposed to have in this world, that's for sure. I can't say what they did with it, but I can guess they was lookin' for somebody just like I was—a plant. Jamispur must have known his business; I passed. The hypnoscan couldn't find a trace of Brandy anywhere, nor, apparently, did any of the cosmetic changes show.

Time had no meaning for us, so I don't know how long we just hung around there, but finally this woman also in black and with real short hair came for us and brought us up to the main floor and took us into a room that was nicer than any of us had ever seen. We got cleaned and scrubbed and then perfumed, and our nails got trimmed and painted, they put on real heavy makeup which was foreign to us, pierced our ears and gave us earrings, even did our hair. We liked it, but we also knew we was about to meet our owner.

In all the plannin' back at headquarters, the one thing that never entered anybody's head was that Vogel would see all three of us at the same time. He never allowed nobody else in the Safe Room, that was sure, but three at once wasn't even considered, yet that's what happened. It was the first kinda thing Sam had worried about from the start—there were too many things you couldn't think of. If the number of unexpected and unanticipated things was too high, the thing would go wrong real fast. And we all knew some things would go wrong. That's why you needed a thinkin', experienced human being in there and not just some hypno-programmed anybody. My job was to improvise.

We waited around awhile; we was all excited, and Lavinia whispered, "Dis new massa be one big *stud* to take us all de same time. Don't y'all fuck up, now. A gal kin git *used* t'this shit."

We'd all moved up from tribal to house status, and clearly Lavinia saw visions of makeup and perfume and comfortable living if we all pleased him. It didn't matter that our chains were still on.

It was fairly late at night when they came for us. That same short-haired bitch in black it was—Vogel's secretary or aide or whatever. "You listen good, now," she said coldly. "You are about to be brought up to *Gruppenfuehrer* Vogel, your owner and master. You behave and perform right and he can be most kind. You nigger farm sluts just do whatever he wants and don't screw up. If he isn't pleased, you'll go to the lab and wish you'd never been born. Now—come."

We didn't understand the specifics, but we got the message, and followed her out and up a back stairway—tough in them leg chains—then down a second floor hall past an armed door guard—there was guards all over the place— and into a huge bedroom, the biggest I ever seen anywheres and the most luxurious, too. "Wait here," said the bitch, and left. We heard the outer bedroom door lock. There was stuff all over—valuable stuff, pretty stuff, even sharp stuff that might be used as a weapon. We didn't move. This was the last test, apparently.

Finally, a man came out of a far door, dressed in brown pants and shirt and leather boots. He was a big guy, and chunky, but in real good shape, with a rounded face and short brown hair. He had a small thing in his hands that might have been a short whip or riding crop, and he had on a pistol belt and holster with the pistol in it.

He walked up to us and got a queer half smile on his face. Finally he said, in a rather mild and gentle voice, to each of us in turn, "What is your name?"

"Daisy, suh." "Beth, suh." "Lavinia, suh."

"Come on in back with me."

They said the entrance to the Safe Room was through the bathroom, but they didn't say that the bathroom was bigger'n most folks livin' rooms. The door in the back was open inward, but it looked less like a door than a bank vault, and the wall through it was a good eight inches thick.

The Safe Room itself was about the size of an average bedroom, but there was storage in the walls for all sorts of stuff, a desk and chair, and the whole thing was carpeted in a thick, spongy wool. Vogel closed the door with a chunk.

And I slowly returned. It was a weird sensation, like Brandy was being poured from a bucket into the vast empty spaces of Beth's mind. The setup continued to hold Beth forward, on automatic, but it was almost like I had two minds, and the other one could take control anytime it wanted to. Vogel came over, took off his gun and belt and put it on the desk right in back of me. I knew I could get it before he could react, but I didn't even consider it. It was one of the first tricks I'd fallen for in trainin', and I would have bet my life that the gun was totally empty. There was a clip somewheres real near if he needed it, but anybody who made for that gun would just be trapped.

No matter what happened, I didn't dare make a move till that security light come on, tellin' me that the diversionary attack had started and that the station was being invaded and secured. This room was a vault, all right; I had a little twinge of worry that the warning light might be burnt out or somethin'.

I also figured Vogel was real kinky, but he wasn't as near far out as I had been afraid he might be. He wasn't one of them game-playin' types, anyways—I guess he did enough of that in real life. He had real clever ways of usin' all three of us, though, and once he got naked and got started, showed a few things I filed away for reference. He had a real good body, real hairy, too, and a tight ass, and one humongous pecker. I just let Beth have free rein and waited.

The soft white light in the room suddenly changed, blinking a real weird-lookin' red. He was so turned on and so into it that he didn't notice at first, but when he came up for air he saw it. I never saw a guy come down that fast, but he just got up, pushin' us out of the way, and went to the desk, opened a drawer, and got out a handset phone and plugged it into a wall outlet. The girls just kept goin' on with each other; even I was so turned on at that point it was tough.

Vogel was clearly real pissed at the alarm, and if it had been anything less than it was somebody woulda died on that wall out there. He calmed down the moment he was told, though.

"An attack? Who? Well, try and find out, damn it! Can you hold? I don't care *what* weapons they're using—you hold them! No—I'll wait it out here, but I'll keep the line plugged in. You give me two short buzzes if they breach the wall, one long if you want me to pick up the phone. Have all emergency procedures in full effect as of now!" He put down the phone and turned back to us. "Sorry, loves, but we have a problem. Don't worry—we'll get back to our business, I promise. Now I need you. Get up and help me move this desk."

We didn't feel none too much like work but we got up and helped him pull the desk away. It was pretty easy—the thing was not that heavy—but his kind didn't do no work when he had other folks to do it for him.

We pulled up the carpet where the desk had been and there was a door there with a kind of combination lock built into it, like a safe. The emergency tunnel! We didn't know about the lock, but I wasn't gonna make no move till he twiddled it and then threw the switch and pulled the thing open. A long, deep, black hole was all there was.

I really thought that maybe we was gonna luck out on

this, that he was gonna go down and right into the arms of the station people without me doin' nothin', but clearly he wasn't gonna move right off.

The phone gave a long buzz and he picked it up.

"Yes? All right, then. Best I stay right here for now. The station's on? Good—*what?* Well keep trying the station, man! I don't like the smell of this!"

Uh oh. They had some feelin' that the station had been taken. It probably wouldn't enter their heads in plannin' that it *could* be, but if they tried to call somebody there and either got a strange voice or no answer they'd be suspicious, what with an attack at the front.

Vogel was still naked, but he got his pistol, then reached behind a panel, got a clip, and snapped it into place. I'd guessed right.

I hadn't been able to shoot my little jet of joy juice into him; he had gave me the lower end in our sex play. Now there seemed no way to give him the kiss; it would have to be the hard way.

I moved real fast, pushin' him off balance and then usin' my knee and then put his head between my arms and used the chain as a choker. He twisted me off, but then he grabbed me by the shoulders and while the leg chain made karate useless I brought up my knee with full force and caught his exposed jewels right on the balls. He screamed and let go of me and doubled over, droppin' the pistol in his pain. I got him real good, too, 'cause I had the gun and even had time to make sure I had a shell in the chamber before he was able to come out of it and figure what happened.

The other two girls looked at the whole thing with real shock and horror on their faces, but they just pressed back against the wall.

"Who the hell *are* you?" Vogel gasped.

"You know who I'm with," I replied, keepin' the Beth accent and grammar since it was lousy English but I could say it clear. The Company want you. You be one *baaad* boy!"

He recovered enough to stand, shakily, and look bewildered. "The Company! It would have to be, but—why?"

"It seem you make lots of dem bigwigs scared with dat drug thing you got."

I got to say he really did look surprised. I'd have loved to have gotten more, but the clock was tickin' and the bomb was under my feet. I gestured with the pistol. "'Nuff. Git on down the hole. You can 'splain it yo'self."

He looked a little cagey, and I got to admit I was feelin' a little good right then at it bein' easier than most of the practices. I was right behind him, when suddenly I got hit hard right on the head. It was so unexpected I took a tumble, got tripped up by the leg chains, and fell. Vogel didn't waste no time; he was on me in a second and just about tore that gun from my grip. I got up, still feelin' dizzy and confused, and looked around. That damned muscle-headed Lavinia had hit me over the head with the desk chair!

Vogel was back to himself now. "Not a move!" he cautioned me. "I never had to get dressed one-handed before but I'll manage, and I'll blow your brains out if you so much as twitch!"

I rolled over and looked at Lavinia. "You dumb nigger bitch!" I swore. "I'd'a killed her with my own hands then if I could. She looked so damned smug and proud of herself.

"Don't blame her," Vogel said, not givin' me enough of an openin' to do anything. He got shirt, pants, and boots on real slow and careful. "She doesn't know who or what you are except that you were my enemy. You see, even though we've just met, I'm the only one she's got."

I was mad both at her and at myself. Lavinia was bein' promoted from field to house in the only life she knew. She'd said she could get used to perfume and lipstick and comfortable beds, and she had no idea that there was any alternative—nor had I time to explain to somebody like that the reality of things. Even if she could understand it, she wouldn't believe it. Vogel kicked the trapdoor shut and then moved to the main door, opening it. He pointed the gun at me.

"I wish I had time to find out all the details, or even put you through the hypnoscan now, but I don't. I gather your friends are causing all this ruckus to divert attention from you, and that they've captured the station."

"Give it up, man!" I told him. "Dey gon' blow dis joint if'n I show or not. Dey wan' you live, but dey git you dead if'n dey hav'ta."

"I thought so. The fact is, I don't know if you're what you say you are, and I don't know if I'm being set up or not, but until I can sort this out I'm not going to surrender to anyone, particularly not to some nigger bitch or on her say-so. *Get up!*"

I made it to my feet, though I felt achy. Gettin' hit by a chair ain't the small thing you see on TV.

He turned to the two others. "You two remain here until someone comes. I won't forget this, Lavinia, I promise. Make yourselves at home in the bedroom. Use and enjoy anything you find."

Yeah, for a few minutes, until the joint blows, I thought sourly, but nobody was gonna listen to me.

"Now you listen to me," he said to be with a real cold tone that could freeze blood. "I saw your moves, I know what you can do, but you don't try *anything*. Once we're outside here, you'll be observed by security and guards. Even if you somehow overpower me, and I'm ready for you now, you will only get cut down by others. You cannot reach your friends and they cannot reach you. If you want to live, you'll do just what I say.

He had a point, and if he was leavin' the place I sure wanted out, too. Once we was out of the buildin', it would be up to Sam and the rest to get me out. I was ready to do my part, but suicide wasn't it. We was now on Plan B. Not so good and a lot riskier, but the object was to get him out of his safe and guarded place where he could get took.

We went into the hall, and some of the sentries had their eyebrows raised by seein' me marched out at gunpoint, but they snapped to. "Ready the drome!" he called to one, then said to the other, "You have the key for these things. Give it here and watch her. She's a bitch!"

The sentry produced a small key, and Vogel took the time to unlock the hand manacles on one side and then hook 'em back around so that my hands were now chained behind my back. Then he pushed me forward, gun at the ready, to some stairs and then, to my surprise, up not one but two flights. A dome shape was goin' back with a lot of noise above us, and I could see we was in open air, on the roof, and there was a small, funny-lookin' helicopter there. *That* wasn't in no briefin' books!

He opened a door, pushed me into one seat, then got in on the other and started the thing. It started with a quiet whine, then a big roar as the blades got to speed. It was some kind of jet helicopter but different than any I'd seen. All the instruments was in German.

We went up a little, then he pushed somethin' and pulled back and we went straight up so fast I felt like the breath was bein' knocked out of me. When he cut it and hovered, we was so far up that you could see the whole compound down there. There was still some fightin' on two sides, and all sorts of runnin' around, and it was all lit up like a Christmas tree.

Vogel started the chopper forward, slow at first, like he was waitin' for somethin'. What it was was a tremendous set of explosions that made the whole place down there look like World War III. Buildings, includin' the big manor house, just blew apart like they was toys. The station blew, too, in one hell of a blast that also seemed to trigger a whole bunch of funny blue-white lights, like a solid Labyrinth cube. The station shimmered, then just—winked out. Just like that. There was nothin' left of it but one monster hole in the ground.

Sam was supposed to be on the B team, the Just In Case team, so I could only hope and pray he still was and hadn't decided at the last minute to meet me in the station.

Vogel gave a satisfied laugh, then pushed us forward at maximum speed into the night sky.

"What now?" I asked Vogel as we sped into the night sky.

"I am the stationmaster for this world," he replied. "No one knows the setup here, the weak points, the Labyrinth accesses and modifications like I do. I have enough knowledge of the security system and its goals to get through safely if I pick the right access track and don't go through a switch. We don't have far to go once inside. There I can take stock of things, with enough equipment to discover what I must know and perhaps make contact with others."

"You 'spect me to just sit 'round all dat time?"

He chuckled. "My dear, are you that naive? You are on a mission into an alternate world and you have failed in your objective and you have failed to elude capture. Surely you realize that they cannot allow this. You know too much, and you might be of value to someone against their interests. Everyone can be broken. *Everyone.* Were I, however, to try to break you or subject you to physical, mental, or artificially induced interrogation, it would be automatic. You would be blocked out, the process reversed, and you would again be only poor, sweet Beth, my willing, eager, and appallingly dumb slave. I couldn't even bring you back with hypnoscan and the best equipment."

It wasn't no bed of roses in that little chopper naked and in chains, but I got a real sick feelin' when he said that so confident and smug, 'cause I knew deep down in my gut he was tellin' the truth.

"Don't let that worry you," he said smoothly. "In fact, if I had to flee, they gave me a perfect tool and assistant. You will be a great help to me. It will be amusing to watch it happen more slowly. Beth, all of her, is still inside you, whole and complete. Your willpower keeps her down now, but the more tired you get and the more you sleep the more she will merge with you. Those are powerful programs, and very complete, since they have to fool even the devices that create them. It's still for their protection—at your expense." He laughed, but suddenly got real cold and crazy. "You listen to me, bitch! You are my property! I *own* you! What sanity you have depends on me. If I put this down and let you go right now, you would become Beth instantly in *this* world, a world where power is everything and your skin alone marks you as having none."

I figured he was tryin' to scare me, and he was doin' a pretty good job. He was sure right that I wouldn't last long in these parts alone. He was also right in that all of Beth was still in my head, and I almost had to fight her to keep from actin' like her. The only chance I had now was Sam and Bill and that crowd. I knew they was coverin' the most likely substations, and they also said that somehow they could track me—but that was no sure thing, if we got away clean before they knew it. That was some takeoff and nobody figured on this chopper. What if they thought we was both dead? That scared me the most, 'cause that left me as Vogel's slave forever.

I dozed off after a while; I couldn't help it. I was dead

tired and there wasn't much more to say. Trouble was, I dreamed, and I didn't dream Brandy's dreams. I started to, but they were all made up of my fears and I ran from 'em—into Beth. Those were simple, pleasant, secure dreams, of lots of sex and no worries or cares or responsibilities.

The helicopter landed, wakin' me up, but I just lay there, half asleep, not really awake. It was daylight now and the sun was shinin' and it looked like a pretty day. My arms hurt and I couldn't remember why. Chained in back . . . I must be bein' punished for somethin', but what?

Vogel came back and got in and looked at me carefully. "Beth?" he asked.

"Yessuh?"

"Now, listen close. You got a demon inside you, a real bad one that wants to hurt you and me and everybody. You can feel it in your head. I bet it's trying to get in right now."

And it was. I felt it, comin' in like a mass of mud.

"You can fight it, Beth. Don't let it in! You must fight it with everything you have! You *will* fight it. You will not let it in!"

But Beth couldn't really fight it, the knowledge and understanding, and I was more or less back in control, but shaken. Vogel saw this, but didn't seem terribly upset. "You ought not to fight it," he said. "It is inevitable. Here—I will prove it."

He got me out of the helicopter and then undid my arm bracelets and chains. The relief was enormous, almost orgasmic, both the ultimate pleasure and pain at the same time.

We was in a grassy meadow and there was cows in the distance, but the sun was fairly warm and the air humid and it felt okay after that gray chill.

"There's a farm just two kilometers that way," he told me, "and a town another two beyond that. You want to get away, just go ahead. I won't stop you or shoot you. Go to the farm and see what reception you get. Go to the town and see what happens. Or, perhaps, go wild in the fields here and try and live on what garbage you can steal until you're caught. Go ahead."

I looked around. "You made yo' point," I told him, and

actually for the first time I could at least understand the poor, late Lavinia. Even slaves in the old south had a place they might run to, if they had the guts and the energy, up north. Not here. Not anywhere. Latin America, maybe, but I didn't know enough about the rest of this world to know for sure or how far down. And them old runaways, they didn't have to fight no Beth every time they got tired or slept. Even if all the shackles were off, there was just no place to run. Hell, I didn't even have any idea where in hell we was!

He unpacked a basket that had sandwiches and a jug of what proved to be cider and gave me some. There was enough Beth in me to find the meat in the sandwiches unappetizing and the cider pretty bad tastin', but I managed. After, he told me to pick up all the stuff and repack the basket and put it in the chopper and I did. There wasn't anything else to do but play along. It was all out of my hands now and I knew it. I'd just have to be good.

But I sure would like to get Vogel someday in a world where the black people were on top. There were some—I asked once.

Vogel surprised me by also removin' my leg chains. Not bad treatment for somebody who'd kicked him in the balls and cost him his empire.

"A final demonstration," he said, enjoyin' it. "I need some sleep, and the men with the gasoline can't be here for a few hours. Since I still can't be certain you won't try to grab my pistol and overpower me, I will lock myself in the cabin. Unfortunately, that means you remain outside. Go where you will, but not out of sight, please. Almost anyone who found you around here would be far less kind than I, and you would lose any hope that your friends could find us." And, with that, he climbed into the cabin and locked both doors and settled in.

This, I decided, was the nuttiest situation I could imagine. I was stark naked in some cow pasture, and I was free and my kidnapper had locked himself in to protect himself from me.

As a demonstration, though, it beat all the lectures in the world.

There was no way I was gonna live in no cow pasture, and

trees and hills of any size was few and far between here.
Last thing I wanted to be was a slave to a bunch of
farmhands, and the town would have the usual Nazi everything. I sure wasn't about to kill myself so long as there was
any hope of bein' rescued, but I thought I might do it if it
was this for life or death. So I just moved out a little into the
warm sun and sat down in the grass and waited.

The gas truck came a couple of hours later, driven by two
typical cracker types. I pounded on the door and woke up
Vogel and he got up and came out. The two drivers just
stared at me and I thought at first it was because I was
naked, but then I realized they probably never saw a black
person before in their lives.

Vogel noticed it, too, and enjoyed every minute of it.
"You want to feel her up a little? Go ahead. She likes it." He
took a manacle with chain and held it sorta like a whip.
"She won't do nothin', will you, Beth?"

I hated his guts but the only protest I could manage in
this situation was to not reply. It was a horrible situation,
almost but not quite a rape, but just as degrading and
humiliating, and I flipped out. Brandy shut off and Beth
took over, as Vogel figured would happen. The only thing
Beth had was her body; her skin limited anything she might
want to do or anyplace she might want to go, and any mind
was a liability. She wound up givin' both of 'em blow jobs
and enjoyin' every minute of it. That's how Vogel paid most
of the gas bill.

We was in the air when I managed to creep back into
control, and now I knew what havin' a split personality was
like. I was so completely disgusted and humiliated that I
was on the edge of just givin' up and lettin' Beth take over.
The only thing that stopped me was that I knew I was this
man's and this *world's* prisoner, but I was damn well not his
property or slave. It was the only part of me I could still
control, and I had too much pride and too much hate for
him to let him have that, too.

It was clear Vogel felt he wasn't bein' chased—they'd
have caught up to us by now—and he was in no real hurry.
If he'd made a run for the stations closest to his Pennsylvania retreat, they'd have nabbed him, but if two, three, or
more days went by with no sign, and even in this tight

dictatorship no records comin' back to their contacts, they'd slack off. They had to. The way both the headquarters people and Vogel talked, it would take hundreds of folks to stake out all the possibilities. They could spare that many for a day or two, but not for real long.

I wanted Sam, bad. I needed him. More, I needed just to know that he was still alive. That had been one hell of a bang, and I don't think they was the ones who triggered it.

Turned out, too, that Vogel wasn't out of the woods, neither, 'cause he didn't dare use much of his influence for anything that might get his location reported back to someplace where it could be noted by our people. He did, however, have money. That helicopter was outfitted partly as a permanent getaway car, complete with fake and convincin' Nazi IDs and a fair amount of money. He just got a charge out of using me instead when he could. Still, he couldn't keep outta notice and with farms and real small towns forever; he was gettin' nervous 'bout his own people here now. Three days after we set out, he made for this real hot, dry, dusty desert place with big, tall, purple mountains in the distance. There musta been mining there sometime long ago, 'cause on the desert floor but up against the mountains there was this tiny, broke-down ghost town. Not much, about a half dozen buildin's that looked worse than any slum.

He picked the place well. Nobody, not even no roads, around for a hundred miles, a hot baked nothin' of a place, but with a kind of sandy ground that showed every track around. Ain't nobody been 'round that place in a long time, I thought. *He's gonna get away with it!* I thought in somethin' of a panic. *That fucking son of a bitch is gonna do it, and take me with him!* I knew where he was headin'—sorta. There was all sorts of time lines in which people just never developed at all, or anything else, for that matter, that could think. Some of 'em was right in the middle of otherwise populated worlds, and some had been rigged up by bigwigs both in the Corporation and by traitors to it as safe worlds.

Vogel no longer even worried about me, even when I wasn't Beth. Truth was, even though I had my full knowledge and identity, most times, more and more I just was actin' and thinkin' like Beth 'cause it didn't do no good to fight. The longer we kept from bein' caught by anybody, the harder it was to fight it. My last hope, the shit still in that tooth compartment, was dashed 'cause whenever I was under that kind of sexual thing Beth took over. It might as well not be there.

Vogel left me there while he checked out the buildings, bein' as cautious and sure as he could. He came back and pointed. "There's a trail up to an old mine there. Get the supply basket, particularly the water, and come with me."

I got it, although it was heavy and a little awkward.

That trail wasn't much these days, particularly for bare feet and carryin' that basket, but I kept up with him. It was a long way up from the town and hot and dry as could be, and Vogel stopped every once in a while and had me bring him a bottle to drink. He didn't give me none 'though I was dry as hell, and I was so far gone by that point it never even occurred to me to take a drink without permission. It wasn't until we was halfway there that he let me have the last half of a warm beer he was drinkin'. It was a strong brew on a mostly empty stomach on a hot day and I got feelin' a little high from it.

We was high, too. Lookin' down the helicopter was far enough below that it was blurry to me, and everything beyond was too blurred to see. On top of everything else, my vision treatments was wearin' off fast and I was goin' back to bein' legally blind without no glasses. We finally reached the ledge where the mine entrance was—more broke-down timbers and an old musty hole—and he let me have another beer and he had the last one.

"I put in this substation myself several years ago. Just me and three others, none of whom lived to tell of its existence," Vogel said. "It's a known weak spot, but the Company ignored it because it was clearly inside a mountain. They didn't know about this mine."

I giggled, feelin' pretty drunk on only one and a half beers. "Dat damn thecurity juth as fulla holes as always was," I muttered, more to myself than to Vogel. "But if you on the squah wit' th' Comp'ny, den why you build dis at all?"

"A good question, so I'll answer it. Graft, mostly. Most

stationmasters need a little just to do their jobs. That hypnoscan, for example, was wonderful for insuring loyalty and changing minds, but it's illegal here. Places like this make getting that kind of thing possible. I haven't had to use it in years, though. There are better methods. It's handy now."

He got up. "Stand up and stick close to me. Get me the flashlight out of the basket and hand it to me. We're going to leave this burning hellhole."

I got up and followed him into the mine. It was dirty and dingy but almost immediately it was cooler. The flashlight lit up the place, but it was still bad lookin'. It went in and then curved around and down a bit. Some of them rafters was real old, and every once in a while some dirt and stuff would come down on or around us.

There was an old iron gate at the end of it, with a thick, rusted lock on it. Vogel didn't have the key, but he didn't need it. With my help the whole gate came free, lock, door, and all, and we put it to one side. Beyond that was a bunch of machinery, painted black so it didn't show, and Vogel turned it on. Just beyond in the tunnel, there was a sound like an electric motor whine, then a pulsing, and then he threw another set of switches and the Labyrinth line appeared, then did its usual thing of dividin' and dividin' again.

For a minute I had a thought. Once in there, I had a place to run—anyplace but out into one of the other worlds. Just to a switch point. He wouldn't dare follow but so far. 'Course, he had the gun, but I still figured it was worth the chance. Vogel, unfortunately, had the same idea.

He grabbed the basket, moved some stuff, and came up with the arm and leg chains. My hopes sank. No way I was gonna dodge bullets wearin' *those*. If I'd'a known he put them in there, or had my full wits in me, I'd'a chucked them things.

He turned to me, his back to the Labyrinth, and turned me around and pulled my hands behind me. He fixed the chains, then turned—and looked straight into two mean-lookin' guys with big, fancy guns.

He turned back and saw two more guys with guns blockin' our way back out again. He grabbed me and put me in front of him, back against the wall, pistol out. This was one tough dude.

"Stay back or she's dead!" he shouted. "You let me through and I'll give her back to you!"

"You're in no position to deal, Vogel," said one of the men who had to have come in through the Labyrinth. "The idea was to get *you*. It was her job, too, and in a way she did the job anyway. Kill her and you have no leverage. Shoot any of us and we'll have to try and shoot you even if it's right through her."

"Oh, great," I muttered. He had one hand on his pistol, the other wrapped around the chain holding my hands in back of me. Freak-out Beth was nowhere around now. She couldn't handle this kinda situation. Me, it took two seconds to figure the odds—either we'd be there a long time, or Vogel would shoot and take his chances. He wasn't the type to surrender peacefully or they wouldn't'a needed me in the first place.

Using all my muscle power, I twisted my body and fell to the stone floor. Vogel, his hand wrapped in the chain, had no choice but to fall with me. His gun went off, and the shot ricocheted all over the place, but if it hit anybody it wasn't clear. They was on him in a minute, tossin' the gun away and haulin' him up back to his feet none too gentle. One of the men from in back, the entrance side, ran forward to me.

"Brandy! My God! You all right?"

"Tham!" I managed, and then we was huggin' and kissin' and both of us was cryin'. One of the men found the key to the chains and gave it to Sam, who undid them and handed them over. The leg chains got put on Vogel; they had plain old handcuffs for his hands.

"How did you—?" I managed.

"We didn't foresee this kind of getaway," he told me, "but we still had the monitor on to your encoder so we could tell when you went into the Safe Room and start the show. All of a sudden the thing went nuts, and we got a reading of straight up and over. We got everybody back and radioed the men in the station to get back in the Labyrinth. Most of them made it. We followed you by land for a while but it wasn't possible, and by the time we got something in the air you were out of range. We've been going nuts trying to find you ever since."

He helped me up. I was still shaky and I knew I was gonna have a bunch of bruises. "Den how did—dis place . . .?"

"Every world where the Company has a station they have satellites to monitor communications and general conditions. Back home, ours can read a newspaper. Theirs can find all the encoded people and give a fix. He led a real zigzag route over two thirds of the country and he was real clever about it, but when we got two fixes on this spot we knew he had to be heading here, even though we didn't have it down as a possible. He couldn't use Oregon or Mendocino, the only other two possibilities over here, because we had them covered. It had to be here. We got here about an hour before you did—close—but time enough to radio back to Bill in Oregon and have him monitor the weak point on the Labyrinth side while Sergei and I staked this place out."

"Den why didn't you take him when we git heah?"

"First, we wanted him—and you—alive. This was the least risky. And we didn't really know where the substation was until we followed you up. We figured the tunnel was the best bet. You saw how he was even in here. Figure the odds if we'd tried to take him in the open."

It made sense. "Den—it's ovah? I kin get back to tawkin' normal?"

"It's over, babe. Let's go back to the doc and then home and collect. I figure they owe us a cool five million smackers. Haji—lead the way! We want *out!*"

Bye-bye Beth. It's for your own good, too.

The two men from the Labyrinth side led the way, with Sergei and Sam and me bringin' up the rear and a very sour-lookin' Vogel in the middle. It felt real *good* to see *him* in chains. A coupla times we passed windows out to worlds that looked right for him and I half expected him to make a break for it, but he didn't.

We made a coupla switch points on the way back to headquarters and I was feelin' *good*. Fact was, the man had been right—they got Vogel 'cause Vogel had me. The crazy

thing was, if I had made any kinda break for it, or if he'd
dumped me and gone it alone, he *might* just have made it
out. He was just so damned arrogant that he was gonna
break this uppity nigress that he never thought of this kind
of trackin'.

We was in the main line now, almost home. Most of the
world pictures mirrored to us looked a lot like headquarters.

They hit us first with a concussion grenade that knocked
everybody silly, then came at us from the sides and top. I
don't know how many there were, I was feelin' so groggy
from the concussion, but I looked up and saw bodies
everywhere and the flashes of guns we couldn't hear but
could kill just the same. The concussion grenade didn't
make no noise, neither, but it was like a big fist knockin' us
flat.

There were six of them—I got the sense of both men and
women, all dressed in black and hooded and with firearms.
Our people managed to get two of 'em, but the others
looked around and started firin' at random into just about
everybody. I saw the whole thing like it was slow motion; I
saw Sam jump as one of the black-masked killers brought
his gun around on me and jump the guy from the front. I
saw the flash and then saw part of Sam's head explode in
blood and he was knocked down right on top of me. I guess
they figured they got me, too, 'cause they lit out on the run
to the next cubes and out of my sight.

Sam was a bloody mess and he looked as dead as the
others, but I thought I saw some signs of life there. There
was a switching cube just three back and I figured the best
thing I could do to save what lives there was to save was to
make it back there and get help on the double.

We wondered how the big man was gonna take Vogel out,
and now we knew. It made perfect sense in 20–20 hind-
sight. Vogel was to be hauled to headquarters. They knew
just where in the Labyrinth he'd have to pass, and, most of
all, they knew it was us just twenty minutes or so after we
nabbed him. I didn't think of anything like that right then,
just Sam.

The last thing I expected out of this was for *me* to be the
survivor.

5.

Just One More for Sam

I will say they came right quick—almost too quick, I remember thinkin'. I couldn't help wonderin' if some of them folks gettin' to the dead and dyin' and gettin' emergency medical and transport through the Labyrinth wasn't some of the same folks who done the shootin'. A security alert went out for all of 'em up and down the line, and nobody not authorized or unexpected came past either switch point. Now, sure, there was a lot of worlds goin' toward the headquarters junction, but these people had to know the Labyrinth, have almost unlimited access to it, and have some kind of communications that allowed them to know, at three different substation points, just when to jump in and jump us.

They not only had vehicles in the Labyrinth when they wanted them, they had at least one that was a small hospital all by itself, but Sam was the only one they loaded in and he didn't look long for this world. They pumped so many bullets into Vogel's fat head that it wasn't nothin' but a grease spot, but then they went and shot everybody else. They shot me, too, it turned out, only I didn't even notice until they rushed to give me medical help. The bullet tore a nasty gash right in my left side, but it didn't hit nothin' fatal or even cripplin'.

By the time this little scooterlike thing with a seat on it come for me, Sam and the big medical truck was long gone. All I wanted to do now was to follow them, to be with him at the last. Last thing I wanted was Sam dyin' without me there.

So help me, they still made us go through the whole routine at the entrance to headquarters, although I was

93

okay. The best medical knowledge anywhere was just inside, but I wondered how long it took 'em to test Sam and spray their damned rays before they got him where he had to go.

Still, they didn't waste no time gettin' me to the surface and off to what could only be called their big medical center. It was out in the boondocks just like Mayar's place, but it was an enormous complex of buildings, rounded, cubed, A-framed, and everything else, and it went up and out for a long ways.

They finally gave me a shot for the pain, though frankly I was too keyed up emotionally and physically to feel much, and I dozed in spite of myself for most of the trip.

It was still kinda weird and frightenin' to be rushed into this place with all these golden perfect people around talkin' away in that singsong language and not bein' able to talk to them or understand what they was sayin' or doin'. They put me in some kind of pack and treated the wound almost by remote control, but the itching and pain stopped almost at once and when I had the thing taken off there was a kind of feltlike bandage over it and just about no feelin' right there at all. Some kind of anesthetic in the bandage, I guessed.

I kept tryin' to get some word on Sam, who I knew had to be brought to this place, but all I got were shrugs and apologetic looks. They took me to a small room with a bed and a window that didn't look out on much, as well as a sink and bathroom, and kinda signed to me to stay there. I didn't have much choice, really.

I had had one hell of a day. I'd gone from despair and surrender as a damned slave on that Nazi world to complete joy and relief at bein' rescued to even worse seein' Sam get it like that—and in the head, too. Thing was, he was blockin' the finish-off shot to me. He got it savin' my life. That made me feel even more miserable.

After a couple hours of just layin' there, Bill Markham came in, lookin' like death warmed over himself. He needed a bath and a shave and he looked like he hadn't slept in a week, but he'd come as soon as he'd got the word and could get in here. I was relieved to see somebody, anybody, I could talk to.

"Sam's here," he told me right off, "and he's still alive. That's the good news. The bad news is that the slug took a chunk out of his skull on the right side and we don't know just what damage there is. He's in what passes for brain surgery here now, and will be for some time. There's nothing to do but wait." He sank down tiredly in the one little chair near the bed. "I'm really sorry, Brandy. *I should have guessed!* I feel like a complete idiot!"

"No, none of us seen it, Bill. Now dat dey gon' and done it, it be de only thing dey could do. When dey go bad, dey go *weal* bad."

He looked up, but he didn't really believe a word of it. Fact was, I was kickin' myself over it, too. Damn it, we'd had a runnin' gun battle through the Labyrinth and into another world once. Only made sense that what you could do one way you could do the other—if you had the information. We was all too smug. Even Bill admitted that Vogel's getaway substation was unknown to security. This whole thing was just too damned complicated and the Labyrinth itself had just too many entrances and exits to ever secure it. No wonder they was able to run this drug or whatever back and forth for a while without gettin' caught —and then only by lucky accident.

He looked over at me. "Look, there's nothing to see in the surgery, and all your medical records were transferred here by Jamispur. They tell me you lost some blood but that your wound's a lucky one and it should heal completely in a week to ten days. Maybe you should think of using this waiting time to get them to restore you. Get rid of Beth, get your teeth and jaw back on so you talk normally, that kind of thing. You want to be ready when Sam wakes up."

I knew he was just tryin' to divert me. Yeah, when Sam wakes up. *If* Sam wakes up . . . Still, I sure as hell didn't want to stay this way any longer than I had to.

They used Jamispur's hypnoscan records to fix that first, since that was the biggest headache, and while I was under they used the time to do some of the corrective dental work needed. Beth wasn't erased, exactly, but she became a memory, not a personality, like somebody you once knew real good and close. I liked it that way. I wanted to remember Beth, and all the Beths in all them worlds out there. Anytime in the future when I was feelin' sorry for myself or wallowing in self-pity I'd just think of Beth and the others and know just what blessin's I had.

I couldn't talk at all after the dental and facial stuff, but by then several English speakers were around for my benefit. That hypnoscan could be damned useful as well as dangerous.

They told me that Markham had simply passed out and was sent to bed with a sedative to sleep it off, but then they took me down to see Sam. He was in a special wing just for head injuries, the most common and still the hardest things to deal with.

They understood a hell of a lot more about the brain than we did. I think they knew just how it worked and could do tricks with it, but head injuries were no less tragic here for all that. They could even grow new brain tissue, something the body has problems with, but they couldn't replace what you lost, only give a replacement place for something else to be written. Sam might have lots of problems, even memory problems, when he woke up—*if* he woke up.

He wasn't much to see. They had him floatin' in a tank covered in some kinda liquid that sure wasn't water, his head down to his big nose encased in a special kind of bandage, all sorts of tubes leadin' to and from his body to big machines. I was afraid he'd drown, but they assured me that he was gettin' all they could give. Even they didn't know if it'd be enough, though.

In that chamber I couldn't even kiss him or talk to him or hold his hand. It was tough.

He had plenty of brain activity, so he wasn't brain dead, but they didn't know much more. He might be out for days, for weeks, for months, even forever. There was no way of tellin' now 'cept to monitor and wait.

Within a day I could talk again, and I got to admit that from that point on I never again was the least bit self-conscious or embarrassed about how I talked. Anybody didn't like it, piss on them. In fact, that whole experience really changed me for the better in a lot of ways. I was a lot more humble now 'bout my own strong will. Damn, just *bein'* in that damned world started breakin' me. The technicians at the Center—that's what they called the medical place, just the Center—told me that, yeah, it was true, if they'd started torturin' me or used hypnoscans or drugs on me while I was in control I'd revert to Beth, but just the fact that Vogel knew that kept him from doin' it. He loved breakin' people. That was his hobby and his fun. No fun in trippin' somebody over when you don't figure she really knows what you want to know anyhow.

But he was lyin' through his teeth 'bout me turnin' into Beth slow and on my own. Fact was, the Beth personality was there, but it was real weak compared to mine. *He* planted that seed, and I swallowed it, and just 'cause I swallowed it Beth was able to get control. Vogel was right when he said anybody can be broken, but in the end *you're* the one that breaks you. He didn't really want Beth; he wanted an obedient slave girl who had all my knowledge and talents and abilities. And just 'cause his kind was the bosses on that Nazi world didn't mean we didn't have 'em just like him on our world, or most any world.

I was stronger, too, because of that mission. More self-confident, I think, but also knowin' my limits. I was ready now to not worry what anybody else thought about me and just be me and cope with whatever came along.

I didn't have them put me back all the way, I admit. I never was able to grow or keep straight hair before, and with my own more rounded face I kinda liked the look. They told me it would keep growin' straight so long as I only cut it at the ends. If I ever shaved my head it'd come back the old way. I also kept that creamy complexion. Folks spend millions tryin' to get a nice, even, perfect complexion like that.

My body was toughened by those days I spent with no clothes in all weather. I found it damned hard just to wear shoes and so went barefoot most of the time. The golden people's saris felt okay, but I knew I was gonna haveta ease back into more normal clothes.

Fact was, I was ready to go out and enjoy life and conquer the damned world, and I didn't care if I was starvin' and shunned so long as I was free, but it just didn't mean a damned thing without Sam.

The trouble was, I couldn't imagine life without Sam, and at the same time I was already easin' into just that. All that stuff I spouted to him about risks and gettin' hit by a truck—I didn't really believe that. Besides, we was talkin'

about if somethin' happened to me. I just never even
imagined that anything would take Sam from me 'cept'n my
own death.

After a few days, I met Bill Markham and Aldrath Prang
for a debriefin' and brain session.

"You set us up," I told them. "One of you, anyways, with
that damned dinner meet. Whichever one it was was
handed the time, place, and all the rest on a platter—and
you *still* didn't catch him!"

"It was one of Mayar Eldrith's schemes," Aldrath told
me. "He is a senior vice president and chairman of the
Security Committee. In other words, he is my boss. I was
powerless to prevent it, although I recommended strongly
against it."

"Yeah," I said, "and what's he say now that he's lost
Vogel and maybe killed Sam and the others?"

"The usual," the security chief replied with a shrug. "He
is blaming it on me and on security in general."

Bill grunted. "He *is* on our list, isn't he?"

"Near the top," Aldrath admitted. "But he is also near
the top in both social, class, and corporate power. You see
the problem. These are all high-ranking, extremely powerful men."

"Who would know enough 'bout security's ways and all
that would be needed to have set up this thing?" I asked
them. "I mean, not all of 'em could pull this off, could
they?"

"Any of them might," Aldrath replied, "although some
are more likely than others. Certainly the vice president
could do it effectively without even touching it himself, and
Mukasa Lamdukur is in charge of day-to-day operations."

"The one with the airhead mistress."

He nodded. "Alas, so. And Basuti Alimati, who is something of a fanatical personality but whose office handles
much of the routine business communications between our
many divisions. I cannot rule out the other two, since
Dringa heads Research and Development and Hanrin holds
the security purse strings, but neither of those two have as
much day-to-day interaction with operations. They would
need a good number of support and managerial personnel
to do the actual work. Neither is particularly technically
oriented."

Even Bill was surprised. "You mean the head of R & D isn't technically oriented?"

"He authorizes a lot of things depending on what his advisors, both technical and political, recommend, but he understands little. He is a typical executive. What can I say? Basuti and Mukasa, on the other hand, are both inquisitive and highly intelligent and make a point of learning as much as possible about their responsibilities. Mayar understands almost nothing, being a politician, but if he wished he could through his vast power and position arrange practically anything."

None of that helped much. We still had five big, fat suspects, no real motive, no real clear knowledge of the plot, and while two was most likely suspects and one was in the best position to do just about anything, the fact was the least likely suspects couldn't be ruled out. Back to square one.

"Listen, like I told your men, I didn't get much out of Vogel, but whatever else that bastard was I don't think he was no traitor. He was real surprised and real upset when he learned that it was the Company after his hide, and the reason he didn't face us was 'cause whoever he got his orders from was high enough up that it woulda been his neck in a noose. He was had, though, by this dude. I think he got routine orders from somebody to set this thing up and he didn't think it was crazy 'cause he had the perfect setup to experiment on people, and he didn't ask no questions not only 'cause it was from so high up but also 'cause he was gettin' payoffs for it, like that hypnoscan in the basement. Imagine a paranoid like him with a hypnoscan!"

"Agreed. He knew and we blew it," Bill said. "I mean, our computer simulations actually said that an attempt within the Labyrinth was a likely thing, but that was if the whole plan went down pretty much as it was. When he escaped with you and then lost us for over a day and a half, all our resources went into locating and then tracking you. I was constantly shifting people inside the Labyrinth from one track to another to cover all the possibilities. The fact was, the other dangers just weren't important if we didn't have Vogel alive in the first place. When we got him, we were just so damned happy and smug we forgot to put

everything else in place before moving him. It really was
our fault, and I don't know any way around that."

"All right, I'll buy that," I told them. Hell, if they wanted
the guilt trip, let 'em have it. Their lapse was understand-
able but, damn it, it *was* their fault. I had my own problems
to worry about—I couldn't do their job, too. "The thing is,
what happens now?"

The question seemed to catch both of 'em off guard.
"What do you mean?" Aldrath asked.

"You got a skunk, a traitor, high up. Somebody who
makes even Vogel look human. That skunk's gone to a
whole lotta trouble to set somethin' up that is definitely
aimed at the Company, maybe at its heart, and it comes
right out of the Security Committee."

"But we lost Vogel!" Bill protested.

"Yeah, so you lost Vogel—*but so did he!*"

That seemed to hit the both of 'em like some new
concussion grenade. I guess in a way they was just like
Vogel—you get so much power, you get so arrogant and
self-confident, you can't see your damned nose in front of
your face.

"Go on," said Aldrath Prang.

"Look, how long you figure this has been goin' on? This
drug thing, I mean?"

"Two, maybe three years so far. Why?"

"What's two or three years to a guy fifty to seventy who
expects to live another hundred to hundred and fifty years?
That's why he's takin' the time to experiment and movin'
so slow and cautious. But we just blew a lot of that research
down the drain. We don't have it, but neither does our big
boy, and he ain't gonna get no more from Vogel or his
world. They wasn't done—that's clear. How long was it
supposed to go on? Another year? Five? Or maybe until
they found out what they wanted to know no matter what.
Well, they ain't found it yet 'cause they was still doin'
research and experiments. We don't know what they're
lookin' for and why, but it's pretty damned clear that if they
don't find it then there's no plot, no threat, no scheme.
They just lost their main man and the technicians who done
most of the work, but they still need the work and now the
heat's on real hard. Now, he's got two choices. Either open

up somewheres else and start from scratch, or step up in a place he's already at. You tell me which one's less risky and less trouble."

Bill thought a moment. "Aldrath, who knows about that second world except us and your immediate staff? Was it in your report to the committee?"

"No. Since we were doing only surveillance activities there, I thought it prudent not to mention it or we might drive the operation totally underground. They do not even know we intercepted the courier. They were told that we discovered it by accident during routine checks of Vogel's station." He paused a moment. "Sometimes you find it best and prudent to tell your superiors only what they need to know. We needed a plan for Vogel, lots of manpower and appropriations, all the rest. We had to take a station, have an attacking force, plus all the monitoring both in that world and within the Labyrinth. The committee had to be told."

"And I'd say that would be used, since it already is set up," Bill added. "To try the same thing that they did with Vogel with a new stationmaster would be too risky for words now that we know how he did it, and it would take a long time. I think you're right. I think they'll step it up where they already are and go with what they have. If it goes bad, then they can always start new."

Somethin' just sorta snapped inside me. Maybe it was my brains, but it all come together. "Look," I told them, "I want this bastard. I want him bad. You know the odds on Sam. They grow longer every day, every week. I tell you, if he goes, there ain't much I got to live for and that's the truth. All I got is a burnin' hatred and will to get this man and nail his hide to Sam's tank."

Bill looked at me and shook his head. "You've done your bit, Brandy. More than done it. You have millions, you're still young and attractive, you still have quite a life ahead no matter what happens to Sam. You're in shock now, and grief, too, and I can't say you're going to ever forget that, but you'll learn to live with it just like others have. Besides, what if Sam comes out of it and you're back in the fire again?"

I didn't really believe that, any of it. I accepted that

much. I had no family, no friends, and all I could look forward to was the best friends money could buy. I wasn't real unhappy in that broke-down office in Camden with the roaches and shit once Sam was there. Half of me was down in that damned tank or in splatter on the Labyrinth floor. I didn't *want* to learn to live with it.

"I want this bastard no matter what the cost, and I think Sam would, too."

Bill sighed, and I could almost see his brain workin'. Half of him was wracked with guilt and embarrassment over blowin' this at the end, and the other half was real tempted. He really wanted me to do it; he just didn't want me on his conscience right next to Sam.

"Look," he said carefully, "this isn't the same thing. We don't have a Vogel to snatch here. We don't even have a station or operation on that world, just some agents, a communications link, and some weak points. They only have access to it because the Pennsylvania weak point is between two heavily traveled worlds and the Labyrinth comes on for brief periods spontaneously there, and we can't build a substation without getting the authority and approval of the committee. There's no spy satellites, no big team with all sorts of connections, nothing. There's no backup."

"If I can be watched and get word out, then that's the only backup I'll need. If I get in too deep, even the damned United States Marines ain't gonna be no help to me."

"It's a string of hookers and the mob, you know," Bill reminded me. "To get close there, you run a real risk of getting hooked on this stuff yourself, even without meaning to. You're over the age they like, but if they find out who you are or suspect you're working for us, they'll do it."

When you been broke as a naked slave in chains, bein' hooked don't seem so damned horrible no more. "I know the risks. But if I nail this bastard, it'll be worth it."

"Yeah, but what if you do and then Sam comes around? So we break 'em, but you're hooked for good or die from a supply cutoff. No, I can't allow it."

"You told me they could break the addiction. Here, probably."

"We have had some success, yes," Aldrath admitted, "but

it is very unpleasant and very ugly and quite often results in irreversible brain damage. Come, let us go over and we'll let you see just what we are facing and what you are truly talking about."

We went to one of the separate buildings, away from the main center. This was a security building, with all sorts of controls on gettin' in and gettin' out, but with Aldrath Prang along there weren't too many doors you couldn't get through.

In some ways it was hard to think of the Center as a hospital, since even though you had patients and some regular kind of rooms none of the treatment rooms or labs looked anything like treatment rooms or labs. We went into this room that looked more like some computer room or library. There was a bunch of screens, chairs, and both microphones and keyboards all around, 'cept them keyboards had about a hundred keys and the symbols on them made Arabic or Chinese look real familiar. Aldrath sat down at one and typed a few things and the screen came on. It looked like one of them medical shows where they blow up the blood or cells to giant size.

"There is the enemy," he told us. It all looked like icky brown slime to me with lots of little things floatin' in it. "I'll blow it up and you can see it face-to-face."

The thing zoomed in, and suddenly there was a real pretty pattern of multicolored see-through shapes. They looked kinda like them Christmas stars with all the points comin' out like sunbursts, but somehow they all fit together. Inside, they seemed to be made up of millions of little strings, like jellied shredded wheat.

"I never seen nothin' like that," I told him.

"Neither had we," he replied. "Separately, they aren't much, and the amount of magnification needed to get them this large and this clear is enormous. They're not quite as big as a common virus, but much more complex. The raw stuff has a different pattern than you see here—really colorless, with fewer spikes and more tightly packed granules. When it invades a host, it makes the entire trip through the bloodstream in a minute or so and finally settles in the brain, but it takes a grand tour first. When it settles in, it changes, and it's never the same twice in any two individuals. It adapts to what it finds in incredible ways. At the start, it seizes control of vital chemical areas of the brain, turns off the body's defenses but only to it, then reproduces and grows to a certain size that the body can support without harming it, then stops. As a body manager, it's actually quite good and unique to each individual."

"You mean—it thinks?"

"No, we're pretty sure it doesn't, not in any sense we think of it. It can live only in a host, and its sole imperative seems to be survival of itself and its host. It cleans house, and much more efficiently gets rid of invading bacteria, viruses, you name it. Cancerous and precancerous conditions are identified, attacked, and dissolved. Arteries are unblocked. Body chemistry works at maximum efficiency. Hosts are actually healthier and in better condition than any human we find naturally."

"You make it sound almost like somethin' worth havin'."

"We think that in the world where it evolved, it *is* something worth having. The only way you can catch it is by sexual transmission. I could take a vialful of the stuff and inject it directly into you and you couldn't get it, since it would be individually adapted to its host. To reproduce, it actually builds a cluster of virgin and unadapted units encased in a gelatinlike shell with a mind of its own and some real power. It not only goes in with sperm, it can appear in females as well and actually invade upstream, as it were, through the penis of the male. The world where it comes from has no addiction problem, since they live with it naturally the same as we live with a host of beneficial bacteria, and, as I said, it pays its own freight by making a more efficient body. We know that host is a Type One because it's close enough to us that this thing can adapt, recognize, and use our body so well, but it's not a hundred percent."

I nodded. "Bill told us. It can't keep livin' in our bodies, right?"

"Right. First of all, there seems to be something, some element, that it needs that our bodies lack. It forms its reproductive units, but they don't work. They fall apart and are gobbled by the would-be host's immune system. Therefore, it can't reproduce—but it doesn't know that and keeps trying anyway. Second, this element, which defies isolation, is present in the clusters we see, but since no more can be made in our bodies it starts to break down and be expelled or changed, perhaps by the chemicals of our own bodies, into harmless material. We suspect the latter, since that would explain why we can't find it. Within thirty-six hours the thing starts to die, and starts killing the host in the process. Only a fresh infusion of virgin material will restore it. Hence, we have a dangerous and deadly addiction."

He turned back to us. "You see, we can't even take material from another host and inject it, since it changes to be specific only to that host and it's using every bit of it for its own use anyway. The virgin cells won't grow on their own—they need a host—and so we can't make our own supply. Since the carrier in the drug modules appears to be semen, we've made a genetic analysis of the host and we're trying to find the world it comes from. The problem is, we've not yet found an exact match and there are hundreds of thousands of worlds in this genetic category. We'll find it, eventually, but it takes lots of time. I mean, you just can't walk in to every world, walk up to the nearest male, and demand a semen sample for lab analysis."

Yeah, I could see that. Pardon me, sir, but we in our protective suits to keep from catchin' nasty diseases want you to lie down and jerk off into this here tube for us . . .

"But Bill said you could cure it."

Aldrath sighed. "Sort of. The trick is to get a host when the thing is in full control, not breaking down. Then the subject is somewhat frozen and suspended, life support slowed, and the entire organism is then attacked at one time throughout the body. It *is* a foreign organism; our scanners can isolate it and attack it with equal strength all through the body. That kills it, and keeps it from killing the host, but it doesn't replace the body chemicals the thing was managing. We then have to keep the host in suspension for many weeks while we stimulate the right areas of the brain and get it used to doing things the old way again. Then the *body* is okay, but the mind is something else. Most of them resist cures to the last moment. When we cure them, they feel terrible physically and they would go back on the stuff in a moment no matter what the price, even months later—which is all we've had to study this. It requires the hypnoscan and psychiatric techniques to remove that craving. The hypnoscan is a wonderful invention, but it cures nothing. It can only add and subtract and distort."

"I see."

"Only slightly. All of our subjects came from projects run by Vogel, outside of his compound, and snatched in convincing ways so neither he nor his people knew we were involved. We've found none without some evidence of brain damage, although we suspect this was the result of experiments or somebody not getting their injection in time. The long-term users also retain their habit patterns. Their inhibitions remain suppressed, their selfishness remains high, their sexual drives become insatiable in an attempt to recapture that ultimate high. No one has yet completed therapy sufficiently to be restored to total normalcy. Come on. I'll show you just what we're up against."

We went down to a lower section of the building that began to look more like a luxury jail than a hospital. I seen good-lookin' young guys and pretty young girls sittin' there in rooms in near constant masturbation. The weird thing was, you could talk to 'em and they'd talk back, but they never stopped. Others seemed to act normal, but had problems talkin' or writin' or rememberin' what they just said, and others with jerky muscle movements like the palsy. The best ones seemed tired, run-down, not ambitious or much interested in doin' things.

"We could wipe out much of their memories—get rid of the longing for the high—but to do that we'd have to rebuild their personalities," Aldrath told us. "Our only real hope is to find the world where this stuff comes from. If we had just one individual from that world and could compare him or her to one of us with it, we could find the critical chemical difference. Then we could synthesize it, stabilize the organism, and find a way to tame this beast. Cure the addiction, block the reproduction, and those who have it would be able to live normal, productive lives in the best of health and get its advantages without its terrible drawbacks."

I nodded and we walked back out into the sunshine and fresh air. I was shaken by what I saw, but also angry. I didn't want no *thing* livin' inside me, but them people and a lot more was goin' through hell because they didn't have the thing's parents' address. Somebody did, but they didn't want us to know it.

"That's the bottom line, Brandy," Bill told me. "I don't want you in there, like that. I couldn't handle that on my conscience."

"But volunteers ain't standin' in line to infiltrate this mess."

"To say the least. It's a real trap, since anybody we send in who gets addicted becomes controlled by them and for their own self-preservation goes over to the other side. We can't snatch and interrogate the underworld figures involved, since they really don't seem to have any knowledge beyond ours worth blowing the only other lead we have. We've considered a switch of some of theirs for some of ours—the big boys, I mean—but it seems the reason these people were chosen is that there are no good candidates who would work for us against them inside that organization. The only possibles are counterparts who are the same people inside and out and already bosses themselves—not likely to want to work for us—or the kind of people who would take the job but wind up enticed by the power of this thing and be just as bad as the ones they replaced."

"We still don't know where it comes from or how it gets into our courier network," Aldrath added. "The actual couriers who deliver it get messages to pick it up at different points every time, and only after it's already dropped. There's been no pattern in those drop points that we can find, and no single individual or group can be linked to most of the drops."

I nodded sadly. It shook me bad to see that and know just what sufferin' was goin' on. The worst part was that nobody did all this just to trap hookers or hook the kind of folks we seen in that hospital wing. What did they plan to do? What was they lookin' for? An immunity agent, so they couldn't get hooked? Probably, but that wasn't all of it, since you'd need one hell of a population of the world these come from jerkin' off all the time to supply any huge amounts of the stuff. A way to make it work just as good without shots in us as it did in the people it came from? That didn't make no sense, neither, since that would mean no addiction and no control. It didn't make no sense. I did have a thought, though.

"What if they got it in here, to this world?" I asked them. "You could just keep a few big men on a string and rule it all."

"We thought of that, of course," Aldrath replied. "Our first thought, really. But controls are very strict. We do not allow it in, and our equipment is set to it. No virgin material was ever here—that work was done elsewhere. Even if it was surgically embedded in your body, we'd pick it up, since it's an alien compound with a unique structure. Anything that would shield it from our instruments would show up the shielding. The computer scanners can't be altered by anyone without exactly what was done being public. Not even the President or Chairman of the Board could smuggle that stuff in."

"Yeah, but what if they snuck in one of the folks from the world that has these natural?"

"First of all, he'd be pretty obvious since he'd have to have sex to spread it and I'm afraid our people are— clannish. They wouldn't do it here, on this world, other than with their own kind, and rape would be pretty quickly reported, particularly by a Type One individual. They might hook a few people before they were caught, but they wouldn't get close to the classes with the power by then and, once caught, we could find the home world this thing comes from from the one who came in. Besides, one of the things we do when you enter is read your genetic code. We *know* their basic genetic code, and we're even attempting to clone some cells to see what they really look like and give us more of a limited range to hunt for them, but so far without success. Clones in any case don't come out as full-blown adults; it takes the same time as with natural development. So far we've had no real luck, and the code only gives us that vast range of worlds I talked about. Unfortunately, it's a pretty common species type, almost as common as our own. To further minimize the risk, no one from that family of genetic relatives is permitted in here at all. And nobody from here, once they take a post in the Corporation, leaves."

It did seem like they thought of everything this time.

Sure, you might hook a young one out explorin', but he'd never come back 'cause he couldn't get his supply of the stuff while he waited around for twenty or thirty years to get an important job, if then. This was a puzzler, all right. If not hookin' the Board, then what? Or, rather, who?

"What about transport and switchmen?" I suggested. "Control them and it don't matter what happens here."

"We know what it looks like so we can test for it," Aldrath said. "We test everyone four to six times a year for a variety of things, and anytime we suspect or see anything unusual or have someone in a critical area. They didn't even hook their couriers for that reason. You might hook some stationmasters, but what does that get you in the end?"

Bill thought for a moment, then said, "It could get forbidden stuff in and out of places. Ever think of that?"

"Of course. But Vogel got his hypnoscan without it, and there's not much beyond this organism that's so dangerous and so valuable to make it worth the risk. Besides, if that was all, why test it? Why hook fifty young, pretty girls and make them sell sex for hire? Other substances do as well for that. Why only women down there? Vogel's people experimented on men and women equally, with equal results. We have lots of pieces, but whenever you build a frame they don't go together."

I couldn't help thinkin' how Sam woulda loved this—*did* love this. Even though he was against my goin' undercover, he still had real joy at the puzzle itself and a real yen to solve it. So did I. Havin' seen the price, though, I just couldn't quite talk myself into it. The price of solvin' this one was a one-way ticket to hell.

After six weeks, I went back home. Sam was still in the tank and there was no change, and I was beginnin' to get used to the idea that there might never be. There was sure no reason to hang around; headquarters world was friendlier and more comfortable than Vogel's for me, but I was still an outsider in more ways than one.

Goin' home, though, proved only a temporary relief. The agency was pretty well a dead duck; Sam had handed off his cases to other PIs before we left and there wasn't much to pick up on, and I just didn't feel much like tryin' for new business. I might no longer care what that class of people thought of me, but that didn't mean they was gonna keep comin' in with new jobs. Sure, I could have picked up some work just from the Company—but it woulda been charity work, just Bill and the rest tryin' to give me somethin' to do.

Not that I had to do much. At first them bastards tried to get away with payin' just half the money, since they didn't have Vogel alive, but I shamed 'em into the full amount. I didn't need it; just the two and a half million was more than I ever expected to see in my life. It was just the principle of the thing, damn it.

I took a quarter of a million out and put it in liquid funds so I had cash and let Whitlock at Tri-State Savings keep and invest the rest. Then I got out all the bills we owed, big and small, and paid them all off. It was kinda rough lookin' at the check register and seein' Sam's handwritin' on most of the stubs.

In fact, Sam haunted everything. I kept wakin' up in that apartment expectin' to find him next to me, or maybe in the livin' room or kitchen. The phone would ring with somethin' or other and I'd instantly think it was Sam callin' from Pittsburgh or some other place and have it picked up before I realized that it couldn't be him.

There wasn't no sense in keepin' the office, so I closed it down and sublet it to the end of the lease. I didn't want to stay in town no more, neither. Seems like once you got money word gets around fast, and every fast-buck artist and get-rich-quick schemer and con artist finds you real fast. I had to get out of town, go off by myself awhile, but I couldn't think of anyplace I wanted to move to lock, stock, and barrel. I went up to New York for a while, rented a shabby little studio apartment just off Greenwich Village, under the name Beth Parker. I know, I know, but I was feelin' more'n a little like poor Beth right then, kinda lost without nobody around. I picked New York 'cause I was always a city girl at heart, and I didn't really know nobody up there and nobody knew me. The Company arranged for driver's license, credit cards, and a local bank account in that name. With the straight hair and smooth complexion even some of my relatives wouldn't't'a knowed me anyways.

I was rich, but I didn't *feel* rich, and I didn't want nobody to know that I was. Sam had married me when I was a ghetto girl in cockroach heaven. I took very little with me, and bought what I needed from second-hand stores in Manhattan. When I was bored and lonely and depressed I ate a lot, and since that was the case most of the time I satisfied my every whim. Started smokin' cigarettes again, too, and quickly got up past two packs a day. Every kind of drug you can think of and a lot you never heard of were easy in the Village, and I tried some of the ones I knew about. They helped for a while, but I knew I was only runnin' from myself.

I at least started one thing I always meant to do and never had. There was a congregation of black Jews in New York and I went up there and started takin' classes in instruction. They was a little surprised—the Jewish faith takes converts, but doesn't go after 'em, and you really have to work to join that religion—but I found it real interestin' and a real relief from the Bible thumpers of my childhood. Sam wasn't exactly the world's most religious Jew, but deep down it wasn't just cultural. Deep down he really believed it, and that was more than I could say about myself, so it seemed to make sense. Actually, tellin' the rabbi about Sam—and his condition—without, of course, revealin' the hows and wheres, hurt me a little 'cause he got real skeptical. "If Sam were a Catholic, I think you'd be entering a nunnery now," he said. It took some time to convince him that I really meant it.

New York's not the best place to be alone, though, particularly if you're a woman. Go into a bar and either ten guys would try and put the make on you—and five women, too, if you stayed in the Village—or you'd be wallflowered out. Same with discos and other dance places, and it didn't feel right goin' to the theater alone. About the only place was the movies, and I went to see a bunch of 'em. And, yeah, I did allow myself to get picked up a few times and I even went to bed with a couple of one-night stands. I needed it. I thought—hoped—Sam would understand. They was like the drugs, though. They helped, but only for a little while.

I called Bill's office in Philadelphia often about Sam, but

it was always the same news. No change. Finally, one night, I was standin' there naked lookin' at myself in a mirror and thinkin' how fast and easy the fat goes on and how hard it is to get off. I finally had it out with myself in that mirror, too.

Okay, girl, now what? You keep on like this, you'll slit your wrists in a year or wind up in a permanent heroin haze. You got so much money you could light your cigarettes with it. You can go anywhere you want, do anything you want, and what good is it doin' you? You don't want to go nowheres or do nothin'. You can go out and buy some business and run it, but you don't know no business but investigations and you done all you could in that. You could just screw around, until you got to be a fifty-year-old three-hundred-pound diabetic who had to buy it. If this was reversed the way you thought it could be, you knew Sam could handle it, but you can't. Find some nice guy and shack up with him? You already played with that, and you know that wouldn't be fair to him or you. It'd be a lie, a let's pretend.

Yeah, that was part of it, too. *You don't know no business but investigations . . .*

Anyone who gets close enough to learn anything will probably get hooked . . .

That other world is the only thing they got left . . .

There's no possible cure for these people unless we find the origin world . . .

"*Sam? Do you think it's possible to do it? Do you think I can do it?*"

My conversion would have to wait. God knew how I felt, anyways. The next day I took the train back down to Philadelphia and arranged with the Company to visit Sam at the Center.

Aldrath Prang met me personally when I arrived, which surprised me. "News?" I asked him.

"Some. Not about your husband, although there are some recent encouraging signs of increased brain activity. I thought you had a right to be informed of the progress, or lack of it, we're making."

"I'm very interested."

"You were quite right about the shift of activity. Larger quantities are going to the other target world, and they seem to be preparing to set up some facilities in a South American country where absolute privacy and absolute license can be bought and paid for. They're still limited to the one Pennsylvania access, but they seem to have recently completed a minor substation. It's no more elaborate than Vogel's or Cranston's and far less versatile, but it gives them some freedom."

"Yeah? That costs money and lots of expert manpower, don't it?"

"It does, but they seem to be willing to pay any price—and able to do so—and most of a substation could be built, in unrelated modules far apart, within your own country right now, requiring only some small but vital sections to be added from other worlds. It's not difficult to do, unfortunately. The competition, as you know, has a number of safe worlds with just such substations. One could easily be dismantled and reestablished component by component. They did basically that in setting up the ambush in the Labyrinth. Which reminds me—how is your wound?"

"Gone," I told him, and that was the literal truth. I never seen nothin' like it. When it was ready to go, that bandage, which withstood showers and rain and all the rest, just fell off and there was nothin' there. No scars, no marks of any kind, no skin discoloration. It was a hell of a gash, yet you couldn't even tell now that anything had ever happened there. "But gettin' back to the other—what about the bad guys? I mean, there's got to be a couple who really know what's goin' on now, both local and from off-world. They need a Vogel type for this."

"There is, alas, no shortage of Vogel types. A number of locals may be being raised up and prepped—there is also no end to the scientific amoralist who would jump at the chance of a project like this, although the same problem exists as existed with Vogel's researchers. They are experimenting along given lines with a license to freelance off on their own, but none are actually told what they are looking for. The only off-world presences are a man who is overseeing the South American operation and a woman who is handling things up north. The man is called Dr. Carlos, the woman is known only as Addison, both cover names, naturally. So far we have been unable to get photographs, let alone more intimate data, on the pair, except that Carlos is dark, looks like an Indian—that's the description, I can only offer it—and speaks with an odd accent, and this Addison is young, not terribly attractive, and has very short hair, wears glasses, and is described as a cold fish who likes men's clothing. We suspect that they were part of Vogel's team on his world and were not present at the compound when it blew and therefore used other exits."

"Better than nothin', but not much. And you can't catch 'em at the substation?"

"We have it covered all the time, but no. Only the couriers. Remember, though, they did have access to a stationmaster who could both legitimately and illegitimately request sufficient spare parts for almost anything, and we didn't know about the one Vogel tried to use."

That stopped me. "You mean it's possible there's another someplace there? One you don't know about?"

"It's possible. There are a thousand weak points of one degree or another across any world from the Arctic to Antarctica. We have very few people who even know of this world and we are limited that way. Sensing, let alone tracing, a power drain and tracking it to its source is bad enough with full resources."

"Uh huh. Like tracin' a phone call." I *did* see, too. With all them points, so long as they turned the power on, used it, and shut down real fast, that small a drain might not even be noticed and definitely not traceable. The bet was it wasn't noplace geographically convenient, though. If it was, they wouldn't be riskin' improvin' the Pennsylvania substation unless that was some kind of diversion—and if it was, then they knew we was on to 'em so why set up all this new stuff? No, bet on the other station bein' in the middle of nowhere, like the Andes or the Congo or maybe Fiji. Useful, but not convenient. And to get enough bread and people to do anything major, they have to tip off the man behind it. It was real tricky.

"Any progress on your science detective work?"

He shook his head. "We're as far as we can go without new people to try new things on, and we don't dare pull any from this other world or they will pack and run. We have well-placed operatives there, but they can't get too close and at the minimum safe distance it's too far to learn much more than this."

"The Security Committee's still in the dark about all this?"

"Yes, but not for much longer. We can't go on static like this or we just watch them do their job in ignorance. Sooner or later we will have to vastly expand, increase our monitoring, and perhaps go in with all we have. That takes money and people and technical support and that means the committee. It might drive them underground, or we might get lucky. At least it will set them back, and if we're fortunate enough to nab an Addison or Carlos we might well win."

"Not without somebody inside, you won't. See, *they* got somebody inside—right here. Without somebody to tell, gettin' a Carlos or Addison would be sheer luck."

I asked him two favors. One was to visit the ex-addicts again, the other to see Sam—alone.

"No problem, but there are few patients left now. We had several suicides, and a few whom we were able to treat with hypnotherapy and find places for. The few left are those for whom, for one reason or another, we have found no place, but who can be monitored against doing away with themselves."

The patient I decided to talk to was named Donna, and she was at one time a secretary in the Atlanta of Vogel's world. She had fallen in love with a young Party man with ambition, fed him some information on her bosses that would help his advancement, and then got caught doing it. She had been tried by a Party court and sentenced to "useful imprisonment," which meant being sent to the Montrose Hospital and Asylum near Houston, site of many medical and psychological experiments on humans and one in which Vogel's people had a part.

It was unnerving to talk to her. She had stuck in my mind from before because she was one of the ones who had stayed naked in her room always feeling herself up. She still was. She was also a little unnerved by me; I don't think she'd ever seen a black woman clothed and with more than one thought in her head before and she couldn't quite believe it.

"Every day they'd take me in a little room and give me a

jolt of juice," she told me. "It didn't take right away. You
get that rush—" She shivered and closed her eyes, remem-
bering it, and it took a minute or so for her to pick it up
again. "—then you get a little sick and that's it. After a week
or so, though, it took."

"What's it like?"

"You ever had an orgasm? Well, it's like that, only all over
your body and a thousand times more intense. Like nothing
else. You come out of it, but you don't feel down, you feel
good, but you want that rush again. You live for it. It's what
keeps you going—the thought that every day you'll get it
again, always as good. The rest of the day—well, it's kinda
funny. You're all right—I mean, you feel great, the best you
ever felt—but you get these urges. Compulsions, really. You
never know when they'll come on. You slowly get real
turned on, I mean real up, and then you can't think of
anything but sex, and you got to have it, and you stay up at
real high tension until you do. Another time, you just got to
exercise. You only feel good doing it. You get hungry
sometimes for crazy things, like you're pregnant or something, but other stuff, things you've always loved, taste
horrible. It's like you're not really in control of yourself, but
yet you're still you. You lose all modesty, all integrity, all
the brakes. Inhibitions, that's the word. Brakes get put on,
but not by you. Almost in spite of you. I can't explain it. It's
like you lose all sense of what's right and wrong, but
something else decides—and it might not decide the way
you would have."

"It sounds like you become some kinda robot or something."

"Uh uh. It's not like that at all. You're still you, and
there's lots of time in the day when you are. You know
what's happened, but you don't really care. You're basically
free—they never even bothered to watch over me most of
the time and I was never locked in—but you won't go.
There's no way you're going to miss your next juice shot.
That's the control. If the one person in the world who can
give it to you asked you to stand on your head or shoot
somebody, you might feel bad about it but you wouldn't
hesitate to do it. If you had an unlimited supply of the juice
you'd tell 'em to stuff it, but if it's obey orders or no juice,
you'll strangle your own mother."

"You sound bright, intelligent, and you're not hooked anymore. Why do you stay here—like that?"

"It's what I mean that I can't really describe," she told me. "The juice needs its own juice. It changes you. First time they tell you to do something horrible or disgusting and you won't, so they don't give you the juice and you go to hell real fast. One thing they wanted to know was whether they could cause the stuff to change the body and brain if one particular thing was demanded to get your jolt and they kept it from you for a while. They ordered me to go, every evening, down to the military and staff wings, stark naked, and proposition every man and woman I could find and do whatever they wanted. Every night. I fought it. Some of them were brutal, sadists and the like. They kept me from the juice for a while until I finally had to agree. They did this every night for weeks. Finally, the juice learned. One day, I woke up, and that was all I wanted to do. It told me when to eat and like that, but the rest of the time I only wanted that. I was totally turned on and I stayed turned on. Not in the head—it was physical."

"It made you a raging nymphomaniac?"

"I guess that's the right word. I didn't want clothes, I didn't want anything except I was compelled to go down and do that. I *wanted* to do it. I *had* to do it. I lost any will to fight—anything. I still can't. My voice got higher, my breasts and hips got bigger, everything."

"But that's over now," I said. "It's not there anymore."

"I'd take it again in a minute, if I could," she told me. "Right now they got me on half a dozen drugs. Otherwise I'd be all over you begging for it. They say my brain's permanently locked in that pattern—chemicals and all, and that my hormone level is monstrous. The drugs I'm taking now are blockers, that keep the worst of it from being triggered, but without them I wouldn't even be human. I'd just be a bitch in heat all the time."

"But—can't they do nothin' for you? I mean, physically?"

"Sure. A oophorectomy and brain surgery. They say I'd come out sexless, a nothing. That's bad enough, but they say there'd be side effects because of where the damage and changes are and what they know from having to replace the areas in natural brain damage. At the very least they say I'd have no feelings. No love, no hate, no envy, no greed, no friendship, no loyalty, no compassion, no mercy, no—nothing. I would think, and remember, but I'd be like a machine. I still have feelings. I wouldn't want to be some machine. No hopes, no ambitions, nothing. If that's the way it is, I'd rather stay right here, just like this."

It was hard to think of this pretty, intelligent young woman a neutered machine, and I could see her point—and the Center's. She was still a fund for research and information. They could "cure" her, sorta, but since the cure would be worse than the disease they wouldn't force it.

The interview was sobering in a number of ways. I didn't underestimate what them Nazis who could gas millions and make lampshades outta 'em and sleep like babies and even go to church every Sunday could come up with. The scariest thing was, somebody with a real strong will and sense of identity and purpose could break even heroin, though it sure wasn't easy, or at least live a fairly normal life on methadone. But *this*—no self-cure possible, no methadone-style alternative, and if you got cured you wound up like Donna between a rock and a hard place.

Donna, though, made me mad. She was bright, alert, good-lookin', and she had real potential. Anybody born and raised in a south where Martin Luther King got gassed as a kid if he got born at all and who come from some Nazi background to boot who could learn to talk to me and accept me as an equal human being in that time could adapt to other, better societies. They cheated her—and how many others? They never saved more than two dozen here, all they could sneak out and treat without revealin' their interest. How many more Donnas died in agony when we took Vogel out as supplier? Hundreds? Thousands? How many more was they gonna make in this other place, and maybe other places as well if they went underground again or got whatever they was goin' after with these projects. And for what? So some shithead born to power and gold silverware here could get a little more personal power.

Then, too, Donna got me to thinkin' 'bout Sam, who I was gonna go see now. Different cause, but they both had brain damage, and there was still only so much that could be done. Sam was all wrapped up and still floatin' in that tank, but for the first time I began to wonder not just if he would ever wake up but whether it would be a blessin' if he did. Would he remember me? Be palsied? Be unable to tie his own shoes?

"Sam, I know you can't hear me or understand me, though they say my voice gets through at least," I said outside the window lookin' at his chamber, "but I'm gonna talk anyways, 'cause I never made a big decision or took a big case without talkin' it over with you.

"I can't hack it alone, Sam, not back home. Without you, there's only one thing I'm good at and that's investigations. I know the last one didn't go none too well, but that was them and their experts and their damned computers. There's a lot of innocent, good folks bein' crippled and put through hell out there, Sam. Bein' put through it by a whole bunch of cruds at least as bad as Vogel. I'm gonna take a crack at 'em. All of 'em. I *want* the bastards. I want the ones who did this to you and are doin' worse to others and who'll be in charge of all this if whatever they're plannin' comes off. The damn company's foul enough as it is; I can't sit back when I see firsthand that it might well wind up in the hands of Vogels and Hitlers and all the rest. Maybe I can't lick it. Maybe it's bigger'n I am. Maybe I'm just gonna sell myself into slavery and hell. But I *got* to try, 'cause there ain't nobody else and it needs doin'. If I can't be Nora Charles to your Nick, then there's nothin' for me back home.

"It'll be just my luck if you come outta that damn pool ten minutes after I'm stuck beyond any hope myself, but if you do, then you just play support like always, 'cause the only hope I got is findin' the source world and nailin' them bastards to the wall. You'll cuss and scream and yell, but you'll break it with or without me, 'cause we're the best, Sam. We're a damn sight better than this fancy security and we're better than their crooks." I stopped a moment. I was cryin' too much, and I really wanted him to thrash around in there and scream at me, but nothin' happened and the monitors showed no real change in his condition.

"So, so long, sweetheart. The problems of two crazy people don't amount to a hill of beans in this crazy world."

I walked out and went to find Aldrath Prang.

6.

The Shadow Dancers

"You must understand what you are contemplating. The dangers involved . . ." Aldrath Prang told me gravely.

"I know the risks. Look, I'm not goin' in there to get captured or to get hooked. If I can keep from either one, I swear I plan on doin' just fine without 'em. I'm realistic enough t'know I might and I'm willin' to take that risk just like I was riskin' as much for you three months ago. Besides, don't give me no jive, Aldrath. You been expectin' me to do this for some time and probably got itchy when I took so long."

He looked hurt but you got to be a decent actor in his line of work.

"I assure you I did not. However, I am willing to listen and see if you have any chance."

"Like on the last one, huh? Look, this is strictly me and you. No big operation, no giant backup team. If they don't catch me I won't need backup, and if they do it won't make no difference, now will it? What I'll need from you, aside from a complete briefin' on this world, these people, all you know to now and who you got workin' the case so I don't shoot the wrong fella, access in, free access to the Labyrinth if I got to get out, and some way to monitor me so I can get information out to the right people, meanin' you, without gettin' caught."

"We have a resident agent there now, somebody local but she knows about us, and she uses local talent who don't know about us. She will have to know, and at least arrange signals and means of passing messages—if you can pass them."

"They don't keep these folks locked up, do they? Why bother?"

"Good point. The other question is, *if* they catch you and hook you instead of killing you outright, will you want to pass anything to us? Those who have this thing inside them have an overwhelming urge to self-preservation at all costs."

"Then we got to agree absolute to the opposite," I told him. "We got to agree that if I get hooked and then make no attempt to communicate within, say, a month of my first observed opportunity, you'll come in and snatch me."

"But that might kill you! At the very least—well, you visited and talked with Donna."

I nodded. "That's why. If it takes self-preservation, or preservation of that thing, to keep me motivated, that should do it."

He nodded. "Yes, yes. Very clever and original. All right. But just what do you propose to do?"

"I don't know and that's the God's honest truth. I won't know till I'm briefed and then there on the scene with time to check it all out and learn all the ropes. Uh—will I have any trouble like in Vogel's world?"

"If you mean color, no. At least, not any more than you would have operating in your own. You will be in a rough democracy which has the same sort of failings and virtues as your own, although it's different. But—I can't let you go in alone, with no plan, no backup."

"Sure you can, if you want results. That's part of your problem all along. You're so Mister Future, high tech, computer modeled and the rest you don't have no gut abilities or feelin's. That's why you keep lockin' the barn door after the horse has already gone."

"Such confidence. Anyone can be broken."

"Yeah. Vogel came damned close to doin' it to me, so it don't take a lot to break me, but I was ready the first opportunity I got to wring his damned neck. I ain't never gonna be no Beth again. I might hav'ta act like her, or worse, but I'll never *become* her. I got you all to thank for that much, and Vogel, too. I learned the difference between *havin'* to be a Beth and *wantin'* to be a Beth. That Donna girl down there—for all her problems and for all that she's a shadow of what she coulda been 'cause of this, doesn't *like* it. She's broken, body and soul; she's been raped in the mind as well as the body. Even if she didn't have no permanent brain damage she'd be broken and in shock. But if she could get the ones who did it to her, she would. If she could pass judgment on 'em, she'd demand justice. That's the difference."

"All right." He sighed. "I'll make the preparations. Fewer than six people will know, all under my control except the resident agent and her people, who you'll have to watch out for." He paused a moment. "You know, you're taking me at face value, too. If I were in your position, I, too, would be a suspect."

"You are," I told him honestly, "but I got to trust somebody. It's that thing about *feelin's* again. I can't get it out of my head that you really love what you do, that you wouldn't do nothin' else, and that the only thing that could scare you would be if you had to quit. I can't see how you could be bribed to sell out, and somehow I kinda suspect you got somethin' on everybody who could fire you."

He smiled, but said nothin'.

The next few days I spent goin' over all the materials. I didn't trust no hypnoscan, but I'm a quick study when I'm on a case. I memorized everything I could of this world, the important people, the way the opposition's organization was set up. Aldrath, in the meantime, arranged to transfer some of *my* funds into slush funds in the money of the new world, so I wouldn't even be takin' a dime from the Company on this.

We agreed only on objectives. How much did the players in the game there know? Who knew the most? Did they have any orders on what they was doin', or was all the stuff they did directed from above by the two controllers? Who were Addison and Carlos? Could they be snatched? I didn't expect to hand the whole thing over—that woulda been beyond belief—but if we could get one of them, another Vogel type, we'd have what we needed. Incriminating, absolute evidence against their boss who *would* tell Aldrath what he needed to know about the rest of it. If I could also somehow put together just what it was they was plottin' to do, then we would be able to make sure that nobody else could do it.

I went back home one last time, to close out a few things and register a will. It was funny; just like last time, I was calm, I didn't have nightmares or other scary ideas—I was all business. Not even this late in the game, not this time. I don't think I was committin' suicide in a noble cause, not now. I think it was just that, like Aldrath, I knew and loved my job and I did one thing well and this time *I* was in control.

All that stuff about clearin' up personal things back home was really an excuse to see Bill Markham without nobody suspectin' or knowin' nothin' about it. I had the idea that Bill's remorse over Sam was genuine, and even though he was white and blue-eyed, he was one of my own kind. Since his office was in the same downtown bank buildin' as my account and financial advisors, it wasn't hard to arrange a meet.

I told him what I was gonna do, and he did all the usual things and said all the usual things, and a little bit more. I asked him if he trusted Aldrath Prang.

"Yes and no," he replied. "If you mean, do I think he's got any interest in this except catching these people, no. If he could nail a Company director it would be the highlight of his life. On the other hand, he sees people as game pieces, not human beings. I guess it comes with the territory. If he thought he could get more from exposing or sacrificing you, or me, or all of us, he'd weigh the odds and then do it and feel he was right. Are you sure he didn't plant this idea in your head somehow?"

It was a sobering question. "I don't *think* so, but with all them gadgets who'd ever know for sure? Do *you*? About yourself, I mean? You can get *too* paranoid in this job and then you're as crazy as Vogel. Bill, what the hell would you have me do?"

He sighed. "You see the *Inquirer* this morning?"

"Nope. Why?"

"They had to cordon off four blocks of Philadelphia—right here—because an interracial couple moved into one of those white working class neighborhoods and there was rioting, mob violence, and all the racist talk in the world. We've elected black politicians, even mayors, and we're decades after full legal civil rights and lots of progress, yet this still happens—not far off down south, but right here."

"I know a little bit about that myself," I reminded him.

"I'm real sorry to hear it, but what's that got to do with this?"

"That's the kind of hatred and violence and unreasoning fear and madness that breeds Vogels and Hitlers and all the rest. They're not just out there, on other worlds, or over there, in other countries, or down there in Mississippi or someplace. They're *right here*. Over there, you're going to be on unfamiliar ground, at a distinct disadvantage, on their turf and alone. If you have to fight this type of thing, wouldn't it make more sense to fight it here?"

I thought about that. "Bill, what you say is true and maybe I'm nuts, but I think I'm right on this. Our little Hitlers and Klansmen and the rest do a good bit of damage here, but that kinda thing's part of what we have to live through and fight all the time. This is the Company, damn it! Good old G.O.D., Inc. They didn't pick them initials for nothin'. That's power. Real power. Lord knows they're a pretty unpleasant bunch as it is, but suppose instead of a Board *they* had a Hitler? Never mind this drug shit, I'm talkin' 'bout the Company. I got just a taste of what we folks could do to ourselves with a Hitler a few months back without the Company's power and resources and knowledge. They could impose that on lots of worlds and hold 'em till the end of time. Billions, trillions of human bein's, all of 'em their toys and playthings forever. Uh, uh, Bill."

"Damn it! You're only going to get yourself killed—or worse!"

"If Sam's uncle knew what was comin' back in the thirties and he had a big family but he also had one shot at bumpin' off Hitler, even though he'd get caught and tortured to death, I think he'd'a done it. Instead they sent that family to Auschwitz, where they lived hell for years, and only one distant cousin survived at all and him a broken man. Better to have gotten Hitler."

Bill nodded, but made one last try. "A worst-case scenario. You get in, they catch you and hook you and try to turn you to them. Sam survives, recovers, and in the meantime you find yourself blocked and trapped, learning nothing. Finally we take you out, as we would have to, and rush you to the Center, and you wind up like this Donna, say."

"Then I'd say I'd still be better off than bein' Beth all my life, or walkin' aimlessly around through life watchin' this thing go down bad and always wonderin' if I coulda done something to prevent it. And it wouldn't be nice, but Sam would be no worse off than if Vogel had killed me."

He threw up his hands. "All right, then! It's your funeral! Now, what do you want *me* to do?"

"Be an independent monitor. Use whatever you can to keep some independent track of me—without Aldrath knowin'. And be here in case they double-cross me so somebody gets what I know."

He thought a moment. "I'm pretty limited here, and I'm just a regional security man. Compared to Aldrath, I'm next to powerless. But I'll do all that I can, I promise you that. I'll tell you something nobody is supposed to know that may help. When we went in for Vogel, we also went into his two chief experimental labs in North Carolina and Houston. That's how we got Donna and some of the others you saw still in advanced stages. We also captured more than three hundred doses of the stuff. Some of it went to research, of course, but some didn't get reported. Some of us wanted to make sure that nobody got *us* hooked so we had no way out and no supply to get to the Center fully charged. I have more than a month's supply in a safe-deposit box in this very bank. As far as we know it'll keep almost forever at normal temperatures and conditions. I doubt if I could get a line of communication in there much; you'll be on your own with just Aldrath's few people. But if it really goes bad, and you can manage somehow to get into the Labyrinth and get here, I can keep you going until the Center."

I stared at him. "If it comes to that, you better damned well be here and answer your phone."

It was like our world, and it wasn't nothin' like our world, all at the same time. In *this* world, we lost the Revolutionary War. Washington was hung as a traitor and Benedict Arnold was a great hero. The French Revolution started different, but it still happened and it wound up the same, so they had a real fight with Napoleon anyways. The British claimed and seized most of what we called the Louisiana Purchase by force, not cash. Texas and California revolted and set up their own republics, which Britain recognized and helped defend. California later came into the Empire after the gold rush. That's more history than I knew in school, but that's what they told me happened.

So we had in the end a Dominion of North America, except Texas and some parts of New Mexico and Arizona. Spain hung on to Mexico and most of Spanish Latin America 'cept Brazil and the places the Brits had colonies, but they mostly governed themselves.

Britain wiped our slavery in the whole Empire in the eighteen thirties, but it was the old pattern here, convertin' slaves into sharecroppers. As machines and industry grew up, as we had it, in the north, a lot of black folks went up there lookin' for work and you had the ghettos formin' anyways pretty much as they looked back home. But, in a number of ways, it was worse.

There hadn't been near as many wars, they hadn't yet discovered the bomb or transistors, for that matter, airplanes was still for the rich and was real funny lookin', and radio was there but TV, while invented, wasn't a big commercial thing and wasn't in nobody's homes. The public schools was really private schools, and the ones for the poor folks was lousy. There was still segregation of sorts, too; not no back-of-the-bus stuff, but there was black schools and white schools, black neighborhoods and white neighborhoods, and the blacks, as usual, got the poorest education, lousiest jobs, and most of the unemployment. Not that there wasn't black doctors, dentists, lawyers, and the rest, but they came from black colleges and had black practices. You needed money to vote, and that was where the power was. This was an America without the Votin' Rights Act, the Civil Rights Act, and a lot of the rest.

Each of the commonwealths, which was what they called states, was much bigger—Pennsylvania, which still called itself a commonwealth in my world—went all the way to the Mississippi, for example, and parts of Canada and Michigan were in New York. They ran themselves like little independent countries 'cept for money, trade, and foreign affairs, which was taken care of by a national Parliament with only them powers. The country's capital was Philadelphia, of all places. Washington, D.C., just didn't exist. It was like steppin' back in time to the forties, or maybe the thirties. The cars looked funny and old-fashioned and drove on the left side of the road with the steerin' wheel on the right, and although they had penicillin and a few other things medicine wasn't that great, neither.

The American pound was the currency, divided into twenty shillin's or a hundred pennies. Football was soccer, somebody did invent basketball but there was cricket fields instead of baseball. The national drink was tea, but somehow Coke and Pepsi managed to get invented but beer was the standard. The pound bought about what a dollar buys here, but the average wage was less than a hundred pounds a week. What medical care there was, though, was free, only if you had money you could see somebody real good and real quick. Abortions was illegal and back-alley affairs, and the only birth control they seemed to have was condoms. I had the Center do their version of tyin' my tubes; it was quick, painless, and you couldn't tell, but it relieved my mind a little in a place like this.

I had to come in down in Tennessee; they forced the weak point open just long enough to get me in and close it down again. The other side controlled the only regular substation —and it was theirs, not ours—and that was in Pennsylvania near State College, which wasn't called that or nothin' else, there bein' no Penn State there. There was only a few sleepy little farm towns around there—and the country estate of one George Thomas Wycliffe, a real nice name for a country gentlemen who happened to be the boss of organized crime from New York to the Virginia border. It also happened to completely contain not just the weak point there but also just about all views of the weak point.

I stepped out into the late afternoon of what in my world would be the Tennessee countryside but was now just the Boone District of the Commonwealth of Virginia and the Labyrinth closed behind me. Aldrath worked it so it opened when it did by forcing a spontaneous opening of the thing so one of his agents could go to a world nearby on that track on some pretend mission. Fact was, only three people really knew I was here—Aldrath Prang, Bill Markham—and Aldrath's resident agent in the world who was meetin' me. She was supposed to be born here, and knew her way around. Even she was told as little as she could, only that I was on some mission for Aldrath. To her, too, I was Beth Parker. No sense in takin' a chance that this Carlos or Addison might know who Brandy Parker Horowitz really was.

She was there, all right; a thin, slightly built young woman maybe five two or three, with shoulder-length black hair. Her face was long and she had a real sharp nose and thin lips. She was wearin' a fur jacket, knee-length skirt, and high-heeled boots. Me, I had on a blue wool sweater, jeans, and sneakers, and I had one of my satchel handbags packed with toiletries and stuff and a small suitcase with just things I thought I might need and might not be able to pick up here.

"Hello," she called to me. "Over here." She had one of those middle voices and middle accents that seemed just about average for American women. I half expected some kind of British accent or something, but I guess we was already polluted in our talk by the time of the Revolution. Of course, the Canadians of my world had been with the British and they didn't sound like no Brits, now that I thought of it. As I went over to her, though, I could see on her face that it wasn't exactly what she was expectin'.

"I'm Beth Parker," I told her, bein' friendly as I could.

"Lindy Crockett," she responded, but she didn't offer a hand. "I—I've seen that thing work a couple of times, but it always gives me the chills. Sorry."

"That's okay. Somethin' else is botherin' you, though. Better clear the air right now; I'm gonna hav'ta depend on you a lot from here on in."

"Uh—nothing, really. I just wasn't expecting you to be a Negro."

My old defenses went up automatically, but I was under control. This wasn't my world and I wasn't invited, I invited myself. I might not like the place much, but it was better to have a comment like that than to be what that meant in, say, Vogel's old world.

"You got problems with that? If so, we better try to set up some alternate people right now, before this goes much further."

"Uh, no, no. It may even work to our advantage once we

begin, but it does complicate things a little. We're going to have a very long drive, and this commonwealth has some pretty rigid segregation laws. Until we get out of Virginia, there might be some problems just finding restaurants we could eat in or motor inns if we need to sleep. I planned on driving to Richmond and taking the train from there, giving you a feel for the place and briefing you as best I can, but we wouldn't even be in the same cars.''

Just like home, huh, Aldrath? Of course, they *was* still blockin' off a whole neighborhood of the good old northern City of Brotherly Love back home 'cause a black woman moved into a neighborhood, and my daddy grew up in a place and society like this.

"Then how 'bout we drive north instead of the train?" I suggested. "Or would a black woman and a white woman in a car prove embarrassin'?"

"Not so long as we were both women, no. The roads aren't too great, but we could go up to Huntington and get the train east from Cincinnati to Philadelphia. If I got a compartment we wouldn't have problems.''

"Let's do it, then. Anything else?"

"Well, women in pants are pretty rare in this country, and those shoes aren't seen much off the squash courts. Did you bring anything else to wear?"

"Well, I got one skirt in there and some high boots, but I didn't expect to risk my lone pair of pantyhose so early."

She stared at me. "What are pantyhose?"

Now I knew I was livin' in a primitive place.

I changed in the woods and got pronounced all right to travel, although I got the idea that my stuff was a little out of style here. We hiked over the fields and through the woods to a country road where a small car was parked to one side. It was a real tiny, boxy car and it bounced a lot, but the only real problem I had with it was that I was sittin' where I felt I should be drivin' and she was sittin' in the passenger side with a steerin' wheel and we drove opposite of all I was used to. It took some gettin' used to, I'll tell you. Crockett also was the kind of driver who liked to go sixty on roads you wouldn't dare do thirty on and brake at the last minute.

She was a cigarette smoker, though, and relieved that I was, too. She smoked these long, thin, unfiltered things, though, and I began to realize that I better hoard my two cartons 'cause I was universes away from any more Virginia Slims menthol.

Lindy—her real name was Linda but nobody called her that—was originally from Buffalo but she went east like so many did in my world to make her fame and fortune in New York. Most women here were housewives and you could still live here on one income, but the professional types tended to wind up as secretaries and clerks. Lindy was from the well-off middle class, and she'd gotten a law degree from one of the two colleges in the whole east that let women study law. She never could get into no law firm, though, and couldn't get much business on her own, so she wound up a full lawyer workin' as a legal secretary for a big law firm. She met a guy there who did their PI work, they got married, and she moved over to be *his* secretary. About a year and a half later the husband died from pneumonia he caught on a long stakeout and she inherited the business. She was twenty-six then.

The thing wasn't no Spade & Marlowe, though. It was a nice, comfortable operation with five full-time male investigators all of whom were willin' to let her be the boss so long as they kept doin' all the real work. It was only after a while that she discovered that one of her most regular clients who had 'em goin' all over and doin' all sorts of seemingly crazy things was really the Company. Because there really wasn't no Company here, only a few of Aldrath's agents tryin' to run down what they could, security employed a bunch of private eye companies to help it get information. Since some of her agents had contacts inside "Big Georgie" Wycliffe's organization, she was the one they finally picked as resident agent.

"In a sense, it saved my agency," she told me. "A number of the men didn't like working for a woman and were looking around to jump to other agencies, and business was drying up. Not any more. Plenty of cash, plenty of work, as you probably know."

Yeah, I knew what the Company could do, even if it wasn't in a world where it was set up and fully operating.

"The Gurneys—sorry, the National Police—have been

trying to nail him for years, but he always slips away," she said about Big Georgie. "He came up as a dock union leader and made the big time by being smarter and tougher than anyone else. He got where he is by a combination of big favors, mostly assassinations, for the higher-ups and while still a union leader he seized control of the illegal narcotics trade and made millions. Opium, heroin, cocaine —you name it, he controls it, north of the Mason-Dixon Line. Officially, if you can believe it, he is a brewer in northern New Jersey and also a tea importer. He's highly visible, at charitable events, sporting events, and the like, but very well protected and insulated by a top organizational staff."

"And you think he knows about the Labyrinth and the rest?"

"He knows, because what is being done is being done by his subordinates in his territory. It couldn't be otherwise. The main man for this horrible new drug, though, is a lieutenant named Arnie Siegel who controls the narcotics underworld in the south New Jersey and Philadelphia areas. He works this part of the operation out of Atlantic City, New Jersey, rather than Philadelphia because the mob owns and controls Atlantic City, while Philadelphia is the headquarters of the National Police. They run the Philadelphia vice, too, and own some of the best politicians money can buy, but there's no use in tweaking them *too* far."

I nodded. "But so far this operation is only the fifty prostitutes? No more?"

"That we know of, although things do appear to be changing. The work done up on the farm—the estate up-country—on the gate there seems to be very extensive, and they wouldn't do that if they weren't planning some real expansion. We also believe that they are importing a lot more of the drug than before, and one dose a day is not only the minimum but the maximum you need. Any more has no real effect on an addict. Then there's this Addison woman. She tends to show up now and again, much more in the last few months than ever before, but she never uses the Pennsylvania gate. She has also been seen in the large compound they're building in Guiana."

"Then why don't you have pictures of her? At least I'd think you would have them places staked out as best you could."

"We do, and we've had half a dozen chances, brief ones, to photograph her and a couple of opportunities to photograph Dr. Carlos, but no matter what the photos turn out too blurry to be used. They must have some sort of device that makes it impossible. That's all we can figure."

Well, to folks who could build and run the Labyrinth, a gadget like that would be no trouble at all, I thought. Still, it brought up a real point. "If they don't want their pictures taken that bad, then there must be somebody somewheres who might recognize them," I pointed out. "That means they ain't no flunkies and messengers. Have you tried composite sketches?"

"Oh, yes. We sent some fairly detailed ones to security, but they were unable to get anything from them. It's another of those mysteries."

"Other than this Addison, has there been any contact between this Carlos and Siegel? Anything?"

"We think there must be, but we haven't been able to document anything as yet. Consider that the National Police at least know of the drug and are scared by it, too. They think it's locally made and they're scared stiff that it might be mass-produced for general use. They, and we, have staked out, bugged, and tapped both operations as much as humanly possible and come up with nothing at all. The odds are very good that Wycliffe and Siegel have anti-bugging technology far in advance of ours. For them, this is a strictly business proposition. They are getting new technology for their operations that make a joke out of the police efforts, and in exchange they are doing this on the side. None of it, however, makes sense. I mean, why hook fifty young girls on it, all under nineteen when hooked, when you can use far more conventional drugs the same way? And why no men?"

"Any link between the fifty? Families? Anything?"

"The first thing we looked for. Most are runaways or the sort that decided to go on the street on their own. None come from powerful or influential families, although a few are from the middle class, God help us. They are all well built and attractive, but none are much more than that. The bulk are white, but there are some Negro girls in there and also some Chinese girls. At the start, when there were only a dozen or so, they were kept together, but now they're in small groups working in various cities along the eastern seaboard, no more than six to eight. Siegel keeps three around his personal home at the Jersey shore as virtually his slaves, although even they occasionally work the streets."

Well, we managed to make it to Huntington. After bein' Vogel's Beth I didn't mind eatin' mostly carry-out food and mostly sleepin' in the car. The train ride was real nice—we don't have trains like this back home, I'll tell you—and most everybody just assumed I was Lindy's personal maid or something like that. Their assumptions pissed me off a little, but I played along with it because it was handy and the laugh was on them. Most of the train crew was black, though—the porters, cooks, waiters, that sort of thing—and every damned black man on there seemed to think he was God's gift to women and were the most arrogant bunch I ever was around.

Philadelphia was very much different and still pretty much the same. There was no Schuykull Expressway or I-95 or like that—no expressways to speak of at all, and no U.S. 1 as such, either—but it was still a big city, it was still laid out based on Market and Chestnut, and it had elevated railways, streetcars down every street, and trolley buses, too. The downtown buildings, even the new ones, tended to look old-fashioned and not all box and glass, but it was familiar enough, and out on all sides was the row houses and tiny streets lookin' much the same. They had a couple of northern bridges across the Delaware, but the big ones I was used to, like the Franklin, Whitman, and Ross, just didn't exist. Most folks took ferries across the Delaware to Camden, which was more wide open than in my world.

Blacks lived in their own sections and only there, comin' out only to work or shop, but things wasn't so bad otherwise. Philadelphia stores took the same money no matter what the color, although some of the big department stores had separate dressin' rooms for colored and white. On the other hand, you rode anywhere on the trolley or train you wanted and all but the fancy restaurants didn't care if you ate there so long as you had the money. The most real trouble I had was that I kept lookin' the wrong way before steppin' into a street and almost got run over, and when a streetcar—they called 'em trams—or somethin' stopped, I half the time would have to keep from walkin' to the wrong side, without the door. Same with taxis, which were all real old-fashioned types and black.

Still, I managed to pick up a decent and in-style ward-robe. Seemed most skirts was at or above the knee, and worn with stockings and real high high-heeled leather boots with fur trim. While they hadn't thought of pantyhose yet, they did have nylons. Tops were mostly blouses, although you could get leather open vests to match the boots and stuff. Bras were real old-fashioned and real stiff, but all "decent" women wore 'em. My biggest problem used to be fit. I needed a lot of half-sizes and I got real wide feet, and it's always been a problem to get a good fit, which was why I dressed so casual and cheap most times even after I had money, but in Lindy's world they actually would measure and tailor stuff for you and have you pick it up—in twenty-four hours! There was something to be said for this world. Guys came out and pumped your gas and cleaned your car windows and checked your oil all automatically, for example.

I admit I had trouble gettin' cabs and the attention of salesclerks and waitresses, and I knew why, but white folks almost never did—even if the waitresses or cab drivers or clerks themselves was black, which some were. I ain't sure it was the color itself so much as in this place bein' black signaled "poor."

Once I started to feel comfortable gettin' around here— learnin' the rules, you might say—and got all the briefings I could, it was time to go to work. Lindy had a service where you could call collect from most any phone anyplace and either get hold of her or leave detailed messages, even information, that would be taken and passed on in strict confidence. She also had contracts with local agencies in Philadelphia and New Jersey who'd come runnin' if I called with the right code words. I also had a driver's license, passport and other documents, and a bank account as Beth

Louise Parker in an Atlantic City bank. I needed to have some ready cash around, since they didn't get around to inventin' the MasterCard there yet and I wasn't a likely candidate for individual store accounts. I did like the fact that all my IDs listed my right birth date but the wrong year. It was nice to be so suddenly under thirty again, even if only on paper and only by half a year.

Atlantic City was never much in early November, and here it didn't have the casinos. The boardwalk was mostly deserted, most of its businesses shut down till summer, and the place was left to the permanent residents. The rest of the city didn't look no better than it did in my world; the whole place looked and smelled like the worst of Camden. I took a small apartment in the black section of the city that was no great shakes as a furnished apartment but wasn't no roach motel, neither. I also hired a small car—no problem parkin' on the streets in November—that was old and sad-lookin' but ran okay, but it took a little time for me to make a turn and wind up on the left side of the road.

The general agreement was that I would call Lindy's special number once a week without fail, even if I had nothin' to report. Of course, I could use it sooner to get information and the like if I needed. If she didn't hear from me for two straight weeks, she would assume that I was taken and check up on me. If she couldn't find me or I didn't report for a full six weeks, she would communicate with Aldrath to send in the Marines.

I spent a couple of weeks gettin' to know the city and its haunts and own special rules, and checkin' out Mr. Siegel and his operation. He had a real nice house right on the ocean down near Ocean City, with high fences and a gate and gate guard. The land around there is so flat that there was no way to really see inside except by air or by boat. Since I knew what kind of crates these people flew and a balloon would be a little obvious, that left boat and I was no sailor, particularly in fall's rough seas and changing weather. They said that Siegel tried to buy here a few years before and was told it was "restricted"—no Jews allowed. So all of a sudden a lot of houses down here started catchin' fire, and there was a real crime wave, and lots of businesses them WASP folks had suddenly went bad or had troubles, and then this strictly blonde and blue-eyed bank came in and made nice offers and bought a lot of the property—and that's how Siegel came not only to have the place, but privacy, too.

But Siegel wasn't no prisoner. He liked goin' down to the lowlife sections, to the bars and clubs he owned and the projects he controlled, and he spent some time in the Oceanside Tea and Spice Company, Ltd., offices, which was just a big warehouse and a small, stucco office in front. He drove a fancy-lookin' red Daimler sports car and was pretty easy to spot or find.

He turned out to be young, fairly good-lookin', thin and trim with a thick, bushy moustache. He was said to be somethin' of a health nut, and drank little if at all, didn't smoke, and swung both ways. He'd go to bed with women, yeah, but he didn't have much other use for 'em, 'cept to wait on him maybe. You had to know your place around him. I took one look at him and knew that if he hadn't been Jewish he and Vogel's blackshirts woulda gotten along just fine.

He didn't manage nothin' personally, of course, and particularly not illegal stuff like prostitutes, since the law would just love to get him on most any technicality. That didn't stop him from visitin' the worst districts and payin' calls on the little fish who worked for him. They was just old friends, see, and what they done for a livin' was no bother to him. Their boss? Heaven forbid! He was in the tea and spice business and that paid just fine . . .

I needed to get closer in to get a real look at things, and that was one thing I'd done many times before. After you cruise a district for a while you get a feel for it, and this one wasn't much different than most. I got to admit I didn't exactly get excited over dressin' down to it, since them streetwalkers wanted to advertise and I was still havin' trouble with a November chill and a brisk wind from the ocean just with a short skirt, but it was part of the job. The uniform of the place wasn't that much different. Real high spiked heels, fishnet stockings, a real short leather skirt and top that left little to the imagination, real heavy makeup with some sparkles mixed in, and the only concession to cold weather allowed, a fur coat, usually rabbit, that was *never* buttoned. There was always new girls comin' on and old ones vanishin', so that wasn't no big thing, but it took some outside detective work to give the right answers if questions came up, and they always did.

Armed with all that, I had no trouble fittin' right in and almost vanishin' into the scenery. This was the kind of neighborhood I grew up in, and these were the same kind of people I always knew. There were, however, some problems I knew I'd have to face. I'd used an identity as a whore many times, but only for a day or two, on stakeouts and like that. Now I had to blend in and stay in for some time, till folks got used to me and talked relaxed and felt I was one of them. That meant movin' into a flophouse room right in the district with only the stuff I'd be expected to have—stuff that could fit in a handbag, mostly—and very little money. I could stay independent for a while, but there was no question I'd have to turn a few tricks to be completely accepted. Gettin' a barmaid's job or somethin' like that was out of the question; November was the off season and there was only so much of anything, even tricks, to go around.

So, in a way, I finally completed my destiny and it was anything but glamorous or even particularly pleasant, but I actually took money for sex. Not bad money, either, considerin' my expenses and the fact I didn't have to split with no pimp. Not that several didn't try to move in, but I managed to put 'em off without them gettin' too riled. That wouldn't last forever, but I didn't plan on this bein' forever.

Still and all, doin' a few tricks and scorin' a little pot did just what I hoped. In under two weeks' time, I was a part of the scenery and I had enough credibility to sit around a burger joint or places like that and just talk friendly to people. I started learnin' one hell of a lot, and I even got some warnings about Siegel. They bought my story—ex-stripper from Philadelphia who got married to a real stud and took a hike the second time he beat me up. It was familiar.

My best friend and source turned out to be a guy named Harley who ran the only porn shop I ever seen with a sandwich thing on the side. Harley was fat and fiftyish and only about five feet tall and as flaming swishy as a three-pound note, but he liked to talk to "the girls." I think he wished he was one of us. One night we got to talkin' 'bout the odd types even for the district.

"You seen a shadow dancer yet? Now *there's* one to give you the creeps!" he said, shiverin'.

"Huh? I heard that name used by some folks talkin' to other folks. What's it mean?"

"That's what we call 'em on the street. A string of half a dozen girls run by Fast Eddie Small—one of Arnie's pimps. All real young, real pretty. They work the streets like bitches in heat, sometimes do real *vulgar* strip shows—it's an art form, you know, or should be. You know—you were one."

I nodded. "Yeah, but where's the name come from?"

"They got hooked on something new, some new drug we think they're making in a lab someplace and it's *scary!* Not like dope—hell, half the streetwalkers here have fifty-pound-a-day habits. They're like, well, *slaves,* damn it. They wash his car, they clean his house, they do everything he tells 'em. He has fun showin' them off to people, making them do *disgusting* things just to show what a big man he is. I mean, I look in your eyes and I see a *person* there. You look in their eyes and you get a chill. Nothin' there. Not even hope. Shadows of pretty girls dancin' to Fast Eddie's tune. I hear there are others around, in Philadelphia, New York, Baltimore, all over. You watch out and stay away from them. I don't want to ever look in your eyes and see only a shadow dancer there."

Well, of course, to stay away I had to know how to find one, and where, and where they sometimes did their simply *vulgar* shows, too. Fast Eddie and his girls worked out of a joint called the Purple Pussycat about three blocks over diagonally from the bright lights, on the edge of the district. I'd been warned more than once not to work that area, that no freelancers were allowed. I decided to check it out first, so I went back to the original apartment where most of my things were. I put my hair up and put a blonde wig on over it. It looked good, but it was pretty obviously a wig and not a dye job.

One thing I learned on the street was that Lindy had been right. Any girl who put on long, tight pants, and went braless under a shirt or sweater, was automatically a lesbian to just about everybody. I didn't want to get roughed up or raped or anything bad by workin' in an exclusive territory, and respectable women just didn't go into them neighborhoods or places alone. Some butch girls, though, got a real charge out of strip shows, although they usually went in pairs or more. Still, this was a more repressed society than mine, and I'd already seen a couple of women come down to the district, usually under wigs, glasses, and the like, alone to see a show and even pay a female hooker for a good time they didn't dare have or try in their ordinary lives. Lots of closeted gay men did it with male hookers, after all.

So it might not be unusual for a black lesbian, whose culture was real macho, to come over in disguise and see a show and maybe try for a good time. My eyes ain't great, like I said, but I used contact lenses I brought with me when I was on the streets and regular glasses off-hours. Now I got my tinted sunglasses, even though it was night. It was the right added touch. I did have to go out and buy a butch leather jacket, to make it just right, but while the saleswoman looked at me real odd she sold me the coat and took the money.

About nine-thirty that night, I took a taxi up to the Purple Pussycat. The driver hardly said a word to me. I got out a block or so before the club, so I could kinda cruise the area. It wasn't a lot of joints and shit like the main street of the district, just real run-down old houses and a mission and the one club near the end of the block with a garish neon sign and blinkin' lights, but I could see why Arnie wanted it. The corner near the club was one of the main drags in or out of Atlantic City, and it was on a main feeder street to there. The lights at the intersection was maybe five minutes long one way and three the other. In season, you could probably proposition or check out a hundred cars, and a john lookin' for it would be able to find it and set somethin' up without ever bein' obvious. There was even a big arrow sign on both streets for the club sayin', FREE CAR PARK IN REAR!

There wasn't much traffic now, particularly on a Wednesday, and nobody seemed to be workin' that intersection.

Now, undercover work's like method actin' only more so—you really got to get into and live the part, 'cause if an actor bombs she maybe gets tomatoes or boos, but if

somebody undercover makes a slip, just one, they can wind
up floatin' in the ocean. That's why when I moved into the
district I had to take some tricks, like it or not. If I didn't,
they'd smell cop or narc or somethin' and it was bye-bye
Brandy. I'd played a few dykes in my time, too—sometimes
it was the only way to get information—and I had it down
pretty good. Like back home, this only had to be a one-night
stand, but I would be pretty damned conspicuous.

I stuck a cigarette in the side of my mouth, lit it, and
walked into the Purple Pussycat.

As expected, it wasn't exactly New Year's Eve in there.
Maybe a dozen customers, all men in suits and ties, one
barmaid and one cocktail waitress. They all gave me a look
when I came in, but I could see right away that their first
impression was exactly what I wanted. The juke box, which
was piped into the whole place, was playin' some jazzy
French song with naughty lyrics. I sat down at an empty
table and the mere fact that not one of them guys in there
made a move was nice.

The waitress had on a sort of bikini, though they didn't
call 'em that in this world, the fishnet stockings, and spiked
heels, all with purple glitter stuff in them. She came up to
me. "What'cha havin', honey?" She looked like she should
be out findin' johns, but she didn't look like no shadow
dancer.

"Rum and Coke," I told her. I'd eaten well before this,
and also drank a whole glass of buttermilk. I figured I might
have to drink a fair amount.

Now, one trick in this kinda thing is that you got to show
you got money, and a fair amount, without showin' so
much that somebody's tempted to just take it the easy way.
I brought a hundred pounds, not super dangerous money
but still an average week's salary in this world, and I
brought it in mostly smaller bills. The money was different
colors and sizes for different amounts so it was clearly not a
huge wad in real value to an experienced spotter—like the
waitress—but it was a huge wad physically and it made an
impression. She gave my order to the barmaid, waited,
brought it, got paid and saw the wad, then vanished in the
back for a minute before reappearing.

For a while, nothin' happened, but I saw that none of the

guys left and a couple more came in. My first rum and Coke tasted mostly like Coke, but my second tasted mostly like rum—the over-a-hundred-proof variety. I was mostly through it when the show they was all waitin' for started.

It used canned music and hokey lights and the runway down the center of the bar, but the show was like no other these joints ever did. I knew from the joints on the strip that what they had in prudery everywhere else they didn't have in their shows, at least not here. There seemed little you could do in a joint like this that was against the law. But this—this was somethin' else.

The show involved three girls with the best bodies I ever seen in my life, one white and a real blonde, one black, and one Chinese. They got naked 'cept for real high spiked heels in record time—no pasties, no *nothin'*—and then they started really doin' it to each other in ways I never even dreamed of. I didn't even know the human body could bend that way or that three girls could do it to one another all at the same time with no conflict of interest, as it were—and all to the beat of the music! And they was all three clearly really enjoyin' it.

It didn't take too long to see what Harley meant. The three girls didn't look *real* somehow. For one thing, they looked *absolutely perfect,* and I do mean *perfect.* They had them lady bodybuilder's muscles, too—had to to do the kind of things they was doin' and hold them positions while doin' 'em. There was also somethin' else, harder to describe. A feelin', really, but real just the same, 'cause Harley and the folks who'd named them felt it, too. An emptiness, somehow. The feelin' that you was watchin' three perfect and perfected Disneyland robots, not livin', thinkin', feelin' women. *Shadow dancers . . .*

I was told by everybody that all the shadow dancers was twenty-one or under, even by Lindy, but that was true only of the white girl and the Chinese girl. The black girl was older, though she still looked real young and fantastic. I couldn't take my eyes off her, almost from the start.

The black shadow dancer was me.

7.

Unmasking in Hell

All right, all right, I knew right off from seein' her that it couldn't be no accident. It broke all their rules, for one thing. But *this* Brandy was me and wasn't me. I kept my straight hair from Beth; she had my old bush neatly trimmed. And my body—nobody human's body—never looked that perfect, that good, or could.

Fact was, the more I watched, the more I got turned on myself. Really turned on. They could do it to a stone, no matter which sex. But I was a pro, and I knew somethin' was not right. The odds against a Brandy bein' in this world was about even—we wasn't that far off my world's line and it was possible Daddy would have married the same woman, maybe even founded an agency. The odds of that Brandy bein' a stripper or whore wasn't all that low, neither. Fact was, I knew I was pretty much that in most of the worlds where I existed at all. But the odds of my bein' in this particular bar in Atlantic City in November as a victim of what I was out investigatin' and just happen to be a performer the night I show was beyond any odds of hittin' a jackpot lottery I knew.

There was no doubt that these bastards knew I was here, who I was, and why I was here. The only thing I couldn't be clear on was if they did this every night till I finally showed up or whether they had made me that night. Yeah, I knew who that dancer was, but did she, or they, know who *I* was? That was a big question. I had to guess they didn't—not yet, anyways. Why bother with this show if they did? Just slip somethin' in the drink and they had me. I had to figure they trotted out their Brandy every time there was a black woman in the house, with or without friends and companions. This was bait, and you don't bother to feed bait to a hooked fish.

Thing was, I was hooked good and proper, but I wasn't 'bout to get reeled in right then if I could help it. One thing they hoped to do was to throw me so off guard I couldn't think straight and they come close—but only close. It was tough, though, when the act was over and they all bounded from the runway to the center bar counter and then into the place itself, naked, wet, and drippin'. And the black one, the other me, came straight over to me.

"Hey, sista'!" she whispered in my ear. "Don't that look *good?* I seen ya here, feelin' yo'self up. Want a private lesson?"

My voice never sounded like my voice to me, but it was close enough to know it really was. Not the accent, though. She was more ghetto-southern, more damned *ignorant*-soundin', too, in the way she used the words. Damn it, though! I was tempted! Not so much by the real offer as by getting this girl, this other me, alone somewhere in a room. Just us. But, then, that's what they figured on. *And this wasn't me!* Maybe we was genetically the same, maybe even the same fingerprints, but this Brandy had taken a different route than me a long time ago and made a lot more wrong choices, and we was literally worlds apart. On the other hand, "sister" was more than just a friendly term here.

"No," I answered huskily, tryin' to lower my voice a little 'cause it always sounded higher to me than it really was. "I just ain't up to you girls." And weren't *that* the truth!

She pressed a little, and I was real nervous she'd see through it all and feel who I was, but she didn't. You don't look the same lookin' at another you as you look even in a mirror. She backed off while I played it cool, and then started workin' the guys. I relaxed a bit, but continued to drink. I was real shaken, but I wanted out of that place in one piece and without tippin', and if they was lookin' for me then I didn't want to leave while *she* was still in the same room.

They all three got customers with no problems and disappeared in the back, and the barmaid come back over. "What's the matter hon? No guts when it counts?"

I looked up at her. "Not with *them.* There was just *somethin'* . . . I dunno. Now *you* I could go for."

There was something in the waitress's eyes and expression when I made that first comment. "I understand," she whispered, more like talkin' to herself. "Hon, after watchin' *that* I might take you up on it, but not tonight. I got to work till two and I been here since four. You come 'round tomorrow this time, though, when I don't work late, and maybe we'll watch the show and have a little fun, huh?"

"Maybe I will," I told her. "My name's Sam, by the way. Short for Samantha but I never use that." I took a twenty out and slipped it to her as a tip. She took it real smooth.

"I'm Deb. You come 'round tomorrow a little earlier, like eight, and we'll see."

I finished my drink, got up, and walked slowly out of the bar and onto the street. I had to walk a couple of blocks over just to get some distance, then waited in the cold until I finally got a cab back to my apartment. My mind was really in a kinda roar, and I needed to sort things out.

First I called Camden information and tried numbers for Harold Parker, Spade & Marlowe, and a few more. I drew a blank, but I kinda expected to. I wanted to call in to Lindy or her people locally and run this thing down, but I wasn't sure I could. Fact was, they knew I was in this world and workin' to find them. The only ones who knew and could get the word out would be Aldrath, Bill Markham, or—Lindy. Not necessarily Lindy herself, but definitely folks within her organization. If so, I couldn't use her, or them, much again.

Things started to tumble into place now, bit by bit. Maybe this world was a damn sight more important to this whole plot than Aldrath and Bill had been led to believe. Maybe Vogel took care of the far-out research, but *this* world was the center of the actual plot, whatever it was. No investigator is ever any better than the quality of his or her information. Aldrath depended on Lindy's organization for most of the information that he got. Maybe, in fact, Vogel was a red herring, somebody to be discovered as a big player in the game when in fact he was a side operation.

If they was feedin' a stock line, and givin' just enough information that some of Aldrath's boys could independently check out as right, then they had it made here. They might even, in the end, raid both Fast Eddie's harem and even the compound in Guiana and blow it to hell and never really touch what was goin' on here. But, then, why reveal the Guiana thing at all—unless that, too, was a cover, the base to be exposed. That was research, while this was some kinda little thing involvin' the local mob.

Then I showed up and got involved. I'm a real danger, not to the operation, but to Lindy or whoever it was in Lindy's crew that was really workin' for the opposition. They got to send out my reports—Aldrath will be expectin' 'em. So they decide to see just how far I can get, and even set a trap with an alternate me.

That only made sense to a point, though. That other Brandy weren't no new addict; she'd been hooked for a long time to get that look about her and get so practiced at that act. That meant they had her before we got involved, maybe long before we ever was brought in to go after Vogel. They just switched her here to Atlantic City 'cause they knew it was flypaper and honey to me. And there was only one reason they'd have another me all set up before all that took place.

They was plannin' a switch. Her for me. But either somethin' went wrong or we got directly involved and they couldn't risk it. No, wait—Vogel. That was the key. They was gonna pull the switch *after* the Vogel job, which they'd been plannin' in that Security Committee for months before tellin' us. That meant my not gettin' shot serious in the tunnel wasn't no accident. That also meant that Sam was supposed to be shot, maybe killed. That's why they took the time to shoot everybody. They couldn't be sure in that small area and time which was Sam.

Then why hadn't they made the switch? I looked at myself in the mirror once more and then I knew. *I kept my hair straight and my complexion a little lighter and smoother!* They couldn't move this big-time equipment over here; the heat was on too much. They couldn't get enough big medical shit over to make it take. They didn't have Doc's or the Center's big experts and gadgets where they could make her over into me. That explained somethin' else, too. Why they might get Vogel a hypnoscan.

Maybe there weren't no Brandy in this world. Maybe she was from someplace else, just like me. I know there was a couple in worlds just near our own. Ones that went bad. Ones that never met Sam. The competition had used folks from one of them worlds the first time we'd tangled. Maybe this one was from the same one.

But why me? And why make a switch with somebody like me? I didn't work for the Company. About the only one I could see was Bill Markham, and they could try for him without me if they really wanted to. Or was it even worse?

Could somebody be a good-enough shot and a cool-enough head to nail everybody in a Labyrinth cube 'cept Sam and me, and then nail me in an unimportant spot and Sam exactly in a way that would cause what happened? Maybe not, but even if Sam had died I'd'a had special status with the Company. Access to the Labyrinth, access even to headquarters. But that didn't make no sense, neither. I had a special, unique, unbreakable code inside me. I knew it was unbreakable 'cause if it was breakable they had all sorts of ways of sneakin' in and out. That twin of mine might be able to learn how I walked, talked, thought, and be made over to be a perfect double, but she could never have that code.

Still, I knew now I was on to somethin', and it was big. I was sure right to have gotten involved—I now had proof positive that the enemy was plannin' to draft me, anyways.

Still and all, there was a number of missin' pieces. Even grantin' they had some way to get her in headquarters as me, so what? It'd hav'ta be real quick, since they hadn't managed to get any of this damned super drug in and she was sure on it. Most she'd dare risk would be a few hours. What could *I* do in just a few hours, takin' nothin' in with me and dependin' on Aldrath's folks to get 'round the place and even translate? The answer was nothin'. A big, fat zero.

That was the thing 'bout this case. Every time you thought you had somethin' figured, it just asked another crazy question. Still, I was gettin' more and more convinced that the answers to many of 'em was right here—or, over there, in the Purple Pussycat. Trouble was, they was layin' for me, and if they missed me tonight they might not miss me again.

I had a sudden bad feelin' and told the driver to let me out a block down and around the corner from the apartment. I was pretty sure they never knew 'bout my street-walker life, but they did know Beth Louise Parker, and her bank, and the apartment she had in her own name. I'd gone back there tonight for the first time in a couple of weeks. I guess they got sloppy. After all, I walked in dressed like a whore but I'd left to go shoppin' as me and come back, then walked out dressed like a dyke. I had to figure they'd be on their guard and fully staffed this time. Trouble was, my streetwalker clothes was up there, and all I had on me was a hundred and twenty-one pounds. I had another two hundred and fifty up there, enough to use for a switch without goin' to the bank where they was sure to stake me out.

I hadn't figured on this. I was on the run from the people who was supposed to help and support me while the people I was tryin' to check out still hadn't discovered me. Without Crockett I didn't have a way in to the Labyrinth or any way to contact Aldrath; they'd just keep sendin' progress reports from me out and everything would look real fine.

Thing was, this was now pretty clearly the place where the real action was, not no backwater joint. More than that, they knew from the start through Crockett's people that security knew about this place and they didn't seem to be slowin' down. Why should they? They was puttin' up a real nice front here, showin' Aldrath just what he wanted to see but not enough to get him to take any real direct action. That was bad, too, 'cause it meant more'n likely that they were very close to findin' what they were tryin' to find, or maybe they'd found it and were just makin' sure. This thing was both a drug and a disease; you don't let somethin' like that loose in alien worlds until you make sure you can't get it yourself.

I checked the area around my apartment. Normally you wouldn't see nothin', but I'd done a hundred stakeouts myself and I knew just what to look for. I was pretty sure they weren't in the apartment itself; the place was real close with nosy neighbors and paper-thin walls and if they got in for more than a visit they'd be noticed. This was one time in this world when it was a real advantage bein' black; the Crockett types wouldn't have no Spade & Marlowe to use, or wouldn't think to use 'em, and white PIs would stand out in *this* neighborhood. Of course, Siegel probably had loads

of black gunsels to call on—the mob always was somethin'
of an equal opportunity employer—so it paid to be careful.

There was a medium-sized black car parked with its
lights out about half a block down from the apartment with
two men in it. That was one. In the alley behind, where the
fire escapes was, I thought I could see movement beyond
the trash containers, like somebody shiftin' uncomfortable
from the cold. If they didn't have nobody inside, though, I
could probably just walk right in bold as brass. The problem would be if one of 'em was bright enough to figure out
why that whore went in, I come out, and there was nobody
else there. You got to be thin and light to be a second-story
type, and I was neither. I turned and headed down to the
district.

Harley squinted. "That really *you*, luv? I didn't know you
was no lezzie. Not that it makes no difference here."

"I'm not, but it's a disguise," I told him. "My ex caught
up with me and he's got an in with Siegel. I got to blow,
Harley, but I can't get back in my darktown flat to get my
money, my workin' clothes, or even my damned contact
lenses and regular glasses." I told him about the place, and
the stakeout.

"You got some money, then?"

"Some cash up there, and I put the rest of what I had in a
local bank. That's what he's mad about. I got his money.
And I can't get to it 'cause they figured out the name it was
under, 'cause the flat's under that name, too." I never knew
how important an automatic teller machine was till now,
but first they had to invent the computer here, and a phone
system where you didn't need no manual switchboard
operators.

Harley chuckled. "Got the stash in a bank, huh? Well,
let's see. I think I know a fella who might be able to get the
small stuff out of your apartment, particularly if it's bein'
watched. He likes that kind of thing. You make a list of stuff
that can be carried in no more than a handbag. I'll make a
call and see if he's interested. He keeps the cash, of course."

I nodded. "Okay, but then what do *I* do?"

"When he gets your checkbook, you write one out the
way I tell you. Not to me, and not for a big amount, but
some. How much you got in there?"

"Lots."

"Three hundred quid?"

"Yeah, more'n that."

"I can see why he's interested and why you laid low. Okay, you give me a check for three hundred and I give you two hundred. Fair?"

Of course it wasn't, but I was in no position to argue. "Fair."

"All right, then. You give me the address and particulars and we'll see what we can do."

I spent the night in a small room in back of his store, uncomfortably but it was a place to hide at least. I didn't wake up until well after noon, then blew some money buyin' some sandwiches from the clerk at the store. The clerk had been told I was stayin' there but not why. You don't go far askin' too many questions down here.

Harley come in about two, lookin' like the cat that just swallowed the canary, carryin' a shoppin' bag. In it was my glasses, contacts, checkbook, fake IDs, makeup, toiletries, and the rest. No cash and no clothes, but I coulda kissed him. I wrote the check and now had a fair amount of money for the time.

I had been tryin' to figure what to do next, and I pretty well decided I had only a couple choices. I could either give up, stay in this world, and go somewheres outside Wycliffe's territory and work the streets—I could never use the fake identity again, after all, so I had no education, no records, and I was a female member of a race that had thirty-percent unemployment here now—or I could keep goin'. This Deb was a way in, but a real risky one. I needed more than a one-night stand to get information, and my money was limited, so I needed an edge. On a crazy thought I checked out somethin' I never even thought of. Back when they did that dental work they loaded that tooth with shit that was supposed to make Vogel real nice, only I never got a chance to use it. I figured when they put my face back they took it out, but since now half my teeth was capped and they left 'em that way I decided to check. I scrunched up my mouth the way I was supposed to and pushed. The loaded tooth moved.

That was no guarantee they'd left it loaded, but maybe

the Center just hadn't noticed or known about it. It was worth a try. Of course, I didn't really know much about what it did or how long it lasted, but it couldn't hurt and might give me an edge.

I got some locals in the district to help. I needed to look different than this other Brandy even when I wasn't dressed like this and with dark glasses. When you never was able to have straight hair, and then you did, you didn't want to go back, but even though it broke my heart I had it cut real, real short and styled in a man's style. My face would never look like a man's or boy's, but it sure changed my looks. I hid the documents in a place that was as safe as any, and got a fresh wardrobe that, with the leather jacket, made me about as butch as they come. Private ownership of guns wasn't allowed and it woulda cost me more than I could raise to get one quick, but a nasty little needle-tipped switchblade with a real strong spring was only five quid if you knew where to get it, and after a few weeks down here, I knew. I had to still go with the blonde wig, and I just hoped nobody had second thoughts about the one there the night before or compared notes with the watchers on the apartment.

Thursday was a busier night, but other people was workin' the Purple Pussycat. Deb was in there, but out of uniform and in fairly ordinary street clothes, sittin' and talkin' to the barmaid. Even though she wasn't dressed like she belonged there, there was that hardness in the face and coldness in the mannerisms that everybody on the street got that said she was right at home. She came right over when I sat down in a small booth.

"Hello, there. Buy me a drink and watch the early show first?" she suggested, real friendly and professional. I had to wonder if she did this normally with girls or if this was a new experiment. Work in these joints long enough, though, and you see and do most everything.

The show started at eight-fifteen, and was pretty much the same as the night before but had one extra girl, another black girl more in keepin' with the other two and not my twin. This time I was ready for it and began to look at the others. There was just somethin' 'bout them, something different even from the other Brandy. Black, white, and yellow, but they was almost the same height, they had near identical perfect builds, and their faces, while different, didn't seem all that much different. They all had the same noses, kinda, small and neat, and the same size mouths, and their eyes looked a little different but even the blonde had brown eyes. Their hair was different—the blonde's was shoulder-length and straight, the black girl's was short and curly, but big curls, not the natural type I normally had or that my twin still had, and the yellow girl had a pageboy with bangs. Still, one seemed no thicker or thinner than the other, and you could almost see any hairstyle on the other two.

Why fifty girls, all female, all just workin' the streets and clubs? Why no men? Why these fifty? Did most of 'em look kinda the same? Suppose all three of them up there had dark brown hair and golden skin . . .

They finished up and went to work the crowd, ignorin' us. Deb sighed, turned, and said, "My place or yours?"

"Yours," I told her. "Mine ain't exactly a nice place right now."

She lived in a room about a block in back of the place. It was a pretty run-down row house that had been made into little tiny apartments with just a tiny refrigerator, hot pot, and plug-in portable stove for cookin'. It was a little messy but it had that lived-in look. Odds were that Fast Eddie owned the place. I pulled out one of my few remainin' reefers and we split it, then started to get to it. The reefer had made it easier for me to turn tricks on the street and it made it easier to do this, too. It ain't bad and can be a lot of fun, but when you get all hot and up there ain't nothin' to put where you want or need it. I did manage to toggle that trick tooth and turn it some, and some sweet kinda liquid, not much, come out and got delivered into her mouth by tongue.

Took me a bit to realize she'd stopped doin' much and was just lettin' it happen with a dreamy smile on her face, eyes closed. I figured I might as well go for the whole nine yards. I started nibblin' her ear and whispered, "You love me, you want me, you need me, now and forever," which wasn't exactly how the whispers usually went. "All the men was just for money but this is the real thing. You'd do anything for me, believe anything I said, trust me forever. Don't try to explain it or think about it, it just is and it's wonderful."

And she smiled, mumbled, and repeated it—and repeated it again. Suddenly her eyes opened, and she looked at me like it was for the first time, like the wonder in a little kid's face at a new toy, and then she really tore into it so passionately I just let it rip.

I didn't know how long the stuff would last, but it was *powerful* stuff all right, if you hadn't been immunized to it. It was hours before it stopped, and then she insisted on cookin' somethin' for me and generally actin' like a cross between a puppy dog and a little kid. "Might as well," I sighed, feelin' really achy. "I ain't got no place to go anyways."

She was startled. "What d'ya mean?"

"I mean I got fired and tossed, lock, stock, and barrel. I been walkin' the streets, sleepin' in women's flophouses, and watchin' my money go down."

"Stay here, then!"

"But—"

"Look, I know this sounds crazy, 'cause it does to me, but I think I'm in love with you. You don't owe me nothin'. I owe *you*, 'cause I never thought I'd have this feelin' again." She was a mixed-race girl, mostly white but a noticeable quarter black, which was why I hit on her, but it was still kinda funny to hear her start talkin' like me.

"I like you, too," I told her, and I did. I felt sorry for her more than anything. "But ain't no way I can stay here without payin' some freight."

"It's okay. It wouldn't even be like you was the first one or only one around here like that. A lotta girls 'round here can't get close to no men. They all act alike under the skin. We lean on each other a lot. Maybe I can get Fast Eddie to find you a job 'round here."

Funny thing was, she did. To this day I ain't sure if that potion was strong or just a little temporary thing that worked as a starter set for what might already have been there in her head 'cause it seemed so natural for her. Of course, the potion made it quick and painless. By the time she took me 'round to meet Fast Eddie Small a couple of days later I'd already kinda settled in and knew most of the girls in the house. And that's how I became Samantha "Sam" Marlowe, my third undercover identity. I ditched the wig and used the dark glasses, which I was gettin' used to even in dark places. I had the contacts but decided not to use 'em since they didn't have the real thin contacts here and I thought it was a little too much of an invite to compare faces with Brandy the Shadow Dancer.

Fast Eddie looked like a guy who sold furniture. Thin, mid-fifties, moustache, little gray eyes, balding and graying, always in a brown or gray tweed suit and real thin tie, usually with a cigar in his mouth. I was real nervous about meetin' him since he almost surely saw Brandy most times and also knew to look out for another with straight hair, but with gum in my mouth, a real Brando manner, and dressed like I was it never seemed to enter his head. "I don't really need nobody so I can't do much," he told me, "but just 'cause it's Deb I'll make an exception. You'll help clean up the place after it closes, mop up, restock the bar, that kind of thing. Thirty a week for part-time on trial. After that, we'll see."

I took the job, and I was on the inside. The basic expenses for all the "employees" was taken care of, and they turned their money over to Small 'cept for twenty percent, although Deb as waitress made a flat eighty a week and got to keep ten percent of any fringes. Of course, she skimmed like they all did, so it wasn't too bad. It bothered me a little that I took so easy to the dominant role in the relationship, in bed, even on the street, but I learned a lot in a very little time.

There was six shadow dancers workin' the place and two more out at Siegel's. Small was married with two mostly grown kids and a house out of town. He didn't mistreat his string more than the usual, and he always had whatever drugs his "ladies" required on hand. About half of 'em was on smack, the other half took various stuff as it suited them. All but the shadow dancers. They lived together in a small set of rooms just above the club, and while you couldn't avoid 'em you didn't stay 'round them long. They seemed free to come and go days, and they did, but not far. Every day they'd do a run 'round a track at a junior high that had closed down and was boarded up now. They bought and fixed their own food, and you could hear 'em up there sometimes exercisin' or liftin' weights or whatever, too. They was always real made-up, even for their runs, and that helped. Still, I tried to make sure that Brandy and Sam was never seen in the same room together again.

They had funny names that sounded like sororities. Beta, Delta, Zeta, Lambda, Rho, and Iota. All but Rho had simple nicknames like Bet, Del, Zee, Lam, and Ta. Letters of the Greek alphabet, like they was some kinda clinical experimental samples. All six really did look similar in size, shape, and build; you could draw 'em in outline, make their hair any color or style you wanted and color their skin any which way and you really couldn't tell which was which. They wasn't no runaways, that's for sure. They was either picked 'cause they had that look, or bred that way. None of 'em had that hard look to 'em, neither; they all looked kinda empty, and lost, like this life and these ways was all they ever knew or could think of, and all they ever imagined the future would be. Shadow people without souls, Harley had said, and that was pretty close to the truth. Only their Brandy was different—larger, with distinct black features and speech, and with natural woolly hair in a mane that was shorter than I used to wear it and better kept but pretty much the same.

It was okay till I literally bumped into her one day. She was with one of the other girls, the black one, Beta, and they come 'round the corner in their fancy-lookin' furs and heels and I was comin' the other way and we collided. Nothin' much, but we stopped for a minute and looked at each other. She just smiled and said, in a real mellow voice, "Hey, sis, don' worry none. It's all cool."

"My fault," I mumbled, tryin' to keep my diction up and my voice and head down. "Sorry."

All the other girls had high, sweet voices that sounded almost alike. "Hey, you know, she look somethin' like you," Beta noted to my distress. "I seen her 'round th' club."

"I clean up there nights," I told them bruskly. "Look, gotta go, nice talkin' and all that." And I hurried off, even though I was only goin' out for cigarettes.

We parted quickly, but I could hear Brandy Two's voice say clearly, "I don't look like no bull dyke."

I breathed hard and tried to think about what to do next. I could run, but then they'd know, and like the shadow dancers I had no place to run to. Here in this district was the only friends I had in this world I could count on. Was it time, maybe, to take on another identity? I went and got the cigarettes and came back to the room and stuck some jazz on the radio. When nothin' happened for a while, I started to relax and followed my normal routine.

It was Sunday night—or, rather, Monday morning. Sundays was busy nights 'cause most bars and clubs was closed all day by law; only in an entertainment district could they stay open, so we got a lot more business from as far away as Philadelphia.

I cleaned up and was gettin' ready to go when one of the shadow dancers came down and looked out at me. "Hey! Sammy girl! The *man* wants t'see ya upstairs. Now."

I frowned. I didn't like this. Fast Eddie still here at three-forty in the mornin'? I could run out the front door but if it was trouble he'd have that covered. Better to bluff it through.

"Okay, okay, tell him to keep his shirt on," I mumbled. "I'll be up as soon as I finish here." And I did take a little time, just to be on the safe side, then went back and up the back stairs to the only part that wasn't reserved for the shadow dancers—the small back office. I knocked, and got a muffled "Come in," and I opened the door and saw Eddie Small there in shirtsleeves workin' on the books. He seemed alone. He kept on with the books a minute, maybe gettin' even with me not runnin' when he called, then closed the ledger, leaned back in his creaky desk chair, and took a pull on his cigar.

"You're one hell of a detective, Horowitz," he said. "Best I ever seen in forty years in this racket."

I had that trapped-rat feelin', but I had to play the part. "What the hell's *that* supposed to mean?"

"It's a compliment. Even with pictures and a description in a town this size, we couldn't find you. Anybody who can disappear into a place that's strange to them in every way and wind up workin' for their mark day in and day out and havin' the mark pick up most of the tab is impressive, I got to tell you. I am really impressed. Even when Beta mentioned your resemblance to Brandy to everybody, most of us, me included, just dismissed it."

"Look, Mr. Small, I don't know what all this is about, but—"

"Stow it! It's over. The game's done. Call it my paranoid nature, but it's kept me out of prison for forty years, not countin' a few nights in the pokey here and there. We still weren't sure we were right, but we had an easy way to tell. We sent a guy up and he dusted a few parts of your place for fingerprints. Know what? You got the same prints as our dancer, Brandy. Now ain't that an impossibility?"

"So what's gonna happen now?"

"Well, the original plan was to let you come back home the grieving widow, then switch our Brandy for you, but it proved too hot to do. Then we get word you're comin' in here so it looked like a possibility, but when you got here you had different hair and coloring. We couldn't straighten that hair of hers in a million years. So I said, hey? Why bother? We don't need to switch if we got the real one. Then you take a powder and we can't find you. To be honest, we did think it was you that night in the club, but when you came back and then moved in we just threw the idea out of our mind. And here you are."

"I assume the exits are all covered."

He just smiled and shrugged.

"Well, what now?" I noticed he let me do all that damned work for him downstairs before he nabbed me. At least I wouldn't have gotten no further tryin' to walk or fight my way out.

"Like the old saying goes, one Brandy is a necessity, two are a luxury. We can afford luxury, but we'll take necessity. It's up to you."

Two gunsels I never even seen or heard was now in back of me in the hall. They marched me down it to a small room all the way forward, frontin' on the street, but the lone big window in it had them burglar bars set in. Half the room was filled with a double bed; there was a radiator down at the other end on full and bangin' slightly. Right next to it was an old, seedy-lookin' and stained bare toilet and above it a rusted, stained, and tiny one-faucet sink. The bed had only a yellow blanket and pillow without pillowcase on it, but it had one of them iron headboards and posts at the feet. The only inside light, barely enough, came from a tiny little bare frosted bulb in a wall fixture and from the streetlights outside. Then they took my glasses and I couldn't even see *them*, let alone most of the room.

It was the start of one of them nightmares a lot of women have. They stripped me, then tied my hands to the headboard and my feet out to the two bedposts. I was braced for a rape, maybe a gang rape, but even that wasn't what they had in mind. Fast Eddie dismissed the gunsels and came in the room.

"Comfy?"

"Go to hell!"

"Almost certainly. That knowledge alone makes it so much easier on me in this line of work. Don't worry. Just a little pressure on your right thigh and then you'll have a really wonderful time. Of course, it almost always fails the first time. Some people need a week or two, and a very few just won't be hooked, but your other self in there only took three days so I expect about the same. We'll take care of Debbie and your things, so don't worry. I'll even have your counterpart come in to see to all your needs while you're here. I'm sure you and she have *lots* to talk about."

"Oh, no! Oh, God, no!" I know they warned me, but I never really believed it would happen, not down deep.

I couldn't do nothin', and then I felt somethin' press on my thigh and felt a small burning sensation. It seemed to sink in and grow, then swallow my whole right side, makin' it a little tingly, and then my head exploded.

I cannot describe it. It's impossible to describe and you get tingly just doin' it. The best I can do is ask you to imagine the ten best orgasms you ever had and combine it with the feelin' and high from the most potent drugs ever invented. Somewhere in your brain you got somethin' like a button, and when you enjoy somethin' or feel real good it gets pressed some. Super drugs can press it more than any natural high, but they go maybe a third of the way. This thing pushed it to the floor. Pure pleasure. Absolute.

Beyond measure, beyond description, and sustained for a long time. The noises outside, the room, the light, the bed and straps, they all don't exist no more. You ain't even aware of 'em. You ain't thinkin' at all. It's impossible. You just relax and it's *everything*.

You do come down, of course, but it's real slow and gentle, not like the crash with pure coke or anything like that. There's no crash at all, just a slow ease back to reality. You feel real good. *Real* good. Everything is heightened and pleasant and amusing. Traffic noise, a creaky floorboard, the radiator clang, or the flush of a toilet down the hall are all the music of heaven. You see beautiful patterns in lights and shadows. I wanted to move, 'cause movin' made it all prettier and things rubbin' on my skin felt nice. I couldn't see too good, and it was still dark, but that didn't bother me none, neither.

It was a surprise to find I could move. I wasn't flipped out or nothin', I remembered where I was and what was causin' this—I just didn't care much. But my arms wasn't tied at all, and I had somethin' fixed to my leg. Another chain, like all this started out. Naked and in chains. Just one, though, a leg chain. Somebody was here and did all this while I was havin' a fine time and I never even noticed.

I was still high. Colors seemed to make pretty musical sounds and sounds caused pretty light patterns. I was also real turned on; 'bout as turned on as I could get. I was so wet I was drippin', and my nipples were so aroused it was heaven to rub 'em, yet I could think fairly clearly. That was the crazy part—I could think clearly. All of a sudden I knew just how that girl back at the Center, Donna, felt. It was all done with brain chemicals, they said, so she must be like this all the time.

It wasn't as bad as I thought. In fact, it was like seein' the world and everything in it, including yourself, in whole new ways. It was like I felt when I was on high-class pot, only better, with everything sharper and more beautiful. Like pot, though, you might have some pain or discomfort and even notice it but you just didn't mind. It wasn't allowed.

I got up, then down on all fours and followed the chain. It was very solidly attached to the radiator, it seemed, and the radiator was hot. Up close, I could actually see fuzzy purples and reds comin' off the radiator and flowin' up and over in the room. I made it over to the toilet, then sat down and peed. I also had some gas. I can't describe what that felt like, but it was somehow very, very funny.

It was gettin' to be dawn, and I suddenly felt tired. I made my way back to the bed in the little room and flopped back on the bed and just lay there a while. Then I went, very pleasantly, to sleep. It was a pleasant glow, and while I must've dreamed I don't remember what about.

I woke to the sound of the boomin' jazz from the club below, so I knew it was four o'clock. I opened my eyes and instinctively reached for my glasses, but they weren't there of course. The really great feelin' had gone, and I didn't feel real good at all. My stomach was sour, I had bad gas, and I felt real dizzy. I didn't really hear the lock turn and the door open, but I noticed somethin' and watched as a dark blur come into the room.

"I guess you ain't feelin' none too good right now," I heard Brandy Two's voice say over the music. "I knows how it is first times. It git a whole lot bettah the more you have it."

"I guess they told you who I am," I managed. My voice sounded like a frog's to me.

"Yeah. I knowed d'ere was ones like you befo' dey put me on de juice. You jus' the first I ever seed in person. I dunno. I think we look mo' like sistahs den twins."

She had a much heavier dialect than mine all the time, and clearly a lot less learnin' even though I did a lot on my own in spite of school. Just from that, I guessed she was probably at least a functional illiterate. And they was gonna replace *me* with *her* and get away with it? I didn't know much 'bout them hypnoscans, but I had a real feelin' they was much better at makin' you dumber and ignorant than the other way 'round.

"Dis heah's toast and orange juice," she told me. "Best take somethin' in yo' tummy but go real slow."

"I'm nearly blind without my glasses," I told her. "You'll have to help me."

"Huh. I don't see de best in de bus'ness, but de juice it clear up some of it. It do the same fo' you, most like."

She helped me, and I managed some toast, but I was very

thirsty and drank the orange juice right down. She wouldn't get more, but did keep filling the small plastic cup with water from the tap. I wanted to question her in great detail, find out everything about her, but it was slow going. I was dehydrated and really more than a little ill.

"Yo' body and de juice dey have a big fight," she told me. "Dat's what you feel now. Tomorrow it be a lot betta', and betta' and betta' afta' dat. Soon you neva' feel sick no mo'. De juice, it don't let nothin' bad happen t'ya. No colds, no sniffles, nothin'. No VD, neitha."

"But it makes you a slave to it," I noted.

"Well, yeah, but ya gotta figua, honey. I was hooked on smack so long I don't 'member when I wasn't. Dis is *much* betta'—give you somethin' back for it 'cept a high, and de high it give is the best. Ain't hooked on smack, neither, no mo'. No, no. Even de needle marks dey *gone.*"

And that, of course, was the bottom line for her. She'd been hooked on heroin since she was a teen—probably from that same gang element I came so close to makin' my life—and she was always hustlin' for bucks to feed her habit, always subject to the will of the dealer or pimp. There were a million stories like hers out there; the only difference here was that she was me, another me, who'd made one different choice. She had my brains, such as they were, and all the rest, but she'd wasted them.

Daddy and me we had that fight, and he stalked to his room and me to mine and I packed and was on my way out when I heard him sobbin' in his room. I stopped, turned, and went in . . .

Maybe Daddy didn't cry for her, and so she left for the streets. Or maybe she just didn't hear, or didn't go in. I knew I'd hesitated long and hard before doin' it. Was that it? Was the world, all the worlds, all the lives of all the people in them, like this? A single moment, a single decision in the heat of anger and emotion, a little thing goin' one way and not the other . . . How much good and bad in anybody's life turns on moments like that, without even thinkin' 'bout them? Somebody too busy with their taxes to play with their kid, or lettin' the kid cry 'cause she had to *learn*—or maybe not lettin' the kid cry. Too proud to

make up after a fight with your husband, or goin' back to a
husband even though he keeps beatin' you. All that.

Sure, we both wound up in the same hole in the end, but
think of all the good things and good times I had before
then. She got the same shaft, but she never knew anything
but.

She couldn't stay long, and seemed almost apologetic
about the whole thing, but she took the tray and left the
room and made sure that door was locked. After a while, it
got dark again, but I didn't bother to turn on no lights.
What was the use when I couldn't even clearly see the
bottom of the bed from the top of it? She left the little
plastic cup, and I couldn't believe how thirsty I was. Drink
four or five cupfuls, then pee about fifteen minutes or three
songs later, then drink more.

I checked my chain and nearly burned myself, but it was
real clear that the other end was welded on to that radiator.
Short of a welder's torch or a hacksaw and a lot of time, I
wasn't gonna break it easy. I went over to the window; the
blinkin' lights from the Purple Pussycat signs gave off real
pretty patterns and constantly changed the look inside the
room. I thought the windows themselves were frosted over
from the cold outside and the heat within, but with my eyes
I couldn't be sure. With luck I might break the glass but I'd
never get them bars out—they was sunk in concrete sills.
All I'd do was wind up freezin' my ass off when it already
was uneven in the room and if I caught anybody's attention
at all down there it would probably be the wrong folks. If I
had my glasses and a lockpick I might have been able to
pick the lock on the leg shackle, but probably not.

Later on, Brandy Two came again, this time with what
seemed to be a coldcut sub, a piece of chocolate cake, and
two opened bottles of beer. I found I was real hungry now,
and it went down just fine. I coulda used cigarettes, though,
but she told me they was not allowed. Too much danger in
givin' me a fire. They didn't even give me silverware, and
the beer bottles turned out to be clear plastic and fairly soft.

I could smell her perfumes and tell she was real made up
and all now, and she had on her show outfit, which
wouldn't last on her long, and her heels. The early show.

"Cain't talk now but I be back lata on," she promised. I listened to the show as I chugged the bottle.

It was late when she came back, but we talked for a little bit. Not about us, though; I don't think either of us was ready for that yet. They had to blame somebody for the breach so they blamed Deb; she was bein' shipped someplace out of state. Word was she'd be lucky if they didn't kill her just to make an example out of her.

She was probably too well known locally for that, I tried to tell myself, feelin' guilty about it. If she turned up dead there might be eyes turned this way that couldn't be bought so easily.

I was also right about Brandy Two. She—we—didn't exist in this world. She'd been in a string in a Camden that sounded frighteningly close to my old world when some mob men had come for her. They drugged her and she woke up a prisoner in an awful place that sounded a lot like Vogel's estate. There they both hooked and conditioned her, but then she was brought down here and kept for a long while at the country estate in what I thought of as central Pennsylvania. They didn't hypnoscan and made no attempt to brief her or rehearse her to be me, which was another thing that didn't make sense. Then she was brought down here and with her larger size and distinctive looks she was rehearsed and worked into the show act. It wasn't a whole lot more information than I had before.

Then, late in the evening, she gave me the second shot. If anything, it was better than before and seemed longer and it also seemed slower coming down. The dizziness was worse and I had diarrhea bad, but that was all.

From Brandy Two I also learned about the life of a shadow dancer. She had not heard the term but liked it. You always felt a little high and a little turned on and mostly great, but during the coming down period you was *suggestible,* at least that's how I see it. A new shot of juice in under twenty to twenty-four hours had no real effect. It was like injecting distilled water. Withdrawal, for Brandy Two, started at thirty hours and got worse and worse. By forty hours she would be in hell. That's how they "conditioned" you. They let you go into withdrawal, then told you what you had to do and gave it to you. When you woke up in that mellow, suggestible time they reminded you of what was expected. They didn't need to do this too much, 'cause while the juice wasn't smart or nothin' it kinda pushed you to do whatever it took to keep gettin' a new supply as needed. No matter how crazy or against your nature it was, it became just like normal to you in no time.

I thought 'bout Donna bein' forced to go through that barracks, day after day. Them patterns was damned hard to break.

After the third day they didn't give me a regular shot. They waited to see if withdrawal would come on. On the fourth day, it did. In its early stages it was almost as bad as heroin withdrawal; you got real sick, bad sick—upchuckin', the runs, hot and cold spells, everything at once. I was hooked and I knew it.

Fast Eddie Small was blunt about it. "Until they decide when or if they're gonna use you and for what you're stuck here," he told me. "Until your hair grows out enough to get styled decent, you'll have to wear a wig. Wear it any time, all the time, you ain't in these rooms. Brandy'll get you all the right jewelry, cosmetics, perfumes, powders, and like that. Use what she don't. You *never* leave here without 'em on and on right. You want to work into the act, fine. You don't, then you go down after wearin' nothin' more than the girls do at the end—and nothin' less—and you get customers. Two a night minimum, twenty-five minimum a trick. If you don't have enough in the club, then you go out and get 'em. They pay the barmaid, satisfaction guaranteed, get it?"

"Yeah, I get it," I replied, wishin' I could rip his guts out. "You mean I got to work the streets in nothin' but shoes with it twenty degrees out there?"

"Naw, I got heart. A big heart." One of the girls—Lambda, I think, the blonde—went when he snapped his fingers and brought back absolutely the most *gorgeous, sumptuous* fur coat I ever seen. It was gray, but otherwise close to the coats the girls were wearin' when I made my fatal bump into them. It was silver fox, mink lined, and it had a belt around its middle and two deep pockets inside. "You wear this and you take care of it. If it needs repairs or cleanin' you tell the barmaid. Now, you get this straight. You want more of a wardrobe, you *earn* it by goin' over your quota. You don't handle money, *never.* You want somethin', you come see me or one of my people and you convince us you're worth it. One way is to follow all our rules. You all got the same rules. You follow them and you'll learn fast enough. You break the rules, any of 'em, or you see one of the other girls breakin' the rules, and you get real hell."

He was really enjoyin' this. It was a real turn-on for him. I hated his stinkin' guts. The only thing worse than big Hitlers was little Hitlers.

I was unchained, unlocked, and left on my own. I didn't know if there was any guards around, but I never saw none. He didn't need 'em. Brandy took me under her wing, though. "Can't call you no Brandy, too. Both of us'll go nuts," she noted.

"That's okay, just call me Beth. I kinda feel like I come full circle on this case now anyways." And that's the way we agreed it would be.

In a way, it was worse, 'cause now I was the property of *two* masters, one allegedly human, the other inside me. I found out what that was like real quick. First, my sniffles, which I'd had since God knew when, just went away, as did all of my old sinus problems, but that was only the tip of it. You sure followed a routine, like it or not.

When you was supposed to eat, you got hungry—and I mean *hungry.* It became an overpowering urge, the only thing you could think of till you ate, but it was a little specific. You got more irresistible and otherwise repulsive cravin's than a pregnant woman. Pumpkin washed down with pickle juice. Raw hamburger with chocolate sauce. Steamed fish à la mode. Now, it wasn't always that way, but it often was, particularly the first few weeks. The other girls swore to me that it stopped after a while and only popped up after that occasionally, but until then I could tell one of the bar staff what I wanted and they'd hold their nose and go get it. I had to fix it myself, though, in a neat but antique kitchen they had. And when you wasn't hungry, you couldn't even look at anything at all.

The upstairs of the club went over into the row house next door, I found. Even after workin' there I hadn't knowed that before. They was kinda like dorm rooms, but each one had a double bed, small closet, a switched speaker that would bring the bar music in with volume control, and some fancy lights. There was two bathrooms with both tub and shower on each floor, one at each end. The sheets were pink, purple, or crimson satin with down comforters. We was all responsible for keepin' our rooms absolutely clean and neat and perfect, and either Eddie or one of his boys could pop in at any time to inspect them like some Army sergeant. All of us was responsible for keepin' up the inside of the house, includin' scrubbin' halls and common areas, vacuumin' with real antique-style cleaners, kitchen, bathrooms, and the rest.

On the top floor was a room that was somethin' of a gym, with weights, exercise machines, and all the rest. *That* was 'cause this *thing* inside us wanted a perfect house to live in, which was us, so just like the meals you got these—well, not urges, really, more like *compulsions.* To run, to lift weights, exercise every part of your body you could every day. It wasn't easy at the start, but when you did what this thing wanted you got little pleasure jolts; when you didn't, you got misery. You did it.

Likewise, I no longer wanted cigarettes. Couldn't stand to have one in my mouth, though it didn't bother me none to be in a smoke-filled bar. You could drink, but the more you drank the more you went to the bathroom and you never got drunk or even tipsy.

And when it decided you was to have sex, you got so tense and worked up that nothin' else mattered. You *had* to have it. Male, female, horse—I don't think it mattered none. Only the knowledge that you had to turn two tricks to get the juice kept your mind in the act.

Of course, I was still a naughty and disobedient girl at the start with anything this shit inside didn't force me to do, like Fast Eddie's rules, but they took me down a few pegs in a hurry. They let you go real deep into withdrawal, just to the edge of where it might really start causin' brain or nervous system damage, then they'd stand there and keep insistin' that you repeat all the rules and swear to obey 'em. There was no way you couldn't. The sickness was bad enough and got worse and worse and you knew it could never get no better but that you could be all well and feelin' great in just a minute or so if you swore on your mother's grave to obey, and then that thing would start pushin' the pain button in your head slowly down, more and more, till you couldn't stand it no more.

You didn't get that far but once.

They reinforced it when you came out of the pure pleasure high and loved the world by havin' somebody there whisperin' all the rules and havin' you repeat 'em and swear to act just that way. One day you just wake up, and doin' everything *their* way is the most normal and natural thing in the whole world. You know it's not the way you used to do it or think about it and not the way other folks do, but it's the norm for you and you do it automatically. It wasn't like no hypnosis or conditionin'; they could change the rules any old time and that would be the new normal thing.

Turnin' two tricks in Atlantic City deep in winter wasn't always possible no matter what the decrees. There was snowstorms and power outages and bad rain and ice storms, and not many people. Christmas through New Year's was great, though, with lots of parties and winter getaway specials and the like, although it was real depressin' for us to see the Christmas lights and displays and people shoppin' and feel isolated, alone, and left out.

By "us" I mean Brandy two and me. The other girls, they didn't seem none too touched by Christmas or much else. They didn't seem to remember no past at all, no growin' up, nothin' but bein' what they were. Even with the never-ending compulsions there was time, and thinkin' was still there, and memory, too, good as old. My eyesight gradually improved to where I could see pretty good from a distance and close up was blurry. It was much better for gettin' around, but it was hell to read anything like a book. To Brandy, the idea that anybody'd read books for fun was near impossible for her to her in her head. As I suspected, her own readin' was on the Dick and Jane level.

After New Year's they moved us up to New York, which was a surprise, to a club in the Manhattan entertainment district where almost anything went so long as you gave the customer value for his money and didn't roll or stiff him. The district's boundaries were pretty clear but unwritten;

the law and the adult entertainment district kept their ends up. Outside the district, *wham*! Inside—well, just keep it there. Of course, it wasn't immune from things like robbery, murder, rollin', and hard drug sellin', but the fact was it was pretty well self-policed and while there was drugs aplenty there was no big scorin' to be done there. You did that uptown in Harlem or over in The Bronx.

By the end of January, I'd undergone some radical changes that at the time I was only partly aware of. My body was lean and muscular, the best it probably could ever be. I could run for miles and hardly work up a sweat. If I flexed all my muscles, I looked like one of them female bodybuilders, and I think I could bench press more than Sam ever could. They paired Brandy Two and me in a duo strip and sex act as The Double Brandys, of course, and slowly my skin was goin' back to its normal tone, which was her tone, and my hair was gettin' all woolly and curly as it used to be. Whatever tricks the Center had pulled was bein' undone. By spring, we figured a trim for her and we would be so identical that even we couldn't tell each other apart. Only our dialects and our relative educations told any difference. We even had the exact tastes in perfumes, lipsticks, and cosmetics of all kinds, even toothpastes.

Mentally, it was strange. On the one hand, you lived for that glorious hour of the juice, and you spent part of the time tryin' to recapture it, push it just a little. You did that by followin' your impulses, which was guided by the juice itself. The normal physical things that brought intense pleasure, like orgasms, produced much more intense feelin's of pleasure, so you went for 'em.

Kinky was normal. We'd take walks in the afternoon wearin' only the shoes and coats and think nothin' of it, and not be cold, and we'd window shop or even go into stores and look over fashions and mentally dress each other, sometimes try on things. I didn't feel no sense of right and wrong when it came to me. We didn't steal stuff we liked only 'cause we understood that gettin' caught and goin' to jail was a death sentence with no juice. No guilt, no shame. When we saw somethin' we wanted, we had to beg and plead like little kids and hope they'd buy it for us, and we didn't care. If you wanted to do it and it wouldn't cause

punishment or death, you did it. When I was workin'
freelance on the street I always felt guilty 'cause of Sam.
Now I had no guilt, no shame, no conscience, no pride,
neither.

And that was the other crazy thing, 'cause I thought about
Sam a lot. Not just Sam, but *especially* Sam. I still loved
him, wanted him, and cared for him. I still remembered it
all.

And I still wanted to solve this damned puzzle if I could.
That was part of me, part of my nature, as much a pleasure
giver as the rest and also in my best interests. I don't know
if they thought of that or not, or if they cared. Whether or
not I could bring myself to deliver that solution wrapped
and sealed to Aldrath or Bill Markham even if I got the
chance I didn't know—I really did love the juice most of
all. Deep down, I didn't know if there was any way I could
consciously and deliberately cut it off on my own. Bill was
kiddin' himself with his thirty doses; you didn't *want* to get
to the Center even if they gave you a complete cure, 'cause
you could never feel that intense pleasure again. That's
what hung up Donna and some of the others in the end.
Even if physically cured, they couldn't forget the yen for
that feelin' and recapturin' even a slice of it meant everything to them.

Fact was, I wanted to solve it all not to bring nobody to
justice or stop no plot but 'cause these folks had pulled out
before and left those on the juice to die in agony. What they
done to others they could do to me, anytime, anyplace. The
only fear I had was fear of not gettin' the juice.

I wanted to be this way forever.

8.

Unravelling Threads

Brandy Two was as fascinated by me as I was by her. The idea that I'd taken over the agency, educated myself, and married a white guy she found both incredible and unbelievable, but Fast Eddie's respect for the old me was more than enough testimony. The problem was, she'd gone wrong even earlier than me. Mama died even younger in her world, and Daddy stuck her—as he almost did me—with a couple of cousins who didn't give a damn. She'd been into drugs early, maybe in grammar school, and she was even wilder as a teen than I had been. She'd been caught stealin' when she was only fourteen, and when Daddy threw a fit she'd run away all the way to Washington—which existed in her world as in mine—and had run the streets. By sixteen she had a habit and was in the string of one of them pimps with the fancy coats and Superfly image. Daddy had tried to find her, of course, but considerin' how hard it is to find runaway kids who want to be found, it's pure luck if you find one that don't.

She was a whore 'cause she'd been one all her adult life and didn't know how to be, or imagine she could be, nothin' else. It all went into the body, the looks, the moves. She had always been dependent for everything, and the mind was the one thing in her kinda life that it was better off not payin' much attention to. She didn't read and had no knowledge of or interest in the world. The fact that I'd come from the same start and I'd made somethin' of myself gave her somethin' of a feelin' of worth by association, but it was too late for her to change, she thought, and what was the use anyway? We was both stuck in the same groove. In a real way, she was less my twin than my shadow; she looked like me, but there was nothin' left down there.

169

The problem was, as time rolled on, I was becomin' more and more like her. On the road, we was even further removed from Small and Siegel and all that lay behind 'em. We slept, ate, exercised, had as much sex as we could with anybody, worked out new routines for the act, and for fun went to stores and tried on all sorts of clothes to make us look even sexier, experimented with new cosmetics and perfumes, and spent a long time in mirrors gettin' it right. The future was the next jolt of juice.

The only thing that tempted me durin' that time was tryin' to go thirty hours between juice jolts. They generally gave us a week's supply at a time, since you couldn't overdose on it and even with a week you wasn't goin' nowheres. I figured at the end of a week I'd have an extra, and then maybe I'd go over to Lindy Crockett's place some afternoon, hold her down, and give her a taste of the stuff. I never did, though. It's the curse of an addiction that you never give it away or delay gettin' it when you got it and it's due.

We went back down to Atlantic City at the beginnin' of May to get ready for the high season at the club there, and for the first time I was back in the same town as Small and Siegel. By now it was clear that I was stuck and that I couldn't do or learn much more than I did unless things was taken out of my hands and moved from a different source. My big worry was that Aldrath would get itchy after all them faked reports from me and nothin' really happenin' and decide to come snatch me. I didn't want to be snatched or cured, no matter what the price. What I wanted was a way to be independent of the beck and call of the bastards who doled it out.

I mean, name me a girl over thirty, or a guy, either, who suddenly had the body of their dreams and found keepin' it that way a pleasure? Who couldn't get sick if they stood all day in the wind and rain. Who had been an old thirty-two and now looked a young twenty-five. Add to that an absence of hangups, of any guilt, second thoughts, regrets for anything you done from that point on, and a high, charged-up energy level that kept you always active, always feelin' good, never feelin' bored or down in the dumps, and just a little bit playfully high all the time. The only real problem was the man who doled out the juice. You had to dance to whatever tune he played or it all came crashin' in, and you was never secure he just wouldn't end it someday.

"Get all your things packed up," Fast Eddie told us. "You're goin' for a little ride."

I was shocked and surprised, but you don't ask no questions in Fast Eddie's string. Pack up for what? And where? Another club, another city? It was just gettin' real nice and warm in Atlantic City and the crowds was startin' to pick up, at least on the weekends. I put on my metallic blue dress that was real short and super-revealin', as was almost all my stuff, with matchin' shoes and made myself up to go. Then I packed the rest in this big steamer trunk, all I had in this world, closed it, and took it downstairs. It was awkward goin', but even though the trunk musta weighed a hundred pounds or more packed, I had no trouble movin' and partly carryin' it. I was damned strong and proud of it.

I was relieved to see that my twin also had her marchin' orders. I no longer was surprised that we'd independently picked the same clothes and even jewelry and makeup. On the basic conversation level we didn't even have to talk much; each of us kinda knew what the other was thinkin'. Not mind readin'—just the same tastes and likes and thought patterns. I looked at her and she shrugged and I knew she didn't have no more warning nor inklin' of what was goin' on than I did.

Fast Eddie rarely paid direct, individual attention to nobody, but he was there now. A huge black car pulled up just outside, and the driver got out, opened the trunk, then waited.

"Okay, girls, there's your ride," Small told us. "Sorry to lose you but the Boss wanted some fresh faces."

The Boss—Siegel? I wasn't too sure I liked this, but he was the man from whom all juice flowed, so there wasn't no way out. We got our trunks barely in the "boot" of the big car, then got in the backseat. The driver and one of Small's henchmen got in the front, and off we went, south and out of town. I figured we had to be headin' for Siegel's place on the ocean, and I was right.

It was real isolated, like I said, with a big gate and high fence around the whole forty acres that kept any spyin' down. The fences was masked on the ground side by a twelve-foot-high hedge wall, then went right down into the beach and about to the low tide point, gettin' a little lower as they went. Way out in the water was a squared-off stone breakwater that kept things mostly calm inside the house and discouraged spyin' from the sea. At the end was a pier and slip at which was a big and fancy-lookin' wooden yacht as well as a couple of smaller boats. The yacht was moored in line with the beach, so it kinda blocked a straight view in. You could spy on Arnie Siegel's place from the sea, but you had to be pretty damned obvious about it. The grounds was green and landscaped, with lotsa trees and bushes and low hedges. A staff spent a lot of time in the spring and summer and fall keepin' it that way.

The house itself was enormous; part brick, part wood, maybe three stories tall and a city block around and all covered with ivy. Back before all this, when I was checkin' Siegel out, I learned that the house was the former official summer residence of the Governor General of America, the guy who represented the King in this country. This was supposed to be some place, and you could bet with bein' able to tap into some of the Company's technology it was near impossible for anybody in this world to get into or out of or learn much. There weren't no soldiers or nothin' like that, but I couldn't shake the funniest feelin' that I was goin' back to Vogel's castle.

"You goils ain't here to gawk, you're here to woik," snapped Marty, the Fast Eddie man who'd come with us. He had a real New Yauk accent. He wasn't, however, no man with the juice.

"Work at what?" I asked him. "Looks like he got 'nuff folks here to run this place."

Marty gave this sneering smile, like he got when he was pickin' wings off flies. "You'll see."

A young man in casual dress came out of the side entrance—we was goin' in the servant's entrance, of course —and he was one of the most gorgeous hunks you ever could see. One of them super musclemen, well over six feet, blond, blue-eyed. I never saw no man looked that good who wasn't gay.

"You two follow me," he ordered in this boomin' voice that still had a trace of gentle lisp in it. *I knew it,* I thought. We went in and down a narrow flight of stairs, then walked down this hall past storerooms and stuff to near the end, then entered one room that had no windows. It was almost surely built as another storeroom, but it had been made over. The walls was paneled, the floor was smooth polished wood so glossy you could see your reflection in it, and there was half a wall of free-standin' closets and dressers and a vanity with mirror as well as a full-length mirror which proved to be a slidin' door leadin' to a tiled bathroom with toilet, sink, and a shower big enough for two, but no tub. The main room had two chairs, one at the vanity, the other in a corner, and a queen-sized bed. But the thing you noticed most was the ceilin', which was low and completely covered with mirror squares. The light came from floor and table lamps, all of which seemed to have soft pink-colored bulbs in them. It was some kinda room, 'cept it woulda been nice with some windows and if it still didn't have a damp cellar kinda feel and smell to it.

"I am Alan Nordstrom, the manager of Mr. Siegel's estate," he told us. "Mr. Siegel is a rich and powerful man, and the only one who can give you what you need. He gives it to me and I give it to you, so you obey either one of us. Got that?"

"Yes, sir," we both responded in unison.

"Now, men like Mr. Siegel aren't like ordinary men. He has everything he needs and he can buy anything he wants, so he tends to get turned on by the few things nobody else can have. There's precious art all over—you don't touch it. There's original sculpture all over. You don't touch that, either. That's all you two are to him—part of his collection, for his personal use and enjoyment. When he's here and wants you, you're his, to do whatever he commands and take whatever he gives. Other times you're subject to every other person in this house from me down to the gardener. If they order you or I order you to do something, you do it. Anybody wants your body, that's fine, too. There's a speaker over there in the vanity so you can be called any time of the day or night. You get called, you come running.

"Anything you want to do, you ask permission. You go back down that hall, up those stairs, and see whoever's in the first room on the right. That's the security manager, and there's always somebody on. You use this bathroom and only this bathroom. You never use the pool or enter the main house unless ordered. The grounds and the ocean are okay if you're free and ask permission and get it, but the water's still pretty cold right now. You always smile and you always say 'sir' or 'ma'am' and 'please' and 'thank you' to any white folks. And unless you're ordered to do otherwise, while you're here, inside and out, you'll wear nothing. Nothing at all, except panties when you do your monthly bleeding. You pick up your meals from the kitchen after everybody else eats, and you take it out and bring it down here, then clean up the mess and bring it back. Now— *strip!*"

"Why, dat's slavery—sir," Brandy Two said softly.

"No it's not. Anytime either of you don't like it here, you are free to leave. If you complain, or smart-mouth anybody, or we don't like the way you do things, we might even toss you out. You see, Mr. Siegel likes practical pets, but he's allergic to dogs."

We stripped, but if looks coulda killed we'd'a burned this bastard to a crisp. Slaves, pets—his own damned brand of Vogel's Nazism. And this guy with a name like Arnold Siegel!

But, of course, Arnie Siegel had never heard of no Adolf Hitler or death camps. They didn't have that in this world's history. The last big bad guy was Napoleon. Ten to one he heard from somebody from the competition about Vogel's thing and never even knowed the history behind it, and how he'd have been gassed no matter how much money and power he had. No race or ethnic group was immune. Catholics stepped on Jews for centuries. Moslems step on Jews, Jews blow up Moslems in my world. Some free blacks in the old south owned slaves, and Liberia was made by freed American blacks enslavin' the Africans.

This was a radical change for us from anything we'd had up to now, and they meant every word of it and also understood just what kinda hold the juice had on us. They reinforced it by bringin' on withdrawal and makin' their demands until we crawled and begged and would do or say anything, and then they used that mellow time after the high to tell us just how to act and how to behave. And, like before, one day you wake up and it's the way things are. You still don't hav'ta like it and you don't hav'ta enjoy it, but you obey all the rules instinctively and you don't even *think* of disobeying. This was all the shit they learned in Vogel's world refined.

The one odd thing was that they wanted us both called Brandy, nothin' else, and they wanted us always together. Sleep together, eat together, run, work, play together, even be a duo when gettin' fucked. It was like they was tryin' to make us identical, at the lowest level. I had a hunch the honeymoon was over and they was preparin' us for somethin', though right then it didn't seem like much.

Fact was, we wasn't treated too bad. The cooks always made up what we wanted, the rooms got cleaned, and there was always some members of some gang or another in the house who wanted to do it with twins. Nordstrom was more of a Tinkerbell than even I had thought, and he pretty well hated and looked down on women in general, but because of that he didn't like us around him much. He was a real turkey when he *did* use us for somethin', but that wasn't very often.

Arnie Siegel, on the other hand, was an icy cool charmer. You got the idea that the guy could be sittin' there sippin' sherry and in gentle good humor reminisce with a chuckle about the time he murdered his parents inch by inch with a knife. I doubt if he did that, but he sure was the type. The fact that he was good-lookin', even handsome, almost a movie star type of look, only made it worse. He liked to cuddle sometimes in his big den with the leather furniture, fireplace, hunting trophies and bear rug, and sometimes he'd just be readin' or doin' somethin' on the couch and want us perched on the rug. He was weird. When it got hot, he threw some parties invitin' all sorts of bigwigs—not just crime figures, but politicians, show business types, even cops. When he did, we was allowed to dress real pretty and slinky and sometimes entertain the guests with a dance or strip act, and entertain a lot of important folks in the mirrored bedroom as well. That we liked a lot.

If he had all this and was only number two, you had to wonder what Big Georgie Wycliffe must be like.

Then, one evenin', we was summoned up to the den by the master of the house himself, only this time he wasn't alone. There was a woman with him, one who looked slightly familiar but who I was sure I never had seen before. She was fairly small and if she was well built she took pains to dress to conceal it. She wore a stock professional woman's suit and blouse, blue with faint stripes, and even though she didn't even seem to have lipstick on, let alone eye shadow, I couldn't get it outta my head that she was made-up like mad. She was almost as dark as me but it was more like a temporary suntan than the tan I got, wore thick glasses, and had black hair tied up in a bun. She might have been a top secretary or somethin', but she had real long and perfectly shaped fingernails. Ever try typin' with long nails? Matter of fact, they looked more like the kinda nails we had, and her hands was smooth as a baby's.

They stood there, Arnie and Ms. Cool, and he put us through our paces, makin' us do all sorts of idiotic stuff, even do the two bitches in heat number. We felt like pet dogs doin' tricks. Finally we got up and stood there while she asked us questions.

"Do you mind being here, living like this?" The voice was high and, while cold, reminded me of somethin'.

"No, ma'am," we both responded, which was a lie. We'd be over that damned wall in a minute if we didn't need our juice.

She asked a bunch more innocuous and dumb questions, but she come over to us and started runnin' her nails over my skin and then my twin's, then actually pinchin' our fannies and feelin' us up. It was gross and unusual, particularly since you could see it was out of character for her and she wasn't in the least turned on by it like we was. Still, I got a slight whiff of her perfume and it wasn't no perfume you could get here, but I'd smelled it before. At headquarters. It was real popular among the women there.

"Amazing," she said to Siegel. "I can't tell them apart, even from the reactions. Which of you is Horowitz?"

"I am," we both said at once. I started a bit and gave a puzzled glance at my twin. What the hell was she tryin' to pull, anyways? Did she flip out from bein' with me all that time and sorta take on my background 'cause it was so much better than hers, or what? Damn it, I knew who I was.

And then she had us turn back to back and started askin' rapid-fire questions 'bout my personal life, 'bout Sam, 'bout the Company, lots of stuff, to each of us in turn. The scary thing was, Brandy Two was givin' the same right answers as me, includin' the kind of personal stuff I knew I never told nobody, not even her. Worse, she was answerin' in my tone and my grammar and my vocabulary!

"Amazing," said the cold woman. "Even *they* can't tell anymore!"

"Well, there's one way," Siegel said, reachin' down and gettin' some cards from behind the couch. They had big letters on them, like eye charts. Big enough for even us to read with no glasses.

They showed one card to my twin, and she read, "'Universities are institutions of higher learnin', divided into specialized colleges . . .'"

"Enough!" said the woman, and Siegel came over and held the other side of the card up for me to read.

And I tried. I saw the words clear, but I just couldn't put 'em together right. "'De opp—opra—was de cree—cree—cretin' of de—fam—fam'ly?—team—of . . .'" I couldn't. I could see the words but I couldn't make sense of 'em. He took the card away and put it in front of the other Brandy.

"'The operetta was the creation of the famous team of Gilbert and Sullivan,'" she read flawlessly, and I felt like I could cry.

"It's all right, dear, go back to your quarters," the woman told me. "You, Horowitz, stay here." And *I* was the one dismissed! I damn near ran down to the room, tears flowin', and fell on the bed. Memories crept in, other memories. Memories of bein' on the street as a kid; memories of shootin' up on smack, of workin' the Washington streets. Memories of bein' carried off here, of workin' the club, of seein' *myself* in that room and givin' her the juice and bringin' shit . . . My dialect, my vocabulary, my grammar seemed to crumble even in my thoughts.

My God! It ain't possible! I ain't her! I ain't no whore who make all de wrong moves! Dey be messin' wit' yo' brain, girl! Yeah, that was it. That *had* to be it! *Dey took me—her—to Vogel's place befo' dey bring her here. Why? Dat hypno-thing. Den dey pair us up and dis hypno-thing gits sprung.* But that didn't make no sense, neither. Sure, they might have done all this just to make her a perfect imitation, but if so, they had to mess with my mind, too. Not with the juice; it didn't work that way. Did they have one here? Did they make me forget? *I is Brandy Hor'witz, damn them! I am!*

But was I? No matter how much I went over it and explained it, I couldn't really accept it one way or the other. *I didn't know!* Not for real, not for sure. I tried to get a mental picture of Sam, to hold on to him, to think about all the real small, intimate moments, but he kept slippin' away. Then one of Nordstrom's flunkies come in and give me the juice, and all my troubles and doubts slipped away.

And when I started to come down, but was still in that mellow state, Siegel came in. "Well, Brandy Parker, the games are all over now. We were never sure if we could totally condition or trust Brandy Horowitz, since she had a real strong will and a devious mind, so we had to develop you anyway as a possible replacement. But she came along just fine, so you can go back to being just plain Brandy Parker again. Just put everything about her out of your mind and don't fight it. Go back to being yourself. Don't think about it anymore. Don't fight it. It's too late for you to get her brains and background. You're a whore, you'll always be a whore, and that's the best you can be. Now that we've turned her as we planned, she's no longer your concern."

I smiled at him. You always love everybody when you're comin' down. And when I was all the way down, some of it stuck. No, I didn't believe him—in fact, when you started thinkin' 'bout that cold killer type you had to be suspicious that he bothered to come down in person anyways, let alone explain anything—but I didn't *disbelieve* him, neither. If I was really her, and treated at Vogel's, I would be just this way now. I didn't want to believe it, but I was pretty sure that thing brung your mind down. It might make me unable to read or edit my words, but it couldn't instantly teach somebody *to* read all them big words. It didn't make no sense if they was gonna break, turn, and use the original to then get the two of us to believe we was each other and then send the copy, leavin' the original a copy of *her.* I didn't want to believe it, but no matter how I thought about it it only made sense if she really was Brandy Horowitz and me Brandy Parker.

Worst part was, it didn't make no difference. I might as *well* be Parker, since *she* was off doin' their business and I was stuck here forever like before. I was a lost ball, a shadow dancer, out of the game unless somethin' happened to her before they was done. Just as well. I may be only a whore but I wouldn't have no blood on my hands.

They shipped me back to Atlantic City and put me back in real slinky and sexy clothes, not to work the club but to work the streets. There was hordes of vacationers all over the place and even conventions. I still had both sets of memories in my head but the way I was workin' and the life I was leadin' and the end of all hope brought Brandy Parker supreme. All my thoughts beyond the juice was in turnin' tricks, lotsa tricks, and I did. I didn't get or want a dime of all that money, but it was the only value I had. The more men who would pay for me, and pay top prices for me, the more important I felt. Didn't need no brains. Didn't need no egghead shit. Dat other girl, *she* got dose, and where it git her?

By the end of the season, I no longer thought much about it or had any doubts. Way back in my mind I still cared, still envied her and thought they'd pulled a dirty trick on me, but that was it. Fast Eddie was real happy. "Girl, you're a terror," he said and chuckled. "I ain't never seen no whore pull in over a thousand a week before. Now that things are winding down here, everybody, including the Boss, thinks you should get a step up. You're our special from now on. No more cleaning up or shitwork for you. You're gonna be for the *best* customers."

And I was real thrilled and proud to hear that. I would get diamonds and gold jewelry now, real pretty stuff, and slinky dresses tailored for me, and a suite with two other girls at fancy hotels, and the customers would come to me. Otherwise, I could do what I pleased and enjoy the places. It was the top of the profession.

But Siegel wanted me before I went off on all this. He was entertainin' some very important folks at Mr. Wycliffe's lodge in the mountains, and he wanted me there. It was still fairly warm; I just took a bag with some of my best clothes and had a real excitin' time gettin' there. They flew me up on a private airplane, a little one-engine job that was kinda like a Piper Cub and rough over the mountains, but it was all real pretty. We came down at a private airstrip on the property, and I was real impressed.

Marty was there to meet me, and this time *he* carried the luggage, what there was of it. "Well, goil, you really come up in de woild since dat last time," he said in his Brooklynese.

"I'm de bestest whore dat eva' was," I told him, walkin' real sexy. Then I gave him a move. "Want some choc'late fudge? I even fuck you dese days, my man."

"Eh. Don't tempt me. I got a wife and two kids who think I do now."

The house was a fancy all-wood huntin' lodge, almost like a resort only it was just two stories and had a big deck. There was a glassed-in patio and pool as well. I didn't ask who I was supposed to service, or why; I didn't really care.

It was real nice inside; big fireplace, overstuffed chairs around it, bear rugs and more trophies—but it looked more right here than in Siegel's estate. There was a very small staff on, but they was gettin' ready for some big arrivals, that was for sure, and there was two or three hood types around checkin' it all out. Maybe it was Big Georgie! Wouldn't that be somethin'! Big George's mistress. Top o' de *world*, girl!

Since there wasn't much goin' on, I got the urge to exercise. Normally I had this clingy gym shirt and shorts and shoes for it, but I realized I forgot to pack 'em. Well, the hell with it. I'd give 'em all a thrill. It was my body got me this far; I wasn't the least bit ashamed of showin' it, and barefoot over grass sounded like real fun. This black girl would be turnin' on some white boys, that was for sure.

It was right near sundown, and there was a mist around. It got cool fast in the mountains, but it was plenty warm enough for me. I started out, gettin' all sorts of stares, and began my run. I never knew how far I ran most days, 'cept that it was several miles when I had the time. I just ran as long as the juice made me feel good and stopped when it stopped.

I went till I hit a boundary, which was a real mean barbed-wire fence, then started 'round it, past the airstrip, past the guards with guns and dogs at several places, and all the way around the huge property, up hill and down, in and out of the trees. There was this fair-sized cleared area right in back of the lodge with a little fence around it and a kinda tent roof over it, but with no sides. As I came near, I saw somethin' happen there.

A blue-white line, then another line out of it, then finally the outline of a cube, then another, then another. The Labyrinth! *This* was the Labyrinth! Hell, I could jump that itty bitty fence in nothin' flat and be inside the thing before nobody even noticed. Not that I would. This was proof positive of that. Where could I go? No juice in there, at least none I could find with a steady supply, and for what? I ran on past, up the front steps to the deck, and stopped. It was a great run and I felt great for doin' it. Off in the distance, I heard the motor of another plane comin' in, and I ran to the side and watched the runway lights come on and the little thing land. I turned and saw Marty there, leerin' at me. I couldn't resist it. I went over and put my arms around him.

"Hey! Stop it! Cut it out!" I laughed and teased him and twitched him in his crotch, but finally backed off. "Jeez! I sure as hell like *you* better den dat udder one dey sent through dis mornin'!"

I stopped, mildly interested. "'Nother what?"

"Another you. De other one, only you sure couldn't tell it. Real cool; professional, if you know what I mean. Even packin' a rod in that purse of hers."

I suddenly *was* interested. "A gun? She had a gun?"

"Yep. And walked through dat t'ing out back cool as a cucumber."

What had they been doin' with her all these months? *Jesus!* They was sendin' her off to kill somebody! *Dat's what dis is all 'bout!* But who? Nobody back in the world of them golden folks. Couldn't get no gun in. I searched through her old memories, findin' it uncomfortable, but this had me curious. Got to be goin' back to her home. To do what? To kill that Markham fella, most like. He'd be in de way. Or, maybe not. Could she be far 'nuff gone to kill Sam? Suppose her Sam had woke up and come home, much to somebody's upset. Not near so many Sams in dem worlds as Brandys, and he be harder to switch. But she wouldn't ice him, would she? She love him like crazy. Even wit' all dis brain shit, no way she could do it. Could de juice make her pull dat trigger? Maybe on Markham, but on Sam?

I was shaken by the idea, but there was nothin' *I* could do about it 'cept hope they caught her before she did it.

"You okay?" Marty asked. "You're lookin' a little sick."

"No, it ain't nothin'. Jes' my period comin' on or somethin'." I went inside and up to my room and tried to get the picture out of my mind.

The new plane carried Arnie Siegel. He came in, said hello to the staff and the boys, and went up to his own room to shower and change. I did the same, then put on my best face and jewelry and the slinky metallic blue dress that looked painted on, left nothin' to the imagination, and was slit all the way up in case it did anyways. I did it up right. Fingernails, toenails, his favorite perfume, you name it. I needed to think 'bout somethin' else for a while. By the time I had checked the nylons and garters and slipped on the shoes, Arnie had been done for some time and was back in his office all the way down the hall. His door was open and I could see part of his desk, so I kinda eased down, real hesitant. I didn't want him in no bad mood with me, not now.

He heard me, leaned over, saw me, and said, real friendly-like, "Oh, it's you, Brandy. Come on in if you like."

So I waltzed in, then stopped dead. In front of Arnie on the desk was a briefcase that musta contained hundreds of doses of the juice at the very least.

He saw my look, and smiled, real amused. "Yeah. Impressive, isn't it? Just out of curiosity, what would you do if I gave this case to you? Just a pretend question, you understand."

I thought about it. What *would* I do? My answer was the point of his question. "Nothin', Mr. Siegel. Jes' stash it and keep on goin'."

Even if I had an unlimited supply with no strings, it wouldn't matter. I just had no place to go that was better than what I had now, 'specially after bein' down so far. That other one, *she* might just use it right, but a whore was a whore in every world and it didn't get no better than I had it right here. "I ain't got nobody and noplace *to* go," I told him.

He grinned and closed the case. "And that's why you're here and why you're my number-one girl now. I can't trust many people, you know, but I can trust you. You're somebody I just never have to worry about."

I felt a real glow of pride at that.

"Originally, we kept you around just because we had to have a backup just in case things went bad, but that's all over now. Now and for quite a while I'm keeping you for myself, because I can trust you and there's nothing hidden or phony about you. Speaking of that, you still have any troubles with some of those memories we planted?"

"Yeah, some," I admitted. *Like the past hour.*

"Well, we've got some doctor's equipment here that might help that, which we've been using the past few months, and the doctor in charge is due back tonight. He put it in there and he can get it out, real quick and painless, just like he got it in. Maybe we'll have him take a look at you and take advantage of the fact that it's all here and get rid of her once and for all. I think you'll be a lot happier."

"Yes, suh. Whateva' you say."

I wasn't real sure I wanted to lose what I had of her. Just the idea that I coulda done better than I did if I had a few breaks was kinda nice to feel, even if it was too late for me. But I could see Arnie's point and I didn't want to say nothin' against it. A quick session, then I don't know nothin' 'bout no other Brandys or this Company or no plots or nothin', and I wouldn't *wanna* know. What you see is what you get. Then I wouldn't have this naggin' dirty feelin' in the back of my head, neither, 'bout nobody gettin' shot over juice.

We went on down to dinner, with me on my best behavior. I wasn't none too comfortable at a regular dinner. I never could figure out which fork was what and what you ate with what, but I just sat quiet and followed everybody else's example. Maybe that doc could teach me some manners with that magic machine of his. 'Course, it wasn't really needed. The only high roller tricks was white guys who wanted to see if black girls really did it better and they wouldn't be seen dead in no restaurant with no black woman. Bars, yeah, but not restaurants.

The dinner group was small; just Arnie and me, and Marty, plus two tough-lookin' hoods named Tommy and Sal who I never seen before. They didn't seem to be Arnie's men; I had a hunch this place was gonna have some visits by other big shots in the rackets, like a crime council meetin'. I just smiled pretty, tuned out the men-talk, and passed the peas when asked.

My whole idea about Arnie Siegel was changin' for the better, though. He weren't no Hitler type; oh, he might be a crook, even a big-time one, but all that slave horseshit had been to break and set up that other me. Nothin' personal, strictly business. This Doc Carlos guy didn't show, though; he seemed to have gone out someplace and didn't get back yet. Arnie could tell I was horny, so he gave the invite to Tommy and Sal and both of 'em paid me visits later on that night in the room. They was typical hoods; thought they was Mr. Macho and really weren't even Quickie Delight. After that I gave myself a shot of juice and let it take over. This was earlier than I usually took it, but I had a six-hour window. Thing was, though, I come out of that nice, mellow period about three, maybe four in the mornin', and I usually didn't go to sleep until six or so.

This was a little different comedown than usual, though. Things kept goin' 'round and 'round in my head, and I seemed to see them like pieces in a kid's jigsaw puzzle. They hadn't really been there up front before, and might never have been brought up had I been fully awake and aware or most particularly if Marty hadn't never mentioned the other Brandy goin' off that mornin' and got me worried and depressed over it.

Vogel . . . hypnoscan . . . Beth . . . Aldrath . . . The Security Committee at dinner . . . the ambush in the Labyrinth . . . Lindy Crockett . . . the shadow dancers . . . Brandy Two . . . the juice . . . the woman at Siegel's with the strange perfume . . . "Who won that war, anyway?" . . . Beth again, carryin' Vogel's load up to the mine . . . "be they yellow, black, or white, there's no difference in His sight" . . . "The sensors would detect any raw drug" . . . "the commoners can move to other worlds, and have" . . . "You're a whore and always will be" . . . Donna feelin' herself up . . . Beth . . . Beth . . . Beth . . .

I sat up in bed and my mouth hung open. Them sons of bitches! They done it to me again! And after I swore they couldn't! Never! And they'd'a got clean away with it, too, if only poor, dumb Marty, who didn't know what was goin' on or care so long as he got paid good, hadn't opened his big mouth and said somethin' he shouldn't.

I stopped short. Damn it, they *was* gonna git 'way with it! I knew what they done and what they was gonna do and why and I couldn't do a damned thing about it. So tomorrow sometime they was gonna take me down to this Dr. Carlos and give me a hypnoscan like the one I had to become Beth, only *this* time there wouldn't be no trigger to let my old self back in. I'd be little Brandy Parker, the dumb, ignorant whore and a kinda *trophy* to their success, and wouldn't nobody even look for me since *she* had my looks, my basic memories, and even my fingerprints and eye patterns. 'Cept'n for Marty's slip, I wouldn't even have known at all.

I was so frustrated and angry I wanted to cry, but then I heard voices outside. They was muffled, but you could tell it was a man and a woman and that they wasn't agreein' on much. I slipped off the bed and crept to my door, then opened it a crack. The whole place was pitch dark 'cept for a light shinin' from under the closed door of Arnie's office at the end of the hall. I was just decidin' whether or not to get closer—I could always say I was goin' to the bathroom —when I heard two dull sounds. *Thud! Thud!* They sounded like gunshots done with a silencer!

I rushed forward, and at that moment the door opened and a dark figure clad in black rushed out the door. The light and the action stunned me for a second, and they run right into me and we both fell down. I heard the clatter of somethin' fallin' on the floor, but the other one didn't stop but was up and away down the stairs in nothin' flat. I picked myself up and felt around and got it. *A pistol!* Felt a little light and funny, but it was definitely a pistol. I picked it up and walked into the office and stopped dead in my tracks. Outside there was some yellin' and screamin' and the sound of a few unmuffled shots.

Arnie lay lack in the office chair, head cocked, eyes open and glazed over, a little blood tricklin' from his mouth. There was two neat, red holes in his silk pajamas, and they was gettin' bigger. Somebody ran up the stairs and reached the edge of the doorway. I turned, nearly forgettin' the gun in my hand, to see Marty.

"Mr. Siegel! Somebody ju—*Jesus Christ!*" He saw Arnie, then me. "You dumb broad! You just killed Mr. Siegel!"

"No! Wait! I—" I started, but Marty was goin' for his gun. Somethin' suddenly kicked in and took over for me. The whole thing slowed, like it was some kinda slow-motion movie, and as his hand went to his shoulder holster my hand come up with the pistol in it. I had much better reflexes than Marty, and somethin' else seemed to be controllin' my actions. I shot Marty dead center in the middle of his forehead. He looked surprised, then kinda puzzled, and I kicked him down and started lookin' 'round the office. Then I saw it—the black briefcase, off to one side of the desk. I picked it up and started to move. There was still some commotion outside, but nobody else seemed to be comin' straight in, so I headed for my room and suddenly was thinkin' again, although on a real super-charged level. I thought 'bout ditchin' the gun and preten-din' to be asleep, but I knew that wouldn't wash. There was no way to hide that briefcase in time, and no way I was gonna part with it short of dyin'. With Arnie dead there'd be a new order around, and I wouldn't be worth *shit* to the new guys even if they didn't blame me for this.

I didn't waste no time gettin' dressed. I just threw what I saw into my bag, includin' the shoes, and put it over my shoulder. I had the briefcase in one hand and the gun in the other. I didn't know how many more bullets was in that gun, but it was all I had. I opened the door and saw somebody had come in and turned the main room's lights on. I crept to the top of the stairs, saw two men lookin' around. One of 'em thought to look up, and I plugged him and then his companion with no thought. That kind of accuracy, when both had guns in their hands, was near impossible. The juice—the juice was readin' my danger level and forcin' me to protect it, and me, at any cost!

I made a leap that woulda done Tarzan proud down to the main floor and hit in a crouch without losin' the case or the bag. I stopped tryin' to fight the juice, and suddenly I was a killer machine. I had only one thought: escape. I was like some vicious cornered animal, only I knew the layout and I knew the gun and I knew the only way out I could go.

I made my way back to the kitchen area, then peered outside. It was real dark, but the glow from the house lights lit it up some. Two guards, one with a rifle, was out there arguin' and pointin'—at the Labyrinth.

It was on, right full, all them cubelike shapes dancin' and changin' and ready for use. No way to make any kinda run, so I just held the pistol at my side and walked through the backdoor onto the porch. They turned and their guns come up.

"Hey, boys!" I called to them. "What de hell goin' on, anyways?"

One of 'em cussed but they both relaxed, and then I shot 'em both down with my eyes at more than thirty feet and jumped down onto the lawn. Somebody come at me right then, and I swung the briefcase and caught him on the head, then kicked him hard with my foot. He fell back and doubled over.

There was another one near the Labyrinth I didn't see, and he made right for me. He musta been six three and three hundred pounds and yet so fast I didn't even have time to use the gun. I dropped the briefcase and then kicked him, grabbed him, and brought both my arms, with gun, down on his head so fast I ain't never gonna know what I did or how. I was now only a few feet from the fence, but I couldn't go yet. I had to drop that case and wasn't no way I was goin' without it even if they shot me dead.

I made for it, got it, then looked up and saw a man on the back porch, framed by the house lights, gun held steady by both hands. There was no way I could figure on scoopin' up the case and gettin' off more'n a wild shot while he had me cold, but I went for it anyways, hardly lookin' as I shot him. I turned and looked back to see him fall forward off the porch onto the ground. At that moment I wasn't one to question luck; I jumped that little fence and ran into the Labyrinth just as it seemed to be slowin' down and growin' smaller.

I hit the cube runnin', then rolled and stopped, then crouched and waited to see if anybody was followin' me. Instead, I watched the cube face from which I'd entered slowly fade out to black. Only then did I get back my wits and try to think 'bout what to do next.

First I looked at the pistol. No wonder it made that funny noise! It was made outta somethin' like yellow or gold plastic and you could see a lot of funny works in there. It sure as hell shot somethin' hard and real, though; those was holes in Arnie, not no ray gun burns or shit like that. That also meant it could run outta bullets anytime. Hell, it might be empty now, but I didn't dare test it. That test might be my last bullet, too.

I looked next at the briefcase that was life to me. Hell, maybe it was only six months, maybe a year, but it was more'n *they* tried to give me or woulda if I'd stayed with no Arnie around. I opened the case and felt panic. It wasn't empty, but it nearly was. Only one of them shrink-wrapped packets of juice cubes was in there. Only one. Panicky as hell, I counted them. Four layers of eight each. A month's supply. Probably *my* supply. I still had three in my bag, that meant thirty-five. I had thirty-five days to live.

That meant I had to do somethin', make some hard decisions, but not right away. More worrisome right off was that somebody back there had helped me escape. The other guys I shot, they all fell backwards like they should, but the guy on the porch, the one who had me cold, had fallen *forward*. Maybe that killer was still back there, waitin' for the time to light out for South America or whatever. It was a woman, that was for sure, and I didn't think she planned to kill Arnie. I really didn't. She coulda done that nice and quiet. Most likely it was that strange woman at Siegel's house. That was almost surely Addison, only she didn't look nothin' like the sketches that Crockett bitch showed me.

Maybe Arnie'd gotten greedy, or ambitious. He knowed what was up, that's for sure, but he wouldn't be more than a small part of it. What had they promised him? That he'd replace Big Georgie as crime boss when they took over? It probably sounded good at the time, but he now knew that was just chicken feed. So maybe, after years of setup, Arnie decides when they begin to roll that he'll throw some kinda monkey wrench in the machinery and hold out for more. The only way to know for sure what it was about was to ask Addison, and I was a long way from bein' able to do that yet.

Now I had only a few choices. First switcher I met, I'd hav'ta give a destination. I was one of them lucky few cleared through to headquarters and it was the logical place to go, but I didn't want to go there unless I had to. They'd take all my information, all right, but then I'd wind up in the Center. Maybe if I started into withdrawal and there was no other way I'd do that, but so long as I had juice I sure as hell wouldn't. Requestin' some destination by description, like Brandy two's home world, was risky. Them switchers used translators and so many worlds was alike enough to them that they usually got it wrong anyways. Besides, what would that buy me 'cept a month of freelance whorin'? Crazy fact was, the best chance I had was tryin' to push the case. Get 'em where *I* could call the tune. I didn't give a damn if they took over everything or not no more, but I wanted a personal, guaranteed, lifetime supply of juice they couldn't cut off. It was a lot cheaper price than Arnie probably asked for, and if I was smart about it they wouldn't dare knock me off.

Yeah, I know, it was crazy to think that they would even bother dealin' with me with all the power they had, but that's the thing 'bout bein' hooked. Still, other than that, it made me very cool and logical. I just had killed my first three people and it didn't bother me one bit. I had no inhibitions at all. Now I knew. My twin would kill without a thought if it was that or juice. That was my only lead, then, too. If I was wrong, if I hadn't doped it out right, I was stuck, but if I was right, I had a place to start.

The briefcase didn't seem worth keepin', now. I put the packet in my shoulder bag, and the gun, too.

I knew what they done to me, and I kinda guessed why. Brandy Two and I was even more alike than I figured. Oh, she was a whore, all right, but that didn't mean nothin' when it came to other interests. She'd still come from a readin' family and she read real good. She maybe talked better than I did, too; she might have been a higher class hooker by the time they got her than she was supposed to be. That's why they run her up to Vogel's place first—to get her brains scrambled a little, the same kinda thing as they did to me. Made her a dumb-ass ignorant slut, then sent her down to Siegel till they could get hold of me. Workin' the shadow dancer route, bein' conditioned with slow withdrawal and then suggested to death on the comedown, she was probably all set up as the girl I saw. It's all they needed from her.

Then I showed up, and I didn't look the same no more, and for a while I gave 'em the slip before walkin' right into their hands as I had to sooner or later. This was a patient bunch. They had somethin' else they was gonna use this other Brandy for, somethin' I didn't have worked out yet, but then there I was. Somehow, durin' that time, they had an extra problem, too. If Sam was dead or still in a coma, then I was all wet, but I bet my last shot of juice that he recovered. Watchin' me, they had a healthy respect for him, and he wasn't no easy snatch and switch. More, he'd be a real dangerous enemy 'cause he'd know where I was and sooner or later he'd come and find out, and maybe not alone. So they changed their plans.

And that's the point I was really guessin' on. Suppose Vogel's experimenters found that they could make a juicer do absolutely anything, and I mean *anything*—even kill. But there was a point, someplace, where even the juice couldn't force it. Maybe a percentage of folks just couldn't be made to kill their wives, husbands, or babies. Maybe it was only a few, but it was there no matter what they did, and they needed a Brandy so convincin' that Sam wouldn't have no doubts at all—and they wouldn't, neither. So they had Brandy Two watch me, watch my moves, my mannerisms, my quirks and habits, talk a lot about myself. Maybe she didn't even know then that she was takin' it all in, but she was. We was inseparable.

So, when they was ready, maybe when Sam was just due to come home, they took us to Siegel's estate and stuck us in such a low, degradin' situation we didn't even have no track of days or times, just shot to shot. Then, when we was on our juice high, they bring in this Dr. Carlos and he hooks up the hypnoscan to us and he puts that dumb, ignorant slut version in *me*, probably a real edited version of the real thing, and two triggers. *The cards!* The crazy things on them cards they had us read! More than enough.

All they had to do was start when we was juicin' high, keep us out for a full twenty-four hours, then give us the next day's jolt and let us come out natural. We never woulda knowed we lost a day, not *there*, and Carlos would have a full day to do real fancy work on both our brains.

So when Brandy Two read her card, *bingo*! All her old skills and speech and shit come back, just flowin' in till it dominated the other, and that along with all she'd learned and observed by bein' closer to me than anybody else could for all that time and a friendly hypno-shove convinced her she was me. At the same time, when *I* read *my* card, the Brandy Two lower personality flowed in and my old stuff was shoved to the back. I couldn't read that card 'cause I'd been cut off from my old skills.

But why not just do a Beth number on me? Make me Brandy Two completely and block off the old me entirely? Maybe 'cause they couldn't, quite. When Doc Jamispur done it to me at Mayar's place, he had all the top shit, the best computers and stuff they had. Maybe it took more than a hypnoscan to do it completely. How would I know?

What he done was bad enough. Even *I* believed it. Forcin' that Brandy Two personality and cuttin' the skills—they knew just where to look 'cause they already did it once to *her*—to be up front. Even if you had the old stuff, you could do what they couldn't—forget it or push it all the way back till it rotted. Vogel proved that by bringin' out Beth on the getaway. All he did was talk me into the idea that I was turnin' back into Beth and I couldn't fight it, and I was so ignorant of what they done to me and so in awe of their powers that I swallowed it and started becomin' Beth and trashin' Brandy. This time they was more clever, 'cause I didn't know I'd been hypnoscanned, wasn't ready for it, and when I figured it out they had a real convincin' reason for me to doubt my own identity. Real convincin'. Still, it was one of their stock tricks, and it had worked on me *twice*. Woulda worked, too, if Marty just hadn't shot off his fat mouth and started that old part of me movin'.

Not that it was easy. I knew who I was now, and had my old memories, but Brandy Two was still forward, still in the driver's seat, and I didn't have no Center to get her out. I was stuck with that real southern ghetto dialect, had a hard time handlin' big words, and I wasn't gonna write no incriminatin' statements. I needed to take a chance on somebody who could and who might not turn me in.

If that damned twin of mine hadn't already murdered him.

9.

Plot Counterplot

One thing Bill Markham drove into my head was that long string of numbers for home. I had some trouble pullin' 'em out, but they felt and sounded right when I faced the switcher.

"Thuteen, twenny-nine, two, stroke sev'n," I managed.

The switcher checked. "You are authorized transit to that world," she said. She was one of them that really needed a shave and a haircut. "Proceed straight on and I will autoexit you."

"Any ways I can git a word sent up to Aldrath Prang?" I asked her. I wanted some insurance.

"Executor Aldrath Prang has been relieved of all duties in security," she told me. "I can connect you to Security General if you like."

Aldrath fired! This was goin' along much faster than I thought. "Uh, no thank you, ma'am. It be kinda *personal.*" And I walked straight ahead, and five cubes later walked out into a mess of broke-down concrete surrounded by a high wall. It was a real mess down there, and I was glad it was daylight. It looked from the droppin's and shit that things lived down there I didn't wanna meet.

There was this rickety old ladder, and I climbed it to the top and found myself out in the woods with just this pit or well or whatever it was there, surrounded by a fence with barbed wire all 'round it. There was a gate with a big padlock on it, though, and there was only one thing to do. I took out the gun, prayed it was still loaded, and shot square at the lock. It kinda ricocheted around and away without smashin' the lock like it always does in the movies, but when I pulled the lock came free and I could get outta the gate.

The next question was, where was I and was I in the right world after all? It still looked like Pennsylvania, which made sense—I was on the Pennsylvania track and hadn't really been switched, just told to go straight ahead—but it wasn't any territory I knew.

I tried to find a clear spot, then looked around at the horizon. Nothin' much to see. A farm or somethin' off one way, not much else. Every time we used the damned Labyrinth before it always dumped us at the Company in Oregon where we didn't wanna be and I kinda expected the same thing. This time, though, they'd stuck me at the State College area substation which they didn't use much and wasn't manned. First time I actually ever *wanted* to be in Oregon and I was here!

I listened, and heard the sound of traffic off in the distance. Well, that was somethin'—a road. Someplace along there there just *had* to be a phone. Clutchin' my shoulder bag, I made my way through the woods and down the mountainside toward the road.

Things opened up considerable after a while, and I was lookin' out over green fields and farmland down to a snaky little road with a fair amount of traffic on it. I started down, and was halfway across the open field before I suddenly remembered I was stark naked. It didn't bother me none but it sure would attract a whole lot more attention than I wanted and I didn't want to get picked up and thrown in no jail while they charged me and checked me out. I sat down in the field and checked what I'd chucked into the shoulder bag. Thing was, I'd had time to unpack at the lodge and I hadn't really been thinkin' too good when I made my run for it. I was lucky to have thought of the bag at all.

The only thing I could find was a pair of spike-heeled shoes, not the best for walkin', and the real tight slinky metallic blue dress that matched them that I'd worn to dinner. There was also a topless string bikini lodged in a side pocket that I'd missed, but somehow that didn't seem none too practical. Well, that dress was knee-length, real low cut, and had them slits in the side that left no doubt I wasn't wearin' nothin' under it, but at least it was legal. I also found a small compact, a lipstick, a wide-toothed comb, an emery board, and a small bottle of spray perfume.

That and the long golden pierced earrings I generally kept on was my sole worldly goods.

I got over to a clump of bushes and sat down to see about gettin' it on, and suddenly I felt an overwhelming urge and need to sleep. I knowed I'd been on the go a lot and needed it, but not now. It was the juice, of course, makin' me do what it decided I had to no matter what, and even though I fought it and didn't want to, the next thing I knew it was much later, and the bright sun that had been on my right comin' down was now on my left. I cussed and got up. Not havin' a watch there wasn't no way to tell the time, but the usual sleep was between eight and ten hours. If it was maybe eight when I conked out, it was probably 'bout five now. I looked out at the road and there was a fair amount of traffic goin' the opposite way, which checked out. I didn't know what day or month it was 'cept it was still warm; time didn't run at exactly the same rate in any of the worlds, so all I could know for sure was that it was summer here. Trouble was, I didn't even know the year. I'd been like ten months in Siegel's world, but how much time had passed here in the meantime? Might be a couple of years, and, then again, it might be only May or June here.

I was hungry and sure to get more so, but I didn't have no way to feed myself so that was one thing I had to push off. Wouldn't get no food or phone sittin' here, though, so I squeezed into the dress and, in spite of everything and I guess out of habit, took time to comb my hair, put on fresh lipstick, and a little makeup and even spray a little perfume on. Well, it weren't just vanity and habit; there was only one way I was gonna get fed and get where I was gonna go.

I stuck the shoes back in the bag, though. No use in breakin' my neck with them here.

There was no way to pick a direction, but I saw some road signs 'bout half a mile to my left so I made my way that way. Best to know where I was first. I had trouble readin' 'em when I got to 'em, but finally made out a sign sayin' STATE COLLEGE 10. Well, they'd have phones there, but I didn't figure no big college town would be quick and easy pickin's for me, and it was the wrong way anyways. I crossed the road, struck a real sexy pose, and started hitchin'. I figured it might take four or five minutes tops, but it was even less than that. I didn't mind if I got a dirty old man, and any would-be rapist would find they sure tangled with the wrong girl!

A little sweet-talkin', a nice little sob story in a high sexy voice, and a few moves will get you most anything if you don't have no standards or scruples. I got let off at a big truck stop out in the middle of nowhere, and I didn't have to be there long before I had more than enough offers to get food and even a little cash. Still, it was fairly late by the time I was able to make a phone call, and when I stood at the phone booth I suddenly realized I didn't know what to call. Bill Markham's number was another of those things burned into my mind, but I didn't dare call him unless I had to. He could stop my twin if she hadn't already done the deed and all that, but he'd also have people all over the place and I'd be off to the Center in no time "for my own good." My old number was no good; I'd disconnected it before leavin' and sublet the apartment, puttin' everything in storage.

I finally called Philadelphia information and asked for a Spade & Marlowe number. The agency was dead and gone, but not its client lists, and there might be a service or referral number. There was a number, but it was only a recordin' sayin' that Spade & Marlowe's cases had been transferred to the Marquand Agency and givin' their number. I tried them but nobody answered. I hadn't even thought about this angle. Maybe I had to call Markham anyways. I had one last thought, and that was if Sam had been back long enough to get a place and maybe get his own number, it would be listed. I checked, and, sure enough and to my complete surprise, they *did* have a listin' for a Samuel Horowitz. I called the number and it rang a few times, then got picked up.

"Hello?" come a woman's voice. *Her* voice. *My* voice. I stuck my voice up way high.

"Is Mistah Horowitz theah?" I asked pleasantly.

"No, I'm sorry, he's out of town," Brandy Two replied. "I'm his wife. Can I take a message?"

Like hell you is, honey! "No, thanks. Will he be back soon?"

"Not for a couple of days."

"I'll call agin then. Bye," I responded, and hung up. So Sam was out of town—or maybe just plain out? She'd use that if she'd already iced him, but then why would she still be there? To get Markham, too, maybe? Only way to find out was to get there.

It wasn't all that hard. You just sat there sweet as honey and then picked the fly you wanted to trap. I give him good value for his trouble, so we was both satisfied. I got dropped right near Broad and Market 'bout four-thirty in the mornin', and I had 'bout forty dollars on me at the time. Not a lot, but I walked over to Chestnut and got a room at the YWCA. Not that I wanted to, but it was gettin' on time.

I took my juice, had a good time, then slept until four that afternoon. I rarely ate meat, but I was able to find decent stuff at a health food store and carry out just up the street. I was down to seven bucks, which didn't worry me none, particularly in center city Philadelphia after dark. The only real worry I had was I was havin' trouble gettin' used to the cars bein' back over on the left side of the street again.

A good detective has no problem gettin' an address when she's got a phone number, even though it was too new to be in the book. The number turned out to be for a development up north of the city near Willow Grove, not exactly on the train routes. I caught a late train up as close as I could, then had to use my charms to get a big, black taxi driver to run me there for seven bucks. It turned out to be a bunch of fancy-lookin' duplexes on them little dead-end streets, but that was somethin' of a relief since I was afraid I'd be lookin' at some security apartment tower. The cabbie—Calvin his name was—refused my money and I promised I'd call him through his taxi company as soon as I was free. Maybe I would, too—he was real nice and real good-lookin'—but that was if I wasn't dead or somethin'.

I checked out the house. There was one light burnin' in the front room, but the shades was closed and I couldn't tell if anybody was in there. The rest of the place looked dark. There didn't seem to be no alarm system, but the doors had good bolt locks and the place was air-conditioned so the windows was closed, locked, and secure. Finally, I decided to see if things would go the easy way; I held the gun inside the shoulder bag pointin' at the door and rang the bell. I heard it go a number of times, real loud, but there was no reply. Suddenly the phone rang inside, and for a minute I thought I'd tripped some alarm system, but after eight rings they gave up. There was nobody home, all right.

It took some doin' to get inside without crashin' no loud glass. I was a hell of an athlete by this time, though, and actually managed to jump up and grab hold of the gutter spout on the second floor and pull myself up, rippin' my dress mostly off in the process. Still, there on this little roof overhang, I was at an upstairs window. The lock was one of them simple throw type, so I put the pistol up against the glass right on the flat push part of the lock and fired. The shot was quiet as usual, and damned if the thing didn't turn about halfway and come mostly free. The hole was big enough for a finger, and I managed to tap it around enough and open the window and crawl in. I no sooner got in and shut it than I saw a back light come on, and then somebody come out of the backdoor of the other half of the buildin' and look around. They checked the whole area with a flashlight, includin' Sam's patio, and even shined a light up my way, but they didn't see nothin'.

There was two bedrooms and a bath upstairs. One of the bedrooms was just that; the other was storage and filled with the boxes and trunks I'd left when I stuck everything in storage. Most of my clothes and other stuff was in there, still packed, although *she* had obviously opened stuff and begun to sort it. I could see why she had problems with it; everything was way too big 'cept the shoes. My feet bones didn't shrink or tighten up with the rest of me. I dug out a big old extra long tee shirt that came down halfway to my knees and I used that lonely bikini bottom, even if it did have sparklies all in it. My credit cards and shit was all in safe deposit at Tri-State Bank, so there wasn't much more I could do.

I stuffed the remains of the dress in the shoulder bag, then went into the bathroom. I stuck the bag in behind some shit under the sink so it couldn't be easily seen, except for the juice capsules and the gun. Then I started lookin' for places to hide the juice, and found more, to my surprise. Not a lot—six capsules, hid in my old mink coat still in the trunk. But they was *her* supply. We sure did think alike. Trouble was, how to hide 'em so she wouldn't figure right off where they was. I decided to think like Sam. I had trouble findin' somethin' that worked as a screwdriver, but then I un-screwed a floor plate for the air-conditionin' and stuck all but a couple in there. Those I stuck in a little kitchen baggie and stuck under a seat cushion in the livin' room. It was so obvious nobody'd think of lookin' for it.

The clocks said it was a little after ten. I didn't know anything else to do but sit and try and relax and wait. The kitchen was real basic and clearly not stocked up for any length of time even for one, and there wasn't nothin' in it fit for me to eat.

About ten-fifteen I heard a car drive up and stop, and somebody got out and walked up to the door. I retreated up the stairs as a key entered the lock. I didn't want to be seen till I knew the score and which one I was facin'. I decided I'd just keep quiet, lay low, and wait.

After a while of movin' in and out and packages rustlin', I heard footsteps come up the stairs and *she* came up and went into the bathroom. She was wearin' a sleeveless stretch-type pale pink top and a pair of real tight jeans with sandals. They all looked new, so I figured she'd been shoppin'. Either they staked her some or she'd made it as far as my deposit box.

I was in the dark bedroom, ready with the pistol if need be, but she flushed and come out and went down the hall to the other bedroom and switched on the light. I had a margin nearly to noon the next day before I needed a jolt, but maybe she didn't. I hoped not. I heard her give a little gasp; I guessed she'd noticed the neat hole in the window in there. In a sense, I was actually in her mind, and I didn't hav'ta see her to know what she was doin'. Hole, then check, open the window and look out, then check the walls and see where the bullet bouncin' off went. Her next thought would be to check for her juice stash, and I heard her pull the trunk around, open it, and start feelin' through the pockets of every coat in there and lookin' down the bottom, feelin' the linings to make sure it didn't drop down, then I heard her give a panicky sort of cry.

I crept down the hall and watched her, knowin' how I'd feel. Then she suddenly realized that somebody was there, turned, and froze. She saw the gun first, then me.

"Dey ain't dere, *sista*," I told her. "Dey been moved far, far away."

"You! How'd you even *get* here? What do you want with me?"

"I think you gots the smarts ta' figah dat out yo'self. You *gots* t'know at least what dis part's all 'bout."

She got slowly up and stared at me. "They—they said you'd never even *know!* And even if you did, no way you gonna leave without no juice!"

"I *gots* juice. All *God's* chillun gots juice. Dey keep makin' dese l'il eensy-weensy mistakes wit' dis chile. Go 'head. Tear dis place up. You won't find no juice. Uh, uh, not a drop. Don' worry, though. I gots it all hid nice'n safe. Lots 'n lots of it. Ol' Arnie, he had one *big* stash, and now I got it. Ol' Arnie, he don't need it no mo'. He deader than a cooked rat."

"Somebody sent you. Who?"

"Som'body do know the secret, but I dunno who. Ain't yo' gal Addison, though, even if she *did* pop Arnie two slugs wit' dis selfsame gun. Kills real *quick* 'n *quiet.*"

"Are you gonna—kill me? There can't be two of us in this world."

"Well, dere is now. We goin' downstairs and den we gon' talk a bit 'bout a lotta things. Where we go from dere be up to you."

I was careful, and I had the experience with guns and with handlin' folks who didn't wanna be handled. I think she sensed that, and was also really thrown off by me bein' there at all, so she gave me no trouble. She also seemed to have completely bought the idea that I'd removed all the juice from the house. Hell, *I* kept fallin' for shit like that, so why shouldn't *she?*

So we sat and we talked, and I got some more details on this setup. She swore she didn't know nothin' 'bout no plot when she was shadow dancin' down at Siegel's, and that she had no memories or recollections of her full self, as she called it, until she read that card. She never really doubted who she was, though, even then; it was the basic selfishness of the juice addict that kept her quiet and let me go away confused and broken. I understood; when somebody else held the juice you danced their way.

But she'd spent so much time with me, been so close all that time, she could do me nearly perfect. After that split-up, they flew her up to the lodge and this mysterious

Dr. Carlos for the final touches. The ultimate test, though, she still found unpleasant to talk about but it brought her to this point. They found one of the regular girls at the club, not the dancers but one of the ones who lived where Deb and I had, was givin' information on the sly to the cops. They brought her up to the lodge, and they gave the poor girl to her and then they withheld the juice.

"I resisted," she told me. "I held out longer than I thought I could, but I finally did what they said. Every bit. Not just killin' her, but cuttin', mutilating, while she was strung up screamin'. It was then I knew I'd do *anything* for the juice. I know it's wrong, but, next day, I didn't feel bad, and I didn't have no nightmares. I knew just what I was and where I stood. Killin' this white man of yours—it was no big thing after that. I lost some sleep over figurin' it, but I wouldn't lose sleep over doin' it. If they had you down there, and your Sam strung up, you'd carve him up yourself. Only thing was, you wasn't gonna be strung out with some controller standin' in back with the juice you craved. On your own, they thought you wouldn't be able to do it. At that moment, you either kill yourself or do as they order. There ain't no third way."

The phone rang. She looked at me, and I went over and looked at the phone. It was one of them new styles, with the automatic dial and built-in speakerphone. I figured it was the same one I'd bought for the old apartment. I gestured her over, then hit the speaker on/off button and nodded to her.

"Yes?" she asked into the little mike.

"Brandy," came a woman's cool, familiar voice, "this is Addison. Is everything going all right?"

She looked at me. "Fine. I'm settled in."

"Very well. This is a change of orders. It is very important. Sam Horowitz is on his way home. We aren't sure of the route or timing, but he could be there anytime within a few hours to tomorrow afternoon. You are *not* to kill him. Do you understand?"

She frowned. "But I thought—"

"There has been a change in circumstances. Brandy Horowitz is loose with a large enough supply to cause real trouble for some time. We think she made it to this world. *She* is now your target. She is certain to try to contact Sam, perhaps make an attempt on you. Delay, hold, or restrain her if possible but do not kill her unless you have to. If you spot her, use the contact method to get hold of us immediately. This is quite urgent."

"Lemme get this straight. You don't want me to kill Sam, and you don't want me to kill Brandy, neither, if I can help it? Then other than hold her, what else am I supposed to do?"

"Become Brandy Horowitz. We have other uses for you now. You can play the part. He knows you got addicted. That will cover many lapses and your erratic behavior, and he, too, had some recovery problems. He'll buy it. You *make* him buy it." The line went dead.

I was as amazed as she was at this. Why, after all this trouble, such a change in plans? Did Siegel's death, and the intervention of some third party they didn't know 'bout in my escape, cause 'em to regroup? This didn't make no sense at all to either of us.

"How do you contact dem?" I asked her.

"The Chessworks. It's a toy and game store in central Philadelphia. You call their number and you leave a message for Miss Addison to call you with the one who answers or on the machine if it's after-hours. I used it once already, but it was a man who called back, not her."

"Well, she here now. Guess her wastin' Arnie made troubles. Don't know what dey still want *me* livin' for, though."

"So, what—now?"

Yeah—what now? Sam was safe, at least for now, and I had a way to contact Addison to make a deal. Trouble was, if I did it now she'd know immediately who gave me the number and where I had to be. Sam might be hours, even tomorrow afternoon, gettin' in, and I needed a jolt before that. Worse, it was into prime hours, and the juice only let up on mandatory sex when you had your period. "When you due yo' jolt?" I asked her.

"Anytime now. Past time. Can't you tell?"

Truth was, I *could* tell. She'd been time shifted in her routine 'cause of all that stuff at the lodge.

"Okay. Figured as much. Dat's why I didn't take it all. Thought it might be kinda useful. Left one here fo' ya." I reached under the cushion and palmed the two cubes.

"Now—we goin' upstairs and you gonna get happy fo' a while."

She didn't resist; you don't in those circumstances as I well knew. When you're due, that's the only thing important to you.

"Now, you listen to me," I said coldly. "I got all de rest o' the juice. You know, too, one o' us'd *die* befo' she tell you where her stash is. You betta' play 'long wit' me, girl, or I'll see you go t'hell."

I gave her the jolt and watched it take effect almost enviously. I wanted it bad, too, but it wouldn't be no good to me for a long while yet. Some knowledge of Sam helped next, 'cause it didn't take me long to find what he called his Junior G-Man Detective Set. It was a small box with fingerprint kit, evidence collectors, and a couple pairs of handcuffs.

I rolled her over and she smiled and groaned, then cuffed her hands in back and then cuffed her legs as well. Then I gagged her, left, and turned out the light. She didn't even notice all that.

I went down, called the cab company and asked for Calvin to pick me up, then went back upstairs and got my bag, stuck the gun in it, deep, made my face over a little and combed my hair, then put on the heels, even if they wasn't real suited for what I was wearin'. I was tempted just to have Calvin in, but I had enough sense to realize that if Sam come in durin' it I might have some trouble convincin' him I was the right one.

It was stupid and risky, but when the juice tells you to do somethin', you ain't got no choice at all, and the sight of her up there in high heaven on the bed only tripled the lust.

I was sure as hell gonna give Calvin his seven bucks worth—with one hell of a tip.

Now, I got to admit I took a hell of a risk considerin' the timing and all, but that's how this thing works. The only thing I had left was my brain, and that was workin' good as ever.

Needless to say, when I got back about four in the mornin' I was real extra careful to make sure that everything was just as I left it, includin' a few little things on the doors nobody would notice but would be out of place if they was opened. I even checked the neighborhood for snoops and found none. Finally I went in, checked out the downstairs, then went upstairs real careful-like, and found Brandy Two also pretty much as I left her, only now she was asleep instead of on the super high—or mad, as she almost surely was from the looks of the bed. Wasn't nothin' to do but relax, so I went downstairs and watched a movie on one of them superstations, which felt real good to be able to do after all that had happened, then just gave myself that jolt and disappeared into heaven on the couch.

I remember wakin' up in the blissful comedown for a while, then just driftin' back to sleep. Wasn't no use in doin' nothin' else, nohow. Sam might come home and be confused as hell, but at least I was the first Brandy he'd see.

Which was why it was a real shock to wake up upstairs on the bed, hands cuffed behind my back. I turned and found Brandy Two still there as well, only she was only cuffed by her hands. Sittin' in a chair opposite, holdin' his .38, swiggin' coffee, and lookin' more'n a little tired, was Sam.

I was so damned happy to see him, alive, lookin' well and as I remembered him, that I sat right up. *"Sam!"*

"My mother warned me about all sorts of things," he said real casually, ignorin' my outburst. "She gave me tons of advice on almost every situation in the world. However, I don't think she *ever* covered something like this."

"Welcome back," said my twin. "We been talkin' 'bout you."

"I bet," I shot back. "Bet you been tellin' him de God's honest truth, huh?"

Sam sighed. "I am a detective. I don't even *like* being a detective all that much. Usually it's boring as hell. Unfortunately, it's the only thing anybody ever taught me how to do that paid money. Now I have two women here, cuffed on my bed, which is kinky enough for any detective novel, and both of them look absolutely identical. Both also have a passing resemblance to my wife, but both look like versions of my wife as sculpted by a master sculptor with a massive bribe from her."

"He's puttin' you on, honey," Brandy Two said dryly. "He knowed 'bout the two of us before he ever showed up here."

"They do tend to notice—eventually—when the identical same person passes the same station twice in the same direction without ever going in the *opposite* direction," Sam commented. "Don't worry, Sleeping Beauty, I already know a fair amount of the story. You see, I asked your counterpart here about our little dog Asta, and she said Asta had to be given away. Isn't that just terrible?"

I was cuffed on the bed, but I had to laugh and keep laughin' for a while. Finally I managed, "Right, Mista' Charles."

One thing Sam and my late Daddy had in common was a passion for the old classic detective novels, stories, and films, and I caught it, too. I guess Brandy Two was too damned mad at Daddy to take up that taste in her life. That'll teach her to read them sexy romances. In fact, Sam always reminded me of William Powell in *The Thin Man.* Oh, he don't look or talk like Powell—wish he did—but it's the same *attitude.*

"So why am I cuffed?" I asked him.

"You are cuffed, my dear, because you are hooked on the most addictive substance yet discovered and you apparently have a fair amount of it. You ought to see what it's done to the two of you. Before I can have a—working relationship, let's call it—with either of you, I have to know where the stash is and take control of it. You're the one who knows, so that's why we've been waiting for you to wake up."

"Sam!" I cried. "It's *me!* Damn it, dey give me dis shit-slut talk an' all, but it's *me!*"

"I worked vice, babe. Remember? I've seen many as strong as you be willing to kill their own husbands, mothers, and children for drugs a lot less potent than this one. You have two choices—tell me now or tell me later. If you choose later, then *I* have to make some choices, since I have to go to sleep before either of you needs a fix or I'll keel over and you two need food and recreation, if I remember the stuff's routine right. If it's now, I can relax. If it's later, I have to either start a treasure hunt, which I'm too damned spent to try, or call in somebody to take over, which means Bill Markham and you know what *that* means, or I have to hand-feed the two of you and find some more handcuffs. Now—which is it?"

"Sam—you know I can't do *dat!*"

He stared hard and serious at me. "Brandy! It's *me!*" he said mockingly. "You wanted *me* to trust *you* on that basis. Not the same the other way, huh?"

He had me, and I didn't know how to get out of it.

"For God's sake, tell him!" my twin pleaded. "It's the only way *I'm* gonna get out of these damned cuffs, too."

I didn't know what to do, so I tried a two-way approach. "Sam—I been through hell. I thought you was *dead,* for God's sake! Only wanted t' git even. Screw dem good. And I *can,* Sam. Dat's de honest truth. If'n nothin' else good come out of dis, I got dat. I knows who's who and what it's all 'bout!"

"I have some of it myself," he told me. "After they finally ran some checks to see if I should be taken off life support and found out that the computer instructions for my maintenance in that tank included a certain drug that kept me sound asleep for months, and they brought me out and told me about it, it wasn't hard to figure. It's not enough, babe. Not enough at all. Why do you think they engineered the sacking of Aldrath? Put that young fellow, Dakani Grista, in temporary command? Dakani's young, ambitious, and like most young and ambitious smart boys he wants to feather his own nest. He's not in on this but he's not going to do anything to jeopardize his standing. He got rid of most of Aldrath's top people and replaced them with bureaucratic hacks. Now, if you or I walk in and tell him we know who's behind all this and most of the cast of characters, do you think he'll believe us and move on it? On his own, against one of his patrons and a higher class at that?"

"Not everybody's in dem upper classes," I pointed out.

"True, but they're all well connected to them and work for them. Dakani might put one of them through the ringer if we had solid evidence, but not on either of our deductions or say-so. Aldrath would have. That's why they had to retire him. It wasn't hard. Even knowing what we know you can make a pretty good case for his incompetence. He was too close to the problem. He had Top Man Disease. He believed his reports from his agents in the field and he fed only those reports into his computers and came up with exactly the conclusions and acted in exactly the ways they wanted him to. His only departure from orthodoxy was you, when he let you go in alone, and when this Crockett woman reported you had been captured and hooked on the stuff, he looked more like a fool. Can't you figure out, with all his resources, why he couldn't find the origin world?"

I nodded. "Same thing. Machines tol' him dat de place was bare."

"Right. Or, it was certified as having been looked at and given a clean bill of health. That means we're right back where we started from. They can blow up Vogel's place and most of his experts, they can cover their people for a while more back where you just came from, and they can cover their own asses at headquarters and rely on Dakani's inexperience and eagerness to please to keep it that way, but the origin world's their smoking gun. They can't blow it up, they can't abandon it, and they can't cover up a whole world's evidence. Deliver that world and you expose the cover-ups and maneuverings. Find that world and even Dakani will have to move fast and hard for the same reason he won't act without it—expediency and his own neck. So, babe, you're one hell of a detective but you still ain't got a damned thing."

"And . . . if yo' *does* got the stash? What den? De funny farm fo' us?"

"Uh uh. How much of the stuff *is* there in this stash of yours, anyway?"

" 'Bout thutty-five."

"Well, that's not bad, although I wish it were more. Truth is, after all this time I don't think we have too much longer. The fact that they were bold enough to make all the recent moves they did shows that, and the idea that they were out to eliminate the two of us. I think they're going to make their big move anytime now, and I think as it stands they're going to succeed. The two of you are rather uniquely positioned to act on it. Of course, it would be easier if we could get us a hypnoscan and get rid of that Stepin Fetchit accent of yours—it would be real convenient if the two of you were interchangeable—but that's why they made sure you had it. So they could always tell the two of you apart."

I was startled by that idea, but then I didn't see why I didn't figure it right off. Sure—if she was gonna play me, she had to talk like me, but since we was so damned much alike they had to make dead certain that even if I was discovered or sprung I couldn't pull a switch back on them. I was wrong; they hadn't underestimated me at all. If anything, they'd overdone it.

"But—if yo' git 'em, what happen to us?"

"There are three sides to the question for both of you," he pointed out. "Their side, the Company's side, and your side. Unlike the other two, your side has a vote, but it's only on whose side to belong to. Now, I have the same problem, with minor differences. If I go along with them, even volunteer for their side, I'll probably wind up with Bill Markham's job and vastly increased powers and get the both of you as souvenirs. If I go against them, they'll either have to kill me or when they take power in spite of me they'll probably eliminate me anyway as a potential thorn in their side—unless I win."

"Sounds like you'd be better off changin' sides," Brandy Two noted.

"The way things stand right now, you're probably right," he agreed, "but I have two powerful reasons not to. First, we're late immigrants here. I'm first-generation native born because my father had some foresight and he saw what was coming in Europe and managed to get here. The family was fairly poor, and he was the youngest, so they pooled to send him and my mother here first. By the time he was settled enough to try and help others, it was too late. Where they were sending the Jews you didn't need money. It won't be Jews this time, particularly, but I can still smell it coming. I guess I inherited it from my father. This time it's me asked to be a 'good German' for my own prosperity and safety and the hell with the others. I grew up hating that kind of person for killing my family. I value that hatred too much to compromise it. And, of course, there's one other reason."

He paused, then went on. "They took the only human being I ever loved and they robbed her of her humanity and made her something ugly."

"Sam! No!" I cried out. *"It ain't true!"*

"Yes it is," said Brandy Two sadly. "Honey, my old life weren't much, but it sure as hell was a life. We ain't people no more—we're *property*. We can jive talk all we want 'bout bein' victims and helpless and all that, and we are, but I don't kid myself 'bout what I *am*. Take a look at yo'self, girl! We is *slaves!* Only difference 'tween us and our great grandfathers is dey didn't wanna be no slaves, but we do!''

I turned 'round as best I could and stuck my head facedown in the pillow, sobbing, 'cause I knew right off she was right. If Sam hadn't been there, right in the room, then I woulda rejected the whole thing, put it from my mind. I still loved him, but I'd cheat on him in a minute, betray him in a flash. I *had* betrayed him, already, and all my daddy stood for, too. I would help that bunch of Vogels win, or look the other way, so long as they guaranteed my juice supply. I woulda thought it was wrong and too bad, but I'd'a let it happen, even helped, anyways. Worst part was, if I was in real withdrawal, and they told me I had to kill Sam to get the juice, I really didn't know if I could keep from pullin' that trigger.

No, that wasn't the worst part. The worst part was that I *still* didn't want no cure. If it came down to betrayin' Sam or gettin' the cure, I would probably betray him, even now. I knew it in my bones, just like my damned double did. When Sam made that remark 'bout goin' over to the other side and gettin' us as prizes I got a real feelin' of excitement that it might be so. It was Aldrath's worst-case example when he tried to talk me out of goin' in. I couldn't have Sam and the juice.

And as I thought this, the juice I had reacted. You wasn't allowed to get too depressed. You wasn't allowed to get yourself too messed up. It pushed my blood pressure back down and pushed a few of them chemical buttons in my brain. I still thought, *Yeah, they're both right. I ain't the same person no more. Can't never be. It feels too* good *to be like this.* I turned over again and looked at him.

"You see?" Brandy Two commented plainly. "It's easier when you know what you've become and don't fool yourself no more. Not better, just easier. You just lose your right to judge."

I swallowed hard. "Okay, Sam, so we deal wit' me as I is. So what if I tells ya where de stash is? What happens in a coupl've weeks?"

"I don't know. That's as honest an answer as I can give you," he responded, lookin' and soundin' real sad. "I'm the only one taking a real gamble. Deep down, I have to gamble on both of you to save my hide, and you have to gamble on me not holding out or turning you in. I'm betting on your basic addict selfishness, though. You're both smart girls; it doesn't affect that, which is lucky."

"We're listenin'," Brandy Two assured him.

"If you betray me, you'll be on their side and they'll give you juice—for a while, anyway. They may keep you on it. Then, again, they may just decide that they don't need you anymore and have no place for you. Then it's the end. There's always that risk, and it's strongest when they've won. If there's one thing Brandy—*my* Brandy—knows, it's that the Company top isn't just powerful, it's racist. They needed others for guinea pigs, but neither of you will fit into their final plan. You know what happened to Vogel's victims when they had no further use for them."

I had a real uneasy feelin' when he said this, since that was always the one fear I had since gettin' hooked, and the one fear the juice did not make go away. "Go 'head, we listenin'."

"Play it my way, and we'll have the origin world. The present Company. They're no angels themselves and they really don't give a damn, but when there's no reason to be cruel they take care of their own. They'd never let this shit get out generally—hell, you put a million doses out on the streets of Philadelphia and loads of people, some of them very middle and upper class, would be fighting to get hooked and wouldn't even ask or think about the price they'd pay. You know that. But it's *organic,* sort of. It exists somewhere in nature. A sufficient supply for the few addicts remaining could be insured indefinitely, particularly for the pair that exposed the thing and saved the damned Company's neck."

"Is that really—possible?" Brandy Two asked in wonder. "A lifetime supply, forever?"

"He ain't jivin', sista'," I told her. "Dat's jes' de way dey do stuff." He was right, and it made me feel a lot better to know that I could do the right thing and still be in my own best interests. "We got nothin' to lose if Sam play square wit' us." If the opposition believed I might not shoot Sam for the juice, then I was damn sure Sam couldn't betray me. "Unda' de flo' vent in de upstairs hall, Sam. It all dere."

He relaxed and put the gun away. "No it isn't."

I shot up. *"What!"*

"You may be only a shadow of your former self, but you still think the same. I found them before you even woke up. Now they really *are* no longer in the house."

"Den why—?"

"If you couldn't bring yourself to trust me and tell me, then I had no chance. No chance at all. Now, maybe, if we can give the details to your—sister—here and make *her* believe it, then we have a fighting chance." He gave a weary grin. "Now you two have only one worry, and it's a minor one, all things considered, but I just want you to be a little paranoid, too."

"What dat?" I asked him.

"If, somewhere, there are two Brandys as identical as the two of you, so much so they might have pulled off the switch, then somewhere, almost definitely, there's a Sam Two as well, one with the ethics of a cockroach who decided that being on the vice pad in Bristol was pale stuff compared to millions in the bank in *this* life. The original Sam is recovering from a serious brain injury, remember? That could hide any lapses. You see, that's the reason I was delayed so long. The move was anticipated, but tricky. We now have something on them—maybe. You see, in the Labyrinth, about thirty-six hours ago, one of us blew the other's brains out. That's why you, my would-be replacement bride, were called off. That's the beauty of it. Nobody —not you, not the Company, not the opposition—knows which one I really am. Not for sure."

Damn his hide!

"Chessworks."

"I would like to speak to Miss Addison, please."

"One moment. I'll transfer your call."

Click! Buzz! Whirr! Ring! "Yes?" It was *her* voice all right.

"This is Brandy. We have her."

"Where?"

"Right here at the house. She's good. She actually got the drop on me, but she didn't figure on a double for Sam, too. Neither did I! Why didn't you *tell* me?"

"It was not necessary for you to know. We didn't know if she might contact Markham or someone first to get allies."

"You give her too much credit. She's a shadow dancer, jus' like me. She was hopin' to replace me and use Sam in a scheme to make a deal with you, but she'd *never* give that Company no crack at her. You oughta know that by now."

There was silence for a moment, then Addison said, obviously amused, "Very well, then. This situation has changed from a strong and threatening negative into a positive. Put Sam on, please."

"I'm here," he said. "I'm on the upstairs extension."

"All right. You know your mission. Do it right and do it within the next twenty-five days and you'll live there like a king on those millions. Fail, and you will be remembered when the time comes, I promise you."

"I got the picture," he replied. "It's not like I haven't done it before. Once you bump off yourself you can bump off anybody. What do you want us to do with the broad?"

"I'll have a car at your place in sixty minutes or less, traffic willing. Since you're about to have delicacy problems, I don't think having a Brandy there who is an obvious addict would escape Markham's notice. We'll take both of them for now." She hung up. Abrupt, that girl, but she had a lot on her mind.

"What you s'posed t'do?" I asked him.

"Murder Markham in such a way that it can't be traced to me, preferably make it look like an accident. Dakani's no fool. He kept most of the resident agents, even the ones close to Aldrath, on the job. Markham's chomping at the bit to be let loose on this thing, and Dakani's inclined to promote him and give him some powers. If he failed, the kid could always blame Bill and Aldrath's people; if he succeeded, the kid gets the credit and maybe keeps the job. There are very few people with Bill's experience or track record in playing the game the right way. Hell, if they considered *me* a threat, think what they consider Bill! It's still a pretty small and close organization they've got, out of necessity, and they've still got a hard job ahead no matter what. What's it cost them to get me to waste Bill? If I do, he's out of the way. If I fail, I'm the only one who suffers."

"Makes sense," I agreed. "Real surprised t'hear all dat on de phone, though. If I was Bill I'd have a tap on it."

"Oh, he does," Sam replied. "State of the art for this world, but no high-tech stuff by Company standards. On the other hand, Addison's people have a tap, too, and they can tap into *this* tap. It blocks all calls to the Chessworks prefix from registering or recording on Bill's tap. Same goes for her calls here. They're pretty confident of it."

"They been pretty fuckin' confident of everything," Brandy Two commented sourly. "What you think they're gonna do with *me?*"

"Make you a guinea pig, just like her, before they risk any of their own with this."

"Sam? S'pose dey don't?" I said worriedly. "S'pose dey jus' send us back t' Fast Eddie or worse?"

"Then I'm done," he answered flatly. "But you won't be any worse off than you would have been otherwise, would you?"

I got a little chill. "Sam—hold me once," I asked him. "Hold me like y'used to an' jes' play like it be old times. Please."

And he held me real close and real tight, and he kissed me long and hard, and I knowed there was still the love there. God! How I'd mucked it all up! God! How I wanted him!

The car, a big blue Mercedes, pulled up in about forty minutes. I didn't expect Addison to be in it, and she wasn't; just a big, rough-lookin' black dude in a suit and a young straight-haired, round-faced black woman in a white uniform, like a nurse. We opened the door, and for just a moment I couldn't go out it. I didn't want to go. Somethin' held me back. All I wanted to do was turn around and grab Sam and run for it. Scream for him to make love to me and then put a bullet through my head.

Instead, I walked out, and my twin followed close behind. She and I was at least dressed decent for a change; she'd shopped for more than one outfit.

We got in, both of us lookin' sullen but me most of all, and even as the doors closed and we pulled away I felt like a tremendous hand was reachin' out and tryin' to snatch me back there. It took a while for the feelin' to fade, and it was real curious that the juice hadn't done nothin' to calm it down.

"Now, you two listen up and listen up good," the "nurse" said, turnin' to us. "You just sit there real nice and quiet-like and enjoy the ride. We got some miles to make today. When you two need t' get juiced?"

"After eleven tonight," Brandy Two replied, and I said, "Anytime afta' fo' in the mornin'."

She nodded to herself. "Well, we gonna put you two on an equal basis. Now, we gonna pull over up here and you two are gonna get out and we all gonna go over in the bushes and you're gonna get naked and we'll see if you got any juice on you. Any juice we find, we're gonna *destroy*. You got that? Now, *I* don't have no juice, and Monroe, here, *he* don't have no juice, so if you two girls don't behave and do just like we say we aren't gonna make it to the folks who do. Understand?"

We understood. We even figured on it. I had none, but my twin had four, since that's a natural thing for a shadow dancer to do in these circumstances, and she'd already managed to hide two in the car, keepin' two on her person.

They found all four, although I thought for a moment that old Monroe was gonna miss the one wedged in back of the seat rest. They ain't that easy to destroy, but they had some chemical that would do it. I wondered who the hell they was to know so much, but they never said. Some folks from their force here, probably drawn from the Company's mob ranks, who expected to be real important here when the new folks took over, most likely.

We took the Northwest Extension up to I–80, then headed west. That State College substation had always been leaky for the opposition; there musta been some way they had of usin' it without it registerin' on security's boards, or so I figured. We didn't go all the way there, though; instead, we turned in at a roadside motel where they fed us, then took us to a room in back for which Monroe had the key.

Monroe sent "nurse" Longstreet outside, then turned to us. "Now, which one of you is the fuckin' oreo?"

"Me," we both responded at once. I was real surprised, and signalled her it was okay.

"We both been lib'rated," I told him. "We don't care 'bout no color. What're you? De black Klan?"

That enraged him, and he started in on me. I had real rough, big, nasty bruisers before, but this guy was somethin' of a psycho. The only thing that was savin' me was that the

juice wouldn't let nothin' get real painful without tippin'
the scales the other way. Kinda made you a masochist to get
pleasure for pain, but it was better than the alternative. Fact
was, the only thing savin' *Monroe* was the fact that we both
needed juice.

Suddenly there was loud talkin' outside, and the door
opened and Monroe stopped for a moment and looked up,
mean as hell. Standin' there was Ms. Cool herself, Addison.
I could hear Longstreet cussin' a blue streak outside, but
somebody had her.

Addison took one look, figured what was goin' on even if
she didn't know the reason, and said, fairly firmly, "Just
what the *hell* do you think you're doing?"

"Shut up, bitch! This ain't your business!" Monroe
growled. That was a mistake.

"Girls," Addison said, calm as could be, "you have my
permission, and my support, if you want to kill this idiot."

Monroe gave a big laugh, but it didn't last long. You take
two women bodybuilder types together and no hunk even
Monroe's size and strength was gonna keep us from doin'
damage. It was one hell of a fight, though, 'cause of the big
weight difference, and while we done him some real damage, when Brandy Two kicked him in the gut and sent him
to the floor under the sink, he rebounded, made for his coat,
and I knew he was goin' for his gun.

He never made it. There was this short Pfutt! sound, and
there was a neat hole in the side of his head. He actually
looked surprised; I think he was dumb enough and strong
enough that it took him five full seconds 'fore he realized he
was dead. The recoil hardly moved him. Finally he just sort
of sat down on the floor, stared hard, like he was seein'
somethin' he couldn't understand, then keeled over.

"Messy, but satisfying," noted Addison, putting her
pistol back in her purse. "You—get your clothes on and
both of you come with me," she added, pointin' to me. "I
had hoped to use this place tonight but we're going to have
to have it cleaned up instead."

I got back into my jeans, shirt, and sandals and we
followed her out. I got to admit I was surprised at all this;
she hadn't seemed like the kind to give a damn about stuff
like that as long as it wasn't her. Two big men pushed

Monroe's girlfriend into the room after we left and closed the door. I looked around and figured either everybody else was sound sleepers or business was lousy.

Parked in an outer lot designed for the purpose was a tractor trailer; one of them big rigs. The trailer didn't have no signs or pictures or nothin', just a big dirty silver. Addison leaped up on the ledge like she done this all the time, threw the levers, and opened one side of the back. We hauled ourselves in, and she got in after us. It was pretty dark in there, but soon as she closed and bolted the rear door the lights come on.

Inside was a whole bunch of equipment, some real big, some in crates and some not, and two people. One was a medium-sized fellow in plaid shirt, jeans, and boots who had real dark skin but wasn't black; he kinda looked like some Indian. The other was a woman with a great build, kinda like ours, but with golden skin and brown hair. One of the golden people of the headquarters world.

The truck roared into life, although I ain't sure right then if even they knew where they was goin'. Monroe had sorta screwed up their plans. The man reached in his pocket and took out two little cubes and tossed them to us. "Here," he said, in Spanish-accented English. "Get your fix now. We have much work to do."

I still wasn't sure it was late enough for me, but since these folks had the supply it didn't cost nothin' to try. I was under in real sweet ecstasy in about a minute and a half.

They didn't do nothin' in the comedown period, since they shut off most of the lights and all of 'em seemed to be asleep themselves. We was still movin', but we didn't know to where. I heard my twin give a giggle and turned to her.

"Look at 'em," she said. "The most dangerous people around, and we don't dare do nothin'. That girl one of them bossworld people?"

"Yeah, that's what they look like," I replied.

"Reminds me of somebody, but I can't think who."

I looked over at her. "The rest of the shadow dancers. Different color, different hair, but all the rest of them girls looked just like that. Haven't you figured that much out yet?"

"Uh uh. Not till now. By the way—glad to see you can

talk regular again. Guess they musta done it while we was
out with somethin' in here."

I was flat-out amazed. Until that moment I hadn't
realized that I *was* back to normal—at least, the normal I
was before they run that jive on me at Arnie's. Wasn't
nothin' to read in there, but I could imagine a page in my
mind and know all the words. Somehow, they took that
module out of me that they put in. That meant that one of
these crates, probably the biggest, was a hypnoscan, and
that made the Mex or whatever he was Dr. Carlos. Brandy
Two confirmed it.

"That pig was my main trainer at the lodge. You suppose
he's one of 'em, too?"

I shook my head. "No way. Wrong build, wrong face,
wrong everything. I guess they could make themselves look
like that if they really wanted to, but I don't think they did
it to him. He's like that pair back there, and Crockett, and
Arnie—just hired help. Real smart and skilled hired help,
but that's it."

"You suppose they ran us both through that thing like
they did last time? I mean, they took somethin' out of your
head, but did they put somethin' else in?"

It was a good question, but I was fairly confident they
hadn't. "Uh uh. They can take that shit out in 'bout an
hour, but it takes a *long* time to put things in. *Damn!* I'm
starvin' and I hav'ta go to the bathroom."

"Me, too. So do they, I guess. Got to be somethin' in
here."

We was feelin' good, and we got up and did a little
explorin', tryin' not to wake up nobody. They *did* have one
of them chemical porta-potty things back in a corner, and
that at least took care of the immediate problem. We
wandered back, 'cause there was nothin' else to do.

"You know, that girl she looks kinda Hawaiian. You got
Hawaiians in this world?"

I nodded and looked. "Yeah, 'cept for the brown hair and
maybe a little difference in skin tone, you're right. Never
thought of that. Island kind of folks, anyways. You got my
brains, even if you ain't got my experience. See anything
else peculiar? Take a look at *both* them girls."

She tried, but shook her head. "What do you mean?"

"Addison's one of them, too. You take that makeup off, put down that hair and make it that brown color, and put her in some decent clothes."

"Them eyes ain't right."

"Yeah, they are, under there somewhere. She ain't been medically converted. It's more like some kind of high-tech makeup job, like they might do in their world for show business. That's why the makeup's so heavy. Covers up the seams."

"But her skin's darker—not like ours, but like white folks with real deep suntans."

"More tricks, that's all. Probably takes a bath in some kinda dye that shade, which is a little darker and duller than theirs. Makes a world of difference. The shadow dancers was black, brown, lily-white, and China yellow, but they was all the same. All but us."

Even with the noise and shakin' and rattlin', I guess we was talkin' too loud 'cause Addison stirred, opened her eyes, looked over at us, then got up. "No use," she said. "I can't stay asleep in something like this. I heard you two talking."

"We was just wonderin' whether you started out in actin' or not," I said pointedly. "You do great makeup, and you play parts real good, too."

"You *are* good. Uh—I assume you are this world's Brandy I'm talking to. Since Carlos took that module out you really *are* incredibly identical."

"I am—was—the detective," I told her.

"Well, to answer your question, my parents were performers. The sort of art they practiced has no real equivalent here. It's a traditional form among my people that is both for art and religion. It is practiced only by husband and wife teams, so when my father died the show was over, so to speak."

"I didn't think none of you people *ever* died," I commented.

"It *is* true that we live a long time, and do not suffer the diseases and infirmities you do, but we all die, sooner or later, from age or from accident. His was accidental, in a crash. They loved each other very much. My mother was left with three daughters and no means of support. She was expected to marry again out of convenience, but she could not bring herself to do so. The only chance they had for any future was in one of the colonies, one without major class distinctions. We were neither fish nor fowl, as you say. We were low-class people performing for upper-class patrons. Unless we all found eligible men in our very small profession, we could not continue it. It took money to emigrate and become established, and my sisters were very young. There was a patron, a very powerful man, whom we played for often, who took a liking to me. I could become his mistress, his kept woman, as it were, and he would pay for the emigration of my family. I accepted. I was fifteen years old."

This was something I hadn't expected at all. She was moody, soft, introspective, and had a need to talk. I guess, rollin' along in a semi in the early-mornin' hours and unable to sleep, she just figured some company was better than none. At least she figured we'd understand, although why she felt we would I didn't know.

"Yeah, well, at least you had the silks and furs," Brandy Two commented. "Me, I was just past fourteen when I run away, and I wound up in a run-down row house in Washington, me and six other girls, hooked on smack in another few months 'cause it helped not to think or regret and workin' the streets for a quota. We all got our sob stories, honey."

Addison looked at her, then at me. "No, there's a difference. I look over at the two of you and I see exactly the same person. I listen to you speak, and I hear only slight differences in your speech, and that probably only because this is not my native tongue. But on my right is a woman who came up from nothing and made something of herself and developed her brain, and on my right is the same woman who did none of this. You might have had bad luck, bad breaks, or even made some stupid decisions, but clearly you had choices. Two ways at least to go. I did not. Women in my society are theoretically equal to men, but none, not even in the upper classes, ever can reach a level of decision making, policy making. Middle-class women can have education and careers, but they always work for men carrying out men's projects and goals. In my class, a woman could not even be chief gardener of an upper-class estate.

An assistant, perhaps, but always taking orders from the men."

"It ain't that cool here, neither," I pointed out. "Is that what got you into this?" Hell, in *this* world some of the meanest radicals was women. "Try bein' a black woman in this kinda society and see how far you get."

"Each world has its own problems," Addison said. "I can do nothing for other worlds until I fix my own. That is difficult and dangerous enough."

"Yeah, so you're doin' your sugar daddy's work for him, like always," my twin noted. "You give him his revolution and he gives you the shaft. I seen that too many times before."

"He just wants power, it's true, and he might be no better, perhaps worse, than what we have now, but he is a product of society and he does not understand the concept of *radical*. By the roots. Nothing less will gain what I want. To him, this is a small, limited plot to take over the Board and control it. A few parties, a few party girls with some of the old men, and that's it. I am his link to all of it. He cannot leave. He was brilliant in showing me how even the greatest computers and experts can be fooled if they are fed consistent but faulty information. He is a typical, arrogant upper-class male and I know him far too well. I knew he would never even *think* that he could be a victim of just such a thing. How could he? I am a mere, insignificant woman, a mistress, lover, and actress, carrying out his orders to the letter. A majority of the corporate board as his shadows, dancing to his tunes. That's all his vision allows."

I suddenly saw where she was goin' with all this, and I was appalled. "You have the missin' element now, the thing that the juice needs and we can't make. But to pull it off, then *you* . . ."

She nodded. "Yes. I must become a host, an addict, myself. I am prepared to do this. As you can see from Aeii, here, there is very little physical change in us compared to you. It is not obvious to anyone, which is the point."

"He'll be cautious. He'll catch you. You know damned well he'll run you through one of them mind wringers before he lets you get near him, once it all starts."

"Dear, sweet Carlos, here, will see that it doesn't happen.

Even the great manipulator Jamispur will not be able to detect it, just as Vogel's technicians could not detect you. He will see only what men expect to see when they examine women like me. He will be extra clever, and search for the lone linkage that might trigger a different personality, but it will not be there. One with Jamispur's skills might have detected you at Vogel's, given time, but not even he can detect what is cut off, closed off, no longer there."

"But that's a kind of suicide," Brandy Two pointed out. "What good's your revolution if you can't pull no strings?"

"The strings will be pulled by others. The depth of my commitment is so absolute I will let no consideration stand in my way. I am only the weapon, not the revolution."

"Yeah, so your big man's in charge, he can just send out for juice any old time he wants," I noted. I got a real uneasy feelin' about this, and about anybody who was this much of a fanatic. "Who could stop him?"

She smiled. "He only thinks he knows where it comes from. He does not. Only a precious few know. And after, even I won't know. We do not mean to control the Corporation, we mean to bring it down. All of it, from its corrupt and inbred male leadership to its vicious class distinctions. And once we do that, we will begin instilling justice on other worlds as we can and as we find them."

Well, I had to admit there ain't been no crime chief who was female since Ma Barker, but I wasn't none too sure I'd like these folks better. Seems I remembered old Ma was pretty scary herself. And it seemed to me, anyways, that nobody who could excuse folks like Vogel and Siegel and cause so much torture and sufferin' and death could accept slow, peaceable reform. Who would be marched to the camps in *this* world 'cause they was impossible to reform and reeducate? How many slaves would they make to build their perfect societies? Old Aldrath had it right, I thought, when he said that progress only came if you had worlds to steal from.

"You will be my vanguard," she continued. "You deserve the honor, for depriving me of Vogel just when vital discoveries were made. The two of you will have the honor of paving the way for the salvation of humanity."

10.

Of Rainbow Weeds and Other Matters

The last of the puzzle was comin' clear now; the few things that didn't make no sense was fallin' into place. I ain't too much on subjects like biology or other sciences, but detective work is puzzle solvin', and makin' sense of what evidence you got is the way to solve it. Trouble was, we always thought we was dealin' with one organization, the competition, as any moves against the Company was always called. Now we had that, and a band of fanatic revolutionaries within it even the bad guys didn't know about.

I still can't figure why Addison just come out and told it to us, or why she bothered to have Carlos fix me up. The only thing I could figure was that somehow she thought just 'cause we was bright women stuck by circumstances she thought we'd understand, maybe even applaud. Yeah, maybe in the end that was it. All this secrecy and skulking about in disguise, all this two-timin' and double-crossin' was leadin' up to the climax for her, and since she didn't expect to be able to appreciate it then she just wanted to take a few bows now.

Still, while it was double dangerous to be around her at this stage, the fact was it was lucky beyond any hopes we had. Maybe Sam had her figured all along; maybe, somehow, he knew she needed an audience, and we was the only witnesses around guaranteed not to talk.

Carlos and this Aeii was a lot less friendly, and clearly considered us excess baggage, but they indulged her. Why not? At least instead of tryin' to figure a way to tag along, we was bein' forced to take front row seats.

It was clear that Carlos and Addison had a thing goin'. At

least, he looked at her and treated her like some kinda goddess, and he was the only man around who we ever saw her drop her act and guard. He knew he was gonna lose her, but he was willin'. Like I said, fanatics. I don't know whose world spawned him, but he sure as hell wanted it changed.

My twin and me, we had problems with the juice that they had to handle. Like I said, when the juice says you need somethin', you really need it. Food we got, at roadside places, though not the balance we needed, so we both wound up with some of them funny and otherwise gruesome combinations of things. They also let us run, at roadside rest stops, and we was able to use the space and some of the gear in the truck for other exercises and weights. The sex urge was a problem, since the driver was this tough-lookin' woman in a black outfit and cowboy hat and Carlos was only interested in Addison. The only way out of it was the way we'd had to go when the club was closed and weather kept any chance of gettin' anybody slim to none. I won't go into details, but if you ever wonder what it'd be like to be somebody else and get laid by yourself, ask me. It wasn't all that bad, since we both sure enough knew just what the other liked most. It was kinda like havin' a million great appetizers but no main course, but so long as you got off, the juice didn't know no different.

They all watched us with real distaste, and Addison in particular looked uncomfortable. We was a real example of what she was thinkin' of doin' to herself.

We come into a small private airport somewheres in Ohio, I think, and there was a plane waitin' for us. It was a small job as planes go, but it could take the five of us, with the lady trucker keepin' on the road with all that fancy and illegal gear. It was a straight air charter, called ahead from the road. I figured from this either we wasn't goin' where I thought we was or they decided not to use anyplace the Company might now be monitoring.

We finally landed, after two stops, someplace in Mississippi, which didn't thrill either of us none on the face of it. I got to admit, though, that my twin was far less thrilled than me. In her world Lincoln lost the 1864 election, and President McClellan made peace with the Confederacy. Oh, they got reunited again, long 'bout 1900, but on strict terms that included a state's rights to make its own laws on segregation and race and to leave the union again if the Compact of 1900 was broken. Yeah, the south abolished slavery eventually, but her version of the place sounded more like South Africa than the U.S.A. I knew. The north wasn't so bad—most of the states had their own civil rights acts—but her Mississippi of today was kinda like ours of the twenties. I tried to assure her that *this* Mississippi even had black mayors and councilmen and sheriffs, but I had to admit I still didn't feel comfortable in the place, neither.

By nightfall, we was in a rented station wagon headin' south, first on nice road, then on real back road shit. We finally got to this old deserted shack in the middle of this hot, humid, swamp in the center of the lousiest land in the state. It was run-down and didn't have no phone or electricity or nothin', but it had a pump outside that worked, an old-style outhouse out back that smelled like nothin' else on this or any other Earth, a wood-burnin' old iron stove, a few supplies in sealed containers, and a bunch of mattresses stacked up in a corner that would do for all of us. Addison had stopped at a grocery and picked up a bunch of things, which told us we was gonna be there for a little while but not too long or there'd be a hell of a drive for more.

They put us to work beatin' out the mattresses, wipin' down the place, washin' out the pots and pans, and even choppin' some of the chunks of wood there so they'd fit in the stove for cookin'. We also did the cookin', the servin' on paper plates and with paper cups we'd bought, and the cleanin' up. The way they had us goin', I got the real impression that the only thing these folks found wrong with havin' a low class to do the shitwork was that they was all in it. They wasn't so damned superior as they liked to think they was, but any attempt to point it out was met mostly with anger and threats, not reason. 'Bout the only consolation we had was that the millions of mosquitoes there tried us and dropped dead without no bites of consequence, while them three was near eaten alive and covered with Carlos's salve.

We was there close to two days when that big old truck finally got to us. By that time they'd gone down into the swamps and come back with this thing that was like a flat

piece of roughed-up plastic that floated a little bit off the
ground. There seemed to be some kinda touch controls on
it, though nothin' was marked, so it went up or down to
suit. To move, though, you had to push it, although even if a
couple of us stood on it, anybody could move it as easy as if
it was on flat rails.

Now they needed our muscles, and everybody else's, to
move that shit from the trailer onto the slab. It was a lot of
stuff, and one of them crates had to weigh a ton—took us
two hours just to get it from the back of the trailer to the
edge, bit by bit—but once you had it on the slab it was the
same as all the rest.

I ain't sure if that lady trucker was in on anything or not,
but she got paid off a huge roll of hundred-dollar bills and
she never asked no questions or made more than businesslike comments. I got the strong impression that she got not
just the cash but that they bought and gave her the truck as
well. I guess maybe I wouldn't ask no questions, neither.

Well, once we had it all, they was as anxious as could be
to get out of there. I couldn't figure why we flew down, 'cept,
maybe, none of the others could stand the idea of two more
days and nights in the back of that truck with poor sleep. I
got the idea that if they knowed about Mississippi mosquitoes in summer they might have saved their money and
taken the truck.

A wide path, just wide enough for the sled, as they called
it, had been cut outta the woods, but they had my double
and me take an ax and saw and sickle and clear out what
had grown back since the last time they used the place,
which was more than they'd figured. Still, it only took the
two of us to push all that stuff down to this shallow and
foul-smellin' lake edge. I knowed we was strong, but we
wasn't *that* strong. It was easy to see how small amounts of
goods could be easily transported within the Labyrinth.

At the lake's edge, though, we all had to get up on the
thing and push off with two long, rough poles, one on each
side, walkin' front to back at the same time. This was
clearly another one of them Vogel-type entrances, one that
the Company didn't consider useful, and when we reached
the spot and saw the Labyrinth form, I could see why. All
but a tiny little bit of that set of constantly changin' cubes of

light and force was under the damned water. We headed into it, and wound up in a cube that had a fair amount of that water in it, only it wasn't actin' like water should. It was all broke up and floatin' around, and we all got sloshin' wet with swampy, foul-smellin' water in no time. Still, we was able to jump down in a hurry and push into the next cube where it was dry, but the smell lingered on.

I never been on this track, so I had no idea where the switches was or anything, but just before a switch point we angled up and out the top. It was dry land, anyways, and surrounded by one creepy-lookin' forest. I almost preferred the swamp after seein' these monstrous trees and bushes that seemed all misshapen and was all sorts of colors and not just green. If you can imagine a forty-foot-high mushroom that was all ugly bruise-purple and oozed bloody-lookin' shit outta its top, you get the idea of just one of the horrors of that place.

"Anybody live 'round here?" I asked nervously.

"No," Carlos replied. "There are some great apes on other continents that have rudimentary intelligence, but there are no great apes on this continent. There are dangerous creatures about, though, so once we reach the camp and throw on the protection, do not venture beyond it."

He wasn't exactly warmin' to us, but I think he was gettin' to like havin' two strong folks around to do all the shitwork he and the other two might otherwise have to do. Aeii was probably the same way, but we couldn't be sure. She and Carlos could talk in some language, and she and Addison could talk in that singsong tongue, but she didn't know no English, or at least she acted like she didn't.

We passed through a bunch of poles about ten feet apart that looked like fence posts waitin' for the fence. Once inside, Addison hit a switch on a pole and there was some kind of light beams criss-crossin' between each of the posts. "Don't touch the posts or in between," Addison cautioned us. "It is sensitive to size and shape to a degree so it probably wouldn't kill you, but it might burn all your hair off and probably leave you blind and partially paralyzed." She didn't have to worry. After that, I didn't want to be no closer to them things than I had to be.

The camp itself looked like some African village, with

three big round huts with thatched roofs and a few smaller ones that looked the same 'cept for size. The biggest one, right in the middle, had some kind of hard, very smooth brown floor, and had a kind of straw door that opened big enough to get the whole sled in. Once in, though, it was real hairy movin', since the place already had a bunch of machines in it. It looked like something out of the Center, or at least Doc Jamispur's lab. There was lights, and even power for all this stuff, though from where I couldn't guess. There sure were no wires to the huts.

We got all but the big, heavy one off easy, then managed to tilt the sled enough to get it to mostly slide off with some real group pushin'.

It turned out they had a real setup here. One of the huts had a communal shower with real hot water—it looked like they collected rainwater, purified, and stored it—and toilets. Not our kind, but waterless round types that somehow got rid of the stuff with a chemical spray. Every time you went you had to wash off in the shower, though; nobody thought to pack toilet paper.

The third contained your basic headquarters roughin'-it kitchen, which was a bunch of gadgets that stored food in these funny boxes, then you stuck 'em, box and all, into one of these compartments or another dependin' on if they matched the symbols on the box, waited until a bell rung, and took 'em out. Some was hot, some cold, and others at room temperature, but while we didn't recognize much of what we ate it didn't taste all that bad and the juice approved.

They stuck us in this little hut that was furthest away from the bathroom, but that figured. It wasn't much—a woven straw mat floor, one bed that was barely a double that seemed to be just a big air mattress covered in some soft stuff and all blown up at one end to form a kinda pillow, plus a bowl if you wanted to get water from the supply and keep it handy, and that was it. We waited to take our showers after them, and stuck our nice, new clothes in to soak, although we kinda figured we'd never get that stink out.

None of the others bothered with no clothes 'cept Carlos, who put on some kind of flowered ankle-length skirt and belt. We figured he was both bein' modest as the only man in the world and also it looked right on him, like the kind of thing his people wore wherever they was.

They mostly ignored us and let us do our own thing 'cept for a few hours after we arrived when Carlos and Addison called us into the big hut and he gave us each a cup of some dark liquid. "Drink it—all of it," he ordered.

It tasted lousy goin' down, but after a little while it really revved us up. We went through our needs and routines extra long and extra hard that day, then just dropped into sleep. It wasn't till the next day that Brandy Two said, "We didn't get no juice last night."

"Huh? 'Course we did, 'cause I feel fine."

"We didn't get it. We should both be well into withdrawal right now, but we're fine. I'm even a little higher than usual. You?"

"The same." I got puzzled. This wasn't possible—was it? Not that we kicked it. We hadn't. It was all there, all the same, only we didn't get no jolt and we both felt cheated by it, even a little let down. No super high at all for the first time in almost a year. No mellow comedown. Nothin'. The juice was still runnin' our bodies and our routines okay, but it was kinda on its own.

Later that day, the juice made that same shit in the cup taste like the world's most wonderful wine. "This is it, huh? This is the stuff?"

He nodded. "Not a lab production, though. It is the product of a plant. A very common plant in certain areas. The locals in the world where it grows call it something like ogroppa, or that is as close as we can come to a name that is part word, part grunt. Literally speaking, the name means 'rainbow weed,' since it is quite colorful. It is their staple, as we use maize, rice, bread, or potatoes. Its chemical composition is quite complex and unique to any botany I have known. Even this world's strange plants are distant relatives to ones in our worlds, but this seems to be a crossover between the botany of basic humanity and the botany of the other sentient peoples who are out along the boundaries of Type Two. At some point, a common organism that was parasitic on higher animals in that world moved into the lifeform that are humans there, and a strange relationship developed among a viral organism, a plant, and the humans of that world. The plant will grow most anywhere except in the Arctic and immediate subarctic regions, deserts, and above roughly two thousand meters. The natives take it for granted and have never related it to this parasite inside them, which becomes a symbiont with the plant. They do not even understand that there is anything inside them at all."

"They ain't real clever, huh?" Brandy Two asked.

"Oh, they have the same potential as we do, but this shapes their development. They do not get sick, therefore they have not developed real medicine and biology as we know it. They are excellent farmers and herdsmen, but high mountain barriers, stretches of desert, and wide seas limit them, as the plant will not travel well or for very long without going bad. They are a generally happy people; they have a rich art and folklore tradition, and some remarkable cities similar to those of the ancient native American empires or those of the early Middle East. They progress, but they are not very ambitious. As you can guess, they have a great deal of sex, but they reproduce very slowly. Females there ovulate only a couple of times a year. The only reason you have this irrepressible sex urge is that it thinks you are one of them; it senses potential reproduction almost constantly in you, and not being smart or clever it acts."

"But there ain't no super high with this shit!" I protested. "That ain't fair, when you got to do all the other stuff."

"You will always want it, but we think you will get used to this. We will take specimens and samples from you daily, from now on. Otherwise, you are free to roam about. Later, when we begin to move, you will gain even more freedom."

"Hold on," I said. "You say you knew 'bout this whole thing, this plant, long ago? Then why all this experimentin'?"

"The biochemical problem is, I think, beyond you. It has to do with the way in which the plant's molecules are constructed. The architecture is very alien to what we understand now, and we haven't had the resources of the Corporation or institutions like the Center. Its own requirements for growth and development are not understood. It grows in most Type Zero and all Type One worlds, and looks chemically identical to the original, yet it will not interact with the symbiont. This is the first one that tested out in the lab for interaction, only a week ago. You two are telling me whether it is functionally identical to the parent."

So that was it. They couldn't use Vogel's world no more, 'cause we blew it before they made their breakthrough. And they couldn't test it on them shadow dancers, 'cause that was their own and needed for the plot. They could make more addicts, but that'd require them importin' more juice when the heat was on, and that wouldn't tell them nothin' 'bout long-time addicts. So they had Brandy Two left over from their idea of switchin' for me, and they had me, so we was handy. Guinea pigs, just like Sam said.

It wasn't a hundred percent, but where it failed it wasn't no pain. Some times you just had so much energy you had to burn it off; other times, you got real droopy and just sorta lay around lazily and tripped a little on raindrops or clouds or grass or somethin', just starin' for hours. I could see why they was good artists; probably would blow mean jazz, too.

You really ached for that jolt and high, but we both knew deep down that Carlos was right. We'd always want it, but we didn't *need* it. We was on our own form of methadone.

After we'd get into our horny fever pitch and go at it, Carlos would be there takin' vaginal samples and scrapin's. Took me a couple days to figure out what he was lookin' for, and took him about ten days to find it. In the meantime, Addison left for someplace, come back briefly once, then left again. She was back about four days after Carlos made his discovery, and this time there wasn't no doubt I guessed right all down the line. She didn't have no disguise on, and she was gorgeous.

"I can't believe that's the same girl," my twin remarked. "Jesus! She even turns *me* on and I'm sick of doin' it with women—nothin' personal."

"I know what you mean." Did I *ever!* "They got this, they ain't never gonna have ta go back to the origin world, though. We're dead-ended and it should be clear by now. I can't figure why nobody's moved."

"You *sure* that Sam was your man? I mean, *real* sure?"

"Sure as I can be," I replied without much hesitation. "You heard him and saw him. They wouldn't'a had much prep time to get him ready, and they didn't have Sam under a hypnoscan like they did you and me. I don't think he could have faked it. Besides, even if they coulda, I just *felt* it. I couldn't explain it, I just *felt* it."

"I thought I did, too. He loves you an awful lot, sister. An awful lot. And this hurt him real bad."

"I know," I whispered. "I know."

Addison seemed both nervous and excited when she came over to see us. "Come. Get into the clothing I have brought for you. After all this time, we are finally beyond the testing and the skulking."

She brought two of the sari and sandal combinations common to the world of headquarters, and they fit just fine. Addision, Carlos, and Aeii also got new clothes, but with an added touch. Each had a small, light, but real nasty-lookin' gun. You wasn't real sure how it worked or what it shot, but no matter how futuristic it was, I could recognize a machine gun when I saw one. They checked 'em out, but then put them in a carryin' bag which Carlos carried for now. Clearly you didn't want to be seen with them things when you reached a switch point.

"You two will stay close to each other at all times," she warned us, "and give no warnings or alarms. Come."

Carlos killed the protection gizmo and we walked out. I dunno how that thing guarded when nobody was there; I guess they had some kind of switch down at the Labyrinth entrance.

Carlos carried with him a gadget I'd heard the Company dudes call a forcer, a small but impressive-lookin' little machine that could force a weak point open, briefly, to gain entrance to the Labyrinth from a world at that weak point or to maintain a small signal so that you could do it with the right code the other way. It made safe worlds like this one possible, and I bet that the bright boy who invented it spent the rest of his life wishin' he hadn't.

We got cubin' okay, but the thing looked weak, unsteady, and not too big. Even so, we stepped into it and everybody made it. We walked immediately down one to the switch point, which was bein' handled by a guy in a red uniform who had a face sorta like an orangutan. "Headquarters, security clearance—" and then she gave one of them words or phrases in the headquarters language. Ape-face checked his board, then made a kinda circle with his face which I guess was the same as a nod, and replied through the translator, "Very well. The male, however, is not cleared. Do you wish me to call in for special clearance?"

"That will not be necessary," she replied, real cool now like she usually was. "Only two of us will enter, the rest will remain in a holding cube until we take care of our matter."

"Very well. Cleared in. Specify the two to go at the final switch control point."

We kept goin', wonderin' just what was goin' on. Headquarters? It didn't make no sense. We couldn't take no guns in, and if I guessed right 'bout what this was all leadin' up to, neither Brandy Two or me was much good there. It was a real surprise, then, when we got to the final security checkpoint and Addison specified herself and me to go in.

And suddenly I figured what we was doin', and I got real scared.

We got cleared all right, but when we got to the entry cube and she motioned for the others to wait, I refused to move. That got 'em a little mad, but confused 'em, too. Finally Carlos reached in the gun bag and I thought he was gonna shoot one of us to get the other in, but instead he brought out a pair of them little headsets, givin' one to Addison and one to me, so we could talk to each other.

"What is your problem?" she asked, nervous and irritated. "I won't leave you there."

"Don't make no difference. Once we do this, I figure you don't need us no more. I might just as well yell 'security' once I'm inside as come back out with you and get dumped in some world where they ain't got no juice or no weed or nothin'. If I'm gonna die I'd rather it be with a gun, here and now, then slow from withdrawal, and we know too damn much to be stuck someplace with a pile of the stuff."

"I thought of that," she told me. "Look, right now you are registered in the log as coming in with me, and you will be registered going out and at every switch point from then on. They may never make the connection that there's something odd about it, but we can't take that chance. If we could, there are other ways to force you to do this. After this, we will take you up to the origin world, the world where the thing is natural and the rainbow weed runs wild. It's no paradise, and the people aren't quite human, but there are a few other humans stuck there—men, too—so you will survive. After we have taken over, we will come to liberate all of you, as you will be very useful when we begin to reform the other worlds. Now, come. They will grow suspicious if we wait too long."

I wasn't too sure whether to believe her or not, but I figured I had very little to lose now that the point was made. I went through with her into the entry chamber. We stripped down, got sterilization baths and super scans and everything, then got cleared to come on back, take that little code verification test on the combination eye and scale gadget, then walked into reception. The small staff was there with new clothes like before, and we had no trouble walkin' from there to the high-speed elevator and up to the surface station.

"You're takin' a real risk with this, ain't you?" I whispered to her.

"It had to be done and I had to see it. There was no other way. Now, I will make my call on mundane business from here and we will exit and rejoin the others."

"You mean what you said back there?"

"Why not? Soon you will be joined by many more, from all the worlds the Company now exploits." And, with that, she made her call. I don't know to who or why, but I figured it was some routine thing not at all connected to our business, though I thought it might have been a code call to her high-class lover that all was goin' well.

It was over quick enough, and we made our way back down. The way out was on a different floor from the way in, and not nearly so complicated. You just had a code check, to make sure nobody was sneakin' out who shouldn't be, and then you stepped into the Labyrinth that was always on at this end.

Addison smiled and nodded to Carlos and Aeii, who seemed real pleased, as well they should be. This was one *hell* of a plot.

We had a *long* walk in the Labyrinth after that, the longest I ever remembered. The switches and tracks had shortcuts to help long distances, but we was still talkin' hours and hours of cubes and more cubes, weird landscapes and more weird landscapes. After a while, Carlos and Aeii handed off the bag to Addison after takin' out their own guns and left us. It was just us three now, but somehow that made me feel better, not worse. Addison's fury at Monroe had been real; she had a temper, but I think in her own way she had a sense of honor. I wasn't none too sure the other pair did.

Finally we turned and entered the damndest tunnel in the whole thing I *ever* saw.

All the scenes on all four cube walls for the longest distance was exactly the same. We was lookin' out on some broad grassy range and off in the distance you could see a fellow on horseback. But each scene was just slightly different as you walked through. It was fascinatin'. First of all, the man and the horse was never in the same exact place. Second of all, sometimes the grass was tall, sometimes short, sometimes green, sometimes yellow, and sometimes there was other trees and sometimes there wasn't. The man and the horse and the scene all changed. After a while, that horse seemed to be a purplish thing and the guy on top began to look more and more like some kinda horror movie freak and less and less like a man. Unfortunately, the scene ran out before I could get a real clear look at them, but I got to tell you it was unnervin'.

We was now in Type One territory, and it was weird all 'round. Once they set up a region, they blacked out the worlds they didn't use or want to look at generally and now there was only the occasional scene here or there, almost never with people. You couldn't see much, anyways; they was careful that their stations would always be concealed, so what we'd seen with that horse and rider was some real thin weak point, a natural thing. Now we was back to just stations, and they was as blacked out mostly as the unused worlds.

We stopped in stages at certain worlds, mostly Company setups, I figured, where there was survival shacks, basic Type Zero food and water, and the like. There was also a separate area we could see that looked all crazy and had stuff you wouldn't touch on a bet—Type One stuff. These was worlds like the one we'd left, worlds where people of any kind just never got invented, and they used 'em as rest stops on the inter-world highway. At the first one, Addison pulled out these little necklaces that looked sorta like red pearls, one for each of us. "Put these on," she ordered us, puttin' one on herself. "They contain small broadcast units that contain randomly shifted identity codes while leaving the security clearance intact. They will mask your much weaker identity signals and make it impossible to trace us from this point."

Another question answered. Anytime somebody tells you a system's foolproof, all it means is that you are protected from fools.

They said that pulpweed juice didn't travel, but I guess that's 'cause the folks where it come from never got 'round to inventin' vacuum-sealed storage containers or somethin', 'cause Addison had it and 'cause we didn't get no high, damn it, we didn't even slow 'em down.

We actually took a sleeping period at one of them rest areas. I didn't mind, but I was real surprised that a revolutionary band this well connected hadn't been able to con no vehicle. What the hell—what did we have the right to complain about, anyways? The last thing I wanted to think anything about was the future.

We took three days, judgin' from the sleep periods and the doses of weed juice, before we got near the place. I lost count of the cubes, worlds, switch points, and rest areas. Finally, though, we entered the world at a force point.

It was a right pretty-lookin' place, but not real homey. More like the kind of background you see in all them old John Wayne westerns. Lotsa colors, mesas, rock steeples, and—what do they call them things?—buttes. Never was clear what a butte was, but they had 'em.

The temperature was cool but not cold, maybe high sixties. The sky looked a little bluer than I thought it should be, and I didn't remember no John Wayne movies with green rocks, and blue ones, too, but this place had 'em. It also had little clumps of growths here and there, of sickly purple grasses and clumps of this odd-lookin' plant that had a base like a pale blue cabbage and thick purple stalks growin' out of 'em with round pale pink balls on the ends. The skin and balls looked sorta *metallic,* and as you walked all the colors of the sun seemed to ripple off 'em, like lookin' sideways at a pane of glass in summer.

"This is *it?*" I commented. "Looks kinda *lonely* to me."

"Looks kinda yucky to me," my twin put in.

"There are better places, but this is the only force point developed," Addison told us. "There's a small settlement about fifty kilometers—about thirty miles—that way. An old trail leads down the cliff side here to the bottom, where there's a small river. Follow the river against the stream and you'll hit it. Most of the vegetation is that violet color; plants here use a different system of making food from sunlight than ours do. Don't let it throw you off. Most anything the people here eat, you can eat, and I doubt if the symbiont will let you eat wrongly. The bulk of the Type Zero colony, perhaps a half dozen people, live near the village. You won't have any trouble finding them. The natives are generally friendly and will mostly ignore you unless you do something to provoke them. They're not very pretty to look at, but we aren't that pretty to them, either, and it *is* their world. Go down to the colony. They'll fill you in and get you settled. They'll understand your problems, too. They've all been hooked on this stuff for years."

"That's it?" my twin asked. "You just drop us here and that's the end?"

"That's about it. When I leave, this forcer will be set to open only from the Labyrinth side. It might be quite some time before anyone comes for you. It might well be many years, depending on how smoothly this goes and how many problems the takeover and restructuring of the Company first and then my people goes, but eventually someone will come. In a week, no more, I will be like you, and Addison will be no more, so this is farewell."

"Seems to me you're makin' the biggest sacrifice of all," I noted. "Is it really worth that much? Do you really believe that your people are gonna be any better than the ones now?"

She swallowed hard. "I am not eager for this. Who is eager to die? But I would take a dagger and strike my chest and remove my own heart and crush it if that is what it would take to topple this abomination. I don't know if we will be better rulers than we have now; no one can fully predict the future. I do know that they could not be any worse, and that radical change in a society that has never changed since gaining power will collapse it, force it to rebuild, and along different lines. I will have the necklaces back, please, now. You can keep the dresses and sandals, although no one here cares much if you run nude all the time. The climate here is mild, and if you get a chill you can make your own. This is enough time. Farewell."

We handed her the necklaces, but we wasn't gonna let her get away scot-free. "Wait a minute!" Brandy Two called to her. "You ain't left no juice or weed or nothin'! How do we even know this is the right world?"

She turned. "I would not have brought you all this way just to fool you. Ask your twin. There are many easier places I could have dumped you with far less time and trouble."

"That's true 'nuff," I agreed.

"As for the fix, you won't need it anymore. That round plant with the stalks is the rainbow weed. It grows like wildfire. You'll find it delicious." She pushed the forcer, got a crude cube, and stepped into it. It collapsed almost immediately.

"Can you *believe* her?" my twin commented. "Damn! We spend all that damned time prayin' for the day when the color of your skin don't mean a thing, and we find out that even if everybody was the same color and beautiful, people would *still* figure out a way to divide and hate each other!"

"It *do* give you some discouragement," I agreed. "Damn it, I guess we got a long climb down and a thirty-mile run 'fore we know if we're just a pair of conned turkeys or if we got a future at all."

"Shouldn't we hang around awhile, just in case?"

I shook my head. "Uh uh. We don't know if them necklaces didn't screw up this whole bit, but if they did we're better off findin' folks and seein' what this place is like. If not, they'll find us. Besides, in order to really wrap this up, I wanna talk to them humans stuck here. Besides, don't you remember her sayin' that some of 'em was men? They been havin' to live with rank amateurs all this time.

Maybe us trained professionals can put a little spice in their lives."

We was able to find the trail without much lookin'; it was well worn and well used. Well, I supposed they had to get the damned juice up to this point somehow and fairly regular.

Thirty miles was more than a marathon run, and sure as hell impossible in a sari and sandals. The river was fairly wide but real shallow and there was a flat, worn area all along this shore. More of the trail, we supposed, since off and on we saw some real ugly-lookin' animal shit. Leastwise, we *hoped* it was animal turds. Either that or this world's dudes was *really* huge 'nuff to shit bricks. Purple and orange ones, too.

I don't know if the juice was feelin' at home or not, but it really felt good to run; we paced ourselves but ran for hours before we stopped, and even then we was just startin' to work up a real sweat. The rainbow weed was all over the place, wherever there was sunlight, and we found ourselves just pullin' it up and eatin' the balls and the big round head. I guess it weren't enough, 'cause the juice also had us eatin' grass like we was some kinda cows or somethin', and drinkin' long and hard from the river. It filled us up, though, but also made us kinda drowsy, and 'long 'bout sundown we just found a patch of grass and collapsed. 'Bout the only thing my twin said before we was both dead to the world was, "I ain't sure I like the menu, but we sure as hell won't starve none here."

Which were, of course, my thoughts exactly.

Next day we made real time, and broke outta that badlands and into broad fields. It took a minute to realize that a lot of the landscape was just like the stuff we saw where we come in, only now it was covered in violet and purple and shimmering colors. The path kept on beside the river, sometimes broken by small streams and creeks flowin' in, but we just splashed through 'em. There was clouds in the sky now, and they looked pretty normal; big fluffy cotton balls that made shadows on the ground.

The trail also had several junctions, but we kept to the river path. Hell, that's what we was told to do. Finally, we come in sight of civilization, or what passed for it in these parts. A big clump of what looked like giant mounds or maybe beehives with pointy tops, only made of clay and mud and rock and havin' openin's and ladders and steps. Before we reached it, though, we met our first inhabitant.

He *was* big, in every sense of the word. Built like a wrestler, with big, round eyes, the biggest, flattest nose I ever seen, and skin that was kinda shiny and glitterin' like fish scales. He had big, muscular arms and bigger feet and he needed a manicure somethin' awful. He also had a flowin' mane of thick, curly, dark purple hair and a beard maybe a foot long. He was wearin' a kinda sleeveless dark brown tunic and a knee-length skirt or kilt, but I doubt if there ever was the Einstein what could make shoes for them feet. The hair was about the same color as the grass.

He started talkin' to us, gesturin' wildly, making the damndest gruntin' and blowin' and bellowin' we ever heard, which we took to be the way these dudes talked. It took a couple minutes for us to realize that he didn't even know we was newcomers; he was spoutin' off to us 'bout somethin' like we met every day.

"I guess we all look alike to them, too," Brandy Two noted.

We finally got this big bruiser calmed down enough to take a breath. We tried to show we didn't understand him, come from up there, and was lookin' for our own kind. It was crude, but he turned out to be a bright fella at that and pointed a long, pointy-nailed finger further on, then cocked it. We figured that meant take the next right, so we thanked him and went on.

Any other circumstance I'd'a been scared to death of that creature, but here it almost seemed normal. At least now we knew what the people were like who got permanently married to a virus and a plant.

"I wonder if our hair's gonna turn purple," I muttered. Anything was possible now.

The new trail we took was less used, but still plain enough, and led pretty quick to a small single one of them beehive type huts with two even smaller ones behind. There was a small creek runnin' right beside the property, and in the field was two creatures that looked like hairy purple elephants with no trunks and tails like them old dinosaur pictures.

We slowed down, not sure this was the place, when we saw two women 'bout as pregnant as you can get sittin' outside, naked as we was, sucklin' a couple of little babies. That stopped me. I just hadn't figured on babies.

One was the golden type, the other was darker and built different, not black but maybe Latino. They saw us, and did a real take, then the Latin woman called to us in some language that sounded as bad as old scales and bellow, only more human. "Uh oh," I muttered. "We forgot 'bout the language thing. Bet Addison did, too."

Well, they all started comin' 'round to us after that, and others come out of the houses or in from the field. There was three women, three men, and seven kids, the oldest of which looked maybe two and a half. A man and woman was of the golden people variety, another couple was this Latino-lookin' type, and a third couple was deep-tanned white, he with real blond hair and blue eyes and she with reddish-brown hair and green eyes.

From the looks of the kids, they didn't seem exactly married to their own matched partners. Maybe they was, maybe they wasn't, when the kids showed up, but not lately.

Language was a problem right off, but one of the men, who looked older, though they all looked damned good, at least knowed what English was and knew a language close enough that we could talk with practice, at least on a simple level. With time we could come to some kinda compromise, I felt, but that worried me. If we had that kinda time, we was in deep shit.

We had the time. Weeks, in fact, to kinda settle in and get the feel of the place. There wasn't much work to do 'cept cleanin' up a bit, and gettin' used to the idea of a pit toilet and a creek for runnin' water, but we managed. The women, all pregnant, seemed almost relieved at our arrival. They didn't get the urge as bad, but the men did, and we kinda took some of the pressure off.

And, real hard but real dedicated-like, we got to the point where we could get complicated ideas across to each other, at least the guy who spoke that sorta English, who said his name was Avong Simran, one of the golden people. A real scientist—he showed us his old field expedition gear, much of it still powered and workin' but not much used these days and not much useful day to day here.

They was an exploiter team, the six of them, sent out by the Company like so many to scout out a bunch of worlds in an area where the Company thought there was somethin' possibly worth its while. They was only scouts, the early explorers, but they did a lot of the original work. Each had a specialty—geology, anthropology, two different biology people, one for plants and one for animals, general physics, and general chemistry. They was on the track of some rare trace element, whatever that is, that was valuable to the Company in runnin' its portable gear and which didn't seem all that common among the worlds, and they was like them dudes who go out searchin' for oil, diggin' here, then there, till they hit a gusher. This was maybe the twentieth world they'd looked at in a row, and all the signs said that in the next few worlds this stuff they was lookin' for, which was made in some natural process not real common and takin' millions of years, was there in goodly amounts.

They was kinda surprised to find the folks here so primitive; their near identical twins in some of the other worlds were pretty well advanced. They set up a base camp near this town, adjusted their gear so they had some language ability with these big dudes—they could understand it, but no Type Zero human had all the guts needed to talk it right—and settled in to make their search. In 'bout a month and a half they found some of it in the hills nearby and was all ready to call in more experts with better equipment and move on when all of a sudden the real peaceful folk of this world just went nuts.

For nine days and nights, there was a near orgy of rape and constant sex and not much else, day in and day out. They were not immune. Each of the women got it at least once from one of them big suckers before it was over. Even the men weren't immune; they got raped by these Type One women just the same, drippin' stuff. You don't get much of a hard-on like that, but they had theirs shoved up holes anyways and got covered with wet.

Then, just as suddenly, it was all over and everybody was peaceful and lovin' and kind as before. None of the Type Zeros was in any condition to walk or ride all the way to the force point for weeks, and a couple had broken bones and all was wall-to-wall bruises, but by the time things started to heal they began to see the changes in themselves. We knew the routine real well. They was hooked. They was also smart enough to figure out that they'd caught *somethin'*, and somethin' real dangerous to others, from the local folks. They got up to the force point and sent a "trouble—dangerous infection" message up the line to the Exploration and Exploitation Division, then set out to study the thing even as it changed and held them.

Trouble was, they was an advance party and not a medical man among 'em. Their lab gear was set up for explorin' and survival, not complicated medical studies. The Company—at least they thought it was—sent some stuff that helped, but there was a limit to what they could do. Finally, they decided that two of 'em would set off toward a quarantine area down toward headquarters to be studied. You can guess what happened. They barely made it back in time to save their own lives and sanity, and even now that couple was showin' some lingerin' effects of damage.

They sent all sorts of samples back—blood, urine, even semen—and eventually they got their answer. Some kinda virus of unknown design and construction, they was told. Probably incurable at this stage without damagin' the host. However, it had real possibilities for somethin'. No, they didn't know for what, or why the Company seemed so interested, but that wasn't their job or place. Could the native males be induced by trade goods and ideas to give semen? Well, it turned out they could. Even though they was only real interested in sex once a year durin' that mad orgy time, they could get it up if they had to. It was a hell of a business, but it kept the stranded team in touch with the Company and civilization, gave 'em a feelin' it weren't no total tragedy, and gave 'em a real chance to study this civilization and people.

It took 'em a long time to get the link to the rainbow weed, even though it was right under their noses. You just don't think of a disease that lives off humans needin' somethin' from a plant. The biologists finally figured it after 'bout a year or more when they started seein' other connections between the lower animals and plants of the world. They sent samples and loads of seeds up as part of their studies.

They also studied the people here and compared it to themselves. You'd think that after that orgy time every female would get pregnant, but only a fraction of them did in any given year. The birth rate was low, but the life expectancy was very long. Still and all, in some ways it was a culture without a lot of the shit that tore us apart. Men and women did all the same jobs equally. They didn't have no marriages or stuff, since what was the point of even developin' it, all things considered, but they had a real sense of tribe and community. Weren't no social classes, neither, 'cause when you had a period of time every year when everybody was screwin' everybody else there just was no way to keep no royal families pure. No races, either. Since everybody bred with everybody any real differences got averaged out maybe thousands of years ago. No wars, neither. They had no real idea of private property.

But there was a price. There wasn't much in the way of development, invention, real progress. They got to a point the scientists called Bronze Age culture, and stopped. Guess they just didn't need to go no further. In the same time our ancestors went from Bible times to television and space travel and computers, and the golden people developed all that fancy futuristic shit and the Labyrinth, they maybe invented a better saddle and a better plow.

It didn't seem fair, but it seems like all our warfare and jealousy and hatreds and divisions was the thing that caused real progress, too. If you got rid of all the bad things 'bout human bein's, you didn't go nowheres. Nasty, divisive, warring civilizations with territories and jealousies and kings and all did best, if they didn't destroy each other, which was the odds 'bout half the time. On that scale, them golden people who founded the Company must have been real sweethearts. And I thought *we* was bad!

I tried to explain what was goin' on with what they was sendin' back down the Labyrinth. They didn't really want to believe it, and they didn't like the idea of bein' used that much, but they seemed to care a lot more that somebody'd found a way to live with it back there than with the idea that it was gonna be used to destroy the Company. I guess if you work for a Company that treats you like shit, you don't give a damn what happens to it. They worked for the Company 'cause it had the Labyrinth and the only ticket to what they'd all wanted to do. They sure didn't have no love for it, though.

Since the demands for semen had stopped and most business with the Company stopped, they figured the high-tech boys had figured a way not to need 'em anymore. That was fine with them, so long as they was stuck, but they was still havin' a real tough time convincin' the locals that they didn't need it no more and that they had nothin' to trade for it. I guess that's what the old blowhard we met was complainin' to us about.

They hadn't figured on kids, neither, but it was kinda inevitable when you had to do it every day, sometimes more than once, and the chemicals they used to prevent it was long gone. Unless that juice done more to us than we knew, though, there wouldn't be no black babies around. Still, it was kinda nice to see them little kids, hold 'em, play with 'em. Even Brandy Two, who never let down her hard shell, really took to 'em.

Still, the little colony was just markin' time here. This wasn't their world no more than it was ours, and they didn't really have much place in it. They was just doin' what they could, livin' day by day, and not lookin' much beyond the moment.

Five weeks or so after we got there, we had visitors.

They came in white suits with space helmet type gear and air packs and all the rest. We told 'em they wouldn't have no trouble if they just all kept their pants on all the time and didn't stick around another month and a half until the locals went after everything alive. One of 'em was Bill Markham, and I was never so happy to see nobody in my whole life 'cept Sam.

"I look pretty healthy for a dead man," he admitted to me. "After all, Sam killed me in a pretty fancy car accident about two weeks ago. Made all the papers. I'm getting a little tired of rescuing you from these worlds, though. We have to stop meeting like this."

"You got 'em, then?"

"No. Not yet. Until we were able to analyze that plant we got samples of from that safe world where you two were held there wasn't any way. Now, however, we're ready to act. Don't worry, though. We're pretty well alerted to what they're trying to do and in a very short time, with all the knowledge and technology of the Center, we've learned a lot about this bug. We're setting up the climax now. I thought you'd want in on it."

"Would I! But—where's Sam?"

Markham cleared his throat. "You want the truth?" The way he said it I was afraid somethin' happened to Sam.

"Yeah, Bill. Straight."

"Brandy—Sam's real broken up about all this, no matter what act he put on for you. I'm not sure he can take seeing you much more. You wanted the truth, you got it. To be perfectly frank, the only reason I think he's kept on living was to wrap up this case. I wouldn't give fifty cents for his future once it's closed."

"Not Sam," I responded. "I can't believe that."

"You think he's so much stronger than you? That he rescued you from the depths? You rescued each other. You never believed that, but it's true. In his own way, he needs you as much as you needed him. Just remember what you were like when you thought he was good as dead. Listless, aimless, nothing to live for—you finally decided that it didn't matter if you got hooked, even killed. Like him, you had only the case and you didn't give a damn about yourself or what happened during or after. I have never seen two people so absolutely unlike in all the superficial ways who were so identical underneath. He's not so tough deep down. Maybe, somehow, he could cope with your death, although I'm not too sure of that, but he could never stand to live knowing that you were alive, too. It would tear him to pieces."

"But—I still love him! I'd go back to him!"

"Sure. You'd go back to him, but like this. It'd be like having a wild, promiscuous, totally uninhibited daughter in the house beyond control, not a wife, partner, and lover. I don't know how much ideas of right and wrong, good and evil, wild and limited, you retain, but there's no room the way you are for compromises, self-sacrifice, or selflessness. I think he could take you crippled, or paralyzed, better than this." He sighed. "Well, we better get things and people all packed up and ready to move here. We're on a tight schedule."

"Bill, I—"

"Save it. It can wait. It's between you and Sam, nobody else. You are all under technical arrest, since you're part of the substantial case we're building here."

"Damn it, you shoulda come sooner!"

"We did. You forget that time runs at different rates in many of these worlds. You been here—what? Five, six weeks? But it's only been four days of my time, subjectively, and two of those were spent with computer experts sorting out the garbage from the signals and tracing you here. They have a pretty powerful and clever jammer there. I'd love to get a look at one. If we hadn't had two of you giving off the same identical signal to reinforce it, we'd never have found you."

"Bill—what happens now? To me, I mean?"

"We have essence du rainbow weed in a shot capsule. With a team working here, I think we can probably get enough to last a very long time, until we can isolate and duplicate what it is in these plants here that makes them different from their twins and siblings on other worlds. We'll be taking transports back, and then you'll be extensively debriefed. Then we'll spring our own little trap and try to wrap this up."

"No—that ain't what I meant. After that."

"We'll take you—and your twin—to any home world you want. Yours, hers, it doesn't matter. There's still over four million in the bank. You get half, and you can split it with her if you want. We'll supply you with whatever amount of this junk you need as long as you need it. You'll have money and a supply, you'll have at least fifty years before you even start to look or feel middle-aged, or so they're theorizing now, and nobody pulling your strings unless you want it. You'll have a ball."

"Yeah," I sighed. "We'll have a ball." At the cost of losing Sam.

11.

A Party at Mayar Eldrith's

Nobody who didn't know and understand Sam Horowitz wouldn't'a guessed that he was depressed, upset, or anything but in heaven that evenin'. And it weren't faked or nothin'; he really was supercharged and as excited as a little kid, and he would be until this all was done. Only then, maybe a few days later, would he come crashin' down. That was the bottom line for me; this was the climax of his whole life, and once you done passed the climax, baby, and there's nobody around to share with and care about, what's the use of livin'?

See, when Sam was a little boy he us'ta see all them old detective movies—only they wasn't all that old, then. Between the neighborhood B movies and the early days of TV, though, he musta seen every Thin Man, Philip Marlowe, Sam Spade, Sherlock Holmes, Charlie Chan—you name it. And he went to the library in Baltimore, which is a real big one, and got out and read everything there was by Chandler and Hammett and all the rest.

Now, don't get him wrong. He never did much thinkin' 'bout bein' no cop, let alone no private eye, except maybe in his fantasies. In fact, he hated police work, thought it was the dullest, least thrillin' job in the world. Hell, he didn't even like guns. After four years with the Air Force police and a few more on the Bristol vice squad, he was still scared of 'em, wouldn't have one around unless the safety of somebody innocent—not himself—demanded it. He wasn't even a particularly good shot.

No, what Sam was in love with in the work was pretty much what I got trapped by, too: not the way it was, but the way it *shoulda* been. The way Marlowe and Spade and the Continental Op and Nick and Nora Charles did it.

Now, there was several ways we coulda settled this case, at least, mostly just with a big set of moves and then explain everything in the paperwork and to the legal boys who'd have to prosecute and punish the bad guys. Hell, *I* coulda explained it and wrapped it myself. But the Company owed him, owed *us* for this, and they was willin' to indulge us.

So, there we was at headquarters, at Mayar Eldrith's palatial lodge, where it all began, and we was hostin' a party. Yeah, a real party, too—with all sorts of fancy delicacies and drinks and all the rest. Since Mayar had done the invitin', there wasn't no way to get out of it, neither.

All his life, since he was a kid, Sam had dreamed of havin' all the suspects together in one room while he, the brilliant detective, explained the whole thing to them and unmasked the guilty. Now, finally, he was gonna get his chance, and while I helped fill in a lot of gaps and details and explain a bunch of stuff, by general agreement it was gonna be Sam's show.

I was dressed in this incredibly beautiful soft and satiny violet and golden sari, with fancy open-toed heels. I had a complete makeover for it from experts here, matchin' everything just right, and they had trimmed and shaped my natural bush just right, like one of them gardeners shapes a bush into a piece of art, and they'd streaked it with brown and gold. I had the jewelry to match, and I never looked better or more glamorous in my whole life.

Sam said he'd be damned if he was gonna do his number in a toga; he had the tailors here—mostly computers once the designer got through—make him a good, old-fashioned forties-style white suit, with just the right shirt and tie, and a pair of shiny black patent leather shoes. We was a beautiful, glamorous couple, and we acted just right, but I could feel his sadness and sorrow every time we talked or our eyes met. Kinda, *this is it, baby, but we're going out in style.*

The guests started arrivin' and things was about to get underway. All of 'em, I think, sensed somethin' was up, and maybe a few guessed it was all up, but since they didn't know for sure and still were pretty arrogant and secure, they came anyways. The rest—well, they had to come along if asked.

So here they come, ready or not. Here was Dringa

Lakuka, division chief of research and development, followed by Mukasa Lamdukur, who ran the day-to-day operations of the Security Committee, then the cold and brusk ex-monk, Basuti Alimati, who was chief of Labyrinth communications, and, finally, among the Committee members, Hanrin Sabuuk, the security division's comptroller. Also invited and present was my other self, this time in crimson and silver and with her hair styled differently but still lookin' great; Dakani Grista, the real young acting chief of security operations, and his old boss, now forcibly retired, Aldrath Prang. Last, but not least, was the Security Committee's chief medical advisor, and the man who made me less than I us'ta be, Jamispur Samoka.

It was a chummy men's club; besides me and Brandy Two, the only other women around was Mayar's wife Eyai, who acted as hostess, and a bunch of female servants.

Eyebrows was raised at Sam, dressed the way he was, but the only indignation was at the presence of Aldrath Prang, who clearly was in the doghouse in spades. Seems what done him in was Dakani's toadyness, which also got him a bunch of gold stars. He got nervous and tipped off Lamdukur that Aldrath was tappin' the private lines of the Committee members themselves, and the outrage hadn't died down yet. It was kinda like discoverin' that the head of Scotland Yard was tappin' and tapin' the Queen and the whole damned royal family. Maybe he did; maybe he just didn't have no young, ambitious son of a bitch to rat on him.

I got the idea that these guys didn't see much of each other normally; they spent a lot of time talkin' among themselves and swappin' stories and information, mostly gossip from the look of it. Couldn't go by us—we wasn't the elite; we couldn't speak their singsong language.

They all spoke English, though, thanks to their machines, so Sam could wander in and out and make nice comments while sippin' a bourbon and soda. Finally, though, we had them all seated on this big central couch that was sunk into the livin' room and formed a kinda U, and provided a perfect audience for anybody standin' in front of the old-fashioned fireplace, which was just where Sam was.

"I know you're all curious as to why we've come together

like this," he began, "so maybe we should get this over with. It's been a very long, tough road, even though most of the perpetrators were obvious from the start. I admit there are still one or two details I'm hazy about, but I think perhaps we can fill those in over time."

"We are here only because we respect Mayar Eldrith, sir," Basuti responded in his usually cold manner, kinda remindin' me of Addison at her normal self. "If we have come here to listen to the blatherings of some other-worldly egomaniac who has delusions that he has a greater mind than we have, then I, for one, feel insulted."

"Then you will have to be insulted," Sam shot back, cool and casual. "The kind of attitude you just displayed is at least partly at the root of this whole thing. However, I will put you to the test. I have assured Vice President Mayar that here, tonight, I can show him the traitor—or traitors—in his own ranks, explain the entire plot against the Company, and put an end to that threat. I can do this for several reasons. For one thing, I *am* this ignorant, primitive baboon, but I'm very good at what I do. Because I am totally unrestricted by your culture, class, or racial attitudes, I can cut through them. And, because my wife was willing to put herself into the living hell of a nasty and addictive alien substance, I have the additional details I needed. The plot is not stopped. In fact, it is right now underway. You can dismiss me now, go home, and it will come to pass and it will succeed. In fact, they'd have gotten away with it anyway if they hadn't made it so complex that at least one major mistake was inevitable. Anybody want to leave and let the plot go on?"

They sat and stared at him.

"I thought not. So let's proceed, shall we? This is such a complex plot, although at its root it's as simple a set of motives as all crimes, that it will take some time to put all the pieces together for you, and with your help and cooperation. I beg your indulgence."

"This is intolerable!" muttered Hanrin Sabuuk. "Eldrith, must we put up with this? Why, the man is not even an *employee!*"

"Let the man begin," the vice president said impatiently. "There is money riding on this. He claims he can solve that which has troubled us most these past three years and indisputably. I told him I did not believe he could do what we failed to do. The amount is substantial; would any of you stake your own fortunes with mine?"

"Bah! What do we have to gain if he cannot?" asked Mukasa.

"You wager money, which you value dearly but won't really miss," Sam told them. "My stake is my life, which is forfeit if we fail tonight. It is, I admit, of no value to you but it makes it a very sporting proposition, does it not?"

I gasped. "Sam! No!" But he paid no attention, and the others looked at each other and nodded.

"Very well, continue with this foolishness," said Dringa wearily. "At least it will be amusing."

"Interesting, yes, Director, but amusing—I'm afraid not. Not unless you have a very odd sense of humor. Let's begin right at the beginning. I'm afraid some of what I have to say isn't all that flattering to you all, but bear with me.

"First of all," Sam continued, "let's picture a corporate structure whose positions are basically inherited. This has some advantages if you're one of the lucky families, but it also has disadvantages considering that the only way to gain a position, let alone move up in it, is by somebody above you dying. With near perfect health and a two-hundred-and-fifty-year lifespan, this can be a problem. I hadn't considered this relevant until I was informed about you, Director Basuti. A monk, a dedicated holy man committed to his faith, you literally were *forced* into corporate politics by some unexpected premature deaths in your family line.

"Now, if you're eighty, or a hundred, when this falls on you, and you really like the job, that's probably all right and the way it was intended to be when it was set up. But when it was set up, the average lifespan was only a hundred and twenty and families were much larger. You sow your wild oats among the worlds, work at various jobs within the Company, or do what your heart dictates, as Director Basuti did. Now, suddenly, we have a number of high-ranking men in positions while still relatively young for your people and society. You are all fifty to seventy-five. It might well be another twenty or thirty years before you move up. In the meantime, you have great responsibilities but not great powers. You carry out policy, but you not only do not initiate it you don't even get to argue about it. It must be very frustrating to have to do a job and be expected to do it well, since you can be skipped over for making mistakes when the openings finally come, yet not be able to change or reform policy at all to meet real needs."

They didn't say nothin', but I could see a couple of 'em nodding. He had their attention.

"About four years ago, our subjective time, a small exploiter team was sent far up into Type One territory in the minus direction. It was one of a number sent out all the time by the Office of Exploration and Evaluation, which, I believe, comes under you, Director Dringa. 'Research and development'—such a nice, all-encompassing term."

"It is mine now, but not four years ago," Dringa responded.

"I know, we'll get to that. At any rate, one of these teams, in search of a rare and needed natural substance, blundered into a world with a very nasty trap in the form of a symbiotic viral creature. It didn't show up in the preliminary medical checks or even the quarantine and volunteer example because it is strictly a sexually transmitted organism. You can't even get it by an injection of an infected person's blood. It trades superb health and immunity from virtually any nongenetic disease in exchange for feeding off the host—a harmless amount, too. This, quite naturally, also produces over a period of millennia a totally homogeneous and incredibly long-lived race and creates a situation where a very low birth rate is mandated."

Quickly, Sam filled them in on the background of the world where it was found, and how the expedition caught it and was trapped by it.

"Now, then, they followed all the established procedures. They went to their force point and they sent a report as soon as they could of all that they knew. They also requested quarantine and medical study in a safe world and started out, only to suffer the nightmarish and eventually fatal withdrawal. They got back in time on the hope that there was something in that world that would reverse it. They made it, just in time, but not without a couple suffering some fairly dramatic and permanent brain damage. One of the women is partially paralyzed; one of the men has the active intelligence of perhaps a five-year-old child. They sent this report, too, and it was followed up with research instruments and requests for samples."

"Wait a moment," Hanrin Sabuuk broke in. *"I* was head of R & D at that time, and no such report ever reached me."

"No, it didn't," Sam agreed. "Instead, the reports that reached you and were subsequently fed into your computers listed this world as hostile to human habitation and fatal, and the exploiter team were all declared dead. The supplies and other equipment sent up there, and the samples sent back, were all credited to different teams working in the same region. It was spread out well enough that nothing would have been obvious or flagged. What had happened was this. Someone had to receive the initial signals in the routing, and then see in there something that caught his eye. At first, it was probably no more than petty corruption—the idea of controlling a disease or substance that was highly addictive, perhaps. This person needed to know more, so he enlisted the aid of another, highly ambitious man, a medical scientist in the managerial classes who felt frustrated and confined by the narrow limits imposed on him by the Company. He, in turn, had done some work in a couple of worlds and there had met and recruited to the Company's employ some young scientists in one of those worlds, the most brilliant and impressive of whom was a young man of whom we know very little except that he uses the name Dr. Carlos."

"We do not recruit scientists," Dringa commented. "We have an oversupply as it is."

"Perhaps *you* don't, but the Company has thousands of locals in the worlds on which they have stations, as well as bankers, crime lords, and even private investigators. We don't know what chord was struck between them, but Carlos learned well. He is at least as proficient as his mentor on the medical machines and many other machines of the Company. With these three men, we have the beginnings of a conspiracy. It was Carlos who was set up in a safe world with all the medical and analytical equipment he required. I'm sure we'll be able to discover how they hid the requisition of these machines and their distribution when we trace the serial numbers through the computer network. Carlos, however, was still limited. He didn't have access to the best machines and brightest minds in the Company, and he was woefully short of manpower. I can't prove it, but I believe that it was he who came up with the idea of locating a Nazi-style world, a world in which experimentation on humans existed and a party elite answerable to no one if they held on to power reigned. There was such a world with a Company station. The stationmaster was impersonating a powerful party leader named Rupert Conrad Vogel."

"Ah, yes, we know about him," Mukasa said.

"You do and you don't. You see, they were very clever. Vogel received orders to carry out experiments using supplies of this viral agent with his normal company mail, under a Most Secret clearance. The orders came from very high in the Company hierarchy. He had no reason to doubt them, or that he was doing what the Company wanted. Vogel's own projects were equally clever. The virus was represented as something discovered on that world only recently. They were put to work analyzing it, diagramming it, and, of course, seeing what it would do to human subjects, both its powers and limitations. Vogel got his supplies of the agent—actually the semen of both the trapped humans and males of the native race there, re-packed into injection capsules in minimal doses—with his normal Company pouches. He had no idea they were being smuggled into the mail system by Carlos and those few he had recruited to help him, with the aid of some corrupt people in the transport union. It was perfect, as far as it went, since Vogel supplied the raw data and Carlos could then reinterpret it in light of knowing its true origins."

"But we know all this," Mayar Eldrith pointed out. "You are only filling in the details."

"I asked for patience. During the experimentation, it was discovered that the viral agent reproduced only sexually, but created microscopic, specialized reproductive units. These units were present in male and female subjects, but they were malformed, weak, and tended to break up when expelled from the body. This was very fortunate considering the heightened promiscuity of all the infected subjects, since a few could quickly create a plague, but it also indicated that the reason the thing broke down was because it lacked some certain chemical element. Vogel's people searched for that missing link but couldn't find it, and I doubt if they would have used it if they had. But this very fact turned what had begun as basically an illegal side operation with potential business uses to something else."

"Now we're finally getting somewhere," Basuti grumbled. I noticed, though, that all the others was listenin' real good, and ones like Dakani and Jamispur hadn't said a word.

"Now, I won't take up any of your time detailing the viral agent or how it works. We all know that. But our man back here, the one who started it all, began to think along more ambitious lines. In my world, we once had a woman who became infamous in history as Typhoid Mary. Typhoid was a particularly virulent killer disease, easily transmitted and quite fatal. Mary was found to be literally infested with the disease, but she didn't catch it. She was a carrier, immune herself to its awful effects but able to give it to almost anyone she touched. Now this fellow started to wonder what a Typhoid Mary, or perhaps many Typhoid Marys, would do to this world. Suppose they were introduced as professional courtesans at a party like this one, for the high and mighty. Not everyone would partake, of course, but some would, and there would be other opportunities. Now you begin to go into withdrawal, but someone, an agent for the top man, could offer you not a cure, perhaps, but a daily fix that would keep you going and even cure what you might catch. Ask your doctors—no mind can tolerate that withdrawal, not even any of yours. Right, Jamispur?"

The doc nodded. "It is true. Within a few hours of the onset of withdrawal you would kill your family and cut off your leg for it. It is not a matter of will; the thing is in control of your mind and its sole imperative is survival."

"They wouldn't snare Basuti," Mukasa chuckled. "He has a permanent vow of celibacy." He stopped a moment. "Say—that's *right . . .*"

Eyes went to Basuti, all lookin' at him funny, but he ignored them. "The plot is an infantile concoction of this madman," he said. "First, you would have to find the missing agent. Second, you would have to get that agent into this world, something I find impossible to believe. Third, you would have to have some way of continuing to import it."

"Oh, once they had enough people—most of you, say, and some key security people, they wouldn't need subterfuge. They could get all of it in they wanted," Sam pointed out. "But, you're right. The thing was, that original, stranded exploiter team finally figured it out. It was literally under their noses all the time but it was so obvious and yet so alien they failed to recognize it. The staple food here is haipi, and pardon my mispronunciation. There's some haipi in these snacks right here. Where I come from, it's potatoes, rice, beans—you name it. The rainbow weed was the number-one staple of the origin world. It grew like wildfire all over the place and was eaten all the time in every imaginable way by just about everybody. They long suspected it was something in the diet or something in the forms and balance of radiation in sun, soil, or water, and they very courageously self-experimented to find what it was, but rainbow weed was the last thing they tried because it was everywhere.

"When they discovered this, they sent the seed pods down to Carlos to analyze and grow others, and our man went into action. Under a cover, he had agents on the colonial worlds of your people recruit, perhaps even kidnap, young women under twenty years of age, and, by virtue of his committee authority, flagged their Labyrinth IDs as security recognized and moved them out. Carlos had already prepared a place for them, a camp in a world without Company personnel but near the so-called stroke seven worlds like mine, in a primitive jungle where there was an uncharted weak spot. There the girls were hypnoscanned to be unable to access their entire past, and a new, simpler, rougher past consistent with that world was brought forward. They were given cosmetology treatments to change their hair, alter their eyes, vary their skin color, and the rest. They were hooked on the drug, which made them quite suitable as prostitutes and dancers. The only problem was, Carlos had few people and a lot of other work to do. There was no way he could handle up to fifty girls, as there eventually were, about the limit for the amount of the agent, or 'juice,' that the team up in the origin world could produce and ship, allowing for accidents and unexpected losses. In the end, it was decided to take a leaf from the Company's own method of operation."

They was all ears now, and all of 'em looked downright uncomfortable. I begun to worry that maybe they was *all* in it.

"Oh, I forgot to mention Addison. I shouldn't, she's a key player and there are things even the one here who knows her well doesn't know about her. She had relatives in one of the colony worlds, and she was a mistress of a Security Committee member so she had a security code and legitimate reason to go back and forth. She was, then, the liaison between our man here, who couldn't leave, and Carlos. She had a safe world where she could undergo a rather startling metamorphosis into a cold, plain-looking woman who had only superficial resemblance to the women of this world, and she did it all without high tech machines. She came from a family of professional performers and she knew just how to do it and do it right. She was also a quite accomplished method actress, who, when Addison, was really a different personality. Colored contact lenses and tinted glasses added the final touch. She approached Arnie Siegel, a major criminal boss in the northern hemisphere, about the girls. He was big and powerful enough to cover for her, and she was able to hand him some Company gadgets and secrets that made it easy for him to evade the law and gave him an edge on possibly knocking over his own boss, a fellow named Wycliffe, who was ignorant of the affair. The only ones he let in on it were people he owned, body and soul, such as the master pimp Edward 'Fast Eddie' Small, who would take over Siegel's position when Siegel moved up, and gunmen personally loyal who would oversee the project's security."

"You mean they turned fifty girls of *our race* into whores for this—this—filthy world?" Hanrin Sabuuk seemed real angry and upset at that.

"Yes, because this not only assured them the preservation of the fifty with no effort on their part, and also because by then Aldrath, here, had by sheer accident stumbled into the very existence of this agent, or drug, and knew just from its existence that the plot had to be very ambitious and go very high. His big attention was on Vogel, since that's where the experiments were and he knew Vogel had to know who was behind it, but he sent a couple of agents to scout around this other world and set something up just in case. The agents went completely by the book and followed absolutely standard procedures; as a result, they were led by the nose by ones who already knew the book to Lindy Crockett, a New York private eye with mob connections, and were highly impressed with her. They should have been. She was carefully coached on what to say and do to impress them. She was more than connected; she was the chief private eye agency handling the Wycliffe mob's investigations. From that point on, there was a constant flow of information from Crockett, all of it written by the very people she was supposed to be investigating. It checked out and was mostly truthful; it was just worthless. She gave Aldrath Addison and Carlos, which was safe enough, but said they couldn't be photographed and gave slightly distorted descriptions and sketches so they wouldn't be recognized even if they were next to the sketches. She sent the news of Carlos's operation in Guiana, but only after it had served its purpose and was already pretty well closed down. And you, Aldrath, took that information and fed it into the computer and came to all the conclusions they wanted you to."

Aldrath shrugged. "A detective is only as good as his information."

"But you were so certain that this was a sideline, a minor offshoot, that you didn't even keep permanent security personnel there to independently check it out. You see, you're vulnerable to this because you all have sealed yourself off here, away from the action. All of you are only as good as your information, and your computers believe what they're told to believe. The origin world was listed as lethal and useless, so you ignored it. Nobody even dared poke their head in and check it out. The data banks were sacred, couldn't be tampered with. Maybe they can't be—but all that means is that you tamper with the data you feed into them. You were had. You've got thousands of stations out there. Who's going to check to see if a hypnoscanner was really ordered by a station authorized to get one and that they received it? So long as the order is proper and lawfully entered, and so is the receipt, you don't really know *where* that damned equipment went."

"A physical audit of everything is impossible in so vast a system," Mukasa noted. "We know there's a certain amount of built-in graft, but we try to keep it to acceptable levels."

"Uh huh. The trouble is, you don't know when that level's reached unacceptable. So, now we're set up. They are rolling and they have their active agent. The rainbow weed even grows well and apparently normally in worlds more in our line. Its molecular structure and balance seem identical to the parent's. The trouble is, it doesn't work. The addicts like it, but they still need their shot. It grows quickly, so you plant it every damned place you safely can—on the hundreds and hundreds of safe worlds. Nobody cares about the safe worlds except as havens and rest stops, so nobody ever bothers to look, say, ten, or perhaps a hundred, miles from the rest areas and supplies. I'll bet if you do you'll find this crazy-looking stuff multiplying like crazy. It's going to be the kudzu of parallel worlds."

"What is this kudzu?" Hanrin asked.

"Never mind. You'll see what I mean in time. At just this time, we threw them a real curve. Aldrath revealed that he was going to kidnap Vogel and had sealed off access to Vogel's world. Now Vogel couldn't be reached without betraying a hand. You know that story, too, in gruesome detail. We went crazy trying to figure out how in hell you could know the precise instant from three different parallel worlds that some specific person would be going through the particular entrance cube. Then it hit us. Vogel gave us the slip but took Brandy with him; as a result, we could track him because her security code included a tracker and was superimposed over her old code. The ambush was painfully simple. They simply waited until their devices, *set to Brandy's tracking broadcaster,* all went beep together and moved. The object was first and foremost to kill Vogel, of course, but if they could they were also told to spare Brandy. She got away with a wound, since in that confined space it was impossible to guarantee anything. I got a head wound, which was real bad but not fatal. They couldn't do much, but they were prepared in case anyone survived except Brandy, since they would certainly be rushed to the Center—after quarantine and examination. That gave them, ahead of time, the names of any survivors, namely me, and the nature and extent of the wound. Again, they pulled their favorite trick.

"Care at the Center for most things is automated and computer controlled and monitored. The physician with his diagnostic computer just puts in the treatment and the like and it's done. Knowing it was a head wound and which doctor was alerted, they used the standard security taps on all medical emergencies and intercepted the doctor's instructions, adding a small extra detail, a slightly higher level of a support drug that would keep me comatose indefinitely. It was such a fine difference it took months before any doctor noticed it and questioned it."

"Who could tap into the medical line with such knowledge and finesse?" Mayar asked.

"In a minute, sir. First, why Brandy? Well, first of all, they'd just lost their experimental subjects and the heat was on. It was going to be dangerous to bring in more than small quantities of the needed semen in the future. My death— or, as it turned out, my coma—sent her into severe depression. They knew her well, had her entire mental profile. She would go in after the only lead left. This did them several favors. First, since Brandy went in and would be giving detailed, inside reports, Aldrath would hold off on a major commitment there pending what she found. Second, they could control those reports, via Crockett, and keep Aldrath more concerned about Brandy's safety than about what was actually there. Finally, they already had a Brandy of their own, one taken in the usual manner from a world close to ours but where the duplicate's life was, shall we say, less fortunate and the individual more opportunist."

Brandy Two smiled. "How sweet."

"The idea was an eventual switch. Brandy Two would be primed and sent back as Brandy One. They were very impressed by *our* Brandy, and none too sure that she could or would carry out their orders implicitly, hooked or not. There were a few circumstances in the Vogel tests where people committed suicide rather than face an impossible alternative. They couldn't take the chance. Brandy Two, as Brandy One, would have Aldrath's confidence here and Bill Markham's at home. She would also be an effective test case if they found the right element for their plot, since she could walk right into this world of yours on a security pass."

"Impossible!" Mukasa shouted. "You go too far. It is precisely because such twins exist that we have our unique security codes. Even twins from adjacent worlds who have precisely the same history and development will show up as different individuals under our system."

"And so would both of them—but they don't. They don't, because Brandy One's original code still has the security code and tracker superimposed on it and that drowns out and supersedes the old code. That code is intended to be temporary and so it's not in the master identification system as such."

"But only the security medical technician who imposed it would know that specific code and be able to provide it for duplication!" Mayar pointed out.

"Exactly so. Isn't that right, Chief Medical Security Advisor Jamispur?"

The doc jumped. "Look here, if you're implying that I'm a part of this conspiracy—"

"I apologize, sir. I was not implying anything. I am saying that you are the medical technician who knew and took Carlos under your wing when you were younger. I am saying that you were the ambitious and frustrated scientist tapped by our man to set this all up. That's why you got promoted to Chief Medical Security Advisor, so you could be in the best position for this."

"Now, hold on! *I* picked Jamispur!" Mayar said.

"How?"

"Why—computer records, job performance and proficiency, medical and psychiatric evaluations. The usual. He was the best man for the job."

"Of course he was. Because for several years our man had been letting the computer know all about Jamispur—exactly what they both wanted. He probably scored ninety-nine out of a possible hundred. Doesn't pay to be absolutely perfect. Your computer picked him from among the staff after that tragic flyer 'accident' killed his predecessor.

Garbage in, garbage out. How does it feel to be garbage, Doc?"

"This is outrageous!" Jamispur stormed. "I will not sit here and allow any more of this insanity to continue!"

"Oh, yes, you will," said young Dakani softly, speaking for the first time. The tone left no doubt that the doc was gonna stay, whether tied up and muzzled or comfortable. Dakani and he was the same class; no political or jurisdictional problems there.

"It had to be Jamispur all along. He was the only one who could duplicate the security code. He was the only one who could feed that code to Carlos and his accomplices, via Addison, so that they could set their own tracers for the ambush. He was the only one who had the complete medical and psychiatric history of Brandy One and even had the opportunity right from the start to plant the seed in her mind that if anything happened to me she'd do what she did. As chief medical security advisor, he could tap into any of the Center's lines as well as just call security at the station and know exactly what to do to neutralize me—all by phone, or its equivalent, here, with his trusty little computer and all those wonderful access codes a top security position gives you. What was it, Doc? Ambition? Blackmail? Or did they just keep refusing to let you experiment on your own with people?"

"I have rights here. I do not have to answer to the likes of you," the doc responded kinda surly.

"No doubt. And no doubt you're good enough to have booby-trapped your own mind and memories. We start probing and prying and it all goes away. Don't worry, Doc. We're not even gonna *try* that stuff. We'll just walk you down to this little room, strip you, tie you to the bed so you can't hurt yourself, and give you as many jolts of this stuff you seem to love so much as it takes until you're hooked. We'll let the two ladies, here, handle it all. They know all about how to do it, thanks to you. All we need is a name. It's a name we already know, but your supporting testimony will give Dakani, here, the right of immediate arrest. I'm sure our big man hasn't booby-trapped *his* brain. We'll learn the rest from him."

Jamispur was sweatin' somethin' awful. I didn't even

know these people *could* sweat till then, and it looked mighty sweet to me. "Don't," he managed, his voice just a hoarse whisper. "I'll tell."

"Sorry, Doc, that ain't enough," Sam told him. "You could give any name here and then stall for time, hoping that you'd get sprung. It *has* to be our route, while these gentlemen here remain as the vice president's pampered guests."

Suddenly Jamispur leaped from the couch toward Sam. Me, my twin, and Dakani all moved 'bout the same time, shovin' him back so he fell right into that whole mess of Directors. There was absolute chaos, everybody strugglin' with everybody and shoutin' curses in two languages, nobody clear what was what, when, just like in one of them thirties thrillers, the lights went out and plunged the room into darkness.

There was more shouts, but the lights was back on in maybe a minute and we finally untangled. Well, most of us did. Considerin' how much melodrama we seen so far, I really wasn't all that surprised to see that Jamispur didn't get up. He had one of them fondue forks right through his throat, and he was gaspin' for air but not makin' a sound. By the time we did what we could, he was dead.

Sam looked over at Dakani, who was lookin' back at someplace in the hall. The young man then turned back. "Did you get it?" Sam asked him.

"I got it. But I kind of hoped it wouldn't be fatal."

"Sorry," Sam replied with an apology. "I thought he'd use one of the butter knives. I'm out of the wrong society to even *think* of fondue forks."

Basuti turned, sweatin' too, and wiped his face nervously. "All right—you've convinced us there's a true traitor here, but you've just lost your only identification of him. You'll never get any prints off *that* fork handle. It's a rough-grip handle."

"Nice of you to notice that. You might be a detective yet. Well, I admit I didn't really expect more than an *attempt,* but this will do nicely. I regret not being able to deliver a smoking gun, but I think a smoking fondue fork will do just as well, although from the sound of it I can see why nobody ever used it in the old stories."

I watched Dakani Grista vanish back into another room, then come back, lookin' real grave. I had to hand it to Sam. I never woulda believed that anybody this slick woulda ever gone for it. I mean, our man still had lots of friends around. Bide your time while the doc got juiced and make your getaway.

"I'm afraid you've all been the victim of a very melodramatic setup," Sam told them. "The fact was, though, I really couldn't lose by it. If Jamispur hadn't lunged at me, or tried for a getaway, we wouldn't have pulled it and we'd have taken three to five days to get our absolute evidence. Fortunately, none of you have ever seen a vintage detective thriller movie. I presented the motive, opportunity, and method to commit a murder here tonight, and after all was chaos, partly aided and abetted by my two lovely cohorts in crime here and the very dubious Dakani, we even killed the lights, an obvious setup if ever there was one, but since we had our man backed into a corner and made certain we didn't give him enough time to think about good fortune, he took what appeared to be a wondrous stroke of luck to do away with the only witness who could credibly finger him. And so we can all let Dakani do his duty and get it out in the open now, by fingering the man we—Brandy and I, at least—have known was behind this from the start."

"Mukasa Lamdukur," said the security man, "I hereby suspend your rights under the Security Act on the grounds of treason and murder."

Mukasa stared at him. "You are both insane. You have no right to do this."

"Well, it wasn't hard to figure out once both Brandy and I were thinking straight again," Sam told him. "At that first, brief, dinner meeting in this very room, before the Vogel affair, you made a slip and had to cover it. You betrayed a fairly complete knowledge of my world, something you shouldn't have known unless it had been of particular study and interest to you."

"I told you—I was there, or very near there, when I was young."

"Yes. World War II, I believe. But we were told that no one from your class is allowed to go to any world that does not have a full station and Company operation, for obvious security reasons. The Company wasn't even there in the forties. It didn't establish its first outpost there until the mid-fifties, ten years after the war, and it didn't establish a full station until the sixties. We had been discussing war, so when you made your slip you covered with a war. The war Vogel's side won in his world and lost in ours. Why lie, unless you had something to hide? Unless you had been personally researching the world of Brandy and me with the idea of making a switch and eliminating a number of possible irritants at once? It wasn't enough to hang anything on you that would stick, but it was enough to tell us which one of you it was. When I was able to check, I discovered that, four years ago, you had the communications post now held by Director Basuti, the newest member and the cause of the musical chairs in the group. Communications—who would get the first frantic messages from that exploiter team. Communications—which, by its very nature, is the post that gets all the information fed into the computers first. And now, operations, where you can issue clearances, monitor all security personnel, and get any question answered with no problems."

"You are guessing. You can prove nothing," he snarled.

"Dakani?"

The security man clapped his hands, and a big paintin' on the wall over the fireplace winked out, much to my surprise. It was like some kinda big, flat, square TV screen. The scene on it was of lousy quality but it was clear enough. All of our clearly recognizable outlines was there, and then Jamispur lunges, we go into our act, forcin' him between Basuti and Mukasa, and there is Mukasa's hand, almost by accident, hittin' the fondue fork, takin' it out, and then rolling and stabbin' the doc in the throat while he pushed against the doc's head with his other hand. Then he rolls away.

"I'm not against high tech when it's useful," Sam told them. "We often use infrared and other means to get photos and information in the dark back in my world. I figured they'd have an even more improved model here. We mounted it last night behind the mantelpiece. At least five technicians in various places caught it independently on their own machines. Two were witnessed by representatives of the President and the Chairman."

Mukasa seemed almost to wilt. In a flash he'd gone from the most confident man around to a scared little boy.

"Oh, relax, Mukasa," Sam told him. "The truth is, you just did yourself a favor. When is your mistress, Ioyeo, due back from visiting her sisters and mother in the colonies?"

"S-she's back. Oh, the curses of the Nine Hells, she's *dead,* damn it all. I had to do it. Don't you see? She showed herself to Brandy, here. They *knew* she was Addison. But Ioyeo played around, as she was told to. She's serviced everybody here except Basuti."

"Maybe it was all for the best," I put in. "For her sake, too. Then she never got to make love to you one last time."

He looked strange. "Yes, she did. Last night. That's when I . . . Oh, gods! She just looked up at me, her eyes wide, and even in death she had this look of total surprise."

"Not half as surprised as you gonna be in a few hours, honey," Brandy Two noted sourly.

Dakani was quick. "Did you make love to any other woman since? Or anybody else where semen was exchanged?"

"Why, yes. I felt—charged up. It was the first time I ever had to do anything like that myself and I got—a thrill. It was exciting. It was pure power. I slept like a log afterward, and after I woke up today I had the longest, most passionate session with my wife I've had in years. If she'd turned me on like that in the past ten years I'd never have even had Ioyeo."

Dakani was already on the communicator. I just hoped his missus wasn't feelin' so turned on she had a few boy whores on the side. Hell, this scheme of theirs might work anyways!

Sam looked at him. "It's almost a fitting punishment. You never knew just how much she hated you. You never even guessed how much she hated all of you, this Company, this world, this whole system. She was the fifty-first Typhoid Mary, and the first to come in. She hated you so much that she was willing to destroy her own mind, kill that brilliant if tragic intellect, just to make you the first victim. To spread it beyond any hope of containment. This thing thinks that humans are only turned on for a few days a year, so every day it sees we can screw profitably, it forces us to do just that, early and often. It's just a virus; it doesn't think. Every day is just one of those few to it."

"Oh, my gods and demons!" Mukasa moaned. He knowed now what we already did.

"Carlos, too, sacrificed much," Sam continued. "You see, she loved him. He was—is—a genius, a brilliant man from apparently a very poor and very oppressed race. He had passion, commitment, and was everything she ever dreamed of in a man. He loved her dearly, yet he did this to her, at her request. He is one hell of a man, and, after this, if we can't track him down and pick him up through the agents here, he will be the most dangerous and deadly human being in all the universes."

An obviously shaken Mayar Eldrith got some of his composure back. "But—so she was double-crossing him? *Why?* She had everything. Everything!"

I looked around at all them silver-spoon, upper-class, First Royal Family types and I felt sick. "They ain't never gonna understand, Sam. Let 'em eat cake."

"But what, exactly, was the plot?" Basuti asked us when all had been calmed down. "I can understand motive, yes, on both their parts, but I just can't see how they were going to take control and get that substance in."

"First of all, it didn't matter to Addison—Ioyeo—or Carlos if they *did* get the substance in. They had thirty hours from their last drink of the rainbow weed pulp to get the girls in after the setup and party was all arranged and infect as many upper-class types as possible. Because of Mukasa's last embrace with Ioyeo, we wound up with six cases so far and maybe more. Imagine what half a dozen initial ones would have done. The cornerstone of security and the corporate classes would have been devastated before they knew what hit them. That was all Addison and Carlos wanted. The destruction. But they did have a way, and they made Brandy prove it would work by walking through."

"What? How's that?"

"Once they found the one that worked, or actually a way to get almost any normal rainbow weed to work, they gave it to both Brandys and took samples from their vaginal areas. They found live, complete viral reproductive units there. They gave them pulped but not pureed bulbs that grow on top of the stalks—the seed pods. They contain millions of tiny seeds and they are resistant to tremendous amounts of things. They are, among other things, indigestible but harmless. Only some of those fifty girls, restored to their original looks, being the correct race, would be used to spread the infection. The first, small group, only a couple, would be brought in as mistresses from the colonies under their original codes. Everyone of your race has the right to come here, at least for visits. The families are too closely interrelated. The scanners would pick up swallowed balloons, and even just clusters of foreign things where they shouldn't be. But they were not set to pick up addicts alone—a very complex process, finding one virus that you could only kill by killing the person—but only unusual things. Each of the girls would be fed till they burst with seed pods. Once away, they would be given diarrhetics. The human feces, with the seeds, would have been spread in a private greenhouse. The girls could then conveniently be discovered to be addicts in withdrawal and sent to the Center."

"Yeah," I added. "In just two or three weeks that greenhouse would be up to its armpits in rainbow weed."

"With all the alien races coming in and out and all the field people, it was impossible to scan the normal food and wastes that might show up in the scan, even if that scan showed odd material. It usually did, since people have different foods and diets," Sam pointed out. "Short of forcing everyone, regardless of race or class or what, to take an enema and have their stomach pumped, there's no way to guard against this."

"And what was the secret of the plant's missing ingredient?" Mayar asked.

"It wasn't soil, certainly, nor geographic position. The thing was a plant that converted sunlight into food without chlorophyll. It was sunlight-dependent if it didn't need much else. There are differences in the amount of solar radiation, and the type and degree, even within one world, and they subtly vary every world away. The exact balance of the origin world was required for maximum efficiency. Any variations and it was below maximum photosynthesis. It was actually a slight excess of one of those chemicals that made the difference. You'll have to get the chemists to tell you just why it's not obviously different in analysis, but I think it's the same stuff as on the other worlds, only when it has an excess it converts it somehow into an allied chemical, and that's the one. No excess, no biochemical waste. Any good greenhouse with special lights and the exact radiation balance of the origin world can duplicate it, giving you perfect rainbow weed that will sustain this virus indefinitely."

"Yeah, and if they hadn't made two big mistakes, it'd all worked and most of this world would have been under 'em in a couple of weeks," I pointed out. "One was fallin' for the same trap y'all was in here. Things was goin' so good, and they was so dedicated and radical and ruthless they got real cocky, started doin' side deals they didn't have to do. Me, for example. They figured when I come back from Vogel's place they'd stick me under Jamispur's machines and he could restore me and program me and all the rest. But I got shot, and Sam wasn't dead, so I went to the Center instead, and I had them do it. But not all of it. I ain't never been able to have straight hair in my life and I hate cornrows with a passion. Friend of mine went *bald* wearin' them things. And we girls spend millions a year tryin' to get our complexion creamy smooth and totally even. I kept the hair and the complexion. When I finally showed up down there, I didn't look like my twin. They couldn't make no switch, so they had to nab me and hook me, too."

"Then, when they knew they were near, they got arrogant," Sam said. "They did a quickie search and recruitment for a down-and-out Sam Horowitz who was corrupt as hell. We didn't think they'd do it, but we were ready for them when they did. There aren't very many of me. I'm not sure if that's reassuring or depressing. I nailed him in the Labyrinth. I talked to him first, because I just wasn't sure I could kill myself. I forced him into an available world and we had a talk. He had Nazis and concentration camps in his world, too. He lost the same relatives I had. It didn't bother him a bit. Not a bit. Before I knew it, I'd blown his fucking face in."

"That meant they thought they had Sam Two when they actually had Sam back home," I added. "We had a real go-round. He finally showed us that only by helpin' him did we guarantee our supply. He turned us in and our job was to press, finagle, or in some way get one or both of us to the origin world. See, that was their final and biggest mistake. More'n once they used that damned trackin' gizmo inside me for their own ends, includin' wastin' Vogel. Carlos was so busy and so sure of himself, and Addison had so much on her mind and one corner of it on the clock, they never bothered to take it out or turn it off. Since we was the only two addicts they had left not of their own race, Sam and Bill felt sure that they wouldn't do nothin' bad to us till they had their cure, their agent. We was the only guinea pigs they had."

Sam sighed. "Well, that about wraps it all up." He downed the last of his drink.

"Uh uh. You forgot one thing. Who killed Siegel and then helped me escape into the Labyrinth? That's the only part that has me completely confused," I said.

"Oh, Addison killed Siegel, just as you thought. The only thing unusual was the reason for that argument. It was you."

"Huh? *Me?*"

"Yeah. She wanted you for experimental or sentimental or whatever purposes; she had personally dropped off the load of filled shot capsules earlier in the evening. That's why the Labyrinth was running when you first saw it. The guards knew her, so they didn't think anything was wrong with it. Then she went into town to make some phone calls, probably to discover why Carlos, who should have been there, was not. She was just going back, but saw the office light on and went in to have a talk with him. She had seen you earlier out running, so she knew you were here, and decided to take you with her, probably to their safe world hideout, until the rest of the plans played out. Siegel refused. They got into a bad argument in which Siegel revealed inadvertently how much he knew and understood about all this, which was far more than he should have. Whether this was just his people monitoring Carlos closely and the Brandy Two project or what we'll never know. She lost her temper and shot him. She was used to being in charge, but suddenly it occurred to her that she was in a very bad position in a house completely surrounded by Siegel's most trusted bodyguards. She did a force on the Labyrinth with a remote device, which drew the guards, and she couldn't get away.

"In the meantime, you'd discovered the body, gotten rashly accused of the murder—you know better than to pick up a murder weapon, damn it!—and tried to shoot your way out. Addison had no choice when she saw this. You polished off a number of the guards, and she picked off the rest. This meant you would get away, something she hadn't planned on, but also cleared the way for her to come out, blame you for the crime, and take a leisurely exit of her own."

"Uh huh. Two things wrong there, though. First, where did the rest of the juice go? I shoulda had hundreds of capsules in that case. And, second, how do you know all this? Everybody who was there 'cept me is dead, and I didn't know."

"The rest of the capsules had gone directly into Siegel's office wall safe, of course, to be picked up and sent down to Fast Eddie the next day by plane. The remaining package was yours. He planned on you being around awhile. For some reason, he wanted you bad enough to risk Addison. In the end, for all his power and money, Arnie Siegel was a very lonely man whose own success required him to be totally paranoid at all times. He couldn't have the shadow dancers permanently. You were probably the only human being in his whole world he could trust absolutely. As for my source of information—you're still a hell of a detective. You figure it out." He got up like he was goin' someplace.

"Sam—"

"Not now, Brandy. We'll talk tomorrow." And, with that, he made his excuses and left. I started after him, but Aldrath stopped me, then took me over in a corner.

"I think you proved conclusively tonight that it was time I retired," he said. "It was a rather stunning and embarrassing collection of deduction, hard work, and theatrics, but the root cause was my own failures."

I kept lookin' after where Sam disappeared. My mind wasn't on no more small talk.

"Don't you know how he knew, Brandy?"

I started and turned to him. "Huh?"

"He was there. Once he recovered here and then found out what had happened to you from me, there was no stopping him. He wanted no one notified, not even Crockett. He trusted nobody and nothing. In the close to a year you were shadow dancing, he managed to research and even worm his way into confidences. He had a fair amount of money—he took it in in precious metals and converted it—and he knew his job. In only three months he managed to get a job with the Crockett agency. I have no idea what sort of means he used to come up with the credentials and background, but I suppose he knew just what she would look for and how she'd find it, being in the business himself. He watched over you, Brandy. And he kept me from going in full tilt with squads and invading the operation. He felt we could get far more by letting it run."

"He was sure right." Sam . . . there all the time.

We was fast approachin' that time I didn't want to think about. "What will happen to us? And to the shadow dancers?"

"The events of tonight will not be kept under wraps very long. When Carlos hears that the plot is compromised, he will undoubtedly finish off the shadow dancers and regroup. When he hears that Ioyeo, his Addison, is dead, he will redouble his efforts. He has no clearance to headquarters, but he has a lot of skill and knowledge and equipment and at least a small organization. As Sam said, until we capture or kill him, he will be the most dangerous man alive. Undoubtedly they will be going through every single detail of Jamispur's life trying to figure out the connection. They must have been together quite some time. At least we'll find out who he is and where he came from."

"And us?" We'd been in on everything, but both Brandy Two and me had been kept under close watch and restrictions. We was Typhoid Marys, too.

"Well, everyone with the live reproducible virus will be

under strict quarantine restrictions. You will be kept with your double here tonight and locked in, as before. Tomorrow, you both will be transferred to the Center for tests, after which you will have some hard decisions to make."

"What kinda decisions?"

"Options for the future. Someday, perhaps soon, we might be able to stabilize this thing, but its very nature will require taking something every day for life. Wait for the doctors. They'll explain it."

"Aldrath—promise me. Promise me that you won't let Sam leave till I made them decisions. Will you do that much for me?"

"I think I can guarantee that much. Farewell, Brandy. You and Sam cost me my job, but you saved my world. I have children. I can't be angry with you for that."

Then they came to take me back up to my comfortable prison I shared with my twin. I didn't see Sam till the next day, and it was clear he was comin' off a real drunk. Still, they let me have some time with him.

"Sam—I heard what you done back at Siegel's. Damn it, I *do* love you, Sam. There's gotta be a way for this to work out. For us."

"How?" he managed, his head poundin' somethin' awful. I could tell. I knowed they had hangover cures here and I got the idea he just didn't want one. "Brandy, they're going to convert Carlos's old safe world into a quarantine colony. Any who have the full virus, and any who for some reason wish to join them, will be able to do so. They will be researching this thing for years to come. In a short time that colony will be able to provide a small supply of the semen for capsules, allowing some people limited mobility elsewhere so long as they take the capsules and can't transmit the virus. It'll be a leper colony, but a very pleasant and self-governing one. *Ow!*" He felt his head.

"Sam—you know how hard it is. The only way out for me is to take the cure, and you saw all them folks who took the cure. Not a one of 'em is right. I love you, Sam. I really do. Come with us to this place. It ain't so bad, and we'd still be together. Maybe they need a private eye."

"Forget it, babe. I can do a car chase at a hundred and ten miles an hour through city traffic but I can't stand roller coasters. Know why? I can't stand not to be in full control. Besides, it wouldn't be the way you imagine. You have your full intellect, but it's untempered. You have no inhibitions and no brakes except what is necessary for your own survival. You know that even now you're only being civilized because they'll shoot you if you aren't. You aren't human anymore. Love and lust are synonyms to you. The only meaningful concept of right and wrong you have is that what gives pleasure to you or is necessary for your survival is right. It won't let you get hurt, it won't let you get depressed for long, and there's no guilt, no sense of responsibility. That's why I couldn't take the stuff myself. A Jew without guilt is just a Unitarian. The Almighty would strike me dead for it. Right now, you want me, and you have that cultural and intellectual knowledge of right and wrong, but there's no sense on the gut level. I can't handle that."

"Damn it, Sam! Then I'll take the capsules. Move back in to Philadelphia and our world. It can be like it was before."

"Really? You'd be picking up the cab driver and the laundry man and every jock you met at the health club or on the streets while you exercise. I wouldn't have a wife, I'd have a wildly promiscuous and uncontrollable daughter I couldn't depend on personally or professionally."

"Look—you control the capsules. I'd have to do just what you said, act just the way you wanted."

He looked appalled. "My god! You can't even see how that sounds. I don't want to *own* somebody. I don't want a slave. I want an equal partner who sticks with me and puts up with me because she loves me." He looked up at the security guards and made a motion. "Good-bye, babe. I need a drink."

12.

Fate and Fortune

The doctor's name was Chidra, and he had me strapped down and surrounded by so many gadgets that I couldn't move. They'd already poked and probed and scraped and sampled and quizzed and tested us so much I was dizzy. Now it kinda looked like the moment of truth.

Fact was, I was totally incapable of kickin' the juice, even though I was no longer expectin' that massive high. I felt great, and just a rest or heavy exercise was enough to wash away guilt and lingerin' doubts and memories. I wanted Sam. I loved Sam. But I thought Sam was bein' totally unreasonable. If he really loved me, then he'd take one of my offers. That's how you thought.

"First, since you are intellectually unimpaired, I am going to explain the options to you," Chidra said. "I'm going to be blunt, and I already know your answers so I don't wish or expect any. Just listen. Clear?"

"I guess." What was the point if he already knowed?

"First, you can elect the colony. It won't be fancy, but there will be people there you have known and work will go on studying this thing. You would be provided with all the basics and be expected to submit from time to time to studies, but otherwise it would be a carefree life, much like the life you shared with that stranded exploiter team, with some amenities and no strange natives. I must be blunt. With this thing managing and protecting your body, you might well live a hundred and fifty years. Even if we eventually found a miracle cure or stabilizer that would render you harmless and nondependent, which may be years, even decades away or might not be possible at all, you would remain there, since your patterns would be fixed and

274

there would be, I'm afraid, little purpose or use in allowing you out. You simply have no means to contribute."

It didn't sound too awful. Plenty of sex, lots of room to exercise and play, and no work or responsibilities, plus flush toilets.

"A second choice would be to return to your world where, I'm told, you still have a substantial sum of money that would guarantee supporting you comfortably. Your half would come to a bit under two million dollars, if that means anything to you. I have no idea what a dollar is worth. You would be maintained on the capsule with the pure virus as you were for most of your addiction period. When you needed a supply, thirty days or so at a time, you would go to a Company representative and draw it, like from a bank. You already have a high level of nymphomania; this would probably proceed unchecked."

That sounded even better.

"We would, in either case, make some adjustments that would be in our mutual interests. We would not tamper with your intellect, but we would have to tamper with your memories. We would eliminate all memories of Sam, of your marriage, of your career, of the Company and the Labyrinth. There would be gaping holes in your memories of the past, but you would not be bothered by it and you would never be curious about it or want to know. You would dismiss it if you found it out somehow. You would be perfectly content the way you were.

"The third and only other option would be to allow us to treat the illness and cleanse your body. The cleansing itself is relatively simple and subjectively painless, but curing and treating the results in mind and body would be a long and difficult process with no guarantees. If you want your Sam, though, that's the only road. We've done some fairly good analysis of him, and we believe he will be dead or as good as dead within a year without you, and that's the plain truth."

"I'll bring him around. I'll take number two. You even get the high with that, don't you?"

"I said you weren't to choose. Not now. The reason why you are so secured is that in a few moments I'm going to feed a charge through the body at a low level. It will stun the virus and confuse it. It will not be able to deal with it. There will be no permanent harm, and the whole process will take many hours as we compensate. During that period, and particularly near the end of it, since the virus will adjust eventually and reseize control, you will have your thoughts clear, organized, and unfettered. *Then* I will ask the question again."

"Now, wait a minute, I—"

Suddenly I felt a real sensation through my whole body, kinda like when you touch an electric light socket that ain't grounded but weaker, almost pleasant. After a while, I just went to sleep with it, hardly thinkin' at all.

Now, I know what they done. I even kinda suspected it at the time, but it didn't make no difference. They used that neutralizin' current and a hypnoscanner not to program me, but to feed in subtle visions and suggestions, provoke old feelin's. Memories of life with Sam, of just lyin' there sometimes while he was still asleep and just watchin' him and feelin' love. All his habits, his quirks, his idiosyncracies. Knowin', too, that it was mutual, that he both loved and respected me just the same. And then other visions—one vision. Sam, in the Labyrinth, tryin' to block the killer from shootin' in my direction, takin' the bullet, part of his head splatterin' . . . and what I felt then, and after.

And there was other visions, superimposed one on the other. Me, screwin' Calvin or somebody, havin' a ball, gettin' into that high, always over the sight of Sam's bloody head. The meanin' was clear. All I had to do was nod my head and get a life of highs, pleasure, and ease—all at the expense of Sam, all paid for by Sam's destruction.

And, through it all, I could think. *Really* think, 'cause the juice was too busy handlin' the distractions to block out the negative emotions. Guilt, shame, regret, all was there; I had a sense of right and wrong, good and evil I hadn't had in over a year. I had perspective. Yeah, I'd be happy. Oh, I'd be sad and cry if I was told that Sam blowed his brains out, but it wouldn't last long.

But they was honest. I also got views of them wards of Vogel refugees, of Donna and the rest. What if I did take the cure and wound up crippled or brain damaged? Would *that* be any more of a service to Sam?

And I knowed it would. I knowed that even then, he'd be there, always, doin' what he could, 'cause he loved me. I was the only thing left to him that had any importance, any meanin'.

In the end, the bottom line was, who did I really value most? What was most important to me? Who was more valuable, more precious? With the juice in force, of course, the answer was simple. Self-preservation of me and the juice inside was all there was. But the juice wasn't talkin' now. It was just me, all by myself. I still *loved* the juice, the way it made me feel, but I loved Sam, too. I owed him.

"You simply have no means to contribute."

And there it was, in the doc's own words. Without Sam, I had no reason to exist except for pure pleasure. Brandy One and Brandy Two would merge. It would be as if Sam had never existed, like the agency died with Daddy. Not only Sam, but all that I had accomplished, or might have accomplished, would be gone.

You could live a hundred and fifty years . . .

As a fucking dumb vegetable. What kinda livin' was *that*?

He was there, watchin' over me, even though he was sick at what I'd become . . .

Values . . . worth. *You ain't human,* he said. The juice needed to survive. It needed a host and it needed a weed and both was equal in importance. That's all I was or would be. Some stinkin', worthless weed. Not a human, a *thing* who'd turn its back on somebody who needed me even when that somebody'd been there when I'd needed him. Once he'd been willin' to die for me, and me for him. I was willin' to get in this fix just to avenge him. If I really loved him, no matter what the power and lure of the juice, I oughta have the guts enough to live for him, too.

I was still under; I knowed they wasn't even ready for me to come out of it yet, but I still fought it off and screamed, *"Do it, Doc! Get this thing outta me! Hurry it up and do it now, 'fore it changes my mind!"*

They learned enough from the early ones to know how to do the easy part. They put you in a chamber, out cold, the juice in you and doin' fine, and all at once, evenly through the body, they put this ray that was very specific and very deadly only to it. The death of the juice was instantaneous and uniform throughout the body. There was no chance for it to curl up and mount a defense or do more damage than it done already.

The trouble was, the damage it done makin' you over into a comfortable and controllable home for it was done, and on top of that its absence was more painful and rough than you knew.

All our lives we live with some pain. Gas pains, joint pains, muscle aches, you name it. We tune it out, learn to tell the new pains from the old, the important ones from the routine. With the juice, you didn't have no real pain 'less it was somethin' serious, and then only long enough for the juice to take care of what was wrong. I woke up in real pain. I needed a pill somethin' bad. I was in so much agony that I pleaded with them to put me back on the juice, that I couldn't stand it no more. I knowed Sam was there, but I couldn't see him or talk to him. I couldn't face him with the idea that I was too weak to take this, that I couldn't hack it no more without the juice. They gave me a few pills to help me sleep but that's about all they did. No juice. Lotsa sympathy, no juice.

They was always there, though, watchin' and monitorin', tellin' me it would get better, but it didn't. It got worse and worse and finally I just couldn't stand it no more. I sunk so deep in depression and pain and misery I couldn't even think straight and all I wanted was out. They stopped me twice from killin' myself.

They begun a program of physical and mental therapy and drove me hard. I didn't feel no better, but at least I was doin' somethin'. Fact was, the lousy way I felt was called normalcy. It was somethin' you just didn't know or notice till you didn't have it. Then, when I was ready to at least see Sam, to get some reinforcement, I couldn't.

I was in a kinda isolation ward. Seems the juice took over most of the job of my body's immune system. It took a lot of their medicines and a lot of time to build itself back up where a common cold wouldn't kill me.

They had a lot of pills for me to take without fail, and my mind worked funny tricks there. I kept tryin' to understand why if I had to take these damned pills all the time they just couldn't give me the juice and cure it all at once. God! How I wanted it! I thought about it, craved it constantly.

Finally I was built-up enough to see Sam, but all he had to do was come in and say, "Hi, babe," and I collapsed into his arms and just cried and cried and begged for him to hold me and never let go. A few days later, when they decided that the benefits outweighed any risks, they let him move in with me. I just wanted him to hold me and kiss me and make love to me and nothin' else mattered in the whole damned multiple worlds.

I wore him out, and I knew it. He was exhausted and a little ill himself and wound up with what they called a "minor coronary episode," and that was crazy, too, 'cause all of a sudden he was more of a patient than I was and I was gettin' shit for him and tendin' to him.

The docs got fancy names for it. They claim I subordinated and fixated and all the rest of that crap on Sam. All the energy, all the emotions, all went to Sam and Sam alone. It was, well, like when you first fall deep in love with somebody. You can't think of nothin' or nobody else but them, you damn near worship them, you just wanna be with them always. It kinda wears off and settles in after a while—what they mean when they say the honeymoon's over—and it had some with us, too, but they say this kinda thing might not wear off for years, maybe not ever, this time, and I don't give a damn. Sometimes you just about gotta lose what you most want before you realize how important it is. I had almost murdered half of myself, and it would never happen again. I was Sam's rainbow weed and he was mine and we was each other's juice. Neither of us was much damned good without the other, but together we was one *hell* of a team.

"Sam?"

"Yeah, babe?"

"I love you Sam."

"I love you, too, babe."

"You still gonna love me when I'm old and blind and ugly wrinkled?"

"If you can love me the way I look now, why the hell should I be any different?"

"I don't want it to go back like it was, Sam. You was

miserable with that high-class clientele and chasin' down computer embezzlers in Pittsburgh and I was miserable 'cause I wasn't chasin' down them white collar bastards with you. I don't wanna be separated again by no job or no funny lone wolf missions to other worlds. We're a team or we're nowhere. Even in this business, even though we didn't know it, we was a team. Ain't nothin' gonna break us up again."

"You impressed a lot of people here, babe, including me. Even the bad guys were impressed. They made most of their mistakes because even though they had you on a gold leash they couldn't keep their admiration and fear of you in check. Half that summation was yours, maybe more. God, though, wasn't that *great!* You couldn't sell it to Hollywood. They wouldn't believe it."

"I'm through impressin' nobody but you. I talked myself into this mess in the first place 'cause I kept tryin' to impress all them folks who looked down on blacks, on women, on people with bad grammar or ignorant table manners. All them stupid, *meaningless* rules."

"I always loved you just the way you were," he told me seriously. "I never asked for anything else."

"Then piss on 'em all. If they don't take this coarse, foul-mouthed black bitch the way she is, I don't want 'em. If I ain't learned nothin' else, I sure as hell learned that. Look what that kinda shit caused here. I bet that damned Chairman of the Board shits just like everybody else, just in a gold pot. Hell, them highbrows kept makin' them remarks but we impressed the hell outta them, too! Just bein' what we are and doin' what we do best. Better'n anybody!"

"I don't think we have to impress people when we get home," he said real casual. "I think people have to impress *us.*"

"Huh?"

"Well, even putting aside the post-tax nearly four million we still have in the bank for the Vogel job—you remember how I started that summation? A wager. A fee, if you will. If I lost, I paid with my life. But I'm still here."

"What in hell did you *win?*"

"A retainer, more or less, with fringe benefits. They pay us a flat fee, adjustable for inflation, every month for the rest of our natural lives for the *right* to consult us on Company business. We don't lose the retainer if we refuse the job. That only gives 'em the right to talk. The fringes include medical care, miracle pills and drugs, and everything else that the Center can provide to their own people. We also have unlimited access to the Labyrinth. If we want to get away from it all, we have an infinity of choices."

"Sam—how much of a retainer."

"Well," he sighed, "it starts at ten thousand dollars a month. Of course, it'll come from the Company so we'll have to pay taxes, but it's filtered through a number of foundations and tax gimmicks to minimize things. I figured if we let the foundation let us live in one of its houses and use its cars and stuff we ought to be able to get by for a few years, letting that four million just roll over and multiply."

"Sam, that's over a hundred thousand a year!"

"Sure. Plus expenses. The consultative services of the highest-regarded private eyes in a few thousand known worlds is cheap at that price."

"Oh, my God . . ."

Well, that's most of the good news, anyways. The rest was that the Center's microsurgery techniques was so good that reversin' my sterilization was a breeze for them, though I had a long waitin' period before they was sure my system could take it without hurtin' no kid.

We got to thinkin' 'bout adoption, but never followed up on it. Sam wanted to adopt an Asian baby. I think he just wanted to see the looks on teachers' faces when both parents show up for the PTA, not to mention the bar or bas mitzvah. Oh, yeah—I had to take the instructions over from the start, but now any kid I have will be born of an official Jewish mother. We took a trip to Israel to celebrate, then went down into Kenya and Tanzania and Zimbabwe and Malawi, too. I got to admit it was a charge bein' in places where black folks run the whole thing and people was starin' sideways at *Sam*.

I ain't gonna give you the good vibes jive, though. It took almost a year and a half, longer than the damned case, to get me to where both my mind and body worked reasonably well. I still have dreams of them super highs and periods sometimes when I kinda blank out and flash back to feelin' the bad old mellow times. My eyes got so bad I can't see the end of my nose without glasses, and I need the kind of special high-tech glasses they ain't invented here yet to see reasonable at all. I can't drive 'cause every once in a while when I see a ripplin' effect or some shimmerin' colors I kinda trip out for a few seconds to maybe a minute. I can read fine with the glasses and do, but I gotta keep from concentratin' too hard on any one image, whether it's a printed page or a paintin' or even a big unmovin' object like a parked car, or it kinda does a flip in my head and I'm seein' everything backwards, like in a mirror, sometimes for up to an hour. Sometimes when I stub my toe or hit my head or somethin', instead of pain I get a pleasure rush.

And, every now and then, I get these episodes, as the docs call 'em. Like suddenly gettin' super turned on for no reason at all and usually at the worst possible time and situation. Or I'll get up and put on makeup and jewelry for no real reason and come down and not realize I didn't put no clothes on till somebody points it out, or we'll be eatin' out and I'll pour ketchup on my ice cream and eat it without noticin'. I didn't get away scot-free; that damned thing did some damage up there. I'm gettin' control of the worst of it, though, and Sam's been super supportive.

Then there's my twin, only she ain't so much my twin no more. She didn't have no Sam or nothin', so there was no way she could kick the stuff. She controls her own juice supply now, but she decided that she knowed one thing best and made a deal. She's back workin' for Fast Eddie Small in *that* world, on a fifty-fifty split, still packin' 'em in. They sent Mukasa's brains to the brain laundry, and now he's happily workin' in the labs at that juice leper colony of theirs. His poor wife and *her* lover are there, too, as are the whole set of them from the exploiter team. Hell, their top folks are in charge there.

They still ain't found Carlos, which worries everybody, but they did find forty-two of the fifty shadow dancers in a safe world stop, all with their throats cut. What he's doin' with the other eight I don't want to know. We can't always be savin' their damned world. The cost's been too high, even though the rewards are good. Ioyeo was right about one thing, though; that society and that Company ain't gonna change 'less it's forced to, and the longer they don't the more Ioyeos and Mukasas and Jamispurs they make. Dakani's still got the security post, but also still with "actin'" in front of the name, but he's pretty secure now. He has old Aldrath Prang outside in the Labyrinth and the field seein' how they can keep the kind of computerized foolery from happenin' again. He was by not long ago, and sat and watched our tapes of every Thin Man movie and every Raymond Chandler film ever made.

The way they worked it for us was that Mayar Eldrith got us a Company job. It's well disguised and a new post, but it's one they needed for years. It comes with a two-hundred-and-forty-four-acre estate in central Pennsylvania near Bellefonte and State College, a manor house with fourteen furnished rooms, huge livin' room and fireplace, an indoor hot tub, and an outdoor pool, plus horse stables. Most of it is used for contract farmin'—the trust which is the Company cover here leases out the land to local farmers, mostly for corn. The horses are part of a deal with Penn State's agricultural college and they mostly take care of them, though I'm learnin' to ride a horse and not doin' too bad at it. That leaves our ten grand a month for groceries and livin' expenses and a few luxuries, like the Mercedes sports car and my minks and jewels.

See, in a wooded patch up part of a hillside on the property is this big, round, concrete-lined pit with a fence around it. Seems like the lock on that fence been gettin' broke a lot, posted or not. We see that it ain't used unless it's supposed to. I guess you could call us substationmasters; at least, this one's needed somebody to oversee it for a long time. Makes gettin' visitors and goin' visitin' a breeze, too. We even got a number of local friends now. The area's too cold for too long, but the folks in general are real nice and friendly with none of the usual hangups. It's the university what does it. They don't know nothin' 'bout no Company or Labyrinth, and we intend to keep 'em in the dark.

Well, the docs at the Center finally give me the go-ahead, and it didn't take long at all to get me pregnant. I didn't want to put it off no more, and if this one don't make me swear off it we might have more. We really do love kids, and, just as important, we need something more than just each other to center our lives on. Sam's got his ailments like I got mine, but with the Center's help and some commitment on our part there's no reason we couldn't live to be a hundred or more if we wanted to. But in case one of us didn't, there's gonna be at least one more reason to keep on livin' and doin'. It sure done in the last of my hopes of keepin' my old good looks, though. I'm puttin' on weight like mad and I ain't in no mood to take it off. Sam ain't gonna love me no less fat or thin, so why kill myself? I'm already married—for keeps. If that fat bothers them jocks joggin' up and down the road come snow or sun, then tough shit.

Ain't nothin' I get more of a charge out of than walkin' arm in arm with Sam down College Avenue to a restaurant or over to the university for a show or up to a movie, with my diamond earrings and seven months' belly stickin' out from under my mink coat. I just wanna shout to people. *"I got Sam in love with me and millions of bucks and the acclaim of a people who routinely walk between the worlds and you don't! Eat your hearts out!"*

We got a few disagreements, of course. I was kinda hopin' for fraternal twins and name 'em Nick and Nora, but I know the odds against that. If it's a boy, Sam wants to name him Dashiell. It ain't bad, but any kid who's gonna start life half black and all Jewish don't need nothin' more on his shoulders. Almost in retaliation I threatened if it was a girl to name her Mignon or Agatha, after some pretty good mystery writers of *my* sex. We'll find compromises someplace. After all, *I* get to fill out the birth certificate.

One thing we did agree on, and it was easy. We was in Philadelphia closin' out the last of our business there and we walked by this mall pet store window and in it was a small wire-haired terrier puppy we just couldn't resist.

We named him Asta.